D1490921

THE ELIZABETH WALKER AFFAIR

ALSO BY ROBERT LANE

THE ELIZABETH WALKER AFFAIR

A JAKE TRAVIS NOVEL

ROBERT LANE

Finis Origine Pendet

The End Depends upon the Beginning

THE ELIZABETH WALKER AFFAIR

The sweet petal of love, dried and brittle, its once vibrant colors and intoxicating smell lost in the shards of time, still sparks the silent wild cry of the heart.

—Highlighted passage from a book in Elizabeth Walker's library: *A Collection of Poems from the Scottish Highlands, 1819–1979* Author Unknown

1

There are things we believe because they are true and there are things we believe because we need them to be true, but we treat each with the same sureness.

The charter sailboat *Magic* struggled to find the wind as she came about after spotting a pod of lolling dolphins. Her mainsail flapped in the unsettled breeze and then billowed taut and smooth with the golden mist of sunset. Andrew Keller munched on toasted almonds that had been out of the bag far too long. His eyes tracked the sailboat and the five country flags that fluttered on her mast. It glided past the end of my dock and out toward the mouth of the channel, where her passengers would witness the sun dip out of the cloud-blotched sky and into the emerald sea. Then it would come about again and drift home, a silent vessel sliding through the night.

"You know," he said, running his tongue over his lower lip, "youth is the kingdom of our days. And when you screw it up, you learn that the ache of your mistakes is greater than the joy of your accomplishments."

Andrew never shied away from greeting card prose. When he spoke, the world slipped its grip on reality, the stars twinkled a little closer. Or maybe it was the booze talking, for the stale smell of liquor had chaperoned him into the house. We sat in my screened porch, witnessing the day fade into a deep blue. It would soon be dotted with pinhole lights that winked from across the bay. His sullen gaze wandered over the motionless water. He looked shrunken. Deserted. As if he'd revealed a tender treasure that had been enshrined in his heart, but his Magi gift had elicited no response from his stone-eared companion. His vulnerabilities exposed, he had no choice but to curl up inside, chastising himself and remembering next time to swallow his words instead of sharing them.

He snatched the last of the almonds and tossed them in his mouth. He took another slurp of the midshelf grocery store wine someone had gifted me, propped his feet on the clean glass table, and continued with his lamentation, vulnerabilities be damned.

"My greatest desire became my greatest failure. Tell me if I'm wrong here—but muffing a lay-up at twenty is a little different than an airball at eighty. Youthful mistakes are like throwing a pebble on a still pond—the anguish ripples forever."

"That's a boatload of metaphors."

"Tip of the iceberg, buddy. Tip of the iceberg."

Andrew and I served together in the army, and he'd made an admirable solo effort to keep in touch over the years. He'd called and said he was in town and would like to drop by. He lived about an hour south of me. I'd suggested a bar, but he wanted to see my pad. I always felt a tinge of pity for Andrew. His efforts to endear himself to me had been both genuine and irritating. During our time together defending Lady Liberty, I'd taken him under my wing, displaying a paternal instinct I didn't know I possessed and that hadn't bothered to surface since.

My baffling altruism toward him stemmed from his painful misplacement in the armed forces. Andrew, who'd never exhibited an ounce of athleticism, had as much business slinging a rifle over his shoulder as I did explaining stitch markers to the Pass-a-Grille knitting club. A soulful person, prior to enlisting Andrew had composed music for his own band and planned a career in the invisible art. Something had chased him into the army. Something undisclosed and manacled deep within him. His time in the service was a self-imposed prison term. He served it with sober dignity and steely resolve that garnered admiration while never once betraying the tragic poem that lay within or what dark Baskerville hound nipped at his heels.

"Beautiful view," he said. "Got a woman in your life?"

"I do. A cat as well." The silence that followed disclosed his noninterest in both his question and my response. It was an opening for me to offer a conciliatory remark, but I was unable, or unwilling, to step forth.

The rank odor of low tide sickened the air. I took in an appreciative breath and followed it with a sip of whiskey, thinking of how to absolve myself for my decision not to offer Andrew a courteous invitation to stay for dinner. Kathleen wouldn't be home until close to eight, as she taught a late class on Tuesdays. She'd be beat, and I didn't want Andrew moping around when she staggered through the door. I felt bad about that but shrugged off the momentary remorse. I took another sip of whiskey, its tangy liquid smoke promising a rhapsody it could never deliver.

Andrew scooted up in his chair and placed his feet on

the ground. "You remember that time we binged on *Gladiator* and *Spartacus*?"

"I do," I said with a noncommittal nod. "What brings you to town again?"

He'd been vague when he called. Andrew was the Sofa King of Sarasota and had mentioned that he was in downtown Saint Pete for a meeting.

The Sofa King of Sarasota.

It was impossible to flip through the channels without witnessing his act. His royal robes, rouged cheeks, and ridiculously fake crowns. Women dressed as court attendants sang silly jingles—catchy little ditties—that got seared into your mind. Broyhill, La-Z-Boy, Thomasville. You name it, the king has it. Only the king can deliver the best furniture to your door at the cheapest price. Six locations in Tampa Bay. Visit us today. For his signature signoff, he'd beam into the camera as two winged-hat-wearing court jesters sounded their trumpets. "The king promises you a new life. Sale ends Sunday!"

We like to believe that we pick our careers, but I'm not so sure. Andrew's shtick, like his days in the army, was an act. Andrew Keller had never found his spot in the world, or if he had, he'd been savagely rejected.

The Sofa King of Sarasota said, "Truth is, Jake, I was blowing a little smoke. There's another reason I wanted to see you."

"Oh?"

He leaned forward in his chair. "I heard that after the service you got into a little PI work."

"Peace instigator?"

He arched his eyebrows.

"I locate stolen boats for insurance companies."

4

"Close enough," he said. "The thing is, I screwed up. Twenty years ago."

"If you have trouble with the law, I'm not your guy."

"Oh no." He scrunched his face. "Nothing like that. I've come clean. Set the record straight. Unloaded the guilt."

He clanked his empty glass on the table. A dolphin blew, sounding like the quick draw of a saw through a thin piece of plywood. A great blue heron descended with flapless wings and disappeared behind the seawall and into the fertile hunting grounds of the shallow water. It was close to a full moon, and soon the earth's satellite would electrify the bay with a million white rose petals gleaming in the night.

"Remember what I said about messing up when you're young?" he asked.

I nodded.

"I didn't kiss the girl."

"Man's greatest sin."

"And no greater one, my friend. Elizabeth Phillips, although she is now Elizabeth Walker." He hesitated, as if the very mention of her name hushed the night. Dimmed the moon. "I met her in a church stairwell after a concert. I was out of college and she was in her last year of grad school." He spoke deliberately, measuring his words, as if deciding what to leave in and what to leave out. "She was engaged to some guy who was on the road a lot. We started spending time together. She didn't mind my motormouth. Accepted me for who I was."

He paused, and I wondered if the bulge of silence had my name on it.

"Maybe it was because she was engaged. I . . ." He lowered and swung his head. "I never filled that vacancy in my heart."

He poured himself more wine. I was hoping to wrap

things up, but he appeared to be going in the opposite direction. Andrew never mastered the art of conversation as much as he received a doctorate in talking.

"I was speaking metaphorically about kissing, you know that, right? We kissed plenty of times but never consummated the passion. It was my fault. I just wasn't aggressive enough."

"I don't see how——"

"We decided to go out one night when her fiancé was traveling. I knew she was the one for me, engaged or not. I'd bet my bottom dollar she felt the same way. That night was to be our night. Pause the stars and halt the tide, baby, that girl was mine." He caressed the wineglass with his hand. "It was autumn. Trees were flamed with color and the air was snowing leaves. Paths of gold lined the woods. The first cold front had blown through and all the girls were wearing sweaters and leather boots. Lost love hurts most in the fall."

Andrew went to college in Gainesville, Florida, but I wasn't going to interrupt his reminiscing. Besides, memory is part fiction.

"We didn't know it then, but we were experiencing the final blast of youth before life sucked us in. The waning days before embarking on whole decades that would rush by with no identifying mark. Numbing years with no scar upon the body or song upon the heart. No night wrapped in white satin to brand the time."

He took a slow drink. He kept the glass on his lips, lost in the great mystery of dissolved youth—certainly not in the robust nose of the wine.

"We went to Sam's, some techno-beat club. She was pretty looped—never could hold her liquor. We danced. She smelled of sweet almond—she referred to her perfume as flowers, and that was her favorite. I whirled her off the floor and suddenly she went limp. Nearly passed out from JD and Coke. Her friends hauled her off to the women's room. As they did, she gazed at me and mouthed, 'I'm so sorry.' She knew that was to be our night. Both our lives would be different if . . .' "

"She'd gone a little easier on the Jack?" I said, after he failed to articulate his thoughts.

The great blue heron squawked, as if it, too, registered my glaring poverty of empathy. Andrew slumped in his seat, and I wondered if his presence was a calendar event or a barstool decision. He fumbled with his wineglass and then placed it on the table. I went to the Magnavox and flipped through a stack of records. What to play? Maybe Frank. He always paired well with sappy love stories. He understood that hurt doesn't die. Hurt hurts forever.

"Did you see her again?" I asked, trying to leapfrog the story to a conclusion. I put on a snappy Ella Fitzgerald disc. Andrew didn't need any encouragement.

"I was young," he said, and I wondered if my question had even registered. "I had my music. Books. I wasted it all on the frivolous pursuit of money."

"I wouldn't say you—"

He cut me an irate look. "You think I'm nuts, right? Once on a high and windy hill, I'll be looking at the moon and seeing you, there's a summer place and all that crap. Maybe, but I know this: Our passions are inextinguishable. Our lives are a pale reflection of our soul."

Remember, if you needed a recliner, this was your guy.

"You're being too hard on yourself," I said. Granted, that wasn't a doorbuster, but it was all I could summon. Ella jumped into the night with "Too Darn Hot."

"I never saw her again. We were supposed to go out the

next night, but her fiancé came home. She deserved more than me. I was gutless. A rusted knight on a coin-slot kiddies' horse outside a five-and-dime store. I blew it, man. And she knew it."

"She's the one who got hammered."

He humped his shoulder. "Should never have come to that. Is this the live album, Ella in Berlin?"

"It is."

"You got good taste, man," he said, perking up. "Norman Granz produced that album. 1960. Wrote the liner note too. She forgot the words to 'Mack the Knife' and had to ad-lib her own. And Granz—you know him, right? He did more for jazz and civil rights than anyone will ever know. Why the hell someone hasn't made a movie about him baffles me. A Jew and a black woman, fifteen years after the fall of the Third Reich, fill the largest concert hall in Berlin—I forget the name—and bring down the roof. Art is so much more transformative than war."

"Deutschlandhalle," I said. Andrew and I had spent many nights discussing music until the waking sun put us down. I have a good mind for music. His was better.

He gave a slow nod and glanced down at the rug that needed vacuuming. He ran a finger under his nose. I sensed he could have run with Ella Fitzgerald and Norman Granz to the stars and back. Silence hung between us like a mute observer.

"I saw her last week," he finally said. "At least, I think I saw her. I was at a dinner downtown at the Vinoy."

"Did you talk to her?"

He seemed unaware of my question. Unaware of the world.

"Her hair was different. Blonde. We stared at each other like we were both trying to place the other. But we knew. She always had the kindest eyes I'd ever seen, and you can't change the windows to your soul."

"You thought it was Elizabeth based on kind eyes?" Would I know Kathleen's eyes after not seeing her for twenty years? I wasn't going to find out. "You wouldn't parade that into a court of law."

"That doesn't diminish its credibility," he said with a tone of admonishment. "I can still feel her in my arms on our last night together. That emotion—that embrace—is a moon that orbits my life. Sometimes it's so small it's barely there and other times so bright and dominating I can't even function. It just destroys my day." He leveled his eyes on mine. "The heart has claws, my friend. The heart has claws."

He paused and I wondered if it would be rude of me to ask for a good deal on a couch. The new wood floor in my living room had aged mine beyond reasonable acceptance.

"She turned to join the man she was with. Then she spun around and came back to me. She grabbed me, her hand braceleting my wrist, and said, sotto voce, 'I need to tell you about trumpet.'"

"Trumpet?" I said. "As in Gabriel blow your horn?"

I'd been gazing at the shadowy sailboats moored against the distant mangrove shoreline. When I cast my eyes back to him, Andrew was touching his right wrist as though it were a holy relic. He gave me a sheepish grin, born from the awkwardness of being caught, but he couldn't hide the moisture in his eyes.

Is the king going to break down on my screened porch?

"Yeah," he said. "Strange, right? I have no idea what she was referring to."

I didn't believe him but said, "Was that some code name between you two?"

"Got me, brother," he said, but his attempt at a jovial tone thudded to the floor. "I thought she'd say more, but" he shrugged, "she was gone."

"You can probably look her up and—"

"Her eyes swam with hurt. Like everything was spilling out of her at once. She's in trouble. I know it."

"Legal problems?"

"No," he punched out, exasperated with me. "Her heart, man. She's in pain."

Hadley III snuck in through the cat door. She paused, wisely decided we weren't worth her attention, and slinked into the house.

"I'd like you to find her for me," he said in a quiet voice, as if embarrassed by his outburst.

"She can't be hard to locate."

"My marriage is about to become a statistic. The last thing I need heading into a divorce is a hint of impropriety. A trail of premeditated disloyalty. Even a whiff of it could cost me millions."

"I'm sorry to hear that."

"I've done nothing with my life. Not a damn thing. A lost love. No kids. A business with pencil-thin margins reliant on TV ads that no one watches anymore. I built my sandcastle in the sky. I die? I'm just a picture in the paper, not even on someone's wall. Not even a name on a park bench. Hell, my wife will expense my obit out of my business account."

"You've done—"

"Not even a damn park bench. We don't own our lives. We just rent them, and mine fits me like a cheap suit."

"You can change."

"Just find her, man," he begged. "I can't have phone

calls and text messages on my phone. I need a discreet go-between. I trust you."

"What do you think she needs to tell you?"

"I can't even imagine."

"Yes, you can."

He leveled his eyes at me. "I want to see her, Jake. I *need* to see her."

"Sorry, Andrew." I stood and my left knee cracked. "I'm not the guy to be a discreet facilitator, nor do I see the need for cloak-and-dagger. She can't be hard to find. Tell her you'd like to buy her a drink. I can't imagine a simple inquiry on your part interfering with a divorce proceeding."

"I don't expect you to work for free." He remained seated, pointedly refusing to cede his cause.

"I wouldn't accept money from you. It's just not my type of case." And then, because it had bothered me when he said it, and I felt guilty for not asking at the time, I added, "What did you mean when you said that you've come clean, set the record straight and unloaded the guilt?"

He gave me a look that shriveled me, as if I hadn't measured up to his expectations. He stood. "Nothing. Just running my mouth. Some bullshit about my youth. Hey, I always could lay it on pretty thick, couldn't I?"

He offered his hand and squeezed tight, as if to infect me with his haunting romanticism. I walked him through the house. At the front door, he turned to me.

"You know I'm originally from the north and moved back there after my discharge. But I had to get out."

"The winters?"

"The autumns, man. They just destroyed me."

He sulked into his black car. It crawled down the street and disappeared into the smooth curve in the road that reminded me of a woman's hip when she lies on her side.

His license plate read SOFA. I went back inside my hollow house, poured the rest of the cheap wine down the drain, and wished I'd offered him something better to drink. I opened the refrigerator to get two fillets of grouper and stared into the cold, bright light.

Keller was in trouble. I tried to convince myself that wasn't the case, but he had only flirted in the shadow of the truth. And I had done nothing. I was stuck in the rut of my self-interest and unable to adjust. History offers us only one course, so I'll never know if a plea to stay for dinner or a probing and ardent inquiry, incalculable as those acts might have been, would have made a measurable difference. Alternative history runs rampant and unchecked in our minds. It left me with this: My unwillingness to engage Andrew Keller in his moment of need, my self-centered inability to connect with another human being, led to everything that followed. The consequences lie on me, and me alone.

I believe this.

2

Nothing good comes from a cowboy sitting at the end of your dock. Well, one little stinker did, but I'm light-years ahead of myself.

I eased *Impulse* onto the lift and hit the remote. The boat groaned and squealed up to his level. When *Impulse* was high enough that a surfer's wake from a passing cruiser wouldn't roil her hull, I climbed out.

We exchanged pleasantries and shook hands. I hadn't seen John Wayne since the mess with the cardinal years ago. Wayne was a U.S. marshal out of the Jacksonville office, but his heart, and apparel, never left his home state of Wyoming. At the time our lives had intersected, he had originally suspected me of murder. It was assisted suicide, but he didn't know that at the time. He'd gone on to save my life and Kathleen's as well. Wayne charging the beach with his six-shooter firing is an image I'll carry to my grave. I was indebted to the man.

"Catch anything?" he said.

"Couple of nice trout."

"Need to get them out?"

"They're on ice."

He nodded. A hazy, low cloud that was red at the bottom and iron-furnace white on the top filtered the late April sun. Wayne took a sip from a cardboard cup of coffee. I sat next to him and took a gulp of Corona a.m. It's not day drinking—it's morning drinking. I'd forgotten what a blessing an early cold one was.

"You know a man named Andrew Keller?" he asked.

"Your presence indicates the answer."

"He happen to drop by about a week ago?"

"I think you know that as well."

"Not for certain."

"He did."

"What did you two talk about?"

"Slow down, slim," I said. "Are we talking about the same Andrew Keller? My buddy's a heartbroken furniture salesman pining for the woman who slipped away. A man I hadn't seen or heard from in years who—"

"Suddenly knocks on the door of a friend who spent five years with the Rangers and has had a colorful employment record since then."

He removed his hat, revealing a mane of hair he'd need a jet engine to dry. To behold the man was to challenge the eye, for his face was a weathered testament to life. His meticulously trimmed handlebar moustache rested under eyebrows of unplowed fields of golden wheat. Canyon lines, cut from years and the people who marred those years, creviced his papyrus face. Most of us lotion our lines, but Wayne viewed his yesterdays in the mirror and saw no reason to look away.

"Had you engaged in previous contact with him?" he asked.

"That was the first I'd seen him in over a decade. Close to two."

"What was the purpose of his visit?" Wayne had the fiercest blue eyes I'd ever known. Tiny cubes of ice that sparkled under those fields of gold.

I pushed my beer away. I got the feeling I was on the clock—or perhaps I felt a tad guilty. "He wanted me to track down a woman he'd not seen in nearly twenty years. Said he ran into her in downtown Saint Pete."

"Did he give you the woman's name?"

"Elizabeth Phillips. Last name is now Walker. What's this about?"

Wayne placed his coffee on the bench. A fishing boat raced by and the roar of its three engines fractured the air. A floppy-eared dog rode the bow, its nose searching the air and it ears vibrating wildly behind it. When the sound diminished, Wayne said, "I need to know what he said before I fill you in."

"Horseshit. You want to know what I know before deciding how much to tell me."

"That is correct."

The man was an infuriating blend of manners and honesty. I recounted every word that Andrew Keller had told me. Almost. I left out the part about Elizabeth Walker telling Andrew that she needed to tell him about a trumpet. I don't know why, other than Wayne's presence indicated that Andrew's visit was more than what Andrew had led me to believe.

"Did he mention that Mrs. Walker is married to Charlie Walker, the influential NRA lobbyist in Tallahassee?"

"No. I didn't know that."

"And they didn't exchange any words at the Vinoy?"

"Not that he said." I lied. I justified it by telling myself that Wayne wasn't there on a social call and, based on our previous experience, he knew I played with my cards tight to my chest.

Wayne gave a single nod of his head, a move he favored. "Did he indicate that he had talked to anyone else?"

"He did not." And then, because I'd been so patient and cooperative, I added, "Your turn."

"I'm sorry to tell you this. Andrew Keller was in the wrong place at the wrong time. Two days ago. A convenience store a few miles north of here. An armed robbery went bad. He took a bullet. Two, actually."

"Two?"

"He passed away."

I'd read about the robbery—a glance-over article in a homicide-a-minute world. It had mentioned that an unnamed victim was in critical condition in a hospital. I thought of Andrew as he slumped out of my house. A man I'd opened my cheapest bottle of wine for. A man I didn't invite to stay for dinner even though in another life we'd talked music until the waking sun put us down. A man of pummeled emotions and parched love who I refused to help tilt at windmills. But my thoughts were void of emotions. Those would come later. They would gather in the distant valleys of my conscience and then ambush me just when I thought I was free of my transgressions.

"Why me?" I said, forcing the words out.

Wayne rubbed his chin and placed his hat back on his head. He slanted it over his face, his gaze drifting across the jagged and glinting water of the bay. Soon, the tarpon would run, their silver bellies rolling and thrashing on the surface and glistening under the strengthening sun. Men in boats would drop lines hoping to hook a 110-pound thrill.

You knew when they caught one because they would mark their anchor with a float and the big fish would pull the boat, and the men in it, out toward the open water.

"I'd like to ask you to investigate Mr. Keller's death," Wayne said. "Quietly."

"What happened to being in the wrong place at the wrong time?"

"We have a tape. The armed robber wore a mask. It is our opinion he wasn't there to empty the cash register. He was there to kill Mr. Keller. The robbery was an amateur ruse to disguise his true intent. We want whoever did this to think he got away with it."

"Do the police see it that way?"

He wiped his forehead with the back of his hand. What did the man expect when he dressed as if he were preparing for a January cattle drive? "We asked them to give us a little time. It is important that the official release is that Mr. Keller was an innocent victim and the police have no leads."

"Who sent you, John? This isn't your playground."

The U.S. marshals are under the jurisdiction of the federal courts. They oversee the witness protection system and hunt and transport fugitives. Someone might have called in a favor and he said he knew a guy who owed him. But Wayne wasn't the type of person to leverage a friendship.

"We have an interest in the matter," he said.

"Why would someone want Andrew dead?"

"I do not know."

"Is his death related to him seeing, or alleging to see, Elizabeth Walker?"

"I can't—"

"What *can* you tell me?"

He took his time with that as if he were rolodexing his mind for what to say. "Mr. Walker—this is confidential information—is under investigation for matters that I am not at liberty to discuss. Mr. Keller's death threatens the integrity of our efforts and therefore may jeopardize a lengthy and costly operation that is close to fruition."

"We're talking about the Sofa King of Sarasota. Are you insinuating that he is—was—connected to the chief National Rifle Association lobbyist?"

"He was interested in connecting with the man's wife." He hesitated. "We have a source in Tallahassee we need to protect."

"Maybe he was murdered for totally unrelated reasons."

Wayne gave another single nod. "Through your efforts we may confirm that, and, if that is not the case, determine if our source is in danger."

"Why not bring your source in now?"

"We would lose years of work if we closed it down prematurely."

"Closed what down? Charlie Walker? He's a Clydesdale lobbyist. A major player and as crooked as a fishhook."

Wayne pulled himself a little straighter to catch some shade from the canvas that stretched over the end of the dock.

"Will you do this for us?" he asked.

I spread my hands. "That's it? No other information."

"No, sir."

"I'd swim the ocean for you."

"You'd drown."

"Do it anyways."

We both stood. He reached into his pocket and brought out a flash drive. "This is the tape from the convenience store." He handed it to me. "I know you'll make some noise. But use discretion."

"Do I ever learn what this is all about?"

"When it's over."

"How did you know that Andrew Keller came by my house?"

"We didn't. He had a piece of paper in his pocket. It had your name and address on it. Nothing else."

"That's it?"

"He'd underlined your name. Twice."

"We were once good friends."

"He crossed it out."

3

A wiry man wearing a black mask enters the store. 9:15 a.m. Who robs a store in the morning when the cash register is empty? He must have barked orders, for the three customers hit the ground. Keller included. He is the first to drop. *Keep your head down, Andrew.* The masked man approaches the counter. He grabs a wad of bills from an overweight woman with a trembling mouth. While backpedaling, he shoots the place up, including a double shot to the floor where Keller lay. No one else is injured. No other shots are close to hitting the other customers.

After four viewings, I shut my laptop and called Detective Rambler. We'd become acquaintances when he and his partner arrested me for the murder of the man who had allegedly kidnapped my sister nearly thirty years ago. Like Wayne, he became a friend—that's employing a liberal interpretation of the word—only after being convinced I hadn't committed a murder. That I meet people in such a manner raises disturbing questions about my lifestyle. Fortunately, I excel at pushing bigger issues to another day.

I convinced Rambler that a fresh grouper sandwich was worth his effort. I arrived at Dockside first and nursed an iced tea on the covered patio. The tide was crawling in, and seagrass ran across the top of the water under the bridge and in toward the canals. The dolphins like to feed against the far seawall, but they weren't there. I gazed over the water and felt reflective and thoughtful, but I had nothing to reflect upon and my thoughts were bare, as if a stranger unto myself. It was a combination that had been occurring frequently. At first it was unsettling, but no more. For I've come to realize that it is perfectly acceptable to do lazy backstrokes on a calm sea while staring blankly at the clouds.

Harry, the resident pigeon, did a pigeon walk under the table, pecking the plank floor for scraps of food. I flicked a leftover crumb, but the little guy didn't see it. Other pigeons, unable to rally the nerve, stood on the dock and observed their comrade who, with unexampled bravery, toddled under tables and between patrons' legs.

Rambler pulled out a chair across from me. Harry scuttled off to another table, more annoyed than afraid.

"You got the film?" he said. We'd discussed the case on the phone. He leaned forward and then back, as if testing his chair for a home position. He rolled his long-sleeve shirt halfway to his elbows.

"I do. And you?"

He nodded and scooted his chair a fraction of an inch. His vacant eyes scanned the calm green water and the houses that lined the shore on the other side of the channel. Rambler rarely exhibited comfort in his surroundings.

"A federal marshal asked you to investigate Mr. Keller's death as possibly being premeditated," he said, summarizing what I'd told him on the phone. His voice carried equal part contempt and bewilderment. I wanted to believe that his tone also included a dose of admiration, but that was likely an embellishment.

"The marshal is an acquaintance of mine," I said, although I owed him no explanation.

That earned a harrumph. "We were told not to indicate that the purpose of the robbery might have been murder."

I asked him if the police had gleaned any information off the other victims. He indicated they had not.

"Accent?"

He flipped open his hands. "Little hard to ascertain from 'everyone on the floor' and 'hands on heads.'"

"Much money in the till?"

"Not at that time of day."

"The convenience store," I said. "That's not really a bad part of town, is it?"

"Not till now."

"Did Andrew usually go there?"

He tented his hands and landed a hard glare. He was the one who normally asked the questions. "It's close to one of his stores and part of his routine. Coffee stop. Sometimes gas."

I drilled him on the getaway car—no one claimed to have seen one—and other questions that in aggregate gave me nothing. After we'd devoured fish sandwiches in silence, he reached into a wizened leather notebook he'd brought with him. He unzipped it and handed me a manila folder.

"This was in Mr. Keller's car. We can't make sense of it and have no way of knowing whether it was related to the double shots he took."

Inside the folder were pictures of a woman. "Who am I looking at?" I asked, although I thought I knew.

"Elizabeth Walker. Wife of Charlie Walker. NRA lobbyist. Kingpin of Tallahassee."

Some of the pictures were out of focus, and in others she was partially blocked by people. I recognized the background as the Vinoy hotel, where Keller said he'd run into her. I shifted my attention to her face and my world became unplugged.

Elizabeth Walker, flattened out on a glossy piece of paper, stared at me, her eyes latching onto mine. I had the curious sensation that my life had been scripted long ago, and the woman—and the moment—had arrived. And in that split second, that indivisible element of time, I felt high and cold, as if at an edge and ready to accept the ending. But the sensation pulled back and would not reveal itself to me. I tried to dismiss the bullshit surreal feeling, but as I closed the folder, a shudder tingled up the back of my neck. Elizabeth Walker knew. Knew that I'd seen her. Knew that we were going somewhere high and cold.

"Technically, they should go to the wife," Rambler said from a galaxy away. "But I'm guessing she won't miss them."

Her heart, man. She's in pain.

"Hey, Sam Spade. I'm talking to you."

"Anything else in his car?" I said, rallying my mind from the shadows.

"Why? You think for some reason I'm holding back?"

"Doing my job."

"It's not your job, it's a request. No."

"Keller's phone?"

"You recall the part in the surveillance video where the shooter leans over? He snatched his phone. We got a positive on that. The fat woman behind the counter saw him pocket it."

"Did he grab anyone else's phone?"

"No."

"Can you pull records and see his call history?"

"Sure. Want your windows cleaned too?"

I leaned back in my chair. "I appreciate what you're doing."

Rambler stood. I did likewise.

"Don't call me," he said. "You eat here often?"

"I'll be back in two days."

He strode out of the restaurant and I reclaimed my seat. A light breeze lifted off the water. It blew in the opposite direction of the tide so that surface debris now floated against the current. I broke off a piece of bun I'd held back and tossed it on the floor. Harry, glad that my lunch date had departed, tottered up to it, his head pecking at the floor. I thought of opening the folder but was afraid of the eyes inside. I told myself to forget her. After all, I had other things on my mind. The big day was coming and I worried if Morgan, my neighbor, had everything ready.

Who was I kidding? Morgan would be prepared; was I? And if not now, when; and if not Kathleen, who? A kamikaze pelican smacked the water, and at that precise moment, I understood why my thoughts were empty and I had nothing to reflect upon. Why I was so content doing a lazy backstroke. I didn't know it worked that way, and now that I did, I joined the league of most fortunate men.

4

"She's a beautiful woman," Kathleen said, her admiring gaze on the picture. "But her eyes no longer hold the sparkle they did when she was young."

Pictures of Elizabeth Walker from the folder littered the glass table on the screened porch that still held smudge marks from Andrew Keller's foot. A few pictures were of Elizabeth before she'd transitioned from a brunette to a blonde. Hadley III sniffed one of the brunette pictures and then nestled on top of it, delicately folding her front paws underneath her in a move the beach yoga instructor would swoon over.

"Age," I said absentmindedly to Kathleen's observations.

"I'm not so sure about that. Maybe something more definitive. She lost her father and a brother on the same day?"

"She did. She has another brother, but he's quite a bit younger."

I'd given her details of Elizabeth's personal life that I'd

Googled. Her father, George, was killed in a car accident, along with his oldest son, Benjamin. Her mother also predeceased her. She and Charlie were married three years after the accident. Andrew had mentioned that she was engaged at the time of the accident, but that person was lost to time. Her professional career started in banking, and despite a meteoritic rise, she'd abandoned it to start a prominent nonprofit dedicated to childhood literacy.

"She is the same woman, isn't she?" I asked. Twenty years and a new hair color created doubt in my mind.

Kathleen gathered up Hadley III so that she could view the picture the cat had warmed. She murmured a protest but then laid her head over Kathleen's shoulder. When I picked her up, she'd squirm until I placed her down—and I'm the one who fed her.

"They are," she said. "Take the older photo, add a few years—not many pounds, I give her credit for that—change the hair color and style, and presto. See her eyes? Eyes don't lie."

"You said they lost their sparkle."

"They did. The issue is whether it was the result of corrosive years or a couple of hard punches."

Hadley III leaped from Kathleen's arms and onto the floor, her green cat eyes tracking a gecko climbing the outside of the screen. Kathleen picked up a recent photo of Elizabeth. She traced her hand over the woman's eyes. "Look here. See how her eyebrow is arched in the exact same spot as Elizabeth Phillips's? These two women do their eyes the exact same way. You really doubt they are the same woman?"

I shrugged off my own hesitancy. "Just taking the opposing view."

Morgan popped through the side door carrying a

steaming pot. A French baguette protruded out of his front shorts pocket.

"Same woman or not?" Kathleen said to him. He placed the pot down on a trivet. I grabbed the baguette, broke off the crusty end that had not been deep in his pocket, and stuck it in my mouth.

"No doubt," he said. "Look how she does her eyes. So precise and delicate, yet in both pictures, her eyes are unsure. She needs to paint on her confidence because it doesn't come naturally."

"Exactly," Kathleen said. "Our insecurities never leave us. This woman has looked into a mirror every day since she was sixteen and prepared herself for battle in the same manner."

Kathleen and Morgan saw colors I could not see. I went into the kitchen to gather what we needed for dinner and returned to the porch carrying a bottle of right-bank Bordeaux, butter, utensils, and bowls.

"Why the interest?" Morgan asked. His caramel-blonde hair was tied in a ponytail and he wore a black V-neck T-shirt and khaki shorts. No shoes.

I gave him the recap.

Kathleen said, "I find it difficult to believe that Andrew never saw Elizabeth again after she passed out in his arms."

"It makes you wonder," Morgan said, "what Andrew left out or what really happened. Stories change over time. Our minds prune some memories and fertilize others. Tell the same story five days straight and you will have five different stories. Imagine what twenty years does."

I decided to take nothing for granted. To start from scratch and realize that Andrew Keller might have been even more selective in what he told me than I had originally thought.

Or, for reasons unrevealed, he'd purposely misled me.

I HIT THE VINOY HOTEL THE NEXT AFTERNOON. I flashed a picture of Elizabeth Walker to the front desk, flirted with the bartender with pink and white striped bangs, and questioned a waiter with a head cold while he prepared tables in Marchand's, the dining room. No one recognized Andrew or Elizabeth, although both the bartender and the waiter had worked the night that Andrew purportedly ran into Elizabeth.

It was too nice a day to not take a narcissist chunk out of it. I settled in an outdoor lounge seat under a blue umbrella. A waitress dropped by, and I requested a cigar and a glass of red wine. A gull was next, showing interest in crumbs on the ground. I shooed it away. Harry was the only dirty bird I tolerated. Earlier that day I'd dropped by the convenience store where Keller met his demise. I'd popped some questions, but no answers contributed to the cause. I took a draw from the cigar and puffed the smoke high and to my left so as not to fog a group of women on my right, including one in particular who'd been eyeing me with mounting hostility. I sat there waiting for serendipitous thoughts, assembled by the ageless ingredients of tobacco and alcohol, to drop out of the high, blue Florida sky. They did not. They never do. Yet I felt obligated to give them every opportunity and would not be found guilty of abandoning my post.

It was time to offer my condolences to Andrew's wife and inquire, discreetly, if she was aware of her deceased husband's fiery infatuation with a former lover.

I couldn't imagine that conversation progressing smoothly.

5

Keller's wife pulled out of her garage at 9:45 the following morning before I even had a chance to engage my truck in park. The calling hours had been a few days ago, and I'd opted not to attend. I should have. In lieu of flowers, as requested, I made a donation to the Coalition for Peace—whatever that was.

She navigated her white SUV to a country club, hopped out with tennis racket in hand, and double-timed it into the clubhouse. I took off to get a cup of coffee I didn't need. Twenty minutes after I returned, she strode out of the clubhouse and made a beeline to her car.

"Mrs. Keller?"

She turned. "Yes?"

I gave her my name and said I was a friend of her deceased husband. I offered to buy her a cup of coffee.

"Coffee after tennis? I hardly think so."

"Lunch, Mrs. Keller?"

"Is there an issue?"

"No, ma'am. Andrew came to my house shortly before

he died. I hadn't seen him in years. He had a favor to ask me."

"What kind of favor?"

"That's what lunch is for."

She tilted her head. "Were you at the calling hours? I'm sorry I don't remember you, but there were so many people. Andrew, as you know, knew everyone, though no one knew him."

"I couldn't make it."

"I see. And this favor he asked—it requires that you buy me lunch?"

"Unless it's too great an imposition."

She gave me a rebuking glance. Her black hair, bunched thick on her shoulders, still held moisture from a shower. It had been tied behind her when she'd first arrived. Her feet were planted apart, her head tilted slightly forward. Loose limbed. Alert eyes. Marcy Keller liked to charge the net.

"Did you know him through his work?"

"We met in the army."

"Reeeally." She paused as if rebooting her impression of me. "I don't think he uttered two words about those dark days. All right, I'll bite. There's a French café I'm fond of not far from here."

Over toasted prosciutto and Brie sandwiches and sleepy French accordion music, I relayed my army days with Andrew. I kept it short, for she only pretended to listen. When I finished, she launched into her and Andrew's time together. She did so with surprising openness and no petitioning on my part. How he loved work and music, but she didn't want to settle for two out of three, and they would not have lapped another year.

As if registering her own blatant admissions, she said, "I

can't believe I'm dumping on you. Why are you interested in any of this?"

"Did he ever mention a woman named Elizabeth Phillips?"

She plunked her fork down and leaned back into her chair. "Fantastic. Just super. No. Why would he? Are you buying me lunch just to inform me that Andrew was married to a woman in another state, has three children, and they all want a piece of his business? Is that why you're here, Mr. Travis?"

"Nothing like that." Then I tagged on, "That I know of."

I reviewed my meeting with Andrew. I eased up on the rudderless romantic part and substituted that he was interested in reconnecting with old friends, some fluff about some stage he must have been passing through.

Wayne's marching orders were to keep it quiet, but I had to be the judge of what to say if he wanted results.

"It's possible your husband's death was not accidental."

She squinted her eyes. "What happened to 'I'm a friend looking to make up for lost time'?"

"That was your interpretation, not mine."

"The police told me they weren't investigating it as premeditated murder. That poor Andrew was in the wrong place at the wrong time."

Poor Andrew.

"I'm doing this on my own," I said.

"Is that the best you can do?"

"I'm afraid so."

"I don't trust you."

"Why not?"

"Because I don't. Here is the best *I* can do. I never heard of this Elizabeth Phillips person. Are we done? Oh, wait. I am curious—do you think they did it doggie style?"

"I know nothing that indicates—"

"Save it," she sneered.

"Are you interested in helping me or not?"

"Don't be snotty."

"Don't be cynical."

An older couple came through the door. The man used a walker and greeted the young hostess by her first name. They exchanged kind words and smiles before she showed them to a table by a window. I had asked for the table when we came in, but the hostess indicated it was reserved.

Marcy swayed her head side to side. "Whatever. Listen, it's terrible what happened. I feel so badly for him." She paused and her eyes fell, as if she were reminding herself that she was a grieving widow but having to consciously dial up that number. "He was a gentle man with a tremendous zest for life, but he harbored a distant element that I could never touch. I'd find him at night, alone in the darkness, making love to his drink, listening to his music—literally, music that he composed. When I questioned him, he'd close down. After years of that," she flipped up her hand, "I surrendered. There was a part of the man I never knew. It wasn't the best of marriages. It wasn't the worst. The great American proclamation." She folded her napkin and placed it by her plate. "Is there anything else I can do for you?"

I pulled out a picture of Elizabeth Walker. "Have you ever seen this woman before?"

She stared at the picture, her face expressionless. She brought her hands up, tented them, and nuzzled her nose into her closed fists.

"Is she your Elizabeth . . . whoever?"

"She is."

She clenched her fingers.

"Marcy?"

Nothing.

I said, "You know her."

She put her hands down on the table and her eyes rose to meet mine. "I've never seen her before in my life."

"You're lying."

"That makes two of us." She bristled. "Your interest in Andrew's death has about as much a chance of being casual as I do in hitting a one-handed backhand."

"I need to know."

She stood. "Pity the world doesn't revolve around you."

"How about a little sympathy for the dead."

"How dare you." She stormed out of the restaurant.

The old man at the table by the window gave me a scolding glance.

THE NEXT DAY, AS DOLPHINS FISHED OFF THE SEAWALL across the channel from Dockside, Detective Rambler plopped an envelope on my table, scuttling Harry away.

"Stay for lunch?" I asked. I'd just squirted lemon on a grouper sandwich.

"Some of us have real jobs."

"I hope to be a fireman when I grow up."

He ignored my childish retort. "I'll save you the effort, although I don't know why. Outside of a zillion business calls, a few to his wife and texts to his golfing buddies, there's only one number that might pique your interest. It doesn't seem related to anything else."

Andrew certainly had a business phone as well. I couldn't assume that his cell phone was a complete record of his phone calls.

"And that is?"

"Some hoity-toity law firm in Winter Park."

"Did his company do business with them?"

He snatched a French fry off my plate and stuck it in his mouth. "I should have been a fireman. Everyone thinks their work is dangerous, but all they do is sit around, polish the big red machine, occasionally put out a kitchen fire, and then walk after twenty-five years. High-risk job my ass. How the hell would I know if his firm does business with them? I'm off the case and was never here today. We clear on that?"

"Crystal."

He stole another fry and his eyes got lost over the water. "You eat here every day?"

"Not always. Sometimes—"

"I wasn't really asking." He turned and walked inside. I'd pushed what fragile friendship we had to its limit. It didn't escape me that I considered Rambler a friend far more than he considered me a friend. That we all have an Andrew Keller in our lives—and we are all an Andrew Keller to someone else.

I tried to think of something I could do to fortify my standing with him but drew a blank. Instead, I punched at my phone until I had the address of Chamberlain, Glanis, Newman and Daniels in Winter Park, Florida. A dropdown menu contained a brief bio accompanied by a picture of each of the partners. Underneath the picture was their direct line. I cross-checked Andrew's phone calls. Allison Daniels stared at me from my screen. No smile. What were she and Andrew up to?

"What do you think, Harry?" I said, for he'd come back around after my guest departed. But the pigeon didn't answer, which was probably a good thing.

6

I-4 between Tampa and Orlando is the deadliest stretch of asphalt in the state of Florida. As Winter Park is an oasis in the Orlando nightmare, I had no choice but to battle the tiring traffic. I wondered why Marcy Keller denied recognizing Elizabeth Walker and decided to try my homespun charm on her again. I had trouble picturing her and Andrew together, but perhaps it was the Sofa King of Sarasota who had married her and not Andrew.

I wanted to meet Allison Daniels on neutral ground for fear that if I showed up at her office, I'd sit all day or be escorted out. While rehearsing my opening remarks curbside at her Mediterranean masterpiece on Lake Virginia, the second of four bronze-colored garage doors rolled up. A shiny, deep-blue Beamer backed out. I seemed to possess a knack for arriving when people were leaving. A delicate hand emerged from the window and fluttered at a man trimming bushes. He waved back from underneath a wide hat and then returned to his task. She raced five fast blocks and then swung into a reserved spot on the second level of a parking garage in downtown Winter Park. I took a reserved spot two down from her.

She sprang out of her car, strapped a black leather briefcase across her shoulder, and double-timed it off toward an elevator. Her heels clicked on the concrete and echoed off the low ceiling. Her extended hand held a cup of rocket-fuel coffee—the scepter of the corporate warrior.

"Ms. Daniels," I called out.

The purpose-driven machine did not alter her pace. I repeated myself a little louder while calculating the chances that I had followed the wrong person. She stopped and spun around. She wore a white blouse and a pinstriped jacket. Her charcoal skirt stopped just above her knees, revealing a pair of splendid legs.

"Yes?"

"I'm a friend of Andrew Keller's. I'd like to ask you a few questions."

"And you are?"

She stood motionless, her mind calculating whether I was worth the effort, worth another squandered moment of her precious time. Allison Daniels lived in a world of vapid meetings, droning lunch appointments, and avalanching emails, all of which she assigned critical importance to. But one day they would move on without her, leaving her bedazzled as to where her life went and wondering where she'd gone wrong and what the hell she'd been thinking. My hard opinion and quick judgment—based on such a cursory observance and three monosyllabic words—might have been premature. But I'm right more than I'm wrong, although I'm wrong more than I admit.

I gave her my name, a few lines about Andrew's visit to me, and suggested we meet for lunch, should she be available.

"I've never heard of you. You may call my secretary. He might be able to fit you in."

"I don't want lunch with your secretary."

She pursed her lips. "I'm terribly busy."

"Andrew is terribly dead."

She punched her breath out. "You can walk with me to my office." She pivoted and marched to the elevator in the corner of the garage. She punched the elevator button, disgusted that it hadn't anticipated her prompt arrival, stupid thing that it was.

I positioned myself beside her. She glanced at me. "I didn't mean to be rude. I heard of his death through a mutual friend. Just awful. We hadn't spoken to each other since God knows when. Our firm doesn't do that type of work anymore."

"What kind of work is that?"

"Is what?"

"That you don't do anymore."

"Oh . . . business law."

The elevator groaned to a stop and the door opened. She stepped inside, along with another man who had appeared out of nowhere to stand next to us. I followed the man, fumbling in my shoulder bag.

"I've got a picture here," I said. "Perhaps you can just give it a glance."

"I don't have the time."

"You're not going any faster than the elevator."

"Everything OK, Allison?" The man asked.

"Fine, Kurt. Mr. Travis and I are just concluding a little business."

The elevator opened and Kurt waited for Allison to exit first. I took a step past her and held up the picture of Elizabeth Walker.

"Do you know this woman?" I said.

She started to brush past me but then halted. She snatched the picture from my hand.

"Where was this taken?"

"A hotel."

She handed it back. "And Andrew claims that this woman was . . . who did you say again?"

"He knew her as Elizabeth Phillips before she was married."

A man brushed past us and entered the elevator. "Morning, Allison. We still on for three in the conference room?"

"We are, and if you're late like last time, you're buying lunch for the office the next day."

"Aye aye, captain." The door shut.

"Do you know this woman," I asked again.

She squared off in front of me. "Mr. Travis—"

"Jake."

"—I do not know you or why you are here. Your opening argument about Andrew paying you a visit after twenty-some empty years doesn't impress me. If there was foul play regarding his death, I'm sure the police are more qualified than you to investigate. Now, if you would excuse me and stop your childlike pestering, I have obligations I must attend to."

She trooped through a jungle-green public garden with crisscrossed red bricks and entered the reception lounge of Chamberlain, Glanis, Newman and Daniels. A ficus tree partially blocked her name.

"You lied to me, Ms. Daniels," I said from behind, loud enough to turn heads. "Phone records indicate you and Andrew Keller were in contact prior to his death."

She stopped, turned, and stalked back to me. She kept

coming until our faces were inches apart. "Who are you?" she hissed. I caught a whiff of perfume.

"Andrew Keller bled out on the grimy floor of a gas station convenience store next to a stack of bottled waters on sale for four ninety-nine. I'm the guy who got the call. Rendezvousing with this woman may, in some inconceivable manner, have contributed to his death. You recognized her just now. You and he talked recently, despite your earlier false attestation that 'only God knows when.'"

Allison Daniels backed off a few inches, as if noticing how close she was. "I can give you twenty minutes. Counter at the restaurant at the end of this block at twelve forty-five. Don't be late."

"Aye aye, captain," I said. I expected a smile, but all I got was her back. I didn't think the other side was smiling.

ALLISON SLID ONTO THE stool next to me at 12:55 p.m. I wondered if that would cut into my allotted time. She demanded a spinach quiche without acknowledging the menu. I opted for the grass-fed, nongenetically engineered organic burger with field greens and local organic tomatoes and natural red onions with aged Wisconsin free-range goat cheese. I tacked on two years to my life just by ordering it.

"I appreciate your time," I said, offering a soft opening.

"Your clock's ticking."

"What did you and the late Mr. Keller talk about?" I asked, making no attempt to disguise the tone of my voice.

Her chest rose and fell. She stood, took off her jacket, draped it over the back of the chair, and reclaimed her seat. "Look, it's just a hectic day, that's all. Hectic day, hectic week, hectic . . ." She gave a dismissive flip of her hand.

39

"Your time is your decision."

"Oh puhleeze," she groaned. "I don't need sophomore psych over lunch."

Maybe she did, for her searching, soft green eyes held mine a moment beyond protocol. I wondered if she knew who she really was or made it up every day, but that's just the lens I view the world through.

"I looked into you," she said. "A checkered past, as they say. On whose authority are you here?"

"I can't say."

"That's not going to fly."

"I was asked by a U.S. marshal to look into the death of Andrew Keller. The official statement is that he was the victim of a random crime. We believe Andrew was executed. The purpose of the robbery was to kill him."

"See, you can say. And this woman you're obsessed with?" I was surprised that she hadn't challenged my statement that a U.S. marshal had retained me.

"I'm not obsessed with her."

"Act like it to me."

"She's my only lead—along with you. Andrew claims he dated Mrs. Walker in college. Her maiden name is Phillips. He recently ran into her and was murdered shortly thereafter."

"It could be coincidence. What makes her a lead?"

Our lunches came. My organic burger glowed with Ponce de León health.

"It seems the government may have some interest in her husband."

"Reeeally." She took a draw from her paper straw and pushed her glass forward, like you do when you're signaling for a refill. "Enter the marshal. What can you tell me about that?"

"You first."

"Fine. Are you familiar with Charlie Walker, the NRA's almighty Tallahassee lobbyist? Lord of Guns?"

I nodded as I chewed organic proteins.

"Then you know that woman in your picture is his wife, Elizabeth," she said.

The waiter dropped by and refilled Allison's iced tea. He also added fresh ice to the glass. "You know them?" I asked. "Charlie and Elizabeth?"

"What does that matter?"

"Everything matters."

Allison bobbed her head as if I'd finally spoken her language.

"Charles E. Walker runs the Gunshine State of Florida," she said. "There are some of us—although at times I feel we are doing nothing more than circling the wagons—who do not believe a gun lobbyist should hold the reins of democracy. Who believe the government should aspire to a higher calling than an assault rifle on every kitchen table, a gun next to every teacher's apple, and a Glock for every tot."

I squirmed up in my chair and as I did, my gun, under my sports coat, rubbed up against my lower back.

"Two million people in this state have a concealed carry permit," she said, cutting me an angry glance. "Know how they got it? The Department of Agriculture and Consumer Services. In the state of Florida, it's the same folks who regulate the tomato on your burger who determines who gets to play cowboy or not. Charlie had the licensing moved from the Florida Department of Law Enforcement because the Department of Agriculture can't share in the national database of criminals. This way, even ex-convicts can, and do, get permits to carry a gun. Add that to Stand Your

Ground—the state's legalized murder law—and God's waiting room has become the new old Wild West.

"It only gets better," she said, apparently not done with her tirade. "The head of the Department of Agriculture is no longer an NRA stooge. Undaunted, the NRA is now lobbying to have gun licensing transferred to the Department of Finance that is headed by an unabashed NRA zealot."

She stabbed her quiche with her fork. "Remember Marjory Stoneman Douglas?"

I nodded, choosing to remain quiet and let her vent.

"Seventeen dead kids and the NRA's response? Arm the teachers with handguns. A handgun is no defense against an assault rifle, and the shooter will go for poor Miss Murphy first. This country has more registered guns than people. Yet—beyond all human ability to reason—the NRA's stock answer to gun violence is to issue even more guns. Unfuckingbelievable. These people make big tobacco look like Mother Teresa."

She reached for her iced tea but then stopped, her hand clenched in a miniature fist. "Listen, I didn't mean to jump on my high horse. I've got nothing against hunters—God knows we've got a deer problem, and I've got no issues with someone owning a handgun, but semiautomatics? The Pulse nightclub is just down the road from here. Forty-nine dead. The shooter had a two-thousand-dollar Sig Sauer semiautomatic. It's designed to kill as many people as possible, as quickly as possible and as efficiently as possible. It did its job incredibly well. Even duck hunters are required to a use a plug that limits the magazine to three rounds—the law is intended to give ducks a fighting chance. Why don't we give people the same chance as ducks? Any son of a bitch who groups assault rifles with the Second Amendment is an idiot."

"Do you have an opinion on the matter, Ms. Daniels?" I asked, hoping to lighten her mood.

"It's Mrs." She hissed it out with enough venom to quarantine our corner of the counter.

I wasn't interest in her politics. I was interested in finding who killed Andrew Keller and why. "Elizabeth Walker," I said.

Allison sucked her cheeks in between her teeth and welded her eyes to mine. "You think my mouth is just a loose cannon? It's not, Mr. Travis. My nephew died at Stoneman. My sister . . . it's been tough. It's easy to read the papers when you don't know the victims. It's hard to breathe when you do. No time heals those wounds."

"My deepest sympathies for your sister's loss."

"You and the rest of the circus."

We were quiet for a moment. "I didn't mean that," she said and shook her head. "But the world just goes on in a dispassionate spin. And my sister? Every day for the rest of her life now belongs to the after part. She'll always have that demarcation line. You don't conquer the death of a child. You live with it, and it saddens life forever."

I considered throwing out another worthless condolence but decided that silence was the greatest respect I could show. Allison excused herself as if she were eager to distance herself from me. I asked the waitress, who had refilled my iced tea, for a glass of ice. I was irked that while Allison's drink had received special attention, mine was down to a few surviving shrunken cubes, rendering the tea purgatory cool. As I tapped the new cubes into the glass, Allison returned.

"I've met her," she said. Her words, short as they were, came out before she landed in her chair.

"Elizabeth Walker?"

She nodded. "At fundraisers, political get-togethers. When we all hobnob around each other and pretend we get along. Plastic smiles on our faces while we nurse our drinks as slowly as we can because you sure don't want to get smashed around your adversaries."

"Have you ever considered a different career, Mrs. Daniels?"

"You didn't catch me on the best of days."

The bill came and I fidgeted in my seat to get my wallet out. As I did, I brushed my jacked back, exposing my gun. Allison glanced at it and then quickly looked away. While in my wallet, I fished out a card and handed it to her. She smoothly extracted a card from her purse and palmed it to me.

"What can you tell me about Mrs. Walker?" I asked.

I braced for another broadside attack of cynicism, but she pulled up. "She's nice," she said as if surprised by her own assessment. "Friendly. The perfect hostess. She stays in the background. If she has political views, she certainly doesn't broadcast them. She runs a big nonprofit for childhood literacy. Founded it, actually. From what I hear, she is well respected."

"Kids?"

She shook her head. "I'm not sure what the story is there."

"Anything in her past to indicate that if an old flame approaches her, he needs to be snuffed out?"

"No. But I hardly evaluate people with that thought in mind. You mentioned earlier that the government is looking into Charlie Walker. Your visiting marshal."

"I said they may have some interest in him."

"Same thing."

"That's all I know."

"Liar."

"Not this time."

"But you'll tell me what you can when you can?"

I scooted up in my stool and faced her "Are you going to come clean? Or are we going to dance around it all day?"

"Dance around what?"

"What you and Andrew discussed on the phone call."

She swiped her bright-blue nails across her forehead. "I can't discuss our calls. He was a client."

"Who pays your bills?" I asked.

"We do business succession planning as well as estate planning. Our lobby group, which I run, is largely funded by individuals." She gave me a defeated glance. "There is no profit in civility. Guns? Yes. Organic beef? Yes. Save our manatees? That just tugs at everybody's purse strings. But peace? It's a bankrupt Jesus movement. Fortunately, we have some well-heeled individuals."

I took a chance, for I recalled making a donation in Andrew's name in lieu of flowers. "You're the Coalition for Peace, aren't you?"

She tipped her finger at me and popped her lips.

"How long did you know Andrew Keller?"

"He called after Stoneman. Said he wanted to make a difference. Does that satisfy your curiosity?"

I chose my next words carefully. "Do you think his death was in any manner connected to his relationship with your firm?"

She smoothed her skirt with both hands, pressing down on those splendid legs. "They are nasty people." She shrugged. "I suppose it's possible. But that's way out of line. They don't need to do that to win."

"But *if* they needed to?"

She seemed disquieted by the question. "I don't want to think so."

"How high are you on the NRA's hate list?" I asked.

She chuckled, which surprised me. "I'm sure they throw hatchets at us all day. We are an up-and-coming organization and our donor list is top secret." She glanced at me. "If you're a Republican in this state, you do *not* want to be caught writing us a check. But there are plenty of them out there who disagree with their party's staunch and religious defense of assault rifles. I will miss Andrew Keller. Not only his money but also his understanding that it is acceptable to feel anger toward your opponent but not contempt. Contempt is the enemy of compromise. It racks this state and nation, and so few people know the difference. With luck, perhaps his wife will continue in his name."

I pictured Marcy Keller bouncing into the country club. "I wouldn't count on it."

"You've met her?" Allison asked, her eyes widening.

"I have. Don't let me dissuade you, but their marriage, according to Andrew, was circling the drain. She indicated nothing to the contrary."

She shook her head. "It's never easy." She stood and I did likewise.

"I'll walk you back to the office," I said.

"I've had enough fun today. Besides, I need to drop by the bank." She thanked me for lunch and took a few steps toward the door. She stopped, turned around, and came back.

"We had a fundraiser a couple of years ago," she said. "The one and only time we publicized it. Within a week after the event, many of the women who attended were approached. In restaurants. Getting in and out of their cars. Watching their kids play a sport. They were told that it had come to *their* attention—whoever *they* were—that she had attended an anti-gun event.

"They cornered one of my friends in a grocery store. Told her they'd been watching her ten-year-old daughter at the bus stop in the mornings. Said they heard the neighborhood was bad—total shit—but don't worry, we got an eye on her. We'll protect her. As long as we got guns, that is. But if they take our guns, well, we're sorry, miss, but who knows what might happen to your little one?"

She paused and then added, "I'd like to revise my answer."

"The question?" Although I guessed what we were discussing, I wanted to be rock solid.

"You asked if they could have killed Andrew Keller."

"Your answer?"

"Absolutely."

7

I checked into a swank hotel a block off Park Avenue, as I wanted to talk with Allison again in the morning. She likely knew Charlie and Elizabeth Walker better than she let on. The personal tragedy that her family endured could cloud her judgment, and although I didn't think she'd use me as a vendetta tool, I am often not the best judge of character. She could likely help me more than I could ever help her, if I could help her at all.

Dinner that night was at a bar in a restaurant that had sliding doors opened to a crowded sidewalk patio. The big day was rounding the corner, and I kept thinking I should feel something. Apprehension. Joy. God-stricken fear. But they are rote and common feelings, and none of them were up to the task. The second whiskey on the rocks didn't help much, but it did give me this: *everything will change but nothing will change.* While contemplating the wisdom of yet another drink, three women strolled by on the sidewalk. A blonde with her breasts straining against her dress, a statuesque redhead, and a straight-haired brunette, half a stride ahead of the other two as if clearing the path. The redhead threw her head back when she laughed, revealing a flawless neck. I looked away. When I glanced back, they were gone, as if they were never there.

At the hotel, I talked with Kathleen while sipping a twenty-year port around a firepit in the courtyard. We reviewed the timing and sequence, and I assured her that Morgan knew what he was doing. She worried about the weather. Ever since we'd made our plans, she felt it her daily obligation to bring up the improbable threat of rain and I felt it my obligation to respond with kind firmness that it would be fine, a comment bred from blind faith.

That night I dreamed I was at sea, although I occupied no vessel. I skimmed low above the waves like a wingless bird. A sailboat passed me, its bosomed sail blonde with the evening sun. Its mast was red and thin—too thin, I thought, for the displacement of the haul. I wanted to touch it. Caress it. See if it liked me as much as I liked it. The smooth mahogany lapstrake hull rolled the water, launching voluptuous waves toward an unknown shore, its widening wake spreading like a woman's soft and moist thighs. I swam after it. I ran. I sailed and I jetted. But no matter my effort, it outdistanced me with seemingly no undertaking of its own. The crewless boat gave no recognition of my presence. It coasted into the dying sun and then, with a blink of wakefulness, was gone.

THE NEXT MORNING I did laps in the rooftop pool, thankful that I'd packed an overnight bag. I enjoyed coffee and scarfed down a farmhouse platter at an outside teak table facing a sun-flooded courtyard. Breakfast is better with sunshine.

Farmhouse platter: Brown, organic, free-range chicken eggs; fresh, organic, non-GMO artisan bread; cherry jelly made with traditional French countryside cooking and boasting 100 percent natural fruit with no cane sugar, preservatives, or artificial flavors; and fresh-squeezed organic orange juice muddied with natural pulp. And bacon.

I swung my truck into a reserved space two away from where I had parked the previous day. Allison Daniels screeched in within ten minutes. She spotted me leaning against my truck.

"No," she said, but she didn't turn away. Today's armor was a navy-blue suit with flat-front pants. She wore glasses.

"What's with the Ben Franklins?"

"Don't butter me."

I spread my hands. "It's an innocent question."

"I lost a contact."

"They suit you well." She looked like one of those sassy ads at an optometrist's office.

"What do you want?"

"I need to get close to him. To her."

Allison marched toward me and squared her narrow shoulders. "What did you do? Hang around overnight just to accost me in the parking garage? Again?"

"We can help each other."

"You impress me as a man who can screw things up six ways from Sunday."

"At least I impress you."

"And you need me more than I need you."

"True."

"You have the potential to be my biggest regret."

"Couldn't agree more."

"Give me one good reason why I should help you?"

"I can't."

"Why?"

"You never gave me your sister's name."

She slapped me hard across the face. I saw it coming and fought my instinct to defend myself.

"I didn't mean to be disrespectful," I said.

"Like hell," she spit. "Don't pretend you care. That's all anybody does. And don't *dare* think you can use my family's personal tragedy to your advantage."

I took a step so that our faces were inches apart. Close enough that she might feel the heat coming off my left cheek. Close enough to know that Allison Daniels wore the same perfume, if not every day, at least those two days.

"That's exactly what I plan to do. You want your nephew to die in vain? You think you're a solo act and don't need any help? You need to lose your pretty suit and play at my level. If there's dirt on Walker, let's find it. If you don't have the guts for that, then thank you for your precious time, Captain."

She swallowed hard. Her jaw trembled. She put her hand up, fluttered it across her face, and stormed away. I felt . . . I don't know what I felt.

A car stopped next to me and the window came down. "Hey, pal," a man behind the wheel said. The top button of his dress shirt was undone and the knot of his tie rested underneath it. "That your truck?" He jutted his chin at my truck.

"Are you two eighty-seven?" I asked.

"That's me."

"I'm leaving."

"Yeah, well, it says reserved. What's so hard about that?"

8

Two days after Allison Daniels slapped my cheek—and right around the time that I was considering calling her with an apology for the manner in which I spoke—she texted me an invite to a political fundraiser.

"Masked Friends" was to be held at the pink hotel near my house. Billed as an opportunity to reach across the aisle and mingle with your political antagonist, invites went out to lobbyists and state legislators, and each was encouraged to bring guests, at five hundred a pop. Proceeds went to A Book for Every Child, a nonprofit dedicated to promoting literacy in preschool and early elementary school. I recalled from my research that Elizabeth was the founder of the organization. Allison had also mentioned it during our lunch, although she had not identified it by name. She indicated both Charlie and Elizabeth Walker would be in attendance. She followed up with another text stating that she could play at any damn level she wanted.

The night before the gala, Kathleen and I sat at the end of the dock awaiting the full moon. We rarely missed the show on a clear night. It rose heavy in the sky as if it was fighting gravity and the outcome, although anticipated, was not assured.

"A masquerade ball," Kathleen said. "And they're serious?"

"Judging from the tone of the invite, you're expected to go all in. The goal is to accept that your opposition might be the charming person you're conversing with."

"Clinking glasses with your nemesis. Do the masks ever come off?"

"Allison added that they all know each other, mask or no mask, but in the spirit of détente, you're not supposed to acknowledge anyone by name until midnight."

A breeze ballooned her white shirt as she stroked Hadley III who was curled into a cat ball on her lap. *Magic* slid by coming in from the gulf. A dozen people speckled her bow, their legs dangling over the side like noodles spilling out of an oblong pasta dish. I took a sip of red wine and viewed the lights across the bay through the muted glass. I offered the glass to Kathleen. She took a sip and handed it back to me.

"I saw the doctor today," she said.

"I thought that was next week."

"She had a cancellation."

"And?"

"She said to keep trying. Some women just have trouble. No medical issues. But she mentioned my age. She said every body is different."

"We'll get it."

"You keep saying that."

"What's the worst case," I said. "We adopt?"

"You're fond of that line as well."

That brought a rare and uneasy silence. It was a foreign

53

field for us, and I wondered if it would pass or if it would wedge itself into our lives like a squatter we eventually became comfortable with.

"Do you think they'll allow us?" she said.

"You mean me?"

"There are plenty of children out there. We don't need to go through a public agency. There are private adoption attorneys, and even if . . . that's an issue, there's a child somewhere."

That brought round two of uneasy silence. *That's an issue* meant *if you're an issue.*

My past would likely cause any adoption agency or private lawyer to consider "more qualified" candidates. Kathleen and I had exhausted our words on the subject, but as we had no other paths, we kept rehashing the same piteous story. I didn't want to rupture her fantasy that a stork was coming just for her. It was a Band-Aid belief designed to get her through the most difficult time before reason and intellect took the wheel. Her mind was in self-preservation mode, letting her down gently. At least I hoped that was the case.

Hadley III gingerly stepped off Kathleen's lap—the cat was tentative on the dock—and sniffed my elbow. The moon ascended pale and large and dominated the sky. Orion's belt bowed to its superior brightness, and other stars granted it the stage. When the moon was a shot glass above the horizon, it sparkled the bay like a flat disco ball. The river of light started a mile wide and then narrowed until it ended under our feet. The sun and the moon—the twin forces of life—were lined up just for us. There was no way to sit there and believe anything other than that. No way at all.

Kathleen said, "I want to hold them."

"Them?"

"The sparkly water—the diamonds. I want to hold them in my hands." She rolled up her sleeves.

"I don't think it works that way."

"Hold me."

She kneeled down on the lower boards at the end of the dock. Hadley III took a startled step back but then held her ground. I squatted beside Kathleen and placed my arms around her waist, getting there just before she went in.

"Tighter," she said as she leaned over even farther.

"You know it wo—"

"Hush."

I squeezed her waist to keep her from falling into the bay. The sparkles on the water ran to her and jiggled like tiny, silvery water fairies. Millions of Tinker Bells dancing on the water. She reached into the sea of fairies and cupped her hands together. She raised her hands, but her palms held only dark water. She leaned over again, this time as far out as she could, and I braced myself so we both wouldn't go in. She scooped up a handful of liquid pixie dust. I pulled her back onto the lower deck.

The black water bled through her tight fingers.

LATER THAT NIGHT, AFTER FLIPPING MY PILLOW a few times searching for a cool side, I got out of bed and peeked through the bedroom shutters. The moon was high in the black-domed sky and the water had lost its sparkle. If the bay could not hold the magic fairies, what chance did we have? I made a note to mention that to Kathleen the next day, but I never did, for the night is stingy and does not give us our thoughts back in the morning.

9

If it weren't for her eyes, she would have been unrecognizable.

The "Masked Friends" invitation requested that everyone, at minimum, wear a wig and a mask that shrouded half their face. Kathleen attacked the wig shop on Central Avenue and selected a rug for me as well as wigs for herself and Morgan, who was thrilled beyond earthly reason to be attending a masked ball.

Kathleen, who had chosen to get ready at her condo, emerged from an SUV with flowing black hair and a lightly powdered face. She wore a lavender strapless dress that had white streaks around her waist and then blossomed into a feathery monstrosity nearly five feet wide at the floor. Her mask was the same color as the dress. But her eyes gave her away, for one cannot alter or disguise the clear windows to the soul.

"What do you think?" She twirled around after squeezing through the front door with more effort than one would have anticipated. Another mask, black with satanic green eyes, rested on the back of her head. A dark choker strangled her neck.

"Who thought of the mask in the back?"

"That was me. You like?"

"It's a little creepy."

"Creepy?"

"Enticing."

"Hmm. What time are we meeting Allison?"

"She and her husband will be presenting themselves at seven thirty. We're to meet them at the entrance."

Morgan strolled over from his house. Kathleen executed a 360 for him. "Marvelous," he said. "You're a different woman from behind. You've outdone yourself."

"You don't think it's too creepy, do you?"

"Creepy? Heavens no. It's alluring. Exotic."

She flashed me a look and then curtsied in front of Morgan. "Thank you."

Morgan the Perfect was decked out as a British naval officer from the mid-1800s. An admiral hat extended well beyond his ears and a red and blue naval coat hugged his body. The Union Jack served as his mask.

"What frigate did you board to get that?" I asked him.

"My closet."

"Why on earth would you have that in your closet?" Kathleen asked.

"This is not my first masked ball," he said with aristocratic snobbery.

I was—thanks to Kathleen, for I had nothing to do with it—a 1970s record producer. I'm not sure what a 1970s record producer looked like, but picture a wide collar, moppy hair, and a rapper's collection of gold and silver necklaces hanging both in and out of my open-necked shirt. My psychedelic mask was decorated with the treble and bass clef, which, Morgan corrected me, were the G clef and F clef. If my biggest risk was being discovered as a fraud who didn't know his clefs, then I had nothing to worry about.

Allison said they expected around 160 people. They all arrived at 7:00 p.m.

Pirates. Kings. Queens. Lions. (One lion.) Women with clothing to their necks. Women who left little to the imagination. Men with top hats, baseball caps, topcoats, and no coats. Masks of red and black and white. Green feathers. Purple capes. Wings. Canes. Hair and hair and more hair. Volumes of it piled upon masked faces with electrifying eyes. The hotel staff didn't fit in. They looked as if they were dropped in from a distant galaxy, members of a despondent society who had long ago banned flamboyancy.

Someone touched my elbow.

I turned and faced a woman with a phantom face mask that covered her forehead and cheeks. Her wild and red Rapunzel hair disappeared behind her, appearing again at both sides of her lower back and stopping just above her champion legs.

"It's me, Allison," she whispered.

"Radical," I said. It sounded edgier than *groovy* or *far-out*.

"Charlie Walker has a hawk nose. He's screwed. Hard to miss."

"And Elizabeth?"

"Can't help you much there. Remember the invitation? It urged couples to separate once they arrive. Don't expect her to be hanging around hawk nose."

We exchanged introductions as we edged closer to the entrance table. We were to present our names to either a wolf or a sheep who hid their tablets behind large open

Bibles. A Roman sentry instructed each person to lean in and give their name so as not to tip off their true identity.

"All a ruse," Allison said. "Everyone knows everyone."

"But in the spirit of détente," I said. "Are you solo tonight? I thought your husband was attending."

"He bailed at the last moment. Again. He has yet to accompany me on one of these safaris. I can't decide if that makes me mad at him or if I respect him even more."

"I think he and I would get along."

"I'm sorry I hit you."

"I was out of line."

"You were. I can't believe I have to spend the evening pretending. You can dress up a pig all you want."

"I think you missed the—"

I didn't finish as she leaned over and rasped her name to the wolf. I gave mine to the sheep. As Kathleen, Morgan, and I entered the ballroom, Kathleen squeezed my hand. "I'm going to have a grand time," she gushed. She swiveled through the crowd toward one of the French doors that opened to the second-floor balcony. The creepy green eyes of her mask bounced behind her and then the crowd took her. I turned to say something to Admiral Morgan, but he, too, had set sail.

An orchestra of white, all wearing red masks and conducted by a man in a yellow duck suit, broke into dissonant chords that resolved into the soaring octave jump of *Bali Hai.* The excitement could not be denied. Upon us was a night we would always remember, if not for a lifetime, then at least until the mind could no longer summon the life. It was as if someone gave a party for all humanity, and all humanity came.

. . .

NINETY TEDIOUS MINUTES LATER, I FOUND who I'd been searching for. Hawk Nose had been a breeze; I'd made him within ten minutes. Easily the most popular World War II aviator in the crowd, people flocked around Charlie Walker. The swinging brass balls of the state of Florida didn't go anywhere incognito, nor did he build his influence-dominating empire by hiding behind a mask. Finding his wife was another matter. I wanted to identify her and sequester her away from the crowd.

Wife of the king. Hostess of the gala, for it benefited her charity.

One woman, impersonating a World War II nurse, entertained a constant rotation of masked faces in her conversational circle. She had Carole Lombard hair and a mask with white and gold glitter around its edges. She nodded with discerning politeness. She listened more than she spoke.

Wayne wanted things under the radar, but he knew I didn't fly that low. When a man dressed like a Mississippi riverboat captain stepped away, thinning the coterie that surrounded her, I entered her circle. A woman to her right touched her arm and departed with an "I'll catch up with you later."

The WAC nurse faced me. In a contralto voice, she said, "And you are . . . ?"

They were the same eyes—unsure but willing to take a chance—that had haunted me in the picture of Elizabeth Walker. The borders of my mind blew out and a surge of déjà vu flooded me, just as it had at Dockside when I first viewed her picture. Everything that was about to happen had occurred before and there was nothing to do but to be swept out by the riptide.

"A record producer," I said. "Although I have no clue what one looks like."

"Wasn't Phil Spector a record producer?"

"The wall of sound."

"Yes." She appraised me with a slight smile. "But he's in jail for murder, is he not?"

"Crimes of passion," I said. "What passion would you commit a crime for?"

Her eyes narrowed. "It's not a subject I normally entertain."

A man stepped in front of me with a rude "Excuse me." He placed a hand on my nurse's shoulder, complimented her looks, and laid into her as if they were continuing a conversation. I was out of the game. Politicians. A tougher crowd than I would have imagined.

I sauntered over to the nearest bar, catching a glimpse of Kathleen across the crowded floor. No doubt, it was top dollar to whoever could identify the woman in lavender wearing two masks. My nurse broke away and snaked her way toward the bar. It wasn't a straight path, as she was intercepted at nearly every step. By the time she arrived, she was in serious discussion with a hanger-on about charter school funding.

Either she was Elizabeth Walker or not.

"I'm a friend of Andrew Keller's," I said, staring straight ahead and loud enough for her to hear me. Her head moved forward and her left arm raised, but I couldn't see what she did with it. A woman to her right continued with her manifesto. "This is what needs to be done and done today, don't you agree? They'll listen to you."

"Never heard of him," the bartender said. I hadn't counted on him paying attention. But now that he had, I ran with it.

"Great guy," I said in a still too-loud voice. "Told me a sad story."

"Oh yeah? What was that?" the bartender said, eager to be that caring ear, a flag bearer of his proud profession.

"How he ran into an ex-lover."

The nurse spun so fast that she startled me. She pushed her palm out as if to ward me off. "This is not the place or time." She dashed off.

That's my girl.

I followed her as she mapped her way out of the ballroom and hastened into the wide entrance hall, crammed with creatures of the night. With the orchestra muted, conversations were easier and the politicians and lobbyists of the Sunshine State were hammering deals faster than they were tossing down tomorrow's headaches.

My nurse ducked into a women's room.

Kathleen was at my side. I'd been so intent on tracking my prey, I hadn't noticed her.

"Is that our girl?" she asked.

I nodded my head toward the women's restroom. "I think so, dressed as a World War Two nurse. Tell her some guy you don't know—called himself Phil Spector—asked you to tell her to meet him at the south pool."

"Which pool is that, Phil?"

I love Kathleen more than breakfast, but I've never come to terms with her inexcusable disinterest in the four cardinal points.

"The one with the movie screen."

She sucked on her lower lip and then strode into the women's room.

I took the wide, curved concrete steps down to the courtyard and out to the south pool. The hotel showed a children's movie every Saturday night, and little people in large rafts and inner tubes floated as they watched Truly Scrumptious and Caractacus Potts fall in love in Ian Fleming's *Chitty Chitty Bang Bang*. Their world seemed strangely wholesome and pure. I loitered on the boardwalk, trying to be both easily spotted and yet secluded. The movie, on a screen at the end of the pool, played to a quiet group of enthralled floaters:

"So what we do now?"

"Start swimming."

"I can't swim."

"Then start drowning."

I was thinking of my comment to Wayne, that I'd swim the ocean for him, when she appeared in the shadows. She stopped short of entering the pale light of the resort's lampposts and the low-wattage bulbs strung between unbending palm trees. As "Hushabye Mountain" carried over the pool, I stepped into the darkness and faced the woman who apparently stole Andrew Keller's heart twenty years ago and who in some manner possibly factored in his death. An inexplicable urge to wrap my arms around her jolted me —*did Andrew possess me?*—but it was gone before I could question its cathartic presence.

"Who are you?" she said with anxiety, fear, and hope, as if each word had its own attendant.

"Elizabeth Walker?"

Hesitation. "Yes."

I gave her my name. I told her about Andrew's visit. That he was going through a divorce, and to avoid any complications, wanted me to contact her and arrange a place and time in which they could meet. I talked fast, for I sensed she might bolt at any moment. When I finished, she seemed both relieved and anxious, as if something she'd pined for was finally about to occur.

"I do want to talk to him. Can you arrange that for us?"

For us?

I had assumed she knew that Andrew was dead. But why would she? Although she and her husband had a home on the island across from me, they may have been in Tallahassee the past week. Or Sao Paulo for all I knew. She could have easily missed the obituary of the Sofa King of Sarasota. A galactic crush of sadness darkened the moment. Before me stood a woman on a precipice, blessedly ignorant that the world she occupied had shifted beyond her tenuous control. That yesterday had been her last good day. My words were about to incontrovertibly alter her life.

"I'm sorry to tell you this. Andrew Keller is dead. He died during a robbery at a convenience store. It was a random act."

Her hand shot up to her mouth. "Oh my dear God. When?"

"Little over a week. Two days after he saw you at the Vinoy."

"It was an accident?" She took a step back and crossed her arms in front or her.

"He was in the wrong place at the wrong time."

"Oh God. Oh dear God." Her voice cracked. She squeezed her shoulders. "Oh, poor Andrew. Oh sweet God." Her knees buckled. I thought she might go down.

Touch her, you fool.

I did not reach out to comfort her. I am not that type of person—I am a person who wants to be that type of person. Instead, a man on a mission, I said, "What did you want to talk to him about, Mrs. Walker?"

"What?"

"At the Vinoy. Andrew said you needed to tell him about some trumpet."

She looked at me as if I were a stranger to the human race. She cast her eyes down. The movie played merrily on. Dick Van Dyke told Sally Ann Howes that her father was going to buy his doggie treats business. They were rich and in love. Life was good.

"Not now," she said. She glanced up at me. "Not ever."

"Do you know of any reason or of any person who would want Andrew dead?"

"You said it was an accident."

I remained silent and kept my eyes on her.

She took another step back. "Who are you? Why are you really here?"

"I'm a friend of Andrew's. I don't know anyone tonight." It occurred to me that Andrew's death had broadened the scope of my relationship with him. That seemed surreal, but I had no time for that.

"You're not just his friend," she challenged me.

I hesitated. I didn't want Charlie Walker to know that I was investigating the death of Andrew Keller. Nothing would be gained by tipping my hand to him. But if I wanted information, I'd have to trust somebody. Take that first step.

"I'm the unofficial investigation."

"But that part about him coming to you after we ran into each other—"

"That is exactly how it happened."

Elizabeth Walker looked out toward the heavy and untouchable black of the Gulf of Mexico. The wind kicked up and rattled the palm fronds. A single tear, glistening like one of Kathleen's diamonds in the bay, slid down the cheek of the army nurse from a long-ago war. I couldn't imagine what Seurat painting, what Mahler symphony, that tear held.

She sniffled. "Have you told anyone?"

"Told them what?"

"That you're investigating—my apologies," she said with a note of bitterness. "That you're unofficially investigating his death?"

My mind scrambled as I tried to decide if I should mention Allison Daniels.

"No."

She stepped into me, talking rapidly. "You're lying. You came with the woman wearing two masks who no one knows. Despite the charade, we all know each other and who we don't know. You told her."

"Pillow talk. She has no official capacity. What I meant is that I haven't talked to the players here. I don't know anyone here other than the friends I came with."

"Forget about me. Forget everything Andrew said. For me. For you." She paused and then continued. "I just thought it would be nice to see him again—after all those years."

"You're going to have to do better than that."

"I don't have to do a thing for you."

"Do you know why anyone would want to cause him harm?"

"Enjoy your evening, Mr. Travis."

She turned and hustled up the concrete steps to the balcony. Her abrupt about-face from a near emotional collapse was startling. It lessened my guilt for not reaching out to comfort her, but it left me with this: Who was this masked woman whose emotions, marked by a solitary tear, so chillingly obeyed her intellect?

I followed a few minutes later to the balcony where a

wall of stately French doors opened to the ballroom. The orchestra played "Smoke Gets in Your Eyes," and the luscious melody channeled through the night like a southern breeze. I thought that was a wrap for the evening.

I was wrong.

10

At 11:45 p.m., I spotted Kathleen and Morgan talking with a woman with long auburn hair who appeared to use her hatchet right hand to accentuate every word. As I threaded my way toward them, loud voices erupted from behind me. Allison Daniels and Charlie Walker were in a heated debate, although Allison seemed to be doing most of the talking. Both had their masks off, as, by that hour, did a great many other guests.

I recalibrated my course and snuck up behind Allison. The music had stopped, as the orchestra was reassembling after a break. Allison raised her slurred voice to Walker, her finger wagging in front of his face.

"Not a damn piece of evidence has ever indicated that a person carrying a gun prevents violence. And how can you be pro-life and pro-gun?" she said, her words thick with whatever she'd been washing down her throat. "On what *planet* does that even make sense?"

She'd clearly violated her own doctrine about abstaining from drinking with the enemy.

One of several men standing beside Walker stepped forth. "Perhaps you should leave, Ms. Daniels."

"It's *Mrs.*, you neo-Nazi skinhead. And the blood of children is on your hands."

Oh boy. So much for knowing the difference between anger and contempt—the quality she had so admired in Andrew. I stepped beside her and placed my fingers lightly on her arm. "Let's get some fresh air, shall we?"

Her face crinkled as if she were startled to see me, and who the heck was I in the first place? She tried to shake me off, but I tightened my hand, telling myself that she would thank me in the morning.

"*Shall* we?" she blurted out at me. "Did you really just say *shall* we?"

"Come on, Allison, let's go."

"Fine," she spit out, mad at the world.

"I apologize," I said to Walker and his entourage. "You know she lost her nephew at Stoneman, right? No excuse for tonight's outburst. But it's been terribly difficult for her and her family."

Charlie Walker drilled my eyes as if sending me a warning. But then he rallied with alarming efficiency, the imperturbable lobbyist that he was riding to the evening's rescue.

"Please tell Ms. Daniels—when she is sober of course—that she is forgiven and that I look forward to continuing to work with her. She wears her passions well. Those whom she represents should be proud of her efforts and dedication. We are fortunate to have her in our state." His sonorous voice filled the room and his face broke into an affable smile. Charlie Walker could talk red into blue and hot into cold.

I started to leave, but a snicker by one his stooges didn't

sit well with me. "Just for the record," I said, "*Mrs.* Daniels didn't ask for your forgiveness."

That daggered Walker's smile. Whatever else it did to his facial expression was for others to see as I half walked and half carried Allison to the nearest door. The orchestra broke into "Moonlight Serenade," and the Glenn Miller theme song quieted frayed nerves and soothed the prickly air.

Kathleen and Morgan met me outside by the entrance to the spa. I asked Allison what her room number was.

She looked up at me. "Think I'm bunking with you, pal? Dream on."

"I just—"

"I'm yankin' your chain, music man. Did I call Charlie Walker a neo-Nazi skinhead? Shit. I bet he's thrilled." She punched her breath out. "God, I can't believe I did that. I got to shut my yapper."

"Kathleen will help you up to your room."

"Aye aye, captain." Her eyes widened. "Hey, 'member that? I had to fight not to smile. It's not easy being a hard-ass in a skirt. You try it sometime. Ooh, I bet it's easy for you, gun boy."

She teetered and grabbed the thick concrete rail. Kathleen placed her hand firmly on Allison's elbow. They took a step but then Allison turned to me. "Virginia," she said, drawing the vowels out like whole notes. "My sister's name is Virginia."

The two women stumbled around the outside patio and into a lobby door far from the ballroom. Kathleen would make certain that Allison Daniels was finished socializing for the evening.

Standing next to the side door we'd just come out of, a World War II nurse observed as Kathleen and Allison did their three-legged walk. A woman, who appeared to be an attendant to the court of Louis the Sixteenth, whispered in her ear, but Elizabeth Walker kept her watchful eyes on me.

I don't know anyone other than the friends I came with, I'd told her.

That lie didn't even make it to midnight.

11

Lizzy

He is now to be among you at the calling of your hearts
Rest assured this troubadour is acting on His part

Elizabeth Walker woke up to a morning that belonged in a song: the water still, the sky cloudless, and the sun a welcoming glow of warmth. A friendly breeze graced her skin just enough to let her know that the world was still alive, still good, and that she was not alone. It was as if the Great Spirit was trying to placate her, to make amends for the crushing news about Andrew. She accepted the gift. Why not? She could use a little pick-me-up. After all, her pipe dream had been stupid. Elizabeth Walker commanded a great many words, but on that melodic morning, *stupid* was the reigning monarch.

She finished her walk and stepped into her house. She undraped the earphones from around her neck, dropped them on the kitchen table, grabbed a water from the refrigerator, and plopped into a chair. Her walk, a fraction of the steps she used to log, had exhausted her. She thought about brewing coffee but decided against it. She took half a bottle of water in one long guzzle. The doctor had said it was fine to go about her regular routine but to temper her expectations. Lizzy struggled mightily with that. There was nothing *fine* about any of it. Besides, you never stick *regular* before *routine*. That type of comment made Lizzy think she needed a new doctor, but what was the point?

The previous night had played in her head every inch of the morning walk. It boiled down to this: *Andrew was dead.*

Lizzy kept thinking those three words created the worst combination she had ever heard. Her doctor's *We're sorry, there is nothing we can do for you* had been the previous winner, but now it came up a lame second. Hard to believe it could blow its pole position. Only one worse comment in the universe was possible, but she had nailed place and show. Twenty years, she thought. You decide to right a wrong, and three words land-mine it. Well, that's what you get for lollygagging around. Pretty dumb—no, stupid—to think it could ever have worked out. Not that bad news was totally unexpected. She always knew that life was pregnant with bad things; tragedy waiting to enter the world at any moment.

At first the sudden and palpable yearning for her youth —the searing promise that it represented—had dizzied her. Forging into the past, she embraced the obscene conviction that Wolfe was wrong and cheered her temerity to challenge his great title. But then the banging and inescapable questions: Why now, this blazing infatuation with all things past? This ache for Scarborough Fair? Was her dash backward merely a shrill rebellion to the mollifying advancement of middle age—which in her case came with the diagnosis that she'd be lucky to witness two more seasons—and a blueprint out of her suffocating relationship?

Her relationship.

The painted smile she wore when she and Charlie hosted a dinner or attended a "function." He lived for them. She dreaded them. His energy gained momentum throughout the day, cumulating in those magical hours between seven and ten when backs were slapped, hands were shaken, and cocktails greased the increasingly incestuous relationship between capitalism and democracy. She loathed the niggling pleasantries, the forced smiles, the schadenfreude gossip. ("He always did have a cocktail in his hand." "She's thinking of filing." "They had to place their son in another school—that's twice in three years!") The flirting eyes. The accidental rub. ("Oh, I'm sorry. Elizabeth, right? Wow, you look terrific in that dress. May I get you something to drink?") Standing erect in talking circles when all remnants of genuine concern had petered out and died immediately after—or was it during?—"It's *so* good to see you." A picture to commemorate the event. She and Charlie with their arms around each other, smiling lies into the camera. The silent ride home.

Then at home, the disassembling of the face, the polite good nights, the meaningless kiss, the general blasé agreement that it had been another successful outing. A book on the nightstand beckoning her with its promise of another world, and oh God, she could hardly wait to crawl under the covers and lose herself in the soft light of its pages. (Phew, what a relief!) Who was waiting for her? Daisy and Jay? Julia and Dawsey? The Count and Anna? She would nestle into her sheets, the reward at the end of the day, while Charlie hunkered down in the study, the electrifying momentum of the night carrying him into the single-digit part of the clock as he meticulously planned his next forty-eight hours with unnatural focus. Another evening without a sincere question about her day, although she knew she was eclipsing him. Not in money but in building an institution of substance. Of value. Something to outlive them both. She was creating greatness, yet he barely noticed, so consumed was he in his piddling narrow pursuit: *guns here, guns there, guns, guns everywhere.*

Was her unutterable obsession with everything Andrew a counter to all that, or was it the final gasp of a love affair the world had long forgotten? She was fonder of the questions than of the answers, for questions represented a prairie of hope, and answers signaled dead-end finality—or simply begot more questions.

Weary from the unrelenting whispers of dissatisfaction, from the constant chore of subverting her innermost desires, she'd penned a letter.

Not a letter, really. That would be like calling a two-by-four a house. A kitten a lion. A sentence. A sentence that had taken her ten years to formulate and ten seconds to write. A sentence that was a key to her soul. That was followed by a phone call. And then another. But phone calls are no substitute for a bashful eye. A hopeful glance. An exploratory and light touch upon a shoulder. But neither had wanted to meet just yet, to venture into those unknown waters. Better to cling to hope than to be left with fantasy. He knew nothing of her sickness. What cruel heartbreak that would be, to get together only to be torn asunder. Again. And even though her urge to reconnect had surfaced prior to her death sentence, what doubt would that have spawned? She could hear Andrew's thoughts: *Ahh, the clock's ticking and you want to make amends. Feeling a little guilty, are we? Excuse me, but I think I'll pass.*

Then they met by chance at the Vinoy. She saw it in his eyes. Knew he saw it in hers. She had been unprepared for the cavalcade of emotions. The consuming desire. Her whole body screamed to talk with him. Walk with him. Touch him. Full steam ahead: Burn the books. Crack the records. Rip the bloodied sheets. She had spoken—mouthed, really—a few words. Then she touched him. Hard. Handcuffed his wrist with her hand that, like her voice, had thrust itself out without permission or apology.

Go, hand. Go!

Not that it mattered. Andrew was dead. But it wasn't just Andrew who had died. So had her dreams. Her hope. His death had sucked those out of her life as well, popped them like a balloon. As long as he'd been in the world, so had they. And what wonderful and inspiring companions those silent partners had been. Now they, too, were memory. She thought she knew what an empty world felt like; how terrible to know for certain.

"What's an unofficial investigation?" she said. It had been screaming in her mind all morning.

"Pardon me, ma'am?"

Lizzy faced Ciara, her new housemaid, cook, and second-string confidant.

"Oh, nothing."

Lizzy's cheeks blushed. She caught herself talking out loud more often. She blamed it on the new pills, but they were guiltless. Her voice would soon be silenced forever, and that saddened her. Still, there is dignity to consider. A final act that you perform only once. And, by God, you don't want to be on the stage when the orchestra is yawning.

"Would you like me to change the sheets today?" Ciara asked.

"No. Remember, I said Tuesdays and Fridays," Lizzy said, wishing she had a dollar—forget that—a year for every time she'd given Ciara the schedule. How many ways can you screw up seven days? Quite a few, apparently.

Her previous housemaid, Anna, was on the lam. She'd been ordered out of the country, and officials from the U.S. Immigration and Customs Enforcement—the ICE—were hot on her trail. Anna had been in the States for twenty years, but, like murder, there was no statute of limitations on illegal entry. She had taken sanctuary in a church two months ago. Although they possessed the legal right, the ICE officials refrained from entering churches, hospitals, or schools. While those institutions potentially faced charges for harboring such individuals, the government wisely avoided that nightmare publicity. Both of Anna's daughters, Kimberly and Olivia, were born in the States and continued to live with an uncle and attend school. Her husband was in hiding and doing such a stellar job of it that Anna had not heard from the man in three years. Lizzy visited Anna every week (or was it every couple of days?), and because there is no explanation for such things, no formula for human friendship, the two had grown closer during Anna's self-imposed exile. They had become separated inseparable friends.

Lizzy bankrolled Anna's efforts to stay in the U.S. with her family. That process, while drawn out, was promising, as the courts were lenient on people with a good record and who had been in the country for over ten years. Anna planned to live in the church until she no longer faced forced deportation. Until the presence of the sun or moon on her face no longer threatened to separate her from her daughters and the country she felt was hers.

Lizzy saw the hurt in Ciara's eyes. In a placating tone, she added, "By the way, the spinach soufflé you made the other day was awesome. If you'd don't mind, would you make another one today? Both Charlie and I loved it. Oh, and for the party next week, those mini chocolate raspberry tarts we talked about. Not the cheesecake; those were too heavy."

Ciara nodded, more a curtsy really, and that irritated Lizzy. "Yes, ma'am. I vacuumed the bedroom this morning and I'll do the laundry now."

"No, remember . . . that will be fine. Thank you."

"I brewed you some fresh coffee," Ciara said, eager to do *something* right. Lizzy again saw the confusion in her eyes. *Oh, I don't need this now.*

"Thank you. I was just going to do so myself."

Ciara left and Lizzy stared out the window where pelicans rode the wind above the gulf.

"Anna, Anna, Anna. Why did you leave me now?"

Anna had been with her for seven years. For the first few years, she'd been a kick-ass housekeeper. Happy. Chipper. A flower that blossomed every day. A woman who could not help but cheer those she came in contact with. When she brought her two daughters by, their bulging personalities filled the house. They insisted on sharing goofy YouTube cat videos and pictures of puppies that were impossible not to like. Lizzy and Charlie had no children, and Lizzy found a surrogate family with Anna and her girls. She arranged and pruned her schedule so that she could spend more time in the Saint Pete home and less time in Tallahassee. She slyly convinced Charlie that the gulf-front home was their real home and that she was perfectly fine staying there while he rode north into battle.

Then came the Christmas dishes.

Anna's husband had just taken off. Gone. No trace of the man who had forsaken his fatherly obligations exactly two weeks before Christmas and the day Lizzy had bought herself a discounted chocolate advent calendar because, well, she just she felt like it. Lizzy also felt like having more people around the Christmas table. She insisted over Charlie's weakening objections—he'd never seen the purpose for holidays, untimely interruptions that they were—that Anna and her daughters spend Christmas dinner with them. Normally Charlie's staid relatives dropped by. Lizzy had no family except an estranged brother. She lobbied to the lobbyist that Anna was family to her. Charlie, knowing how the accident twenty years ago had decimated Lizzy's family, had no choice but to acquiesce. His stiff and disapproving posture at the dinner table while Anna—the help, for Pete's sake!—and her girls joined in the festivities gave Lizzy deep satisfaction. She didn't extend the invitation for that purpose, but it was a sweet consequence. It didn't hurt that Charlie's sister, Heather, took an instant and vicarious liking to Anna's girls. Kimberly was approaching those stupefying high school years, with Olivia not far behind, that half the population wouldn't remember by the age of forty. The remaining half, Heather's half, would recount every petty detail with forlorn fondness and sickening accuracy.

Lizzy took a drink from the bottle and was surprised that it was empty. *Drink lots of water,* the doctor had said. *Stay hydrated.* What's that going to add? A few days?

The dishes.

The decision, brewing for years, had finally clamored for recognition that Christmas. *You've got to tell someone sometime, right?* A now-or-never type of gene that had mutated, rallied by her complete acceptance that she had never been in love with her husband. He had been, after all, the runner-up. And if not today, then when? And so while Lizzy washed, Anna dried, Michael Bublé crooned "All I Want for Christmas Is You," and Heather, glued to her seat, relived her glory days with Anna's girls, Lizzy confided in Anna.

She told her everything. (Well, not *that.*)

The love of her life. The accident. The trip to Paris and the part of her that she had left there. Swore her to secrecy. And Anna spilled her secrets. That she had not been born in the United States. That she slept with one eye open. That she believed her husband was not the disinterested father he appeared to be but simply a man who valued his freedom and who wished to remain one step ahead of the threat to that freedom. They'd become the best of friends. Friends who shared dark and beautiful secrets.

No, Lizzy thought, *that's not right.* Friends are people you conjure up in your mind. A media image. You read about them in books, see them on the screen, talk to them at parties, but are they really friends? Sure, she'd met some fine people at the bank and her charitable foundation, but no one had ever clicked.

A sister. That's who Anna was to her. The sister she never had. Even better, for she could create any image of a sister she wanted. From then on, Lizzy considered Anna to be her sister.

Then Anna got wind that the U.S. government, with everything else going on in the world, dearly wanted her back in Guatemala, or at least off domestic soil. What theatrical timing, for Lizzy had decided to make her move. To finally decant her corked grief and to satisfy her unflinching desire to be true to her heart. Anna was to be her crutch. Her cheering sister. But when Lizzy needed Anna the most, Anna had gone to bunk with God. Packing her suitcase along with Lizzy's secrets.

She checked her phone for messages from the attorney she'd hired. *What a towering figure—holed up in his nautical office. It was like he walked out of a Dickens novel.* He'd not been easy to find. A friend who'd triumphed in a vile divorce battle had recommended him. When Lizzy insisted that she wasn't scouting for a divorce attorney, the friend had laughed and said he wasn't a divorce attorney.

"What is he?"

"Who knows, darling? Just go see him."

The attorney (who no one knows what he really does) said it might be months before he got the scent. Laws being what they are and bribery only taking you so far these days.

She brought up her calendar on her phone. *Shoot. I forgot.* More tests at eleven this morning. *Oh God,* she thought. *I know I'm a stranger to you. But hear my voice. Give me time.*

She'd have to tell Charlie about Andrew Keller's death. He would likely have to suppress a victorious smile. Such an unfortunate occurrence—Lizzy's former suitor now off the board. She went into her bedroom, sweeping up books along the way. She'd brought her favorite books down from the Tallahassee house and was in the process of arranging them in her bedroom, a bedroom in which she had chosen to spend her last hours.

She caught herself in the mirror. *Looking a little pale today.* Her mother had always wanted her to apply more makeup. "You are easily the most beautiful woman in the room," she had implored her only daughter between midday drinks. "And with a little work, you can be a striking presence."

As far as Lizzy could tell, "striking presence" was a combination of artfully applied makeup, continual tanning, Botox, expensive articles of clothing a tad too good for the occasion, and a drink in your hand.

But Mrs. Phillips's only daughter hadn't wanted to be the most beautiful woman in the room. She had no desire to invite gazes that would ignite lust into fantasies. Instead, she coveted the solitude of books and became addicted to the wild and stimulating quietness they brought her. They blanketed her on a cold day and breezed her on a hot one. Locked in a love of reading, young Elizabeth Phillips surrendered to the wizardry of words that could feed the sprouting imagination of her fertile mind.

Lizzy realized at an early age that you don't really get to pick who you are, you just need the guts to admit it. Growing up, much to her mother's disdain ("Don't you want to redecorate your room?"), she had a quote from Audrey Hepburn above her bed. "For my whole life, my favorite activity was reading. It's not the most social pastime." Above her dresser was tacked another from the actress, who was a Goodwill Ambassador to UNICEF: "I still read fairy-tales and I like them best of all."

Take that, Mom. Audrey Fucking Hepburn! Breakfast at Tiffany's! *Why don't you go lightly on me, Mom? Golightly. Don't get it, do you?*

She'd read *The Diary of a Young Girl* when she was the author's age and underlined this: "Ordinary people simply don't know what books mean to us." She named her cat Kitty. Her mother was clueless. Her father guessed the reason for the name, which only endeared him to her even more.

Then I let him die.

She loved other things, of course. The smell of a fresh-cut Christmas tree. A child's squeaky voice. And seashells, God's stocking gifts to the world. She kept her hand-harvested collection hidden from Charlie. He always whined, "What are you going to do with all of them?" Why, she thought, do I have to do something with them? They are snowflakes that never melt—so pretty, and no two are alike. Elizabeth's favorite activity was strolling the early-morning and late-afternoon beach in search of seashells. She always wore a shirt with pockets—not easy to find—stuffed with Kleenexes to pad the shells.

Her mother had never relinquished her solo crusade. She slid bitterly to her grave instructing her grown daughter to stand a little straighter and beseeching her to never go out to buy a loaf of bread unless she had dressed for church and to treat every Friday and Saturday night like New Year's Eve, and don't you think just a little more eyeliner would go a long way? She'd spring forth from a rehab center with these same commandments. Then she'd knock herself back into the gutter only to drag her abused liver into yet another treatment facility that she heard was better than the previous shoddy one, before springing free of that "squalored place" and resuming her unrelenting attack on her underachieving daughter, as if the only purpose for her resurrection from the cross of alcohol was to berate Eliza-beth for being hell-bent on not becoming a striking woman despite her goddamn-given attributes.

Oh, Lizzy. I'd give twenty years at the end to look like that again.

She never saw sixty. Lizzy put on just a little too much makeup for her funeral. An eye-popping dress. Her highest heels. She towered unapologetically above the grave, a striking figure, indeed.

Lizzy picked up *Summer Sisters*, *Message in a Bottle*, and a pristine copy of *Sophie's Choice* that she'd read in high school. That was one sad novel. She thought there should be a book scale, like they have for suitcases, to weigh the sadness of a story. She dismissed the thought. For all good books are sad, and what is to gain by measuring tragedy? By out-dueling someone else's misfortune? She arranged the books, as well as a few more she rescued from the teetering stack on her nightstand, on a shelf that clearly had a no vacancy sign posted on it. She went to her closet and did something she rarely did. She pulled the painting out. Its home over the years had been in her different closets, swathed in a sheet and tucked safely behind long evening gowns. For its protection as well as hers.

She unwrapped it.

And then, because all this was too much for her, and all she had ever wanted was to have her own family and to do it right, and she was to blame for that irreversible failure, Elizabeth Walker collapsed on her freshly vacuumed carpet and cried until her trembling, dying body had not a tear left to offer the world.

12

Marcy Keller skipped out of the country club as if she hadn't a care in the world. But this time a man with a sweater tied around his neck accompanied her jaunty exit. She reached up and planted a quick before-anyone-sees-us kiss on Sweater-Man's lips and they parted ways. The flowers had yet to wilt on Andrew's grave.

I didn't think Andrew's support of an anti-gun cause would put a target on his back. At least I hoped not. Wayne had sought me out, leading with Elizabeth Walker. I wanted to gather more information about Mrs. Walker before confronting her again. Marcy had held out the first time we'd met, which meant that she qualified for a second pass. She was ten feet from me, her head buried in her phone, when she spotted me.

"Gotta go," she said. She punched her phone and then landed a hard stare. "I thought we were one and done. I don't know Elizabeth Walker."

"I never told you her married name."

"Well, la-di-da. Bravo for you, Mr. . . . I'm sorry, your name again?"

"You know my name, and you know that Elizabeth Phillips became Elizabeth Walker."

"Au revoir," she said. She reached for the car door.

"Do men really wear sweaters around their necks?"

She spun around. "Pardon me?"

"Your Robert Redford friend."

She sucked on her lower lip. "What's your game? I called the police after the first time you bushwhacked me in a parking lot. You'd be surprised how polite the men in blue are to a grieving widow. They said there is no evidence that Andrew's death, while being investigated as a homicide, was anything other than a random killing."

"That's what—"

"They never heard of you and suggested I call them if you harass me any further. Are you harassing me?"

"It's unfortunate that you consider my interest in trying to find your husband's killer an infringement on your country club time."

Her shoulders slumped. "Tell me how a solitary letter from Andrew's former lover leads to all this?"

"What letter?"

"You don't know?" she said, genuinely surprised.

"No clue."

"I wouldn't put money on that." She cocked her head "Tell you what, Johnny Persistent. Follow me home. I'm all for helping to hang the man who shot Andrew. You can forget turning that other cheek stuff. I'll give you what I got —it ain't much—and then you leave me alone. No more hounding me in parking lots. Deal?"

She didn't wait for an answer but slipped into her car. I climbed into my truck and followed her as we coursed through streets of well-tended houses. She pulled into a circular, paver-bricked driveway with a three-tiered fountain in the center. The Sofa King of Sarasota's house looked like the front cover of a home-decorating magazine for Florida living. Manicured robellini palms anchored each side of the front door, and oversize carriage lamps created a regal entrance. A garage door crawled open and Marcy's car motored into home position.

I followed her through the kitchen and out to an expansive covered lanai with a blue and white tiled pool surrounded by wicker furniture and flowered cushions. If the outside of the house was the cover of the magazine, the patio area was the inside of the same magazine—where every item has a letter next to it that corresponds with an alluring description and an absurd price. At one end of the pool, a raised hot tub circulated a wide stream of translucent water. A cherub with a bulging, algae-green belly held a bouquet of stone flowers next to the hot tub. On the other side of the screen, a row of neatly trimmed wax myrtle framed an undulating golf course of carpeted green.

Marcy went to a refrigerator and took out a bottle of water. While I waited for her to offer me something, she disappeared around a corner. I grabbed a water from the fridge and took a seat on a burgundy sofa.

"Make yourself at home," Marcy said tartly as she came back out to the lanai.

"I don't think Andrew would mind."

She settled into a stuffed chair across from me and placed an envelope on the table. "I don't mean to be presumptuous," she said. "That's not who I am. Andrew and I had some wonderful years together—I'm sure they'll come back to me at some point. But not our last year. We'd grown apart. His business, despite all the ads, was struggling, and we had just," she humped her right shoulder, "lost interest in each other. It happens.

"Now I've got to hire a new general manager and come up with an advertising campaign, seeing as how he was the face of the business."

"The Sofa Queen of Sarasota."

She rolled her eyes. "That's actually under consideration, or, I should say, was. I nixed it fast. Andrew could act, and it *was* all acting. Dressing up in those ri*dic*ulous outfits. And then people thinking that's who he was."

She spit out her last words as if she were disgusted with her late husband. I surveyed the property. "I wouldn't complain too much."

"I wasn't. It's just nothing I could ever do."

She crossed her legs, dangling a shapely limb with a bronze ankle bracelet on it. A shy breeze tinkled chimes. She flipped a finger toward the envelope on the table. "This came about six weeks ago. He went silent the day he got it. Curled up under the water. He never really surfaced after that."

"May I?"

"Why not," she said with a coy smile directed at my bottle of water. "You help yourself to everything else."

The envelope had no return address on it. I opened it and slid out a small piece of stationery. On it, written in cursive, was, "Do you remember Trumpet?"

"What trumpet?" I asked.

"You got me. When he opened the envelope? He just stared at it. I asked him what it was, but he said nothing and never mentioned it again." She spread her hands. "Who knows? Maybe it was some silly love-coded word."

"Who was the letter from?" I asked solely to verify, for I knew the answer.

She gazed out over the golf course, her outstretched arm resting on the chair displaying a collection of gold and silver bracelets. Marcy Keller looked like the house she lived in. I wondered what her description read and what she cost.

"Marcy?"

She sniffled and made a fist of her hand, bringing it up under her nose. "I'm sorry. This has been a lot for me over . . . over a short period of time. You think Andrew was murdered? You insinuated that, didn't you? When we first met?"

I couldn't decide whether she was putting on an act or not. "It's a possibility."

"Do you think I'm a bad person?"

"No."

"But you don't like me."

"I don't know you."

"Andrew dated—no, that's not right. Andrew's true love was Elizabeth Phillips. This was twenty years ago. Not that I didn't have my own ex-lovers. We traded them like war stories."

"You told me you didn't know—"

"And if you believed me, you would never have come back." She uncrossed her legs and straightened her posture. "A woman knows when a man's heart is somewhere else. I spit on my ex-lovers. Andrew? He had but one, and that," she cut me a coquettish look, "was your Elizabeth Phillips. He thought he was being cool and detached when he talked about her. But a woman sees with her soul, not her eyes, hears with her heart, not her ears. I understood his words far beyond him."

Her phone rang. In a voice meant to convey her pitying boredom, she droned that she couldn't talk right now and that she'd call whomever it was back.

"Where were we," she said, leveling her eyes on me. "Ah yes. Romantic Andrew. The trait that attracted me to him was the same trait that built a wall around him. His endearing attribute was his most irritating feature."

"You were married . . . ?" I spread my hands.

"Twelve years."

"Had he been in contact with her?"

"Not that I know of."

"Phone? Mail?"

"Must I repeat myself?"

"When was the last time you two discussed Elizabeth?"

She puffed out her breath, stood, and walked into the house. She came back with a glass of iced tea.

"Would you like something?" she said as an intentional afterthought.

"I'm fine."

"Let's see." She reclaimed her seat and drummed her fingers in a steady beat of indifference on the back of a magazine, as if recalling a conversation with her late husband was an act that required considerable strength. The ad on the back cover was for Sarasota Sofa, including a picture of Andrew in the corner with an oversize crown. It read, THE KING SAYS EVERYTHING HAS TO GO! "That would have been a week or so before he died. He said he ran into her at the Vinoy. Then he admitted that she had been the one who'd sent him the letter about the trombone."

"Trumpet."

"Whatever."

"And what did you say?"

"It wasn't my proudest moment. It rarely is after three drinks. I told him I was going to squeal to my attorney that he was having an affair."

"Was he?"

"I told you—as far as I know, they'd hadn't seen each other in years."

"But you lie," I pointed out.

"When it suits me."

"How did he end up with a peach like you?"

She took a patient sip, her eyes not leaving mine. "We were once both better people."

Her comments did validate Andrew's concern that he didn't need the bad publicity heading into a divorce. Who knows what ugly tactics Marcy was capable of? I wondered if Andrew would have agreed with the first-person plural pronoun in her last statement, but had nothing to gain by defending him, or agitating Marcy.

She gave a sigh, eager to demonstrate that she was filibustering her time away. "I wish I could give you more. He never got over puppy love. Those ridiculous ads he ran? He was hiding from himself. He tried so hard to be someone he wasn't. Andrew forfeited his heart years ago. And . . ." She seemed to have lost her train of thought. "End of story."

She stood and I did likewise. She leaned over and picked up the envelope. "Two things. First, I don't want this." She handed it to me.

"And second?"

"Goodbye." She trilled it out in two distinctive notes and walked away.

13

He might have dressed like a king, but he labored like a serf.

I wanted to check on Andrew's business associates. For all I knew, a disgruntled employee settled a score with him. I should have asked Marcy if she was aware of any threatening situations in which he was involved. I wasn't sure she would have given me a straight answer—although that was no excuse for not asking.

The lineless parking lot of his warehouse west of I-75 hadn't been resurfaced in years. Two lost gulls bickered over a sandwich wrapper. I stepped out of my air-conditioned truck and ultraviolet rays ironed my shoulders. Florida is reversed fruit; the sweetness—the sugary, sea-breeze beaches—is on the outside and the gritty skin is in the middle.

Andrew's half-dozen showrooms in the greater Tamps/Sarasota area were dressy. Clean and inviting. No one could accuse him of corporate overhead. Four mismatched chairs and an end table crowded the waiting area. An off-kilter sunset picture of the Gulf of Mexico was the sole wall decoration. A full-faced woman wearing a blouse of colorful dogs sat behind the desk. Music played faintly from her computer.

"May I help you?" she asked.

My encounter with Marcy was fresh on my mind, and I wanted to get off to a good start. I amped up my charm and beamed my winningest smile. "I've thought of getting a dog, but my cat voted against it."

"I don't care much for either," she said. "Picked this up at the thrift store for a buck. May I help you?"

I introduced myself and told her I was an old friend of Andrew's. That he had dropped by before his murder, and asked if she had time for a few questions.

She glanced at her screen and clicked her mouse. She leaned back in her chair that had a sweater draped over the back of it. "Shoot."

I gave her the spiel. I played down the part that Andrew might have been targeted and stuck with trying to know him better after reconnecting with him after so many years.

"I'm just heartbroken," she said. "He was a wonderful man to work for and now without him, we don't know what will happen. His wife, Marcy—I can't imagine her running it anywhere but into the ground. She keeps herself a mile of sunshine away from this place, and she don't strike me as a penny counter. Mr. Keller knew you can't be taking money out all the time. You got to keep your name in front of the public or they will forget you faster than last year's Super Bowl winner. That was his favorite thing—who even remembers who won the Super Bowl, he'd say. And if they forget that, then what are the chances they remember us when it's time to buy a sofa? Know what I mean? What did you say your name was?"

I gave her my name again and popped some questions about any potential disgruntled employees, mainly to atone for my failure to do so with Marcy. She assured me that Andrew was well liked and wouldn't hesitate to pitch in and unload a delivery truck.

"Andrew's philosophy," she said, "was to have as few employees as possible but to pay them as much as the business could bear. He had a profit-sharing formula and made us all feel part of a team. He was such a sweet man."

An open door behind her led to an empty office that I assumed was Andrew's. It would be nice to look around. I told her that I'd sent him tickets to a Rays game and wondered if he still had them.

She reached into an open box of cereal on her desk, eyeing me warily. "I didn't know he was interested in baseball."

"It was just a chance for us to catch up. We hadn't seen each other in years. I'm sorry, I didn't get your name."

She swallowed. "Didn't give it. Brooke. Let's take a look in his office, but I open all the snail mail and I didn't see anything. Don't mind my slippers. I like my feet to be comfortable, and these are great for knocking around."

She wore blue dolphin slippers, and it wasn't their first day on her feet. I followed her into the office. The wood desk was neat, but the credenza was pancaked with layers of paper and catalogs. A large TV anchored one corner.

"He was always watching himself on that," Brooke said. "Not to stroke his ego but because he wanted to make sure his ads were perfect. Especially the music. He'd nitpick an ad until the music and timing were just right. But he was worried; trying to figure out how to move his act away from the idiot box."

A bookcase next to the TV held a dozen or so cardboard crowns. I picked one up. It was purple with gold trumpets angled in different positions.

"That one just arrived. He special ordered that. Next-day delivery. That wasn't like him at all—to spend a few worthless dollars. Said he liked the trumpets on it. You get them from party sites. You know, I don't see any tickets here." She'd been flipping through a pile of letters on the credenza. "Nope, no tickets."

I turned the crown over, as if trying to decode what a trumpet had to do with Andrew Keller and Elizabeth Walker. "Did he say anything about the trumpets?"

"Just that he liked it."

"Did he ever use trumpets in his crown before?"

"Got me. You know he was always changing his royal garb, don't you? That's what he called it, royal garb."

"What was his plan for it?"

"For what?"

"The trumpet."

"You're working too hard."

I faced the woman in front of me who had puppies on her chest and dolphins on her feet. Her wide eyes punctuated a guileless face.

"Outside of his employees, did Andrew have any enemies?"

She crinkled her face. "Enemies? That sounds so vulgar. You knew him, right? Gentlest soul to ever walk the planet. To be honest, I don't know how he ended up hawking furniture. I always thought he belonged in, I don't know, theater or something. But he had a gift for promotion and that's business 101, I'll tell you that."

I pulled out my phone and held up a picture of Elizabeth Walker. "Have you ever seen this woman before?"

She studied the picture and then craned her neck back

up at me, for dolphin-footed Brooke was likely only a tad over five feet. "Your questions are getting a little pointy."

"Foul play can't be ruled out."

"I kinda thought that's where you were heading."

"Do you know her?"

She gnawed on her thumb knuckle and then lowered her hand. "I was with him for eight years. He treated me well, compensated me even better, and never denied me a day off. I paid his bills—you know all the automatic payment stuff? I set it all up, fixed it all when he got new credit cards. But he kept parts of him so buried I wondered if he could ever find himself."

She paused and I sensed that she was calculating her words. She jutted her head at the credenza. "See the computer, how it faces out to the room?"

I nodded.

"I could see whatever was on his screen when I came in. No biggie. Andrew wasn't into porn; he was into sofas and recliners and pillows and spreadsheets. He said we sold a sofa just to sell a pair of pillows with it. That's where we made the money. But one day—oh, I dunno—'bout a month ago, I came in." She dipped her head at my phone. "She was on his screen. But to answer your question. No, I don't know her."

"Did he say anything about her?"

"I said, 'Who's she?' He switched it off and said she was some model he was thinking of using. But then he changed the subject. He did that when he didn't want to answer a question. And oh boy, was he good at that, just a dandy, let me tell you."

"To your knowledge, did he ever see, hear, or come in contact with her other than what you just said?"

"We at a trial or something? No."

"Do you think she had anything to do with him ordering a new crown with trumpets on it?"

"That's about as crazy as my dolphin feet."

"Do you find your dolphin feet crazy?"

She curled up her lip. "Not at all. He ordered them around the same time I caught him gazing at the woman on the screen. But you're chasing rainbows, and that's dumber than trumpets. You've seen his ads? He was always switching his king outfit. He knew his customers weren't just buying furniture, they were buying him." She paused and said, "What do you know about the woman on the screen?"

"She's a former girlfriend. Name of Elizabeth Walker."

"I *thought* so," she said with a note of triumph, although I sensed she faked the enthusiasm. "I'm a little hurt, though, that he didn't confide in me. I'm an expert at lost love. I met my soul mate at age twelve in Sunday school class. We grew up in the same speed-trap town. And I mean small—a bug zapper and a six-pack was a good Friday night's entertainment. I married her at forty-eight. We look at each other now the same way we did that first Sunday in April."

"What happened to the thirty-six years?"

"Mistakes. Thinking there was something wrong with me. Gay in a rural town is a tough start to life."

"I can imagine."

"I appreciate the comment, but you most certainly cannot. But we don't waste time lamenting lost time. It turned out right. I pinch myself every day."

I thanked her for her time and walked out the door into a vise of heat. It pressed down from the sky and up from the blacktop, shrinking my skin and clogging my breath. I climbed in my truck and sat there in the suffocating air staring at the windowless office door of the Sofa King of

Sarasota. It was all smoke and mirrors; the booming voice behind the curtain, the royal promise of a new sofa delivering a better life. A rich and relaxing life that you worked hard for, that you deserve. Coming to you between ten and twelve this Saturday. Will someone be home? But when the deliverymen pull it out of the truck, it's just a damn chair, and you learn that you can't receive a new life between ten and twelve on a Saturday—but you've always known that.

14

Morgan wedged his foot in the screen door, kicked it the rest of the way open, and stepped into the porch holding a Crock-Pot. A Ziploc bag of fish fillets dangled from his hand.

"Need any help?" I asked, making no effort to move.

"Got it."

"And what is it you got?" Kathleen asked.

"Soup and flounder. I took some down to Harbor House as well."

Morgan and I operated a refugee center for immigrants that we'd recently named Harbor House. All were welcome, and while most were documented immigrants, no questions were asked. Many were families who had court dates one to three years away. We were trustees of the property, and we'd recently hired a part-time worker to help ease the load off Morgan. He taught English as a second language classes, and the huddled masses were rolling in. So far, I'd avoided teaching classes, a maneuver I believed was a blessing to the students. I had become the ad hoc property manager, driver, and resident chef. I also maintained my shifts at the church's thrift store. Those surging responsibilities filled my days.

"Oven on?" he asked.

"Four hundred."

"Be ready in fifteen," he said as he brushed past us into the house. Hadley III perked her head up. She leaped off Kathleen's lap and cat-dashed after Morgan. I refilled Kathleen's wineglass and asked her how her classes were.

"Terrible."

I stood and took her wineglass.

"Hey, you. Give that back."

I mixed an old-fashioned: rye whiskey, Luxardo cherries —unmuddled—a fresh orange peel, and a tablespoon of the cherry juice instead of simple syrup. I added a splash of water to ease the first sip.

I placed it where her wineglass had been.

She gave it a wary glance. "Oh no."

"Take your medicine."

"If you insist."

She took a sip and closed her eyes. The red channel marker blinked on, its pulsating red light skating across the water. Oscar, the young male osprey who'd taken up residence on my dock, settled in for the night on a piling—a black gargoyle, time warped from Dracula's castle.

"Why terrible?" I said.

"I got a talker."

A talker was a person who voiced an opinion on every subject, answered every question, and blotted out every other student. Despite her protest, Kathleen had an affinity for them. She claimed they had so much life inside of them that it bubbled out.

"He or she?"

"She. Tracey."

"Andrew was a talker," I said.

"How is that coming along?"

I downloaded my visits with Marcy and Brooke. She listened without comment while from behind us Maynard Ferguson's trumpet swung through "MacArthur Park." Morgan had put the record on, and I wondered if Andrew had ever played trumpet. The dinner boat with its cutout heads eating inside eased by surprisingly close to the end of the dock. The people on the back deck looked at us looking at them. I got up, went into my bedroom, and came back with a sweater.

"Arms," I said.

She raised her arms and wiggled into the sweater.

"Do you want to talk about Tracey?" I asked, for she had deftly turned the conversation away from her.

"Not really. Do you have the letter?"

I retrieved the letter that Marcy had given me. I handed it to her.

"Not much, is it?" she said.

The question was not meant to be paired with an answer. I took a sip of whiskey and reconsidered my belief in a higher being.

Kathleen said, "Andrew was infatuated with an old flame, who had recently sent him a brief letter, nothing more than a question. He had her picture on his computer, ran into her, or stalked her, at the Vinoy. He solicits you to help find her under the guise that he was getting divorced and didn't want to make waves, and ends up dead a few days later. Then a U.S. marshal asks you to look into it, also for cloudy reasons.

"Oh, let's not forget. Andrew was a big donor to Allison Daniels's foundation. Even in death, he fills the coffers of the Coalition for Peace. Have I missed anything?"

"Yes."

"What?"

"I don't know. That's the problem."

She handed me the letter back. "Anything strike you as unusual?"

I stole a glance at the letter.

Do you remember Trumpet?

"Tell me," I said.

"Capital *T.*"

"Maybe she thought a musical instrument was a proper noun."

"Or a person. Note the absence of 'the.'"

I need to tell you about trumpet, Andrew had told me Elizabeth said to him. But now it was *Trumpet.* And not *the trumpet.*

Morgan presented us with stewed tomato soup filled with chunks of steaming flounder he'd pulled out of the cool sandy bottom at the end of his dock. For a few minutes, I forgot about Andrew Keller and his uninvited trip to my house and the uninvited guilt he had injected into my life.

"I checked the weather," Kathleen said. "It looks fine, and two days is a little short to blow a forecast. Sophia's not exactly a beach person. She's half excited and half afraid."

"And Sally?"

"I can't wait for her to meet you," she said.

"We talked years ago, on the phone, remember? She spewed little white lies that you rehearsed her to say."

"Now *dar*ling," she drew out in a flirtatious voice that conveyed her mastery of all matters between us, "is anything really gained by digging all that up?" She looked at Morgan. "It will be there, right? The sand?"

He put down his fork. "It will be, and if not, I know of other places."

"And then it will disappear? Perhaps forever?"

"More than likely."

"And we'll have pictures and memories of a place and time that no longer exists," Kathleen said.

"All of our yesterdays."

Morgan had a way of wrapping up the world in a few words.

We talked more about our plans, and I assured her that I had all the provisions. She reached over and touched my arm. "I made an appointment with the public adoption agency for next week, since we'll be official."

"I thought you weren't keen on that."

"We need to check it off, don't you agree, Morgan?"

"It doesn't hurt," he said.

"They won't smile upon me," I said, annoyed that she'd enlisted Morgan.

"We don't know that. But if that's true, I'm fine with it. I also made an appointment with another doctor, the whole second-opinion thingamajig."

I thought I should say something, but I was wrung out. She had a high degree of confidence in her primary doctor, Teresa Brick, but I couldn't fault her for seeking other opinions. We both knew the roadblock my past presented. She might make light of it, insisting that there were plenty of children in need of parents and that ours would come regardless of legal and moral considerations, but I wasn't sure the world worked that way. She wasn't a dreamer, nor was she afraid to dream. I thought her fatalistic beliefs were designed to alleviate my guilt. After that, I got lost in a Normandy hedgerow of counterthoughts.

Cool air grazed in off the water and I turned the ceiling fan off. Morgan placed a small plate bearing a piece of flounder on the floor. Hadley III scrunched her hindquarters and patiently ate the fish. A boat with a red dot for a portlight zipped by the dock. Laughter carried over the steady hum of its engine and silence followed in its distant wake.

When it got to be time to retire the day and prepare for the next one, Morgan slipped out the door, his silhouetted figure crossing the lawn. Kathleen, after a second old-fashioned, went to bed to read. I loitered on the porch and breathed her essence, for she never really leaves me. The waning gibbous moon cracked the far mangrove shore. It would soon sparkle the bay with elusive diamonds, and it was my fault that the sparkles fell between her fingers.

ANDREW CAME THAT NIGHT while Kathleen slept with Hadley III nestled against her back, her tail curled tight over her face. He wore the caricature cardboard crown with purple trumpets on it and a business suit, although I'd never seen him in a suit. He kept talking to people who were offstage, and I wondered why he was ignoring me. Then he turned and said, "I know."

"Know what?"

"We weren't really friends, but we can be now, can't we?"

I tried to answer, but I was broken and nothing worked. He gave me a gaze of disappointment, of glum and resigned defeat. Then he was gone.

I got out of bed, went out to the screened porch, and

sat in the darkness. Could I be a better friend to someone after they died than while they were living? Can we do that? Does it count?

It was 5:00 a.m. and sleep had checked out for the night. I pedaled my bike to the beach and took a seat on a concrete bench where the gathering disorder of my life waited for me. The moon lit the low-tide gulf like a Crusader's silver shield. Waves no larger than ears of corn rolled onto the shore. On that bridge between the last hour of night and the launching-pad hour of a new and promising day, I emptied the basement of my soul and vowed to put my old self behind me. To redact my history. To break free of a past that stalked me and haunted my dreams. Dreams so heavy I could barely move my legs in the morning. I needed to tell the colonel I was done. Needed to learn how to leave the house without a gun.

I pledged to disenfranchise myself from what I'd grown into without thought, or at least had arrived at through an unchallenged line of thinking I no longer subscribed to. I didn't know how that would work, but I needed to put it out of my mind for a few days. Andrew would understand. Yet even as I committed myself, I couldn't help but wonder—who would I be if I stopped being who I am?

Enough. It was time to kiss the girl.

15

Kathleen and I were married on a day when the moon pulled the water far from the shore, and part of the earth that had never before breathed air or seen the sky was allowed, if only for a few hours, to shed its liquid overcoat. To break the bond of its double hydrogen atoms and become a new molecule. Our chapel was the bottom of the sea and it would appear for us and only us.

The last day I awoke as a bachelor, I ran the beach under the setting moon and stars as the unseen sun cast hues of pink, yellow, and blue along the low edges of the slumbering eastern sky. I ran thinking of the occupants in the dark homes who would soon stir and leave their dreams —that magnificently uncensored scrambling of the past— on a dented pillow, beckoned forth by the promissory smell of coffee and a daily list of chores. I was married on a day when the new waitress at Seabreeze asked me if I was doing anything special, and I said no, because I fail miserably at talking about the things that really matter. I was married on a day that the trash was collected and the plastic wheels of the trash cans rattled on the pavement, the empty containers resounding like rolling timpani as people retrieved them from the curb and tucked them back beside their homes. The mail came. The neighborhood hummed with lawn mowers. I changed a light bulb in my study that I'd been meaning to do for weeks, but I'd kept forgetting because I wasn't in the study much after dark, although that was all going to change in a way that was unimaginable then and unbelievable now.

Morgan, who served as our officiant, had picked the time and the place, although they were indistinguishable from each other. The time made the place, and the place did not exist without the time. At first I'd thought it a striking and novel idea, but I'd come to accept that time and place are conjoined and cannot be separated.

The catalyst was a tropical depression that had churned offshore the previous fall. Such storms often rearrange the shifting floor of the gulf. Morgan had noticed that a new sandbar had formed with the spring low tide that occurs twice in each lunar month. It would likely not survive the year, as the summer storms would again sculpt the shallow waters to their liking. Kathleen and I had discussed where to tie the knot; the beach at sunset, the church, my back-yard, the hotel. Morgan's boat. But when Morgan pitched the idea, we knew it was meant for us. For it acknowledged that we sleep before birth and we sleep after death, but while awake we are free to cartwheel through our lives and tramp upon the world.

Morgan and Garrett were my best men. Garrett and I had served in the army together and also did contract work for our former colonel. Sally, Kathleen's close friend from Chicago—who I had talked to on the phone when Kathleen had hired me to find her presumably lost brother-in-law and who had lied through her teeth to me—was one of Kathleen's maids of honor. Sophia Escobar, whom she'd become close to after I helped put her husband in jail, was the other. At the last minute, Morgan invited Dusty, a woman from East Tennessee he'd been keeping in touch with.

Kathleen wore an unforgettable slim white dress that fit her like red on a rose. It dragged the ground, and when I'd told her that it would get wet, she'd replied, "It better." Her hair was parted in the middle and curled at the ends. The right side draped over the front of her bare shoulder and the left side was brushed behind her, creating a sense of both exposure and discretion. It also revealed the scar where, years ago, a bullet had cleanly passed through her left shoulder. It took me back to what Garrett and I had been through to secure her life and her new identity.

Everyone had come in a few nights before, and we'd had a blowout dinner at Morgan's. We'd danced under lawn lights. We'd switched partners. I'd forgotten how intimating Sophia Escobar was and how I had trouble looking into Dusty's eyes without wanting her. Garrett and Sally strolled to the end of the dock. His skin blended with the night, and she, dressed in a cream dress, looked like an angel accompanied by a protective dark force. Garrett lost his soul mate to a random shooting years ago, and I wanted them to stay at the end of the dock for a long time—and they did—but I don't know if that meant anything.

AN HOUR AND A HALF BEFORE SUNSET, MORGAN lowered *Impulse* to the level of the dock and we all climbed aboard. The Grady-White was crowded with firewood, wine, a cooler, speakers, a shovel, chairs, decorations, an aluminum tent frame, and seven babbling bodies.

I thrust the throttle down and the boat eventually settled on an even plane. We were embarking on an adventure that no one had ever taken, or would likely take again. It would be impossible for Kathleen and me to ever visit the place of our wedding. That was fine. All stories happen only once, and the good ones never recreate themselves.

Kathleen came up behind Morgan and me at the helm. "What if it's not there?" It was a variation of the question she had asked him a few nights ago. She'd been nervous about the plan for weeks (months), which racked me with guilt as she had enough on her mind.

"Should be," Morgan said.

"You've seen it, right?"

"Not since that last storm blew through."

She slapped him on the back. "Stop it."

I turned the helm over to Morgan as we neared our destination. A few minutes later, he shouted, "All hands on deck." He'd always fantasized about doing what we were about to do, but the situation had never presented itself. He eased back on the throttle. *Impulse* quieted on the water and rolled gently in its own wake. We were nowhere, bobbing in the Gulf of Mexico with Bunces Pass four miles behind us. In front of us, the world of water ran to its fornication point with the sky. There were no boats. No buildings. No sound. Just water, sky, and sun.

Everyone craned their heads, searching for what was not there. The tide was still leaking out for the next hour. Any speck we found would get larger before it disappeared. Morgan, ignoring the GPS monitor, inched closer to nowhere.

"There it is!" Dusty exclaimed, pointing over the bow.

A crown of the ocean's floor broke the surface. It would be exposed for only a few hours until the moon weakened its hold over the earth's surface. A toe of land not on any map, never before seen, and likely never to be seen again.

Our own Brigadoon.

Morgan ran the boat onto the smooth sand. I kicked off my shoes, hopped out, and secured a bow anchor while Garrett dragged one off the aft. Morgan lowered the front steps and we helped the women down. Garrett took the shovel and dug a hole. He stacked the wood in it and set it ablaze. Sophia, Sally, and Dusty hung the poles with crepe paper and decorations that twirled and swung in the fire's warm breeze. When the sun stared at us like a red Cyclops that was half in the sky and half off the edge of the earth, Morgan proclaimed us man and wife. And then, because the tide had shifted, we partied. We ate fresh fish. We drank ancient wine. We slurped oysters and littered the sand with their shells. We danced under the darkening sky. We mixed partners, drinks, and songs.

When we tired of the revelry, we gathered the chairs around the flame. Morgan and I had repositioned the boat twice, as the tide was eager to take back what it had erroneously given. The water crept up behind us, pressing us closer to the hot flames. Soon the back legs of the chairs started to sink in the wet sand. The moment was vanishing, even though it was only a blink ago that we had disembarked with bursting anticipation. Every beginning has an end, and it trims some of the joy out of it all.

We circled closer and closer. Our faces glowed with life and Kathleen's white dress foamed in the waves. We talked and drank and laughed until we could no longer deny that that which we had anticipated for so long had run its course and only the end remained.

We packed everything back into the boat. Dusty insisted we keep the music going until the last person stepped off the sand. A *Titanic* farewell. As I shoved the boat off, she monkeyed over my back carrying the speakers. Morgan idled away and then slowly turned and took us through the night. Behind us, angry tendrils flickered and fought as Hephaestus and Vulcan teamed together to ward off the advancing sea. But it was Poseidon and Neptune who took the field, for they were defending their home, and soon nothing could be seen of our chapel. It was as if we were never there, for there was no *there* to be at.

I sat in the bow with Kathleen snuggled between my legs. We rode the water until distant lights flickered and the darkness took the form of land and the commercial throb of civilization. I whispered in her ear. She whispered back and made me promise. My feelings were unexplainable, for they held no tinge of familiarity.

THAT IS HOW I REMEMBER MY MARRIAGE, MY FORMAL acknowledgment of my incurable thirst for Kathleen and my inability to move forward without her. But like sand, memories shift. I can't tell you what was said on the sandbar that night; after all, the best stories, the ones we keep dearest, happen only once. This assures their permanence between fact and fiction, between dreams and reality. Somewhere south of the mind and north of the heart. Not that it matters. We all know that Brigadoon isn't real. Except for those of us who have been there.

16

"Why would Charlie Walker invite you to his house?" my wife asked. I had received an invitation to Walker's house. Some do-good fundraiser that I hoped Kathleen wouldn't ask me about because at that moment I couldn't remember the cause.

"He wants to keep me close to him."

"How do you know that?"

"It's what I would do."

She twiddled her fork. "Allison's not attending, is she?"

"Not that I know of."

"Shame. Rematches are such crowd-pleasers."

We sat outside at Mangroves in downtown Saint Pete on an absurdly beautiful evening. The heavy smell of water from Tampa Bay mixed with the remnant of the late afternoon heat radiating off the sidewalks. It held notes of charbroiled food that was cut with the passing scent of perfumed, bare-shouldered young women. They catwalked the pavement in tight dresses and high heels like knock-kneed fawns in royal groups of three and four, soliciting the carnal stares of men who had no choice but to notice and then feign indifference.

Kathleen surrendered her fork and stroked the long stem of her wineglass. I took a drink of courage. "What did the new doc say?"

A couple pushing a stroller walked by. The woman had both hands firmly on the handles. The man's left arm circled the woman's waist. Kathleen stared at them as they passed.

"K?"

"She concurred with Dr. Brick," she said and then swung her face to me. "It's not PCOS or endometriosis. It's age. Nothing more than you-waited-too-long-every-woman's-body-is-different."

"So it's still possible," I said and wished I hadn't. She didn't need me encouraging her, as she had likely recalibrated her chances.

"Lottery possible."

The waiter dropped by and refilled her glass. He asked if I wanted another and I told him to put afterburners on it. Someone started playing a saxophone, and a blues melody curved around the street corners and under the tables.

"I've been thinking," she said. "All the people who pass through Harbor House. The way you and Morgan came to operate it when Mac left you the property and money. It has meaning. It's part of us, and I don't see that part diminishing in any capacity. I think something—some*one*—will come from there. It feels right to me. Didn't Hemingway say anything that feels right is right?"

"You don't like Hemingway," I pointed out.

"I might if it would help."

"That's my girl. He said, 'What is moral is what you feel good after, and what is immoral is what you feel bad after.'"

"Oh, that's not what I thought it was. Have *you* ever used it?" She leaned in, as if aware that she'd struck a chord and perhaps opened a therapeutic door.

"I find it generally works," I said but was eager to get the conversation back to her. "Babies don't arrive without parents or guardians."

"You never know."

A woman scurried over to my table and plopped a drink in front of me.

"I heard you were in dire need of this," she said. She twinkled her eyes, fluttered my heart, and skirted out of my life as fast as she had appeared.

Kathleen said, "You think I'm wrong, don't you?"

"Anything is possible," I said.

But we both knew that if that was where we were, then very little was possible. I took a sip of whiskey. It held far more conviction than my previous worthless comment. Undiluted from the melting ice, it was brash, opinionated, and full of feuding tastes as it burned my throat.

After dinner, we strolled across Straub Park toward the water. She dug her nails into the palm of my hand in a rhythmic manner. She had started doing that around a year ago. I wanted to tell her everything would be fine, but I didn't know that.

"Let me believe it, if only for a little bit, OK?" she said.

We went quiet, and in that speechless cave, I questioned what she believed versus what she wanted to believe. If I was even capable of being a father. I worried that Kathleen might be thinking the same things, although we never discussed it, especially now that we were married.

17

A wobbly paddle boarder made her way north, stroking hesitantly in the tranquil water. Farther out, a Jet Ski tour, like ants on a cookie sheet, raced single file in the opposite direction. I was at the hotel having breakfast, waiting for Wayne to arrive. It was the non-clock time of the morning when the atmosphere held the stillness of the night but the rising sun pressed the promise of the day. People shuffled around as if they were awakening from a dream and wanted to savor the moment forever.

Allison called. I'd left her a message to see if she, as well, had received an invitation to Walker's house.

"Are you kidding me? No way," she snapped over the phone "Why would he invite you into his home?"

"You sound like my wife."

"You're married?"

"That's the scuttlebutt."

"You weren't when we first met."

"How do you know?"

"You didn't wear a ring."

"You checked out my fingers?"

"You checked out my legs."

"I wasn't."

"Wasn't what?"

"Married when we met."

"But you are now."

"Apparently. Can we move on?"

"Please. What's the shindig at the house for?"

"Pinellas Early Reading," I said, although the name had escaped me when Kathleen asked the same question.

"Must be his wife's bash," Allison said. "She's the founder of A Book for Every Child. That's the nonprofit I alluded to when we had lunch. It was also the beneficiary of the masked ball. I believe she lends her time to other childhood reading programs as well."

"But you indicated they don't have children."

"Oh, that's right. You can care about literacy only if you've reproduced. How—"

"I didn't—"

"—ignorant of me. How'd a chimp like you score an invitation?"

"He's probably curious about the orangutan that swung to your rescue. Any message you'd like me to pass along?" I nodded at my coffee cup and the waitress filled it to the rim.

"Tell him I'm sorry. I meant to kick him in the nuts."

"I'm not sure the camaraderie stuff worked on you."

"Didn't work for Ginny."

I hesitated. I didn't know Allison Daniels that well and certainly had no right to lecture her. I couldn't imagine her, or her sister's, loss. Yet I wasn't without a morsel of wisdom.

"Bitterness will destroy you," I said.

The phone was silent.

"That's not who I really am," she said.

"You save that part for me?"

"Strange, but I do."

"Why?"

"You pack a gun."

"In my work—"

"Bullshit. Guns kill and that's what you'll do with it."

She disconnected.

Allison's parting shot was reverberating in my head when John Wayne rounded the corner and stopped. His towering head scanned the patio. Without any indication that he saw me, he walked over, scooted back a chair, took off his hat, and sat down.

"You ever wear anything else?" I said. He was Marlboro-manned out in full gear.

"To bed," he said. I thought he would offer further explanation, but a man comfortable in his own skin owes no explanation and gives none.

Thankfully, we ordered breakfast when the waitress made her first pass at Wayne. I was famished as I'd done five predawn miles on the beach and had been at the end of my dock for a Benedictine sunrise.

I brought Wayne up to date. He questioned me on the Allison Daniels-Charlie Walker showdown and showed little interest in Marcy Keller or anything about Keller that didn't relate to the Walkers. He inquired how I'd made the connection between Allison and Andrew. I protected my source, Rambler.

"Why is he inviting you to his house for a fundraiser this evening that supports a cause his wife champions?"

I swallowed a mouthful of hash browns halfway

through the chew. I explained how I came to Allison's protection during the masked ball and that I'd also had a brief and futile conversation with Elizabeth. The invitation could have originated from either encounter.

"Why are you looking into Walker?" I asked. It was time for Wayne to feed me more information if he wanted me to be effective. "And don't hide behind confidentiality. Trust me or don't."

He gave a single nod. "Are you familiar with Limorp Corporation?"

I told him I was. Limorp was Promil spelled backward. Promil—professional military—was military for hire. It operated out of a chain-linked camp buried in the tall pines and moccasin-infested swamps of southern Georgia. I knew a few guys who signed up after their final roll call in the army. It was a legitimate organization used by the U.S. government to augment operations and to occasionally perform solo acts. There was nothing new about outsourcing war. The British hired Hessians to assist in killing the insurgent colonists, the Romans dangled citizenship in front of their mercenaries, and even the Almighty conscripted David to take out the mocking Goliath. I'd considered joining Limorp after my stint but was glad I had not. For I had become increasingly disillusioned with the nation's nauseating glorification of all things military since 9/11—blindly forgetting that these are the same folks who sponsored Vietnam. It is acceptable to unquestionably support the men and women in the field; it is not acceptable to unquestionably support the industrial-military complex that places them there.

Wayne said, "Too many of our armaments are ending up in third-world countries."

"You think Limorp is playing middleman? But why you? That's not your neck of the woods."

"There are some people who are cooperating. They may need protection."

"I don't see . . ." I leaned in across the table and kept my voice low. "Are you telling me that Charlie Walker is in on this and that his wife, Elizabeth, is feeding you information?"

"I said no such thing."

"Do you have someone inside Walker's camp?"

"I can't answer that."

"Elizabeth?"

"I can't confirm or deny."

"Why don't you just speak Latin? We'd make more progress."

"It's a dead language."

I sat back in defeat.

Wayne said, "It's possible that Mr. Keller had gotten close to Mrs. Walker. And if so, she might have told him things."

"He said he hadn't seen her in years."

He placed his elbows on the table, his blue eyes scorching mine. "We can't verify that."

I started to say something but held back, making the rare decision to engage my mind before my mouth. "She's not your main source, is she? Or a source at all. If she were, you'd simply ask her."

His jaw tightened and I took that as nonverbal agreement. I took a sip of coffee. The heightening sun no longer doled out spoonfuls of sunshine. It cast shadows of the hotel farther out from the pink building, warming my legs from the bottom up. The glorious moment of the morning had passed, and no matter what effort you might put forth, it could not be recreated on that day. Beauty and brevity walk hand in hand.

I formulated my thoughts out loud. "You're getting a feed from within Walker's empire. His wife's old flame drops by and gets murdered two days later. Keller aroused someone's suspicion, and fast. He churned up the waters on your investigation and paid for it."

"That's what it looks like."

"Walker's a lobbyist. Why would he get his hands dirty in the gun trade?"

"Money."

"He's using Limorp to launder money?"

"That is our best guess, but—"

"Jesus, John, just tell me."

"We have sources to pro—"

"I got it."

"Try to get close to Mrs. Walker. See what she knows and if she told Mr. Keller anything. It's not a happy marriage. They've danced around with divorce attorneys for years."

I was going to ask how he knew that but was weary of the cat and mouse game.

"Just see if she talked to him," Wayne said in what sounded like a backing-off statement. "We may need to get our person out."

"Assuming she knows something."

"Correct."

"Which she may not."

"Also correct. Mr. Keller's death could be unrelated. But there's nothing obvious that points to personal issues or business problems of that magnitude. You'd make my day if you informed me that his death was due to gambling issues.

If his death was not related to Charles Walker, then we are finished."

"If it was?"

He took a sip of coffee, his thick fingers suffocating the cup. "We may need to get someone out. You may be helpful in that regard."

18

"I'll miss the drawbridge," Kathleen said. She studied her eyes in the truck's visor mirror. When conducting similar exercises in the past, she had never touched or altered them in any manner.

"It's as convenient as a damn hemorrhoid."

"Now sugah," she drawled in a lemony southern accent that was new for her. "You know I de*test* that type of language."

We were on our way to the Walkers' house and stuck behind a car that was too chickenshit to gun it through the yellow blinking light indicating the bridge would soon rise. The bridge was scheduled for demolition, as a new high-rise bridge would displace the need for a drawbridge. I was looking forward to that celebrated day.

"How can you possibly miss an unforeseen interruption?" I asked, wondering if the guy in front of me really thought he was going to have to play Dirty Harry and fly over an opening span if he'd gone on yellow.

Yellow, for Pete's sake.

The four cars, one semitruck, and three lame turtles behind me could have made it. The driver was blindly unaware of the island drawbridge law recently passed by the Florida State legislature. It reads: When approaching a yellow light on a drawbridge, drivers must suppress the gas pedal and aggressively attack the bridge. Failure to comply is punishable by expulsion from the state.

Kathleen, incredibly unmiffed by the scaredy-cat driver, flipped up the visor without having touched her face.

"It reminds me that I'm on island time," she said, done with her Eudora Welty homage. "To adjust myself to that. Don't you agree?"

I emitted a primordial grunt.

"By the way, our appointment is at four tomorrow. I've got a class before, so it will be tight."

"I'll pick you up."

"Do you have the letter?"

"I do."

"I hope it's not an issue."

"If it is?" I asked.

"We'll muddle through."

The letter was from Detective Rambler, stating, in relation to the deceased man who'd been the prime suspect in the abduction of my sister, that I was cleared of all charges and had no involvement in his demise.

If only that was the sole asterisk.

I had also gained unwanted notoriety years ago when, recovering a stolen boat, I'd killed two men in a kill-or-be-killed scenario. It made the papers, as they say. Rambler's letter also absolved me of any legal entanglement concerning that incident. Any adoption agency, private or public, would raise an eyebrow when I walked through the door, assuming they didn't dive under their desks. While the agencies pledged an open mind in the process, few people have ever sat across from someone who was accused of murder or admitted to the lawful taking of another life. We likely had no choice but to pursue a privately arranged adoption. But even those were competitive, with attorneys assuming a fiduciary responsibility to find a safe and nourishing home for the infant.

Bottom line? Anyone with two nickels of intelligence (unlike the numbnuts in the car in front of me) would conclude that there were more suitable candidates, an opinion difficult to contend in the court of common sense. That gave birth to Kathleen's attitude of finding a child in a basket on the front stoop. She clung to irrational hope as a way to defer guilt from me. That was two laps around the mind and all I was good for.

"We still don't know who extended the invitation, do we?" she said, leaving the only thing that mattered to her for another day.

I gave that a second. Elizabeth didn't seem eager to see me again. And her husband? Maybe he wanted to know more about the man who stepped in to save Allison from a complete breakdown.

"Hey, you hear me?"

"Charlie."

"Why?"

"It's business to him, and nothing is more important."

The gate for the drawbridge rose. The car in front of me rolled forward.

"Don't tailgate," Kathleen said. "It's probably an older woman."

"I won't."

"You will."

"No. I—"

"Jake."

"OK."

I eased off the pedal.

CABBAGE PALMS LINED THE WALKERS' DRIVEWAY, and flowering hibiscus bushes pressed against the handsome ranch home that fronted the bay and the Gulf of Mexico. I swung into a valet stand on the street, tossed my fob to a young man hustling in my direction, and escorted Kathleen up the landscaped paver-brick sidewalk. Yellow glowing mushroom lights lit our gilded path.

No zoo animals taking names tonight. We strode without notice through the opened double glass doors into a living room. A wall of folding patio doors allowed for a wide, uninterrupted flow to the outside. In the corner, a woman played a baby grand piano. Next to her, a tall cardboard barometer rested on a table. At the top it read ONE MILLION DOLLARS. Across the bottom it read PINELLAS EARLY READING. And underneath that, A GREAT CHILDHOOD LEADS TO A GREAT LIFE. It appeared as if we were halfway to greatness. The table held brochures and pictures of smiling children. A tax-deductible contribution buys a smiling child. Boy, would that ever solve my problems.

A waitress circulated within striking distance. I snagged two glasses of bubbly and handed one to Kathleen. I guided her by the elbow and led us outside to a swimming pool that glowed from its underwater lights. A pink blow-up swan floated in the pool. It gently bumped off the sides while flashing a spooky and condescending smile at the oblivious guests.

Kathleen wore a floor-length chartreuse dress—I'd called it pale green, and you would've thought I had attacked the sanctity of motherhood—and a shawl. She was a veteran of waterfront parties. I wore tan slacks and a brand-spanking-new navy-blue blazer Kathleen had recently sprung on me. Apparently my previous blue blazer wasn't up to snuff, although the new one looked eerily similar to the pervious one, not to mention the one before that, which, I'm pretty sure, was a dead ringer for the one I had in high school. *Apparel oft proclaims the man.*

Charlie Walker towered behind a raised firepit—a cigar in his mouth, a drink in his hand, and tribal worshipers crowding him. Elizabeth huddled in conversation inside the house. She glanced up and our eyes met. I'm not the best at reading people, but she seemed surprised to see me. Scratch that. She was shocked to see me. My invite had come from Charlie, and he hadn't bothered to share that with his better half.

"See any lost friends?" I said.

"Let's see," she said, scanning the room. "Your buddy is to our right. You want her to yourself?"

"Sure."

"Wow, trigger. Don't kill yourself with enthusiasm." She sighed. "Do you ever tire of these affairs?"

"Immensely."

She pecked me on the cheek. "We got this. I'll crash the men's club. Any instructions?"

"Shake, rattle, and roll."

"Fasten your seat belts."

She draped her shawl around her upper arms and sashayed with alarming confidence toward the men. I took a gulp of bubbly and sashayed toward the women's circle in my gleaming new blazer, which I'm sure created a vibrant buzz. By the time I'd arrived, another man had taken up position as well, which blew my jaw-dropping opening line.

I hadn't thought of one yet, but it would have been a doozy. A real humdinger.

I inserted myself across from Elizabeth. "Is this spot available?"

Instead of tilting her head upward, she shifted her eyes to mine. Her hand tightened around her glass.

"Mr. Travis, correct?" she said. She seemed consigned to her predicament, as if she realized it was foolish to think that our tête-à-tête at the hotel would be one and out.

"Jake," I said.

She introduced me around the circle. Smiles. Nodding heads. Lipstick already smeared on teeth—that's not going to play well in the bathroom mirror. The conversation ramped back up. Everyone stood straight. Poised. The men were serious and the women were more serious, and no one was able to complete a sentence. I pined to be at the end of my dock with Kathleen listening to the dolphins blow.

The man, two to my right, who Elizabeth had introduced as Roger DeRomo, caught my eye. "I work with Charlie Walker," he said. His well-organized face boasted a natural tan that makes the toned Italians the envy of Western civilization. He shifted his weight and added, "I believe you know Allison Daniels."

"I do."

"Terrible what happened to her nephew. Is she doing better?"

"I don't know her that well to know what better is. You witnessed her unfortunate break with decorum at the masked ball."

"You're referring to when she called Charlie a neo-Nazi skinhead?"

"Unless I missed act two."

He chuckled. "Highlight of the evening. Dull parties are

for laggards, Mr. Travis. How did you come to meet Ms. Daniels?"

"Who?"

He paused and cracked an unexpected warm smile. "*Mrs.* Daniels."

The woman to my left, a tall creature with mint breath, started talking to the red dress next to her. Elizabeth Walker, though, kept her attention on DeRomo and me. I explained to DeRomo that I did some business with Allison's firm and that she had invited me to the masked ball. It was a fluffy answer, and I doubt he bought it.

"Are you still involved with her firm?" he asked.

The woman between DeRomo and me said, "Excuse me," in a manner indicating her displeasure with being caught between us. She scuttled off to find more engaging conversation.

I took a step closer to DeRomo, sealing the gap. "My business is not complete."

"And what exactly is that business?"

"What is it you do, Roger?" I countered.

"I'm a lobbyist. My question was more than rhetorical."

I squared off before DeRomo and delivered a right hook just as the competing conversations around the circle hit a pause.

"I'm investigating the murder of Andrew Keller, the Sofa King of Sarasota."

Two—no, make that three—things happened. Elizabeth Walker let out a gasp and dashed away. Roger DeRomo said, "I don't think that's such a good idea." And mint-breath woman said, "The Sofa King of Sarasota? When did *he* die?"

. . .

KATHLEEN EYED HER PREY WITH DULL confidence. Charlie Walker stood with his back to the water. *Makes sense,* she thought. *He wants to survey his kingdom. Keep tabs on who is talking to whom.*

Two men parted as she stepped into the group. "This isn't one of those stodgy men-only clubs, is it?"

Walker said, "We saved the spot for you Ms. . . . ."

She stuck her hand out. "Kathleen Rowe."

"Thank you for supporting Pinellas Early Reading," he said while pumping her hand.

"And thank you for hosting the event," Kathleen said, thinking there was a reason it was called small talk while simultaneously realizing she given her former last name, one that she was keeping for professional purposes only.

"Have we met?" Walker said. He gave her a fake smile that told Kathleen he knew damn well they had met. He took a draw from his cigar, tilted his head back, and let the smoke trail out of his mouth where a swirling breeze confiscated it.

Kathleen fought the urge to raise the shawl around her exposed shoulders. "In a manner of speaking. But we were behind masks."

"Speaking of manners. I apologize. Would you like a cigar?"

The man next to her sniggered. He had inched over so that he occasionally rubbed her shoulders.

"Only if you've got an Ashton eight."

"I prefer Cubans, but the Ashton is a fine cigar. Why are you particular to that brand, Ms. Rowe?"

Kathleen considered appropriate answers. But how

often do such opportunities present themselves? And besides, propriety is boring. Her mind flashed to Bacall and Bogart. *You know how to whistle, don't you?*

"It fits my mouth, Mr. Walker."

The man who had shouldered her spit out his drink. "OK then," another man said, bobbing his head in appreciation—of what? A smile creased Walker's lips. "My wife has always found cigars repulsive," he said. "Is there a trick to making women like them?"

Kathleen decided to rescue the conversation from the high school locker room, although, admittedly, she'd been the one who had Pied Pipered them in.

"No trick, Charlie. A couple of puffs go well with red wine."

"I thought there was more to it," he said in an attempt to keep the game clock running. "Your husband, he's . . ." Walker spread out his hands.

"Flirting with your wife."

Walker eyed Kathleen as if noting her for the first time. "I see. Divide and conquer?"

"More like divide and get to know," Kathleen said, but she thought she could have done better.

"And why, Ms. Rowe, do you wish to know us?"

"Actually, it's Doctor, but please, stick with Kathleen."

"Medical?"

"English literature."

Walker took a step toward Kathleen, effectively cutting the other men out of the conversation. "Even better. One who has studied the soul and not just the bones. Why, Kathleen, the sudden interest in my wife and me?"

"My husband was a friend of Andrew Keller's."

"I'm afraid the name means nothing to me."

"The Sofa King of Sarasota."

"Oh, him," Walker said, but his tone didn't fool Kathleen, for his face showed no further recognition of Keller, which told her that Walker had recognized Keller's name when she first mentioned it. "Forgive me, but what does the death of a furniture salesman have to do with me?"

"Or your wife?"

Walker's eyes narrowed and grooves lined his forehead. "I still don't get the Willy Loman connection."

Kathleen hesitated. *How much should I reveal? Well, the cigar quip isn't going to advance the cause. Can't believe I said that. And I think I'm mom material?*

"You'll need to talk to my husband concerning his interest in the death of a salesman," she said. "Apparently Andrew and Elizabeth knew each other."

"She knew, and knows, a great many people. Yet they do not stalk me."

"Stalk?"

"Forgive me if I don't carry your prestige in language."

"I believe they—your wife and Mr. Keller—made contact prior to his death, which seemed to trouble Mr. Keller. But my husband never got the opportunity to talk to him again."

"He was killed in a random shooting, is that correct?"

"Your memory is improving."

Walker rolled his tongue and shifted his feet. "Let me get this right, *Dr.* Rowe. An old flame of my wife's appears —not due to her calling or desire—and then is murdered in a terrible instance of being in the wrong place at the wrong time. And for some unfathomable reason, you, the wife"— he said "the wife" as if it indicated a lower station in life —"of the deceased man's friend, is, what? Suspicious of me?"

Kathleen inched closer to him. "Charlie?"

"Yes?"

"I never said Andrew was an old flame of Elizabeth's."

The left side of Charlie Walker's lip curled up and froze. He bobbed his head. "If you ever tire of Arthur Miller, give me a call. There's opportunity in Tallahassee for someone like you. I am saddened by Andrew's death, as is my wife. Now if you'll be kind enough to excuse me, I need to attend to other guests."

He brushed passed her. Kathleen brought her shawl around her shoulders, but not until he was gone.

"BUM A LIGHT, BUDDY?" KATHLEEN SAID WHEN WE rejoined.

I handed her a drink, which she instantly took to her lips. We strolled out toward the seawall. I would have steered her to the dock, but it had already attracted a crowd eager to be suspended over water. A three-engine fishing boat hung on a lift. It looked sparkly new, and a single bird had yet to target its black canvas. My boat was the neighborhood dive bar.

"Tell me about your new friends," I said.

"He denied knowing Andrew and then spilled that Andrew was Elizabeth's old flame."

"Impressive. You're the new love of my life."

"Will you miss the old one?"

"It appeared as if one man spit his drink out soon after you joined them."

"I may have injected some questionable humor into the conversation."

"Your stature grows by the moment."

"I'm not so sure of that. And you?"

"I met a man who works with Walker—Roger

DeRomo. I blurted out that I was investigating the death of Andrew Keller."

"Blurted?"

"Afraid so."

"Still ticked that car didn't go over the bridge?"

"Unbelievable."

"How'd Roger Dodger like that?"

"He didn't think that was such a wild idea. At the mention of Andrew's name, Elizabeth cut out." I'd already considered DeRomo's instinctive response. He likely regretted his comment, as all he did by warning me was pique my curiosity.

"When talking, I referred to you as my husband."

"I thought we settled on eunuch."

That got me punched. Despite her advanced degree in letters, Kathleen often resorted to primitive and crude means of communication. It's one reason I'm batty for her, although I've never told her that.

"It felt empowering," she said. "But I don't understand why. That seems against the consensus."

"Our side of the boat."

A woman with a tray of finger desserts stopped by a neighboring foursome. Unlike the other help, who were younger, she was middle aged. Maybe she owned the catering service, or perhaps I was thinking discriminately. I caught her eye and motioned with my finger to have her meander our way. She smiled, was intercepted by another couple on her journey, and then planted herself in front of Kathleen and me. She didn't wear a name tag like the other servers.

She held the tray out toward us. "Dessert?"

"Since you insist," I said and jumped ahead of Kathleen. "Are you with the catering company?"

"No. I work for the Walkers."

Her eyes, under Norman Rockwell cheekbones, were wide and eager to please. I hoped I was right about that. She tilted the tray to Kathleen, who plucked a piece of pineapple upside down cake. "Please do not come by me again tonight."

The woman smiled. "I understand. May I suggest the mini chocolate raspberry tarts? I made them myself using cacao beans."

"One certainly doesn't want to be discourteous." Kathleen took a large tart I had my eyes on. "How long have you worked for the Walkers?"

"Less than a year."

I snagged the runner-up to Kathleen's tart. "We don't know them that well," I said. "But they seem like a lovely couple."

"She is very nice," the woman said.

"What's your name?" I asked.

"Ciara."

"Irish?" She didn't look Irish. She looked and spoke south of the border.

"No. My father liked the music, so I've been told."

"Ciara, I wanted to thank Mrs. Walker before we leave, but she seems to have vanished. Do you know where I could find her?"

Ciara cast her buckeye-brown eyes down at her tray of desserts. "She is not well. She retired to her room."

"Not well, or not feeling well?" Kathleen asked.

She flicked her eyes up to Kathleen. "Both."

"Is she sick?" I asked, wondering if she understood what Kathleen had inferred.

"I cannot talk right now," Ciara said to me. "I am sorry."

"What do you do for the Walkers?" I asked in an attempt to keep her from bolting.

"I am Eli—Mrs. Walker's new assistant." She smiled. "I cook. I clean. I run errands. I arrange and manage her social calendar."

"Do you always use cacao instead of cocoa?" Kathleen asked.

"Yes, ma'am," she said with enthusiasm. She shifted her attention to Kathleen, thankful to be done with me. "My mother told me it was better for you, and I want to help Mrs. Walker."

"And who worked for Mrs. Walker before you?"

"Anna." Ciara's eyes roved Kathleen's face. "I am afraid she misses her terribly. She had her a great many years and they are very close friends."

"Where did she scuttle off to?" I asked.

"Pardon me?" Her eyes darted between the two of us.

"Where did Anna go?" Kathleen said, clarifying my question.

Ciara grabbed the tray with both hands. I imagined it was burdensome. "She is trapped with God."

"How so?" Kathleen asked.

"She has sought sanctuary. She cannot leave the church."

"They want to deport her?" I said.

"Yes. It is terrible. She has been here—in this country—for twenty years. She has children who were born here, go to school here. They, too, sometimes live in the church. Her oldest is—it is so hard to talk about."

"What is her last name?" Kathleen said. "We might be able to help."

Ciara eyed Kathleen warily. "Vargas. Her last name is

Vargas and she is from Guatemala. None of this is a secret. Please excuse me."

Ciara spun around and headed toward the kitchen. I hadn't mentioned Andrew Keller's name to her and wished I had. But if Ciara was new, it was Anna I needed to talk to. Thinking is often the enemy of progress. I strode into the kitchen. It was jammed with catering personnel. Ciara had her back to me, reloading her tray. I came up behind her.

"What my wife said is true," I said. "We might be able to help Anna." She turned, surprised to see me. "I'm associated with a refugee center. We know lawyers who specialize in that area. What church is she at?"

She gave me the name of a downtown church I wasn't familiar with. But I'm not familiar with any church outside of the small island church that owns the thrift store. I attend services there when a friend, Stephen Cole, who has a beautiful voice, performs a solo.

Ciara said, "It is terrible, being . . ."

"Trapped with God?" I said, copying her earlier words.

Her hands shot up to her mouth. "Forgive me for saying such a thing."

"You said you wanted to help Elizabeth. How do cacao beans help her?"

She shook her head and walked away. I had hounded her enough.

On the way out of the kitchen, I snatched a piece of cheesecake and tossed it in my mouth, but it was heavy and not as good as the raspberry tart. I swallowed it thinking that I had figured out what Kathleen meant by marriage being empowering, but we never discussed it.

19

Kathleen and I sat on avocado-green chairs in the cinder-blocked waiting room of the adoption agency, our hung heads staring at the cracked vinyl floor. The rasping AC unit wasn't up to its task and the room felt like a warming oven. Speakers in the ceiling played two songs simultaneously. The chair arms were sticky. There wasn't an inch of my life I wanted to be in that morning.

We had wavered on keeping the appointment. Kathleen had become increasingly and disconcertingly convinced that God, a stranger to us both, had a child for us. Spin it how you want. Woman's intuition. Unflappable belief. We'd decided to try the standard route first, if, for nothing else, to check off that box. But what a sad-sack couple we were. Kathleen's body was not interested in bearing a child, and I was pretty sure the state of Florida had no interest in handing one over to me. Kathleen's unwarranted faith was only because she didn't want me to feel bad that my past had finally caught up with me. That my past had a stranglehold on our future. The wedding seemed like eons ago. Its euphoric vibe swept away with a strong outgoing tide.

An hour later we moped out the front door and into a biting sun that singed us with reality. The state of Florida, despite the letter from Detective Rambler vouching for my Captain Kangaroo personality, felt there were more qualified couples at the moment. I made some dumb joke about raising cats, but Kathleen was in no mood for dumb cat jokes and her dumb husband should have known better, and that hung with me all day.

20

The day I met the woman trapped with God, I stubbed my little toe. Shattered the defenseless pinkie. Its misfortune proved to be an accurate marker of pivotal events, both for that day and for another, more storied day. Therefore, its nonelective sacrifice is noteworthy.

I had a three-hour shift at the church's thrift store. Between the store and Harbor House, Morgan and I found ourselves operating businesses. There is no such thing as a nonprofit business. Either you clear a profit or you shut the doors. No margin, no mission. Roofs needed repairing, termites marched, and insurance premiums continually rose as both foundations were less than a fathom above sea level. That part was a cinch. The people part was a bit more problematic. They got sick. Schedules conflicted. One pleasant, squeaky-voiced woman, whom I hired for the thrift store, was fond of plucking much of the best merchandise for herself when it was first donated. Morgan discovered her marking it up in garage sales, effectively stealing from the church the true value of the item.

I had asked Morgan to accompany me to the church to visit Anna, Elizabeth's former housekeeper. He connects well with people, and I am often a better person when he is by my side. As much as I try to be sensitive with others, I am inconsistent in practice. I wanted to learn more about Elizabeth and arrange a civil introduction. I couldn't build trust stalking her at masked balls or accosting her in her home. Maybe Anna Vargas, Elizabeth Walker's longtime maid and "very close friend," could arrange such a meeting.

Ciara mentioned that Anna had sought asylum, or sanctuary, in a church. There are at least fifty people in the U.S. living in churches, but an accurate number is impossible to calculate, as many cases are not reported for obvious reasons. They cannot leave. If they do, they risk being placed in custody and transported out of the country. In nearly all cases, including Anna's, the individual has family born in the States, but they themselves were not. Like war criminals, such people are being hunted and deported for illegally entering the country.

The toe.

I'd taken an outdoor shower and had not bothered with a towel as the bay was deserted. But then a family in an open-bow boat approached and I hustled for the back door. I smashed the little guy on a stack of paver bricks for a landscaping project that I'd been successfully ignoring. The minor appendage would spend days as white noise pain, until my gun was in my hand, the world was quiet, and my mind was so focused that the toe throbbed in syncopation with my thumping heart. It served as a reminder that the transformative waypoints of our lives are often marked by the most minor and meaningless incidents.

. . .

BUILT IN THE ROARING Twenties, the English Gothic revival church had red bricks and arched white trim. Its stained-glass windows dared anyone to pass by without acknowledging its fortress presence. A worthy place for God to reside and for a woman to hide. The castle front door was locked. Morgan suggested we try the pedestrian doors. As we circumvented the building trying a variety of doors, the late-afternoon sun clamped down on my shirt and beads of sweat trickled down my chest. We hit a door by a rear parking lot speckled with a few dozen cars. Morgan twisted the pitted knob and it swung open.

We entered an airless hall. Narrow banners with stirring words draped the walls. He Died That We May Live. The Way, the Truth, the Life. Arise, Shine, for Your Light Has Come. The last one was laid over a picture of an Easter sunrise ripped right off a postcard. Just standing in front of it made you believe.

"Hear the angels?" I said.

"Choir practice," Morgan said. "That must be what the cars are for."

"I'm going with angels."

He granted me an approving smile.

We wanted to pass on the name of an attorney who might be able to help Anna. Ciara had mentioned that Anna had legal counsel, but it wouldn't hurt to have more than one person working on her behalf. It was a sincere cover, although my true intent was to get in Anna's good graces and enjoin her to arrange a meeting with Elizabeth.

"Mammoth building," Morgan said. "Divide and conquer?"

We agreed to text each other should either of us locate Anna.

I headed away from the sanctuary and toward a smaller

part of the building. "Dona nobis pacem" cannoned through the halls. The canticle faded as I moved farther from the source, although when the sopranos started a new round, their clarion voices pierced the halls. *Grant us peace.* The air was cooler deeper in the church, and I fluffed my shirt a few times so it wouldn't stick to my clammy skin. I passed a banner of white doves and stepped into a brightly lit industrial kitchen.

"May I help you?" a woman asked. Her hair was tied tight behind her. She wore a faded dress that stopped short of her knees.

"I'm looking for Anna Vargas."

Her body stiffened. She held her head straight and clasped her hands in front of her. "I am Anna."

"I'm here to help," I rushed out, fearful that she might get the wrong impression, for she struck me as someone who was prepared to walk the plank. I explained that I knew of a lawyer who may be able to assist her.

"I have a lawyer."

"Two beats one. My friend is here, also searching for you. He has the information." I took my phone out and texted Morgan.

Anna eyed me. "You are not with the ICE?"

"No. I work at a refugee center. We help people." Those were new words for me, and they struck a match.

She relaxed. "I am grateful, full of thanks for the people of this church. They took me in. They keep me. All at risk to themselves. But it is hard. Come, I'll show you were I live." She took a few steps, stopped, and turned. "How do you know of me?"

"I attended a fundraiser at the Walkers'. Ciara mentioned your plight."

She proceeded down a hall and we intercepted Morgan.

I made introductions, and Anna led us into a classroom that had been converted into living quarters. A bed was tight along one wall and a dresser anchored another. A large, circular rug was in the center and a worn couch faced two similarly aged chairs. I wondered if at one time they had been sold by the Sofa King of Sarasota.

"This is my home," Anna said. Then she added with a shy smile, "You saw my kitchen."

"You could cook for Patton's army," I said.

"Yes—although I do not know this Patton you speak of. Most nights it is just me and my girls, although they are busy and cannot make it every night."

"You have daughters?" Morgan asked.

"Two. They are living with relatives but often stay here to keep me company. I like it when they are here. It makes this feel like home. A church can be such a lonely place. It is meant for celebration and worship, not for living. It is either loud and bustling or an empty tomb."

Morgan gave her the attorney's business card. We discussed her predicament. Anna was well versed in her chances of staying in the States. Her odds were good, but the risk resided in the clock, for as the tedious process dragged on, she could be deported before her case was appealed.

"I come here twenty years ago," she told us. She sat on the edge of the couch. "I obey all laws, got a job, married, have children who were born in this country. Are U.S. citizens. But now I must leave? Tear my family apart? Who would make such a law, and who would carry it out? Who would take a mother from her children and her home of *twenty* years because once, when a young girl, I had a dream of a better life?"

Morgan said, "The courts are often lenient for anyone

who has been in the States for over ten years. Hopefully this lawyer, along with the one you are presently working with, can expedite your case, or at least get you a stay of removal."

"I'd like to ask you about Elizabeth Walker," I said, for I was eager to get to my agenda.

"Lizzy?" She perked up. "You know her? You said you were at her house—did you talk with her?"

I explained how we met and then went into Andrew's visit. At the mention of Andrew Keller, her hand shot up to her mouth.

"He came to see you?"

"He did."

"You are a good friend of his?" Her eyes were wide with wonder. She scooted even more forward on the couch.

"I was," I said with false conviction. But I wasn't concerned about that. "Did Elizabeth tell you what happened to Andrew?"

"No."

As I told her about Andrew, her face twisted in pain.

"She did not tell me."

"Do you speak to her often?"

"Every day." She wrapped her arms around herself. "She did not tell me," she repeated, staring at the rug. "She thinks I have enough and she does not want me to worry." She glanced up, her eyes darting nervously between Morgan and me. "Why are you here? It is not just for the attorney."

"We are here for more than one purpose," Morgan said. "But we believe we can help your case."

"I need to know more about Andrew Keller," I said. "His death might not have been random."

"But you just said—"

"I've been told that you and Mrs. Walker are close. I need to talk to her. I've met her twice, and I'm afraid all I did was scare her away from me."

Anna gave me a schoolmarm's disapproving look. She stood and walked to a window. The lower part was cranked open and the sounds of the street poured inside. My eyes scanned her living quarters. A compact refrigerator sat next to her bed. I imagined she didn't want to go to Patton's kitchen every time she needed a snack. A wire from a TV sitting in a corner ran to a window where a white flat antenna, no more than a foot squared, pressed against the glass.

She turned to me, her body backlit by the window. "I need to talk to Lizzy."

Morgan rose and went to her. "Sometimes we do things for friends on their behalf. Things we know are good for them but they cannot see, so we act, we talk, because they cannot."

I kept quiet, thinking anything I said might derail his earnest attempt. She turned back around and spoke to the window, as if her audience was outside of the church.

"They say you find God in silence. But living here? The silence screams." She faced Morgan. "There is nothing here. What this place holds, what it means, is carried in with the people when they come. They take it when they leave. Their laughter. Their children. Their songs and prayers. Their best clothes. Their baptisms. Their burials. None of it stays. I understand that now, although I wish I did not."

She shifted her attention to me. "My friend is dying. She has little time left. And what do you do when that is your tomorrow? You do things to grant peace. Lizzy wanted to make peace with her past. She wanted forgiveness."

"Elizabeth is not well?" I said.

"You do not know?" she asked in a dubious tone.

"We do not," Morgan said.

Anna paused, as if realizing that it was too late to back out. "She has pancreatic cancer. All they can do now is make her comfortable."

"We are so sorry," Morgan said. "For her and for you."

"You are kind," Anna said, looking appreciatively at Morgan. I felt a little left out.

Ciara's comments regarding Lizzy not feeling well came into focus. I considered a conciliatory remark but instead went with, "You said Elizabeth wanted forgiveness. For what?" I moved beside her, as if I were an antenna and by getting closer might understand her better.

She looked startled, as if she suddenly had no clue as to why Morgan and I were there.

"I have said . . . enough. Too much. I need to talk to her."

"You mentioned her past," I said, pressing on. "Are you referring to when her father and brother died in the same crash?"

Anna Vargas looked at me, the sorrow in her eyes as real as the floor under my feet. "A terrible, terrible thing. She must rid herself of it before she dies. This is why I tell you. I *do* know what is right for her. She needs help, for her strength is leaving her. But I cannot talk anymore. I must discuss with Lizzy. Tell her I know about Andrew, and that she was wrong in not telling me, and then perhaps we can arrange a meeting."

Morgan urged Anna to call the attorney. He told Anna that she was familiar with Anna's case and was eager to assist her.

"Thank you," Anna said. "But it is not I who needs help

right now. It is Lizzy. I have time. She does not. I will let you know what she says."

We started to leave, but I turned back to her. "Were Elizabeth and Andrew dating at the time of the accident?" I thought I knew the answer, but verification would be nice.

"Yes."

"And did—"

"Please. I will let you know if she agrees to meet you."

21

Twenty years ago, Elizabeth's father veered off the road and smacked an oak tree. Both he and his oldest son died within twenty-four hours. If Elizabeth and Andrew were dating at the time, such an event would certainly have strained the relationship. Perhaps Elizabeth was so struck by the tragedy that she suffered a breakdown. If so, subsequent years could have fostered guilt about how her reaction affected the arc of her and Andrew's lives. If Anna obtained me an audience with Elizabeth, I wanted to know as much about her and Andrew as I could prior to that meeting. I needed to know the truth so that I could spot a lie.

I sat at Seabreeze, finishing a late breakfast and flipping through the increasingly thin newspaper. I'd switched to my phone, but it had more ads than the paper. I'd given up and was staring at the drawing of Mrs. Beasley on the wall. She had been a carefree mutt that had pranced from one house to another for years as people left food and water out. She preferred the life of a well-fed vagabond to that of sleeping at the same feet every night. The local weekly paper took notice and placed her byline on a social column. Residents would call in to say they had news for Mrs. Beasley, never suspecting that she was a dog. She'd been gone for decades, as were many of the people who knew her and who innocently followed her column.

Marcy called. I'd left her a voice mail earlier.

"I thought we were done," she said.

I ignored her opening gambit and told her what I'd learned about Elizabeth's father and brother.

"Did Andrew discuss the accident much?" I asked.

"Sure. He chatted it up every day. Heck no, he didn't talk about it. Why would he? And why would I listen even if he did? It was a tragedy involving his ex-girlfriend's family. You know—a story to share around the table when people start one-upping each other about bad things that happened to other people."

"And they were dating at the time?" I asked, hoping to build on Anna's simple affirmative answer.

"Pretty sure, but I never got the procession of events right. I do know he broke up his band around that time."

"What band?" I said.

"Andrew had a band. Majestic. Four of them: he, some chick lead singer named Rachel, a rotation of drummers, and Highway."

"Highway?"

"That was his stage name. Played guitar, I think. I don't know much about it, or him. Andrew said they were pretty good, but what would he say—we sucked? That was the end of Andrew's fling with music, except, you know, he wrote all the jingles for his ads. People loved the music in his commercials. He got a greater kick out of that than he did selling furniture. He'd spend hours in his studio working on his commercials, but mostly composing music that no one would ever hear."

"Do you know of anyone who knew him or was close to his band at the time? Anyone I could talk to?"

"We're supposed to be done with each other, remember?"

I closed my eyes and rubbed my face. "Rachel? Highway?"

"Well . . . you might try Rachel. She and Andrew used to keep in touch. I think she's still in the racket, over on the east coast."

"Any place in particular?"

"Don't know. Don't care."

"Last name?"

"See previous comment."

"Thanks. You've been terrific."

"You too."

The line went dead.

ANDREW'S BAND, MAJESTIC, STILL MAINTAINED A glossy website. The band had made numerous attempts to reunite, but without Andrew the comeback gigs were long on promotion and short on tickets. The site mentioned that Rachel Stone performed solo acts in Saint Augustine, where "she was based." Apparently, no one lived anyplace anymore.

More than just about the accident, I hoped that Rachel might be able to tell me about the relationship between Andrew and Elizabeth. I suspected that everything Andrew Keller had told me was metaphorical and that he had walked out of my house with the same well-guarded secrets that he had entered with. Whether it was by choice that those secrets accompanied him to his grave or that it was my fault I hadn't warranted his complete trust was not an issue I felt like debating. Sometimes when you peek into a room, it is wise to shut the door.

I arrived at sunset, which on the east coast is not the Instagram moment it is on the west coast. I booked a room at a beachside bungalow that still maintained some of its charm from the Marilyn Monroe decade and checked my directions for the following morning. There was only one Rachel Stone in the area. She looked pretty hot on the band's website. A late-'90s rocker who straddled youth and middle age with sass and style. I drifted into a rare dreamless sleep, thankful that unlike Mrs. Beasley and Rachel Stone, I had a home.

22

Florida kills.

It kills dreams. It kills excuses. It passes itself off as a geographical answer to all your problems, its magnetic lifestyle seducing you into her fatal borders. It glorifies losing yourself in a bottle. It mocks all you ever yearned for. Your four decades of alarm-clock punching. The gold watch. The pot of gold. The golden years. It tarnishes. It deceives. It rusts you from the inside out. The flowing booze. The flaunting bodies of oiled skin. The synthetic sex. It is all that, but most of all, at its thematic peak, the Florida lifestyle is a religion—an empty promise that some people never stop believing.

One look at Rachel Stone and I knew that she'd lost and Florida had won. In her defense, it was 10:00 a.m. Late for me, but early if your job starts at eight in the evening and winds downs during the lost hours after midnight. But Rachel Stone needed to switch lanes before she became Sunshine State roadkill. I plant flowers every year at crosses on that road.

She lived in a double-wide in a subdivision of double-wides. Even the clubhouse—where a cracked concrete apron surrounded a pool behind a chain-linked fence—was a double-wide. Trash cans lined the streets, which added an exclamation mark to the American dream.

I pounded on the front aluminum door. A thin strip of rubber dangled from the edge. The door opened.

"Rachel Stone?"

She squinted at me through eyes still caved under makeup. She wore faded orange and blue UF Gators athletic shorts and a long-sleeve T-shirt with a blurry image of Stevie Nicks on it. Stringy hair. Bare feet. Smoke skulked out of the house.

"People are up this early?" she said. "What the hell's wrong with this world?" Her breath carried a hint of bourbon-peppermint. I hoped I was wrong about that.

"Are you Rachel Stone?"

"Why are you asking, dreamboat?"

I gave her my name, a little background, and said I had a few questions about Andrew.

"You knew Andrew?" she asked. And then before I could answer, "You saw him right before he died?"

"I did."

"Poor Andrew. I heard about him through friends."

"He wanted me to arrange a meeting with Elizabeth Phillips. Now goes by Walker."

Her eyes widened. "He asked you about Lizzy? Wanted to see her?"

"He did."

"Well, fuck me," she said. "Just lay me down flat. I wondered when someone would come a knockin'." She stepped back into her house. "Welcome to Helldorado. You can leave your shoes on."

She turned and ambled into her house. I trailed her into a cramped living room hung with liquor and tobacco. *The Marvelous Mrs. Maisel* played on the TV.

"You want some coffee?" she asked over her shoulder. "I can't find the ass of an elephant before I get a couple of cups in me."

I told her that would be fine.

On the path to the kitchen, she turned the TV off. "I like watching that in the mornings, but their talking grates on me. I've never known one person with half the self-confidence any of them have, but they still manage to self-destruct, just like everybody else."

"You had it on mute."

"I've seen that ep a dozen times. Wish I had clothes like that. Shit, wish I had a waist like that."

She poured us each a cup. Mine was the Kennedy Space Center with a picture of an astronaut on it. It was scratched and looked like something we'd sell in the thrift store. For a dime.

"Couldn't believe when I heard he died. Jamie called me; she used to be Highway's girl—he was our lead guitar. I hadn't seen Andrew in—God, I don't know. Time just scoots, don't it? Little rascal's like a mouse, always darting ahead of you. Can't believe he went into furniture sales. In his day? He could lay down a melody as good as anyone. That man could make a song out of a cloud. I'm sorry, what did you say your name was again?"

I repeated my name. I didn't know whether her raspy voice was her natural instrument or the result of twenty-some years of abusive singing, smoking, and drinking. She said she needed fresh air and stumbled out the back door. A stained concrete pad served as a patio. Her backyard was a clutter magnet for dying potted plants, yard ornaments, weeds, and one unopened bag of double-processed hardwood mulch. A pergola thick with blue moon wisteria provided shade, although you could only guess what might be slithering around in its rainforest vines.

She brushed back her chestnut hair, as if suddenly aware of her appearance. "I haven't had my shower yet. Late night. Played at the Holiday Inn down on Ponce de Leon. Some pharmaceutical meeting. It's good money and I got a mortgage. I try to save money, but it goes against every natural instinct I have. Was one thirty before I got out. Nearly three before I fell asleep." She paused for a sip of coffee. "Andrew and Elizabeth-Miss-Perfect-Phillips. Why did Andrew want you to look for her?"

I took a taste of steaming coffee. Rachel Stone wasn't afraid of an overroasted bean. "He said he wanted to reacquaint himself with her. That he hadn't seen her in years." And then, to dive the conversation a little deeper, I added, "He thought she might have been the one who got away."

Her face broke into a frown and her eyes fell to the concrete—it needed a good power washing. She arched her eyes up to mine, although her head was still down. "Where you from?"

"Saint Pete."

"Where?"

"Saint Petersburg."

She straightened her head. "You expect me to believe your curiosity about a deceased friend's old flame hauled your early-mornin' cheery face across the state?"

I told her everything. I had nothing to lose, and she wasn't a factor beyond what she told me. She listened as I prattled through the possibility of Andrew being killed due to his involvement with Elizabeth. That Elizabeth's husband was a powerful NRA lobbyist and that Andrew contributed to Allison Daniel's Coalition for Peace.

She asked, as if to clarify a point, "How close did Andrew tell you he and Elizabeth were?"

"He said she was engaged to another man who traveled. Said he never had the courage to kiss the girl. Something he always regretted. But," I added before she came in, "he admitted to speaking metaphorically."

Her eyes showed signs of life as she peered at me from the top of her mug. "First of all, I don't even know what that means. Second—he said that? That he never kissed her? I can attest to their first kiss being in a church stair-well, and honey, it most definitely wasn't their last. You think this all has something to do with Andrew getting killed?"

"Maybe. Thought I'd get your version."

"Tell you what, Jack."

"It's Jake."

"You just said it was Jack."

"I did not."

"You sure about that?"

"I am."

"Either way, I'm taking a shower." She didn't wait for a reply but brushed past me and into her house. "Help your-self to another cup, Jackity-Jake."

I swatted a bug off my arm and went to the kitchen. Several days of dishes cluttered the sink. I rummaged through her refrigerator. When the shower went off, and the pipes clunked in the floor, I broke eggs in a skillet. While they sizzled, I stepped on an ant, poured sour milk down the drain, turned the radio on, and lowered the volume.

Rachel entered the kitchen wearing jeans and a white

shirt. Her hair, still wet, was pinned back. She looked clean but tired, as if the morning shower had lost its magic.

"Eggs?" I presented her with two eggs and toast with orange marmalade.

"Oh my God." She gave me a quizzical stare. "We didn't, like, do anything last night, did we?"

I laughed at her confusion. "No. I thought you could use a little fuel."

She took the plate, and as she did, I reached in and grabbed half a slice of toast. We headed back to her porch. I put my mug on a wrought iron table, nudging a yellowed envelope out of the way.

"You could have fixed something for yourself," she said.

"I already ate."

"Those are my dad's discharge papers from the navy," she said, dipping her head toward the yellowed envelope. "He's long gone and I found those a couple of years ago. What do you do with stuff like that? Seems a shame to stick it in some drawer, you know?"

She guzzled down her breakfast as if it might be snatched away at any moment. I considered her backyard and decided the best bet for Rachel Stone was to trash everything and start clean. Maybe in Maine.

"Andrew and Lizzy," she said when the last of the eggs was gone. "It wasn't exactly what you've been led to believe."

"No?"

"You really don't know?"

I spread my hands.

"They were as hot as French toast, despite her being engaged. But her fiancé was never around. Hell, he wasn't the man for her anyways, *every*one knew that. We were a band, you know that, right?"

"Majestic."

"Yeah, and you got it right. Not the Majestics, just Majestic—like Eagles. Andrew was adamant about that. We were good in our day, which is a weak-ass thing to remain from all your blood, sweat, and tears. If the world doesn't pay attention to you in your prime, it sure as hell doesn't even blink when you commence a sentence with 'in our day.'" She swayed her head. "Those are three sorry-ass words. Andrew, me, and Highway were the core—we rotated through a few stick boys. Andrew had the goods, though. He could write a sticky jingle with a middle eight like nobody's business. And Highway wore his fingers raw practicing his guitar. He and I were a thing for a while till Jamie flaunted her damn perfect body. No woman should be that skinny on one side and so popped out on the other."

"Where is Highway now?"

"Got me. He drank a straight road right off the map."

"Were you and Andrew ever involved?"

She'd been gazing out at her yard, but she came back to me. "Naw. We swung from different trees, know what I mean? And then when Lizzy came into the picture—damn, he just got slammed. It was like he ascended into heaven. Changed everything."

"How so?"

"He doubled down on every moment. Got all serious. He always was, but even more so. His music. What the future would look like. I'm still working on that last one. But she dropped him. And that—that wasn't right, you know? I never seen two people love each other more, and know what?"

She waited for me.

"What?"

She took a sip of her coffee and then held the cup with both hands as if it were her last possession in the world. "If what they had wasn't love, then I don't know what is. I sing it every night, and I don't have a damn clue. I see the eyes of men crawling on me—I don't look like I do now. But I'm nothin' but a false prophet. Leading middle-age corporate America in their inebriated search of the one who's still out there—or the one who got away. Either way, I'm their nightly hard crush.

"I mean, if Andrew and Elizabeth couldn't make a go of it," she curled up her lip, "what's the point, know what I mean?"

"What happened?" I asked. I leaned in on my metal chair and it gave a little more than it should.

"Shit if I know. Prob'ly the accident. You know about that?"

"I do."

"She was never the same. Hell, who could blame her? It shook her—shook *him*." She paused as if going back in time. "He took it just as hard as she did—maybe that's what love is. The band broke up. Andrew wasn't worth a busted piano. Lizzy went to Europe—Paris, I think—for a spell and Andrew split the music scene.

"He joined the army. That's when I knew he was damaged far more than anyone could see." She snorted. "People say drugs are dangerous, but what about love? He surfaced on your side of the sandpit dealing furniture. What a waste. That man had talent. The rest of us? We could ride the coattails of someone like him, but . . . I'm not nothing special. Fuckin' Holiday Inn. We would have laughed our asses off back in the day."

"I bet a lot of people enjoyed your performance last night. I bet you shone on the stage. Broke men's hearts.

Every woman in the audience wished they had the guts to stand in the spotlight and sing like you."

She cracked another crooked smile, deepening a dimple. It was a confident signature move that drove the front row mad.

"You and your eggs and damn marmalade. You're a nice guy, even if you don't know your own name." She twiddled her fingers around her coffee cup. "Word was Elizabeth couldn't handle the double deaths. Cracked her up. So," she popped her lips, "she flew the coop. Andrew missed our gig that night, which I can understand, but two weeks later he walked out on us. Hell, I know he was heartbusted and all, but he had an obligation, you know? What about us? He just pissed on our parade. Quit music. Cold turkey. Joined the *army*." She shook her head. "The whole thing was bizarreville. I tried to keep in touch with him, you know? But he wasn't interested. You can tell when one person isn't as interested in a friendship as the other—I'm not talkin' sex, but friendship, real friendship. Hell, I wonder if he even remembers me."

She paused and then came back in. "We had this song, 'Do You Think of Me,' that I was lead singer on. It was one of my favorites of his." Her head danced back and forth as she sang:
"I'm not talkin' about rock and roll
Not talkin' about sex
There's something I gotta know
Gotta get it off my *chest*
If you never heard my voice
Or saw my face again
Would you remember me
Or would it be, oh, the end?"
She glanced sheepishly at me. "I loved that song. But I

wonder—he split so fast—did he even remember? Or do things really end just like that?"

"You have a nice voice," I said while thinking that Rachel Stone had likely laid her deflated dreams at Andrew's feet.

"Always did have that going for me."

"Whatever happened to the man she was engaged to at the time?"

"I haven't thought of this in a month of blue moons. Lemme see—I heard they eventually married. But it was sometime later."

"She ended up marrying the man she was engaged to when she met Andrew?"

"Pretty sure."

Elizabeth, as far as I knew, had been married only once. She wed Charlie Walker several years after the accident. I had assumed the accident, and her run with Andrew, had put a bullet in the engagement and that she had met Walker after the accident. What if that wasn't the case?

I uncrossed my legs and leaned in, arms on my knees. "Do you remember her fiancé's name?"

"No."

"But he would have known that while he was on the road Andrew was . . ."

"Riding his woman?"

"Right."

"If he didn't know while it was happening, he certainly would have found out soon after. And 'riding' is crude; I shouldn't have said that. They were star-crossed lovers if there ever were any."

I didn't want to lead her. "First name? Last? Anything?"

She shrugged. "Sorry—wait a sec. I might have some-thing to help you."

She dashed to her living room and came back with a yearbook from the University of Florida. "Don't even know if they make these anymore. The guy who Lizzy was engaged to? He was a year ahead of us. He had a beard. That's cool now, right? Was in the seventies, too, but we're talking 1999. So this guy was either way behind or way ahead—take your pick."

She took a seat in a chair next to me and placed the black book on the plastic table in front of us. "What's a Thousand Years?" was scripted across the front.

"Let's see." She flipped through the pages. She smelled like strawberry shampoo. "No." More flipping. "Here's his class. He should be on one of these—there he is." She pointed to a small picture. "See what I mean. A real Grizzly Adams. Like I said, when she came back from Europe, I heard they patched things up, waited a couple of years, and got hitched. Just like they planned all along."

"And he would have known that Andrew and his girlfriend had a serious relationship?"

"You've been listening?"

I leaned over and stared at youthful apple cheeks on top of a full beard. But what really got my attention was the hawk nose. A nose Allison said was hard to hide. I traced my finger under the picture.

Charles E. Walker.

How the hell had I missed that?

She was engaged to some guy who was on the road a lot, Andrew had told me. I foolishly made the assumption that Elizabeth ended the relationship with her fiancé—who I'd never been able to identify—and met Charlie later. And that Andrew was nothing more to Charlie than a man his wife had dated before he came along.

That wasn't the case. While they were in college,

Andrew Keller nearly stole Charlie Walker's fiancée. Twenty years later he resurfaces and threatens to rekindle a romantic flame. He joins forces against Charlie Walker. Then he's murdered. Those thoughts were churning in my head when Rachel, lost in her own mystery, said, "You know what was really sad about her marrying him?"

"Tell me."

"She never loved him. Everyone knew that. Even her."

23

Lizzy
Twenty Years Ago

The union of your spirits here has caused Him to remain
For whenever two or more of you are gathered in His name
There is love

Andrew Keller swept into the room, lifted Lizzy off the ground, and twirled her around.

"There's an art festival in town," he said. "Let's boogie."

She giggled at his outburst. "Boogie? I have a final—"

He lowered her onto the floor and planted a deep kiss on her lips. A kiss normally reserved for a dark bedroom, when insecurities have been flipped off with the light and passions, sensing their freedom, take spirited flight. But Andrew Keller's love for Lizzy was boundless; it paid no homage to time, to light or dark, to customs or decorum. It was potentate of all elements, natural or contrived.

"There'll be hot dogs and kettle corn," he said, his lips hovering over hers.

"You don't say," Lizzy replied in mock surprise.

"And paintings and jewelry. Shaved ice a disgusting color of blue. Kids getting charcoaled caricatures and orchids that look like the faces of baby angels."

"You mean cherubs?"

"Sure, those two."

"Hmm. The usual lineup."

"Hardly," Andrew said. "Word on the street is that Woozles and Doozles will be making an appearance."

"Now we're getting someplace."

He tightened his arms around her. "Even the small green woozles you like so much that sing on foggy nights."

She gave him a peck on the lips. "I do love those little guys."

With Charlie, her world was monotone, but with Andrew, the universe exploded with color and song. Her inner self was free to play. To romp around without the burden of forethought, which dampened who she was and stealthily trimmed the corners out of every day. At first it had been hard to keep up with him, his borderline ludic behavior, then she realized that all she needed to do was relax. That just because you grow up, the child within need not grow down.

"I don't know," Lizzy said, her responsible side kicking in and draining her enthusiasm. "I need to hammer the books today."

She had scripted the day. (She made a list every night, a

habit she still hid from Andrew.) Study, lunch with Andrew, round two of hitting the books, and then she would tell him the news. She didn't want to wait until night. That had been her plan the previous two nights, and how had that worked out? Not well, thank you. She wanted to do it during the day. Under the glare of the sun, before the night circled in. Besides, he had a gig tonight. He was always beat after a couple of hours on the stage. *No*, she thought, *I'm telling him before.* She wasn't worried. In her book-fed wild imagination, she could not conceive of anything coming between her and Andrew.

Their relationship had erupted with a speed that had both baffled and delighted her. Amazed and conquered her. With Charlie it had been a step-by-step process. Love (or some matinee understudy) unveiling itself as if it were an assignment requiring carefully monitored and documented steps. Their time together had been an unvaried process of escalating commitment and comfort that culminated in love —so she assumed. After all, look at all we've done, she'd reasoned. What we have in common. Where we've gone. The friends who surround us. That must be love.

Right?

Right?

But Lizzy, even before Andrew had thundered into her life, had started to doubt that love was evenly spaced stepping-stones of escalating emotions. What is it then, this waltz between the heart and the mind? This confection of emotion? Is it a whisper in an ear? Yes. It is a banging of cymbals? Yes. An immoveable rock? A quiet full moon pressing an open sea? A kiss by Emmanuel?

Yes. Yes and yes. And the velocity—oh sweet Lord—it had stunned her. To think that a kiss in a church stairwell could launch *this*. With Andrew, there were no baby steps.

No process. Had it been too much too fast? She didn't know. She didn't care.

"It's a beautiful day," Andrew said, as if that settled the matter.

"One would hate to disappoint the heartbroken woozles," she said. She gave him another peck on the lips. "Let's go. But I've got to change." She cantered—she couldn't decide whether to walk or run, and Lizzy never could skip worth a darn—into her bedroom. She put on a satin camisole and low-rise jeans. She debated over two pairs of shoes and chose comfort over style.

Five minutes later, they trooped out of Lizzy's off-campus apartment and trekked four blocks to closed streets pitched with white tents. They clutched hands, making them the envy of less romantic couples. What could be more joyful than young lovers at an April Saturday morning art festival in Florida? What bliss could ever top this kingdom of days?

Andrew stuck his nose in the air. "Over here," he said. He pulled Lizzy toward a vendor selling kettle corn. He bought a bag and stuffed a handful in his mouth while Lizzy accepted the change. They ducked in and out of snowcapped tents. In and out of the sun and the shade. In and out of the creative outpourings of fellow humans. They appraised paintings and sculptures. Tasted olive oil and bread and pasta and cheese. Jams and jellies. ("What *is* the difference?" he had postured.) They judged and exchanged both sage and foolish comments on drawings, etchings, glass bulbs, and ceramic bowls. They giggled under their breath at some creations, careful to be out of range so as not to offend the empty-eyed artist. Other works they contemplated as if they were judges at the Louvre or docents at the Uffizi. Do you like this? See what she's done with the light, how your eye follows? Andrew kept asking her, "What do you feel?" He was big on that word. Of all the four-letter words, Lizzy noticed that *feel* was his favorite.

They stopped by a vendor who had a rack of hats outside of her tent.

Lizzy tried on a green baseball cap. "Well?"

"I don't think so," Andrew said.

Pouty face. Her eyes caught a wide-brimmed black hat —so unlike her. She put it on. She lowered it over her forehead and considered herself in a mirror. She touched up her lipstick and lowered the hat a tad more.

Not bad. Mom's right—I do have the goods.

She pirouetted and paraded out to Andrew. She planted her hands on her hips and thrust her left hip out—enough to cause a slight glitch in the earth's rotation. A wobble that, in central Florida, they talk about to this very day.

"How do you like me now, big fella?" She husked out. She worked hard to keep a serious face.

Andrew gave her the once-over. "Damn, woman. You put the hurt on me."

She broke into a giggle. Lizzy felt as if she'd just gotten the best costume out of the costume box.

Andrew stooped down so he could see her eyes. "That is the finest hat in the world."

She pranced around the festival with her head held high. What self-respecting woman wouldn't, knowing she wore the finest hat in the world? As they walked, Andrew whistled a soulful tune.

"That is so pretty," Lizzy said, snuggling up to his side. "What is it?"

"A memory. Songs are long rivers of memories."

"That river got a name, Huck?"

He told her. They wandered into a tent with original oil paintings.

"We should leave," Lizzy said after taking two steps into the tent and sensing the danger. "There's nothing here we can afford."

"They're beautiful, babe. Besides, looking is free. What do you feel about this one?"

He held up a seaside painting of a yellow cottage with opened sea-blue shutters framed by ancient and curved palms. They looked like bent pencils with parsley on top of them. A rowboat rested on the sandy shore. Two oars angled out of the boat and a picnic basket was on the seat. A bird perched on the gunwale, attentively staring at the cottage. Beyond the water lay a small island.

"I love it. You can feel"—yes, she was aware of her word selection—"the couple who aren't seen. The oars. The picnic basket. But where are they? What do they look like?"

"They're inside," Andrew said. "Getting a quick one in before rowing to the island for lunch."

She nudged him. "No, they're not. She's finishing packing lunch. He's gathering fishing gear."

"Don't think so. Pretty sure if you peek through the window you can see them—"

"Stop it. We don't know, do we? And that's the pull, the tension of the painting. Who are our young lovers? What do they look like?"

"Maybe they're old," Andrew said. "Golden Pond material."

A bolt of wonderment struck Lizzy. "That's us inside the cottage. But we don't know whether it's now or decades from now. It can be anytime we want and time can go back and forth. Fix us a lunch, Andrew. Walk me to the rowboat,

Andrew. Stroke us to our deserted island where I'll read you a chapter and you'll sing me a song. Can we do that?"

"We can do anything we want."

His comment, trite as it seemed, baptized her like a waterfall. "We can, can't we?"

"Do you want it?" he said.

"What? The picture? Do *you*?"

"I do."

Lizzy looked at the price tag. "We need to back off, babe. We have no right buying this."

"Silly girl. That wasn't the question."

Andrew toted the well-wrapped painting under his arm for the remainder of the day.

Andrew insisted on sharing a cherry snow cone followed by a pulled pork sandwich. Lizzy contended they should have had the snow cone after the sandwich, and Andrew had countered that wasn't the purpose of street food. That harmless bickering, that playful squabble, was the height of any discord that had ever passed between them.

They came across tables teeming with jungled flowers and plants that they had spotted on the way in. Lizzy knew exactly what she desired but she hadn't wanted to haul it through the show. She went over to the table and picked up a pink orchid.

"I don't think we can afford it," Andrew said.

"Said the man who purchased a painting we'll spend a year paying off."

"Lucky if we can do it in that, but I didn't buy it, you did."

"Uh-uh."

Andrew selected an orchid off another table. "How about this one?"

It was a white orchid with drops of pink on the petals.

"Oh, that's even better."

As Andrew paid, Lizzy considered a bench in the shade next to the creek that cut through the park, its rocky sides forming a border between water and freshly cut grass. I'll tell him now, she thought. Get it over with. *That's what I'll do. It'll be over in five minutes. Bang. Boom. Done.*

She'd already told him that as soon as Charlie got off the road, she was breaking it off with him. Charlie deserved to learn in person, although he'd likely picked up the chatter on the grapevine. No wonder he was cutting his trip short. But Lizzy could only gaze longingly at the bench. She couldn't summon the nerve.

They strolled back to her apartment carrying the painting, the orchid, a baguette, two ruby-red Florida grapefruit, a bag of kettle corn, and two goldfish—Lizzy had named them Larry and Earl—swooshing around in a Ziploc bag. The low, slanted sun shaded her face under the finest hat at the Fourteenth Annual Spring Arts and Crafts Festival. Perhaps even the finest hat in the world. At least the state of Florida would have a serious contender that year.

"Hey, babe," Andrew said as they approached her apartment complex. "I'm gonna need to run."

"What?" She'd been lost in her thoughts. She already regretted that she hadn't led him to the park bench. *You just gotta do it, Lizzy.*

"Extra practice today, remember? We're working on new material."

"You want something to eat first?" she said while thinking, *not another night of keeping it inside of me. I told myself today —that means* today.

"Lord, no," Andrew said. "I can't believe you insisted on that snow cone after kettle corn and be*fore* pulled pork."

"What type of mother will I be?" Her thoughts were seeping out of her.

"The grandest in the world."

Tell him. But instead she said, "It's going to be a late night for me as well. My parents are having a retirement party for a partner of the firm. I've got to make an appearance, but I'll still be back before you."

Her body ached and groaned with disappointment. She was making it harder than it was. Maybe not—for what did she have to measure it by? As they rounded the corner to her street, the weakening sun cast muted tones of fire through the trees. A lamppost flicked on. Andrew froze. He put down the picture and the bags and placed both hands on Lizzy's arms. He flung her hat to the ground.

"What?"

He pressed her back against the lamppost. Her face was shadowed on one side and warmed by a golden beam on the other.

"What?"

Andrew Keller kissed Elizabeth Phillips with every note in Handel's *Messiah*. His hungry tongue explored her mouth, tasting and biting and inhaling her all at once.

When he pulled away, her mouth followed him and they again fused in tangled and unnamable desire. His hands worked up the sides of her rib cage, pressing and squeezing and trying to understand her. Elizabeth Phillips knew that she would carry that kiss forever, that she'd been touched by glory.

Their lips parted and Andrew said, "You are my prayer, my poem. My anthem. My east in the morning, my west in the evening. I will dry your tears with laughter, Elizabeth. I will flower your life with songs. You're beautiful, and I'll love you until the end of time."

"Oh, say it again," she gushed, shocking herself with her uncensored outburst of vestal emotion.

But unable to summon the silken-tongue muse who had serendipitously possessed him, and wrenched of every ounce of feeling, Andrew could only proclaim from the core of his heart, "I'll love you until the end of time."

Tell him now. This moment.

But love froze her. Its salty taste. Its rose-petal touch. It vacuumed the air and wilted reason. She felt nothing except the pole supporting her spine and Andrew's strong hands now behind each of her curved and bony shoulders, for her skin had shrunk off and there was nothing left of her. Nothing at all.

I'll tell him when we get back tonight. No, Lizzy. That's not what you promised yourself.

She didn't want it wrapped in the hot wet love of night. She knew what that would be like. She could lie on her back forever with Andrew on top of her, beside her, in her and around her. His cruel patience. His probing tongue that left no inch of her body unexplored or unloved. His hands that moved over her as if she were made of glass and then without warning, her ungovernable passion would erupt into a million tiny silvery pieces. *No,* Lizzy thought as they took the first steps to the front door of her apartment. *I'm telling him now.*

24

Kathleen and I had just taken delivery of a bookcase purchased from a secondhand furniture store on Central Avenue owned by a hippie couple with dreamy taste. The craftsman-style piece had beveled glass doors that receded above the shelves or could be pulled down. Although similar to one I already had, we had both coveted it the moment we'd laid eyes on it. The only question had been where it would reside—in my study next to its cousin, or in her office at the college. I lost. She didn't have her purse. I paid. Welcome to Married Land.

The bookcase sat next to a flip-up wall calendar. I recalled Andrew's confession that autumns just destroyed him. I wanted to peek at October to see if it was the emotional wrecking ball Andrew made it out to be, but I was on duty.

Kathleen stared blankly at her (should be mine) new-old bookcase. "Little more to the right."

I shifted the bookcase a fraction of an inch. It was the umpteenth time I'd put my shoulder in it.

"Perfect," she said. "So . . . according to Rachel, Andrew misled you. He and Lizzy were a hot item. She was about to dump Charlie and for some reason, she changed her mind."

"Charlie Walker lied as well," I said, thinking Kathleen had gone easy on Andrew. His comments were beyond misleading. "Andrew wasn't just an old flame, as he claimed to you. He was the man who nearly stole his fiancée and was back in Charlie's life as a double nemesis."

"Just a smidgen back to the left."

I followed orders. That's what good married men do.

Kathleen said, "Do you think Charlie Walker had Andrew killed as payback and to eliminate his financial opposition?"

"The motivation is there."

"Double motivation." She plopped down on her chair. "I think you had it right the first time."

"I'm not moving it again."

"I don't blame you. You have love and money colliding. Those are the biggies."

"Major themes."

"That too."

"Walker's too shrewd," I said, taking the opposite side for the sake of debate. "He'd never risk everything over his wife's college suitor riding into town. And Andrew's support of the Coalition for Peace was hardly a threat to Walker."

"I dunno," Kathleen said, cocking her head at the bookcase. "Maybe he hires a button man. You might be overestimating him."

"Andrew told me that he was coming clean. That he had set the record straight."

"What did he mean by that?" Her eyes scrutinized the

bookcase with more attention than any piece of furniture this side of heaven deserved.

"I didn't ask."

"Try this on," she said, flicking her eyes to mine. "Andrew approaches Charlie and says, 'Time's up, pal. It should have been me all along.' That would ignite a short fuse."

"Too confrontational. I should have paid more attention to what he said that night, or at least have been more inquisitive."

"Don't—"

"Maybe whatever he set straight is what put him down." As I spoke, I thought of someone I needed to revisit —someone who I had not asked the proper questions the first time around.

Kathleen sprang up and marched to the bookcase. "Help me out here a little. A baby smidgen—a smidgeneen —to the right." She leaned into it, although her manly effort yielded no results.

"Andrew said he needed to unload the guilt. I assumed he was speaking of a passion that he wasn't true to. It could have been something else."

Kathleen grunted at the immoveable object. "Geez Louise, this brute is heavy. Was he aware of Elizabeth's diagnosis?"

"Not that I know."

She straightened and planted her hands on her hips. "The more we learn, the more we question. My dime is that it all relates to Elizabeth, Andrew, and Charlie and has twenty-year-old roots. It might not seem like it now, but remember, it's all one case."

"It's all one case," I said. "Is that you?"

"Ross Macdonald."

"What do you know about Kenneth Millar?"

"More than you think. You're not going to help me here, are you?"

I walked over and gave her a kiss on the head. "No. It looks fine where it is, although it is noticeably too far to the left."

Her shoulders slumped. "Noticeably? Really? You didn't need to say that."

IF I WANTED TO DELVE INTO MY PAST, AND MY marriage was rocky, who would I confide in, the wife I was contemplating leaving or the woman who I trusted explicitly with my credit cards and business? I hadn't pushed Brooke hard enough or accounted for her being naturally protective of her benevolent boss.

She glanced up when I stepped through the door.

"You're back," she said in a tone I couldn't decipher. No puppies today. Soft music again emitted from her computer.

Her phone rang and she answered as one word, "Sarasotasofa." I wandered back to what passed as the waiting area. I flipped through a worn magazine until she finished with her call.

"You'd think we'd never dealt with a late delivery before," she said when I returned.

"Who's the captain of the ship?"

"That would be me until Marcy's done interviewing, but I think she's just dressing it up to sell, and I don't suppose you came here to discuss the business." She reached into her box of cereal and tossed a few pieces of honey-oats something into her mouth.

I dragged a chair so that it was across from her and took

a seat, elbows on knees. "Andrew was resurrecting his past," I said. "That proved fatal to him. What questions should I have asked you the last time we met?"

Her left cheek punched out with the indentation of her tongue. "Well, for starters, you should have asked me if there was anything unusual in his schedule. But you didn't. You were transfixed on his old flame. You did question me about creditors and potential business problems—which was good—but you got ridiculously sidetracked on trumpets, which was just weird. Oh, and I could tell you aren't in business."

"How so?"

"Business *is* problems. They call it work, not play. Stress, not relaxation. Business, not pleasure. Got it? You get up. You go to battle." She took another snatch of cereal. "I can't stop eatin' this. Most days, I hardly get no lunch. I just sit here munchin' dry cereal all day listening to 'Levon.'"

"You could switch to 'Mona Lisas and Mad Hatters.'"

She flashed a smile and shook her head. "I swear—maybe you and Andy were close. He just loved that song."

I leaned back in the chair. "Did any names surface in the past month that you didn't recognize?"

"Not that I recall."

"Did he take any unusual trips?"

"Nope."

"None?"

"Nope."

She reached into her box and tossed more cereal in her mouth. Something in her face—her attitude—didn't sit right with me. Her double nopes.

"The woman he gazed at on his screen," I said. "Her maiden name was Phillips, but you know that, don't you? And when you saw Elizabeth's picture on his computer screen, you would have insisted he tell you who she was. He didn't use models in his ads. You were performing when you said you thought she was his girlfriend. You played me."

She reached into her box, took a handful, and chewed it slowly, her eyes never dropping from mine. "Truth is, it gets a little boring around here. It was sort of fun batting you around. Do you understand my relationship with Andy?"

"I'm beginning to."

"Yeah? Well, life's too short for beginnings. I'd die for that man." She leaned in. "I figured if you really gave a shit and weren't just dealing it—you never had any baseball tickets; Andrew didn't know a baseball from a grapefruit—you'd come back."

"Here I am."

"Are you giving or dealing?"

I appraised my adversary, who was more gifted in reading people than I'd given her credit for, which is a far easier pill to swallow than admitting to my own gullibility.

"Give. I was never that close to Andrew. But I was close enough that he came to me. Help me or not. It's your choice."

She crinkled her face. "No need to get snotty. It's not like I know you."

"Life's too short to get to know everyone you need to trust."

She bounced her head a few times. "OK—so you finally scored a point. Don't get all bigheaded about it."

"What did you leave out?"

"He asked me to find Dylan Phillips."

It took me a second. "Elizabeth's younger brother?"

"Yup."

"Why?"

"Didn't say."

"No—why did you leave that out?"

"Didn't trust you."

"And now?"

She shrugged. "I do."

"Why did he want to find Dylan Phillips?"

"Dunno."

"He didn't say or you're not—"

"Hey, I'm being straight with you now, got it? He just said he wanted me to find him. Said he was Lizzy's younger brother. That's what he called her—Lizzy."

"No inkling why?"

"No."

"And did he?"

"Get in touch? Far as I know. He—Dylan—lives east of here. Andrew drove out there. Took the day and left. He used to never to do that, you know? Take a day off for no particular reason. I mean, he owned the business, and no one worked harder."

"When was this?"

She sucked on her lower lip. "Two weeks ago? Hold on." She punched her computer. "Three weeks ago tomorrow. I know because we got a truck in from North Carolina and it blew a flat at our loading dock. Took half the day to get it out of here. That skinny-ass driver thought it was my problem. Said he picked up a nail on our lot. I told him the only things on our lot were his cigarette butts and they better damn well be gone when he pulled out."

I considered whether Andrew had wanted to meet—or reintroduce himself—to Elizabeth's younger brother in an effort to gather information on his sister. Perhaps he wanted to pick up some tips on how to approach her. I asked for Dylan's address, and Brooke flirted with her keypad and gave it to me. I inquired if there was anything else that she could think of, whether it seemed pertinent or not. She assured me that Andrew seldom strayed from the task at hand.

"I do wonder," she said as I got up to leave.

"About what?"

"I mean, his last couple of weeks. He was distracted, you know, the picture of Lizzy and looking for her brother. I caught him a few times staring out the window. You've seen the parking lot, right? Makes a desert look pretty. I wonder if all that work, all that dedication, all that effort he put into the business, writing his own jingles, doing his own ads."

I waited for her to continue, but Brooke seemed lost in herself.

"What is it you wonder about?" I prodded her.

"It was like one day he just stopped running." Her eyes searched my face. "Didn't Forrest Gump do that? Just one day stop running?" She shook her head. "But life ain't no movie. I dunno—like it was all an act to cover something up. He sprinted every day, making himself up as he ran. And then," she snapped her fingers, "just like that, he stopped. He seemed to be at peace with himself."

She studied the cereal box, perplexed by its strange presence on her desk.

"Terrible to know a person so well but not know them at all." She flipped her eyes up to me. "Worse yet to realize that person might have felt the same about themselves."

25

Dylan Phillips lived off a county road that ran east out of southern Tampa and looked as if it were hell-bent on running forever. Carved wood animals stood like Yeoman Warders at the juncture of the driveway. A bear. A hawk clutching a stump. A great blue heron with a slender and smooth neck. A ragged Confederate flag rolled in the breeze on top of a rusted pole. A sign read INQUIRE WITHIN.

The driveway, a rain-starved road of dirt, cut through the flat, characterless land marked by Mexican sunflowers that loomed over clumps of pampas grass. It ended at a single-story wood house where rocking chairs lined the covered front porch. Fresh white gravel served as a parking lot, and manicured landscaping crowded the house. A white SUV sat off to the side. A sign on the side read NADINE'S INSTITUTE OF SOUTHERN COOKING, as did a sign above the front door.

I took the two steps onto the porch in one stride, worried that I might have the wrong address. No doorbell. I knocked. A petite black woman opened the door and the heavenly smell of fresh biscuits slapped me hard in the face.

"Hello," she sang like a robin greeting a May morning. "What brings you to my slice of paradise?" She appeared to be in her midthirties. Her thick, dark hair had a streak of yellow in it. A starched white apron disguised her figure. I introduced myself, said I was looking for Dylan Phillips, and apologized if I'd gotten the wrong address.

"Imagine that," she said. "Dylan's suddenly gotten popular."

"Why do you say that?"

"You're the third person this month to knock on my door for him—and you knock the hardest. That's not including the gentleman who wanted to buy a carving." Mirthful eyes accompanied her lyrical voice.

"Who else dropped by?"

"His sister—I didn't even know he had one. And after her another man. Neither stayed longer than it takes a loaf to rise."

"Is he here?"

"He lives out back. This used to be his house, all this property, but I recently bought it and I rent him the room over the barn. I go out there every week and tidy up a bit." She shook her head. "Some men never figured out a hanger. If I may ask, what is the purpose of your visit?"

"I'm worried about his sister and would like to talk to him."

"Well, he doesn't confide in me. Listen, I've got a cooking class starting in fifteen minutes and biscuits are tricky. You can follow me in and then head out back."

"My truck OK where it is?"

"No problem."

"Are you Nadine?"

"Excuse my manners," she said with a smile, for Nadine was the type of person who smiled as she spoke. She thrust out her hand without taking her eyes off mine. "Chief cook and bottle washer. Nadine's Institute of Southern Cooking."

The entrance hall was surprisingly large. The kitchen sported a center island with eight cushioned high-back chairs and room for more. A six-burner gas stove centered the island. Double stainless-steel refrigerators stood behind the stove. A mirror angled in the ceiling allowed those sitting on the stools to see inside the pots on the burners.

"You've got gas out here?" I said, for I lusted after her stovetop. There was no gas on my island.

She opened a heavy oven door. "We do. Surprised me too. It's because of all the new housing developments sprouting up."

She took out a tray of biscuits. "You want a little sugar in these, but just enough to lead the nose—you don't want them to be sweet. I've been using my grandmother's recipe for ages, but that woman couldn't keep her hand off the sugar jar. These are a little hot, but I'll have my class sample them and we'll put them to a vote."

She took another tray out and placed it next to the first one. She gave me a wary eye. "You know Dylan's not right, right?"

"In what way?"

"He's got a burr in his saddle, as my daddy likes to say. Drugs did him bad. There was an accident years ago, when he was about ten. His daddy and older brother died—he's been real messed up ever since. At least he seems to have found peace carving his animals."

"But it's your property."

"It is. When he leaves, I'm going to make that barn into

a gift and kitchenware store. Got blueprints and everything. But seeing as how he used to own all this, I'm being more than considerate in giving him time to move on. Plus, a little rent money doesn't hurt. My business is doing well, but I just eclipsed my first anniversary."

I dipped my head at the tray of biscuits. "Did you make a few extra?"

"Take a few. Dylan never complains about leftovers."

It wasn't so much a barn as a spacious double garage with a second floor. Dormer windows broke the corrugated-metal pitched roof. The first floor, with an open sliding barn door, was set up as a shop. Wood animals in assorted stages of evolution crowded the concrete floor. Outdoor stairs, hugging the side of the building, led up to the second floor. I took the steps two by two and rapped on the windowless door. A pinging noise came from below and in the rear of the building. I retraced my steps and circled behind the barn. A blue car with a canvas draped halfway over its sides was backed into white oleander bushes.

A willowy man, hunched over the remnants of a tree trunk, chipped away with a wood mallet and thin steel file. Both the man and his tools seemed outmatched by the ungainly piece of wood. He wore goggles and had earplugs in. An assortment of different-size chisels, hammers, and files littered the ground.

"Dylan Phillips?" I said loud enough to overcome whatever blared in his ears.

Startled, he looked up and stopped his work. He yanked his earplugs out and raised the goggles over his head.

"Whatdoyouwant?"

His clouded eyes were buried under a bushy head of hair peppered with wood chips.

"Biscuits?" I said and offered him the tray.

He stepped forward and took one. "You looking to buy a carving?"

I said that as much as I admired his work, I was there as a friend of Andrew Keller's and would appreciate a few minutes of his time.

His eyes darted around and he took a step back. He seemed oddly off-balance, as if he'd just gotten off a back-less barstool he'd occupied all afternoon and he could topple at any moment.

"What about him?" he asked, clenching his mallet.

"Is there someplace we can talk?"

"Right here's fine."

I recounted Andrew's visit. How he wanted to recon-nect with Lizzy after they had run into each other at the Vinoy. That he had died a few days later. I added that Nadine had informed me that both Elizabeth and "another man" had visited him.

"You with the law?" he asked.

"No."

"Then why do you care?" He turned the mallet over in his hand.

"There's a possibility that he was not the victim of a random act. That he was the target."

"Really? How'd he die?"

As I explained Andrew's last few minutes, laughter cackled from the house. Nadine's cooking class must be arriving.

Dylan said, "Sounds to me like he was in the wrong place at the wrong time. What do the police think?"

"What you said," I admitted.

"There you go. You talk to my sister?"

"I did."

"And?"

"I thought I'd talk to you."

"She's dying." Dylan blurted his words as much as he spoke them.

"I'm aware of that. How much time does she have?"

His lips curled in a tarnished emotion as he brought a finger up to his mouth. "Poseidon knows."

I gave him for a few seconds to see if he was yanking my chain. "Poseidon?" I said when he failed to elaborate.

"He's coming to take my sister."

"The Greek god?"

"You know he's moody. Totally unpredictable." He jutted his chin out at the stump he'd been chipping away at. "That's going to be him. I think I can appease him—if I can do it right."

"Do you talk to Poseidon often?"

"Do I make fun of what you believe?"

I spread my hands. "No, and I didn't mean to offend you." I wanted to steer the conversation back to saner ground. "What did Andrew want to talk to you about?"

"Nothin'." He swatted his head, as if a gnat had bit him, but I hadn't seen anything.

"We both know that's not true."

He humped his shoulders. "He wanted to know how she was doing since the accident and all. He hadn't seen her for a while. I guess they used to date or something. I told him I was sorry that he wasted his trip, but me and Lizzy were never close and that includes now."

"Are you referring to the accident in which your father and brother died?"

He smirked at me. "That be the one."

"I was sorry to learn of that."

"Sorry?" he spit out at me. "Piece of shit word if there ever was one."

"Did you know Andrew from when they dated?"

"Naw. She was at grad school. I was ten, eleven—whatever. I wasn't really that close to her. I'm what is commonly referred to as an accident."

"Had you seen him in the previous twenty years?"

"You're getting the picture now, biscuit man. Not a glimpse. He introduced himself and blabbered about Lizzy. Wanted to know if I talked to her much and was pretty disappointed when he found out we weren't close. I thought he looked familiar. Then I placed him. The Sofa King, you know? That wacky guy on TV." He swung his head back and forth. "And they think I'm nuts. Imagine all the years I'm watching Lizzy's ex-lover pawning furniture and I don't even know it's him. You think someone would want to kill him?"

"It's possible."

"Got a bad couch and snuffed him out?" He laughed. "Like I said—and people think I got issues. Hell, man, we all got issues." He paused for a moment. "What did Lizzy say to that—him being dead and all?"

"She told me to forget about it."

He crinkled his face. "It?"

"Him and her."

"Well, there you go."

"What did your sister and you discuss?"

"Ask her."

"I'm asking you."

"And I'm telling you to ask her."

"You have no desire to be close to her in her final days?"

"Are you dumb, blind, and mute? Hello, dude. You're standing in front of an accident. She split for college when I was six. Besides, our final days start the day we're born."

"You had to talk about something."

He punched out his breath. "She wanted to say goodbye—think that's any of your business?"

"Just curious."

He meowed like a cat.

It had not been the most agreeable of conversations, and I wanted it to end on a positive note. "Is that an old car you got covered up?"

He gave me an icy stare. "Just a car. If you'll excuse me, I got to get back to work."

He didn't wait for a reply but stuck his earplugs back in and placed the goggles over his eyes, taking his time to adjust them. I tapped him on the back. He took his earplugs out. I handed him my card. "If you think of anything else." He stuck the card in his shirt pocket and then placed the plugs back in his ears.

I strolled down the brick path to Nadine's kitchen. Seven women sat around the counter. The air, like a swollen rain cloud ready to burst, was dense with the smell of bread, fried chicken, and sausage. A pot of white sauce simmered on a low burner and the chicken hissed in a cast-iron skillet.

"Sausage is like garlic," Nadine instructed her rapt audience. "A little goes a long way. I usually make my white gravy with bacon grease, but we'll be making it with sausage today." She spotted me. "There you are. We're making a white sausage gravy. Would you care to join us?"

"Please do," a heavyset woman with a white flower pinned in her hair said. "We need a man's opinion."

"Or just a man," another woman said, soliciting laughs around the counter. Bubbly long-stemmed flutes dotted the counter. A champagne bottle and a carton of pulpless orange juice stood next to the sink.

"Rest your feet," Nadine said. "Our culinary painting will come into focus in about ten minutes."

I pulled out a chair and chatted with the women. Ten minutes later, we all munched on fried chicken that was crispy on the outside and moist on the inside. I sopped up white sausage gravy with fluffy biscuits. Afterward, I mingled as Nadine's flock chirped their way out the door in singsong voices that women reserve for when they talk exclusively to each other, carefree and as happy as they will ever be on that day.

"Give you a hand?" I said when her house was finally empty.

"No need to, but I won't argue."

"How many classes do you do a week?"

"Four. I run a catering business as well, but that's cotton-pickin' work. I want to focus on a cooking institute. Something to teach and preserve the traditions of my ancestors." She handed me a dishtowel to dry with. "How did Dylan seem to you?"

"The cornerstone of sanity."

She laughed. It was a pleasant and inviting sound. I wondered if there was a significant other in her life and, if so, deemed him or her to be a fortunate person.

She placed the cooking pans into a pullout drawer the size of a steamer trunk and I nearly fell ill with kitchen envy. "He's worked hard to straighten up his life. We met at a rehab center where I was a counselor. I was looking to make the leap full time to cooking and he was just trying to keep from leaping. Said he had a place available. It's worked out well, but I worry about him."

I dried a saucepan. "How so?"

She planted her hands on her hips and lost her perennial smile. "After that other man came around, he seemed agitated. I'm afraid he might go back to the drugs."

"Did you ask him what he and the other man talked about?"

"I did, but Dylan is surrounded by a stone wall and he ducks it behind as fast as anybody. You know his story, right? About the accident that killed his father and older brother?"

"I do."

"He never got over that. I wonder if your friend stirred those dormant memories."

"Dylan mentioned Poseidon to me—the Greek god."

Nadine gave a slight nod. "Most times he's fine. But every once in a while, he'll pull that one out. He nearly drowned as a little boy, and the drugs jumped all over that. Did he mention Poseidon once and then drop him?"

"That's about right."

"Then I'm proud of him. We worked with him on that at counseling. Told him if he heard himself talking about Poseidon that he needed to slow down. That was his old self talking. But the truth is, he's always going to be a little lost. He's harmless, and somewhere in his mind, there's a Greek god roaming around."

"Can anything else be done for him?"

"Why? You want to spend the hours and years hauling him to counseling?"

"No."

"I didn't mean to be curt."

"You weren't."

"There is nothing anyone can do. He needs to do it himself and he's doing a good job. Be kind. Treat him with respect."

I folded the dishtowel and gave her my card with the

line to call me if she thought of anything else. On the way out the door, I turned back to her. "One more."

"Yes?"

"I noticed driving in that there's a Confederate flag out by the road."

She nodded, as if she'd heard the question before. "It's his, obviously. No, it doesn't bother me. To him that flag means simple times. He equates it with the old days, before his father and brother died. It doesn't make sense, but that's Dylan. He doesn't have a racist bone in his body."

"But you own the property."

"I think it would upset him to not have it there. Besides, he plans on leaving soon."

"And when he does?"

"That flag is coming down."

26

Lizzy
Twenty Years Ago

Well a man shall leave his mother, and a woman leave her home
They shall travel on to where the two shall be as one

T he kiss in the church stairwell.

   Her right foot mooring the lower step. Her left hand gripping the coarse banister. The clammy feel of the wood. The stuffy smell of the stairwell. Her head pressed against the hard and ungiving wall. Dim voices, but to whom do they belong?

   Elizabeth would remember that moment until death ripped it from her last blink of life. And then death would own it forever.

She'd had no intention of leaving the sanctity of her off-campus apartment on that Sunday night. But a friend called and coerced her into going out for the evening—to hear some band that was supposed to be good. Lizzy tagged along out of a sense of duty. You never want to let a friend down.

Majestic had just performed a benefit concert for homeless families. She was surprised. Shocked, really. The band was good. No—really good. The Christmas Eve and Easter morning chairs were added across the back and along the sides of the massive sanctuary, not that anyone sat. Majestic played a full ninety-minute set, rarely coming up for air. Lizzy couldn't take her eyes off the lead singer and keyboard player. Plenty cute, but that wasn't it. He was so . . . there. As if that performance was the pinnacle of his being. He delivered every phrase with a blue-collar intensity that made Lizzy feel insignificant yet exalted. Alone yet connected. Her mere attendance granted her access into the great circle of—she didn't know, for it was somewhere she'd never been.

Toward the end of the set, he took center stage with his guitar. Lizzy wondered if there were any instruments he didn't play. He broke out of the current playlist. He sang Noel Paul Stookey's "The Wedding Song (There Is Love)." Lizzy had never heard the song before, and it made her afraid of what other beautiful things there were in the world that she was not aware of. It frightened her to realize that she was ignorant of such enchantment. A maiden to stirring passion, she wondered if she was falling in love with him—there and then—and that surprised her because (A) she was already engaged, which means in love, right? and (B) she was a practical person, and it just doesn't work this way.

Halfway through the song, the singer glanced up toward the balcony. Elizabeth nearly fell out of her seat as she tried to get closer to Eden. She couldn't deny her heart's belief that the young man was singing to her and her only. And he was. For, once he spotted her in the balcony, his eyes never left her. From that moment, Andrew Keller and Elizabeth Phillips were fused together. Forever and ever. World without end. Amen.

She and her friends made their way toward the basement and the food. They ran into the band making their way up. The female lead singer trailed Andrew and everyone laughed and talked and no one's feet touched the ground.

"A dollar a kiss for the kids," Andrew said.

He gave a peck on the cheek to any girl holding a dollar, which was every girl on the stairway. Then he got to Lizzy.

These are the first words Andrew Keller spoke to Elizabeth Phillips: "Marry me, my balcony girl."

He kissed her on the lips. She thought she should resist, but the coarse and sticky banister seemed to grant her strength. A Gibraltar in an unsettled and rapidly boiling sea.

He pulled away. She missed him already, but how wrong was that? Vaguely aware of people shuffling around her, she trailed her left index finger over the top of her left eyebrow, a habit her mother had spent years—decades—trying to break. She gushed out a playful, "Excuse me, but do we know each other?"

"I'm Andrew."

She cocked her head and cracked a smile. "Elizabeth."

"Oh my God. Elizabeth?"

"Is that an issue?"

"I *love* your name." He grabbed her hand. "Follow me, Elizabeth, my balcony girl."

"OK."

THEY TALKED FOR HOURS. IT HAD NEVER BEEN both so effortless and so stimulating for her.

Whoa, Nelly, she thought. *First of all, who ever knew that effortless and stimulating even went together? Come on, Liz, you're at it again, trying to rationalize love. Love? Girl, you did not really just think that, did you? This isn't love. It's too fast. Too sudden. Too easy peasy. But what if I never knew what love was? How would I know its knock? Its taste? Face it, I'm always trying to talk myself into that clunker I've got going with Charlie. Is that any way to be before you get hitched?*

They sat in a diner until 3:00 a.m. Elizabeth Phillips, Andrew Keller, and a revolving door of college kids, truckers, bikers, loners, and couples. Everyone scarfing down breakfast. Pancakes. Eggs. Grits. Coffee and more coffee. Someone looked for answers in the jukebox and Tom Petty stepped up. Of course, who else? Lizzy and Andrew talked about art and books and poetry. They ran with music. Green Day. The Red Hot Chili Peppers. U2. Christina Aguilera. Petty and more Petty. Andrew tossed a few others in the ring she'd never heard of and then she sensed he pulled up, not wanting to embarrass her because a vast sea of music rolled within him. They made fun of a man in purple pants sitting by himself and then they felt sad for the man, and Andrew said he didn't like putting people down, and Lizzy said she didn't either but oh my God those pants, and they both suppressed innocent giggles. They vowed never to make fun of another human again except anyone who wore purple pants. Beware: purple pants are fair game.

"What was that song you played by yourself? It was beautiful," Lizzy said when she had returned from the ladies' room. She thought she might feel awkward—the first *"Excuse me, I need to use the restroom"*—but she didn't. There was simply no awkwardness around Andrew.

"You liked it?" he asked.

"I loved it."

He leaned back in the red vinyl booth. "You ever hear of a folk group called Peter, Paul, and Mary?"

She crinkled her nose. "No. I mean, sort of. Did they have a candy bar?"

"They did 'Puff the Magic Dragon.'"

"Oh, sure, I know that."

"No, you don't," he said in a challenging tease. "Sing it."

Lizzy started singing, her head swaying side to side. "Puff, the magic dragon lived by the sea. And something and the something in a land called autumn lee."

Andrew laughed. "You've got a pretty voice."

No one had ever told Lizzy she had a pretty voice. She thought she did but was too shy to ever venture it out of the shower, let alone parade it in public. She beamed inside. *I have a pretty voice.*

"Then why are you laughing?" she said.

"It's 'And frolicked in the autumn mist in a land called Honahlee.'"

"Where?"

"Honahlee."

"Never heard of it."

"You never heard of Honahlee?"

"No." She pouted out her lower lip and shook her head in a playful manner. "Spell it," she said, laying down her own challenge.

Andrew tapped his chin with his finger. "Let's see. H-o-n-a-h-l-e-e."

"And where do you suppose this land might be?" she asked in a throne-like voice.

"East of the sun and west of the moon."

He was referencing a jazz standard written by a Brooks Bowman, a Princeton undergraduate whose promising career ended in a fatal car wreck four days short of his twenty-fourth birthday. Andrew, who possessed a Wikipedia knowledge of songs, liked the song and was haunted by Bowman's tragic death in 1937. He could think of nothing worse than being cut down just when you found your stride. And Andrew had found his stride. It was incontestable that he was widening the gap between himself and other promising musicians. A Bowman-like tragedy was what Andrew feared most in life. All that blocked his star-spangled path. He knew about the twenty-seven club, of course, but those were self-inflected mortal wounds. Andrew, whose idea of a wild bash was one and a half beers, had no intention of nuking his own career.

"And where exactly might that be?" Lizzy demanded.

Andrew feigned exasperation. "It's where magic dragons live. Just beyond the morning star."

"Like Neverland?"

"Yes," he exclaimed, eyeing her appreciatively. "You know where Neverland is?"

"I do. It's 'second star to the right and straight on till morning.'" She delivered Peter Pan's line to Wendy in a clipped voice, as if giving instructions to a passing motorist.

"How do you know that?"

"My dad read it to me and I . . . read a lot. How do you know Peter, Paul, and . . ."

"Mary."

"Right."

"I love all music. 'East of the Sun and West of the Moon' is an oldie. And the song I sang to you? It's called 'Wedding Song,' or 'There Is Love.' One of those goofy songs that has two working titles. Paul wrote it for Peter's wedding, and that was the first time it was performed. Did you like it?"

"It was as if you were singing it just for me."

"And you liked it? I could tell—watching you."

"I loved it," Lizzy said. She thought she sounded drunk. *But I haven't had anything to drink.* "It's the prettiest song I've ever heard." She was going to say the most beautiful, but the word *pretty* was dancing in her head.

Andrew Keller leaned in, his chin resting on his interlocked hands. "It was the first and last time I performed it. I knew if I sang it, you would come."

THEY NEVER DISCUSSED WHEN OR WHERE TO meet again. The usual posturing and arranging the next date seemed so antiquated. Unnecessary. Pity the less fortunate who assume that is the only path. There was no formal move in, for even that reeked of an overture. A plan. When they left the diner holding hands on Monday morning, the next day's paper was in the stand outside the door. It was a new day. A new week. A new life. Andrew and Elizabeth were inseparable from the first kiss in a church stairwell on a Sunday night. There only one tiny glitch.

"I'm engaged," she said. "Sort of. Unofficially. I mean, we've talked about it."

"Oh?"

"He's traveling. When he gets back, I'm breaking it off."

"Certainly not on account of me?" Andrew said. Lizzy thought he was joking and then knew that he was.

"On account of us." She paused. "On account of me. I don't love him."

"You know this?"

"I do now."

Pesky second thoughts being what they are, Lizzy was fearful that she would wake the next morning and groan in reality. That the rising sun would find them in a mire of embarrassment and stale breath confusion. Two Hopper Nighthawks collide and think it's that simple? *Can't be*, she thought. *No way.*

But when she woke that velvet morning, there was no harsh light. No condemning dawn saying she had sinned, that she had been a willing victim of the night. No avoiding eyes. She eagerly accepted the raw morning kiss and all that followed. There would be no lull in the trajectory of their relationship. No leveling off before climbing to even greater altitudes and looking down on the clouds. Let others take the cautious route. They do not know what goddess has passed them by.

Andrew casually leaned against the bedroom doorframe. He held a steaming cup of coffee in his hand. "You like your coffee first thing in the morning and black, right?"

She sat up in bed, smiled, and nodded.

"I'm going to write us a wedding song."

She brushed her hair back with her hand. The sheet slipped off her bare shoulders.

"I'd like that very much."

27

Detective Rambler called as I nailed a gutter on the roof at Harbor House. The sun baked my head because I hadn't put a hat on. Two million hats inside, but lazy me didn't want to climb down the ladder and fetch one. And so I labored on; stupid, lazy, hot and marveling at my dumbassedness.

"Late-model silver Honda. Two door," he said when I answered.

"You trying to pawn off your wife's car?" I said. It was close to two o'clock and I was starving.

He grunted. "We got a tip, some guy driving by at the same time it went down. Said he saw a silver Honda screech out of the parking lot. It had been parked next to Keller's car. Said he noticed Keller's car because of the vanity plate, SOFA. Guy said he looked like he was in a hurry. We think it might have been the perp's car."

I climbed down the ladder and took a seat in a rocking chair on the back porch that faced a pond. A great blue heron stalked the stagnant water, lifting its ballerina legs as it negotiated the high grass.

"Might have been?" I asked, wiping my brow.

"Good enough." He sounded as if he were chewing something. "But he couldn't give us a face."

"You're still working this, aren't you?"

"I don't give a squirrel's tit what the feds say."

I stood and started pacing the creaky floorboards. Morgan burst through the back door and nearly ran into me.

"Your take?" I asked Rambler.

"Hasn't changed. Keller was followed. He was making his rounds, visiting his store in that area. Someone trailed him and tried to make it look like a robbery gone bad." He finished whatever he was eating. "Most victims know their assailant. This was a crime of passion—thought of and executed without much planning. Who commits murder under a surveillance camera?"

"Mr. Dumb Luck?"

"Have a good day."

We disconnected and Morgan said, "Any leads?"

"Nothing to move the case."

Morgan was in long pants and a pressed short-sleeve shirt. "I got a call," he said. "A judge is willing to hear a deportation case and the attorney—the same women who is working on Anna's case—needs me to provide character information. Problem is I have an English class starting in a few minutes. I hate to cancel. These people are eager to learn and their lives have been one disappointment after another. Forty-five minutes. I appreciate it."

"Me? Can't you get—"

He gave me a reassuring squeeze on the arm. "Wash your face. You look like you were roofing without a hat."

He jumped off the porch, and I wondered if I could pretend that I didn't hear him. I scrubbed my face and went into the living room that we had converted into a classroom. Nine faces studied me with uneasiness.

"*¿Sprechen sie Deutsch?*" I said.

Smiles and nods.

"*¿Habla usted Ingles?*"

"*¡Si! Si! Hago! Hago!*" Widening smiles and bobbing heads accompanied their ringing responses.

"Well, I don't," I said, although that didn't diminish their giddy faces.

I held up picture books. I sketched on a chalkboard. I endured giggles behind hand-covered mouths while thinking that I needed to talk to Highway, the guitar player in Andrew's band.

Ten minutes into my injurious teaching career, I asked, through a woman who spoke passable English, if anyone was hungry. Ten minutes after that, I, and my nine new documented immigrant friends, sat around a large outdoor table at Dockside. I—accomplished teacher that I am—instructed each person to say something about themselves in what little English they possessed. The woman who spoke English helped translate. One man reached into his shirt pocket and brought out a soiled piece of paper. He said it was a note from a friend. A friend who supported him. Who wished him luck. Who cheered him on from a distance. The man nodded his head enthusiastically while the woman translated.

I asked the interpreter if he would share what it said. As she talked, graveness shadowed his face. Then she started to read—first in English and then in Spanish for the sake of the others—from the paper that had been in the man's pocket.

"You will do well, for you have great courage, even though you are perceived as someone who is running from your place of birth.

"You are smart, even though you struggle to read.

"You are funny, even though you rarely smile.

"You are a hard worker, because you know the value of work.

"You know love, because you have family.

"You will succeed, because I am with you, even though I am not there. And when you stumble, I will help you up."

She looked at me sheepishly. "He signed it with love."

That sobered the group. I told her to tell the others that if they could all envision one person rooting for them—although rooting proved too difficult a word to translate, so we settled on cheering—their journey, while not necessarily easier, would certainly be more bearable. I asked the waiter for a blank order pad and instructed each of my students to write the name or names of people who supported them. Who believed in them. When they were done, they passed their papers to me one by one. I added my name to the list and handed it back to the person who gave it to me. One woman vaulted out of her chair and planted a wet kiss on my cheek, accompanied by words without meaning. My emotions got all fouled up and I wished I was back on the roof, stupid, lazy, and hot.

I wrote a name and stuck it in my pocket.

I dropped my family off at Harbor House and got antsy waiting for Morgan to return. Anna had never gotten back to me to arrange a meeting with Elizabeth. I decided to talk to Highway first and then take the plunge to see if Charlie Walker was up for a game of one-on-one. See if I could get him to trip up, or at least get a measure of the man. He didn't strike me as the type of man to walk away from a challenge. He did strike me as a man who had a swarm of reasons, both past and present, to want Andrew Keller dead.

28

Rachel told me that Highway, John Henry Morton, lived in Portland, Oregon. I called her, got his number, and gave him a ring. He'd heard through his network that Andrew had died. I explained that I'd talked with Rachel and he corroborated her story that Elizabeth was never the same after the death of her father and brother. His take on Andrew and Elizabeth was that without Elizabeth, Andrew self-destructed.

"Man sold out," John "Highway" Morton told me. "He was the total package and he tanked it. Just a matter of time before we hit it, you know? That man belched melodies. But the accident destroyed Lizzy, and that destroyed him. Want to know the worst part?"

"What was that?"

"They were *so* incredibly good together. I mean, balls-off wonderful. But she—it was just terrible, man. It just demolished her and then him."

"Did he talk to you much about the accident?"

"Tried to."

"Were you close?"

"Like a brother, man. And that's what hurt. Ask you something?"

"Sure."

"The army. That's where you met, right?"

"It was."

"You tell me—what the hell was he doing in the army? No bad feelings, you know—I support the troops and all that shit—but he didn't belong within a moon shot of the armed forces. You agree?"

"He was a total miscast."

"You know why he enlisted?"

"Serve his country?"

He snorted out a laugh. "We're musicians, man. We sing about freedom; we don't die for it. He did it to punish himself. I told him so at the time. Put everything I had into talking him out of it."

"Why would he punish himself?"

"Hold on a sec." He said something to someone else and then came back on the line. "Whatja say?"

I repeated my question.

"Hell if I know, but twenty years gave me this: when he lost Lizzy, he lost himself."

I'd told him to call me with anything he might remember.

"One more thing," he said before I had the chance to disconnect. "You talked to Rachel, right?"

"I did."

"How's that wild thing doing?"

I squeezed my eyes tight. "She's doing well."

"She always marched to her own beat. She'd pet the alligator and shoot the bunny just for the hell of it. Know what I mean?"

"I do."

"Tell her I say hi if you see her again."

"You can tell her yourself."

"Naw, man. That bridge crumbled long ago."

We disconnected, although I wasn't sure he had answered my last question.

I WAS RIGHT ABOUT WALKER. I CALLED HIS OFFICE and proposed that we have lunch; in return, he would never hear from me again. I was lucky. He was in town. I was even luckier. He bit.

Walker kept me waiting fifteen miserable minutes at an outside table at Mangroves. The man who plays his electric keyboard in front of the Museum of Fine Arts sang woefully out of tune. Like a pressurized air organ that needed time to locate pitch and timbre, he groaned inharmonious chords until, mercifully, he found his range.

Walker swooped in and scraped back the chair across from me in an orchestrated entrance. His European-cut suit draped his shoulders. He apologized for being late with a Pepsodent smile that not only lacked a whiff of genuineness but also theatrically broadcast his fictitious interest in me.

I told him I knew about Andrew and Elizabeth. How they tumbled into love when he was on the road. Said I talked to Andrew's bandmates to head off any opposition he might mount. I explained that for whatever reason, Andrew was circling back into Elizabeth's life. That I had interviewed his secretary and knew that he had tried to locate her and her brother.

I didn't divulge that his wife had mouthed words to Andrew when they met by chance at the Vinoy, or that Elizabeth had sent Andrew a one-sentence letter. I didn't want to dynamite my chance with Lizzy should Anna be able to arrange a meeting. I laid out that Andrew Keller, the man who decades ago had nearly stolen his fiancée from him, was one of Allison Daniels's top funders and that the Coalition for Peace was the first serious challenge to the NRA's unquestioned and unopposed dominance in Tallahassee.

Walker listened without comment. His hawkish nose and receding hairline lent him an unassailable air of aristocracy. The intricate crinkles around his eyes looked as if they were the finishing touches of an artist. He possessed a natural demeanor of superiority: Delicately folding a napkin. Elaborately crossing his legs. Shifting his weight in a disturbingly calculated fashion. Drumming his fingers— his whole body attuned to his performance. Not the material to stalk Andrew Keller and kill him. But perhaps, as Kathleen had suggested while lamenting the position of her new bookcase, the material to hire someone to stalk Andrew Keller and do the dirty deed.

I concluded my apparently vapid monologue by reminding Walker that he had denied knowing Andrew Keller yet slipped while talking to Kathleen by calling Keller his wife's "old flame."

"You're lucky I showed today," he said, his gaze following a woman down the sidewalk. Charlie Walker was using every weapon in his arsenal to convey that I was a schlemiel and not worth his effort.

"Oh?"

"I was going to send my attorney, with an order to stop beleaguering me. But I thought it best to extinguish your demonic imagination myself. You think I had Andrew Keller killed?"

"Did you?"

The waiter bombed us. I did a double take, for he was

missing his left arm. Walker placed his order with an exasperated tone. A delivery truck grunted down the street, LITTLE DEBBIE AMERICA'S NUMBER ONE SNACK. The meter maid inched by, car after car, checking the meters and irritating anyone who miscalculated by a few seemingly harmless minutes.

"Apparently your mind is open to wild fabrications," Walker said after I ordered. "I assure you I had nothing to do with his demise. I am saddened by Mr. Keller's death. My wife and he were close at one time. A minor infatuation that ended before it began. I harbor no ill feelings toward him and offered sincere condolences to his family." He gave me a look you'd grant a small child. "As far as him donating to the opposition—your ineptitude in politics is glaring. One does not go around killing donors from the other side of the aisle."

"You lied about knowing Andrew Keller."

"But for all the wrong reasons. Not because he's a threat but because he means so little. He made a pass at my fiancée twenty years ago." He flashed his pearly whites. "It bores me now. It bored me then."

"Losing your fiancée bored you?"

"She came back to me."

"After a hiatus to Europe, correct?"

"Elizabeth took the accident hard. She needed time. My god, her father and older brother—who she adored—killed when some maniac ran a stop sign and they slammed into a tree." He swung his head. "I knew her father, of course. Gem of a man. But I'm sure if he knew that by swerving, he'd kill himself and his son, he would have gunned for the other car. Taken the son of a bitch with him. Wouldn't you do that, Jake?" He suddenly seemed to have an interest in me, as if noticing me for the first time.

"I don't think it works that way," I said.

"You don't answer questions, only ask them?"

We were off subject, and sparring with a professional lobbyist was a little out of my league.

"It's a rhetorical question," I pointed out.

"That's not an answer."

The waiter rescued me. After I fielded a useless, "Is there anything else I can get for you," I asked Walker how the accident affected Elizabeth's family.

"Elizabeth was crushed. Her younger brother—I think he was around eleven when it occurred—got into drugs later. She was never close to Carolyn, her mother, and she died, oh, somewhere around nine years ago. A late casualty of the accident. Terrible thing to see a child in a cradle and a coffin."

"Elizabeth went to Europe after the accident?"

"I encouraged her to go. Paid for part of her trip." He nodded his head a few times, as if he were proud of his support. A real man. "I told her that if she wanted me, I still wanted her. But she had to want me, not him. And to take all the time she wanted."

"How long was she gone?"

He flipped open his hands. "Year or so. We married two years later."

"She did, didn't she?"

"Pardon me?"

"Take all the time she wanted."

He eyed me, rolling his tongue in his cheek. "The pause was good for us both. And now," he tossed his napkin on the table, "we are done with my past. My wife is dying. You have nothing to do with our relationship. Stay away. You will only make her remaining days that much harder. The doctors give her less than two months."

"I am sorry to learn of her poor health."

He stood, towering over me.

"And I am sorry that Andrew Keller is dead. That is the last thing she needs now. Yet incredibly, you think I had a hand in it. I can tell you that I do not know who would even re*mote*ly want to harm the Sofa King of Sarasota. If, by chance, I do, I will contact the police."

He walked away at an unperturbed pace. I wasn't worth his attention and he'd wasted enough of his life on me. He passed a large tousled man walking in my direction. His face was flat and gray, his twitchy head cockeyed, his mouth slightly ajar. His squinted, troubled eyes were locked in an unknown struggle. Across the street, the organ man again lost his pitch. He wrestled with a chord that, try as he might, he could not resolve. The one-armed waiter dropped off the bill.

29

Lizzy
Twenty Years Ago

Well then what's to be the reason for becoming man and wife
Is it love that brings you here or love that gives you life

Lizzy tossed the nearly empty bag of kettle corn from the art festival on the Formica countertop. It slid until it hit the two-slice toaster. Andrew had turned the toaster upside down a few days ago, dumping five years of crumbs out, and telling a disinterested Lizzy that toasters, like everything else, needed to be cleaned.

"That stuff is addictive," she said with equal praise and disgust. She took the newly purchased orchid and placed it on a bookcase. But the plant, with its thin stick to support the flower, was too tall. She moved it to the kitchen counter.

"I don't think so," Andrew said. He took the orchid and placed it on the round table that sat at the end of the couch, angling it out toward the room. He arranged the papers and magazines.

"It does look good there," Lizzy admitted. She straightened out the magazines—one was overlapping the other—while thinking that he would likely be better at such things than she. It wasn't that she didn't like decorating or believe that she didn't possess a unique flair, for what woman doesn't? But decorating presented certain dissonant challenges to her.

"What time do you need to leave?" she asked.

Andrew flopped on the couch and kicked off his shoes. "Twenty minutes. We got some new material to run through. I'll be late getting back. One thirtyish."

All the more reason to tell him now, she thought.

The realization had shocked her. Her body had never reacted well to the pill, which made her worry what other secrets her body might be hiding. They had been careful, and the one time they had done it with no protection, she thought they were OK. *Dumb, Lizzy. Can't you count days?* When she'd verified her trepidation, her first thought wasn't a thought at all. It was an electrical jolt to her body. A seizure. She'd wanted to tell Andrew immediately; after all, it was part his, right?

It? Is that what you call . . . it?

But she kept her secret inside, where it grew every day. She had contemplated her predicament from a concrete bench as she gazed out over the foaming gray waters of the Atlantic Ocean while attending a bridal shower for a friend. She dug her bare feet into the cool sand until her pastel-pink toenails disappeared. She wanted to be clear in her own mind what *she* wanted before she told Andrew. After all, it was her body. Lizzy expected a raging internal battle and did everything she could to promote it, but no opposing forces answered the bugle call. No contentious argument. She could see no foreshadowing cloud hugging a distant horizon.

She resumed the cause the next day and tried to talk herself out of it—like when she was forced to defend opposing views in Mr. Zionletti's ninth-grade debate class. While she put up a spirited counterargument, there was never any doubt. They both wanted children. Their discussions had revolved around the usual points—timing and, the more serious issue, numbers. Two? Three? (He'd mentioned four one time but quickly withdrew upon registering her shock. Four!) They had never explicitly ruled out now. It was, at their age and position in life, assumed.

Relax, she thought. *Andrew will embrace it. Rejoice.*

Rejoice.

Lizzy liked the word. She breathed in the sound like a cool morning mist. She thought the baby would like it as well. If you were an unborn, wouldn't you want your expecting parents to rejoice at your arrival? Rejoice at your birth? Rejoice as they cuddled you in a warm blanket and passed you back and forth like the tiny blood-circulating miracle you were?

Can you name a child Rejoice, she thought? *Bet you somewhere, someone has.*

This will be hard, she reasoned. At our age? At our pitiful income? Certainly a drag to his music career. But none of those arguments stood anymore of a chance than a wisp of wind against a Roman phalanx. This is life. This is good. This is love.

Rejoice.

I think.

Andrew held up the picture they had bought. He positioned it above a lamp and off to the side. Lizzy would have placed it higher on the wall. "Where do you want it, babe? How about here?"

"I dunno," she said absentmindedly. She studied the painting and imagined herself with Andrew in the small seaside cottage with their books and music and little Lizzy or little Andrew. What more could one ever desire? For if you spun the globe and landed in such a spot, wouldn't you be the envy of history?

Now, before you change your mind.

"I've got something to tell you," she said, surprised to hear her own voice and thinking, *This is it. I'm doing it!*

"Hmm." He moved the picture a little to the right, closer to the lamp. "You're supposed to hang things at eye level—which is BS, as everyone is a different height."

Lizzy took Andrew's hand. "Sit with me," she said, impressed with the calm resolution in her voice.

Andrew placed the picture on the end table, leaning it carefully against the wall. It would be twenty-one years and a continent away before the picture would ever hang from a wall.

He sat beside her, draping his arm across her shoulders. "What's up, babe?"

"I need to tell you something."

"You don't like kettle corn? Because I don't need to buy it ever again."

"No, remem—"

"I get it. I leave dishes in the sink." He never left dishes in the sink, she did. He sat up straight and took an arm across his chest. "I pledge to you, I will amend my bachelor ways."

"No, it's nothing like——"

"I haven't written you a wedding song? I'm working on it. But I don't want you to hear it un——"

"I'm pregnant."

There was a pause—a shift—and Lizzy wondered if the rest of humanity felt it as well. As if down the block, around the corner, and in the far reaches of the planet, people looked up from their screens, placed down their hoes, and searched each other's eyes while muttering, "Did you feel . . . something?"

"You're pregnant?"

Oh shit! Now what?

Lizzy had been so focused on her opening statement that she hadn't bothered to draft words beyond that point. But it was too late, for she was having great difficulty thinking at all. She wanted the moment to pass in the worst way, and then she didn't, for it may represent the last breathless prayer of splintered hope.

Could it be the end? Oh please, no, Oh please, no. Oh——

"You have a tiny . . . Snoopy in you?"

"I do." She nodded and cracked a smile. A tear tracked down her cheek, but she was afraid to brush it away. "But I'm hoping it's more like a little Lizzy or Andrew."

Andrew smothered Elizabeth with kisses and hugs. He abruptly drew away.

"You're sure?"

"I am. Oh God, I'm so sorry. Remember that time when I said it was OK? I must have miscal——"

"Did you say you're sorry?" Andrew asked in a puzzled voice.

Lizzy stroked his face. "I know we talked about it. But

with your music, and I don't even have a job yet—I just don't know."

"Do you want it?" he asked.

"Do you?"

"I do. I mean, there's always . . . alternatives, right?"

"Yes," she said. *Please God, no. I will go to church every Sunday until I die.* "We can choose not to have it. Or to give it up."

Andrew kneeled on the floor, as if the excitement of the world rested at her feet. He circled his arms around her legs and looked hard into her eyes. She brought her hand up to her mouth and then combed her fingers through his hair. She leaned over and touched her forehead to his.

"Do *you* want it?" he asked, still on his knees and squeezing her legs as if he were afraid of losing her.

"I do," she declared. It came out strong. Elizabeth Phillips was proud of that.

"I do too."

Lizzy cupped his face in her hands. "I don't want you to want it only be—"

Andrew placed a finger on her lips. "I want it because it's ours. Because it's not an *it* but a Little Lizzy Lizard or an Atom Ant Andrew."

"Or a little Snoopy dog?" Her words were choked with elation and shattered emotions. The moment had passed, and the world was good again. And oh, how shivered and scared she had been.

"Well, should that be the case," Andrew said, "our lives will likely be resigned to freak shows." They both laughed, a reaction born more from relief than from humor.

"Are you sure?" Lizzy said. "That you just don't want Little Lizard or Atom Ant for me, and not really for you? For us?"

"Elizabeth?" he said. He rarely called her by her first name, saying he would prefer to wait until their advanced years in order to grant the name the dignity it deserved.

"What?"

"I'll finish your song."

Tears streaked her cheeks. Why had she ever doubted love's eminence? They had crossed the river. No torrent or sunken rock could ever upend them. There was still all that crap about a job, a nanny, a new apartment, but those were details. A list of to-dos on a notepad and boy oh boy was she good at that. Give Elizabeth Phillips a list and she ruled the world. Harnessed the atoms.

"You're sure?" she said in a perky voice.

"Never ask again," Andrew pronounced.

She sniffled and laughed, although she did not understand the laughter, other than her whole being felt lighter, as though she'd become a fluffy white summer cloud.

"My song?" she said.

"It's the bestest, prettiest song for the bestest, prettiest girl in all of Honahlee."

Lizzy's mind spilled with everything she had kept imprisoned. Things she had been afraid to think about, that she had forcibly turned away at the gate, until this moment had passed. First up—get a job right after graduating. Pronto. That shouldn't be an issue. She was in the top 10 percent of her MBA class and had solid leads from internships. She didn't want Andrew to forfeit his music, and while he made money, it was not a benefit-rich career. They would need a nanny. A new apartment. A crib. Car seat. Baby socks that she'd purposely held off looking at and now she couldn't wait to fondle. Tiny articles of clothing smaller than her outstretched hand. And baby books.

Baby books. Oh, what a wonderful world!

"I made a list," she blurted out, kissing the palm of his hand as it ran over her mouth.

"Imagine that." He glanced up at the clock in the kitchen. "Shit, I gotta run."

"Stay just a moment?" Lizzy pleaded. She wanted the relief to linger. She had, after all, earned this moment.

"I need—"

"Please?"

Her limp body slipped onto the floor.

AFTERWARDS THEY LAY WITH THEIR YOUTHFUL legs entangled around each other, Elizabeth on her back and Andrew on his side. He traced a finger over her body, his eyes transfixed on his finger's sensual path.

"We need a name," he said, not looking at her but keeping his eyes on his finger as it progressed up her flat stomach and between her breasts.

"I need a job," she said.

"I can look as—"

"No," she said sternly. "I've given it a lot of thought. The timing's not bad, and I'm a woman with an MBA. I'll get snatched up." She kissed his finger as it came home to her mouth. "Keep writing your music. Promise me?"

"Promise," he said. "But, you know, we can't call it 'it.' And as much as I like Snoopy, he's a beagle. We need a working title."

"I like that. Working Title."

"Little Working Title. I don't know, babe. It's sorta long." He tucked a strand of hair behind her ear. "Trumpet."

"Trumpet?"

"I always wanted to play trumpet. Such a gorgeous

sound. We'll call her—or him—Trumpet. A little noise-maker running around in our imagined seaside cottage."

Lizzy smiled. "Trumpet."

"And I know why there are no people in the picture," Andrew said, reversing his finger and now running it down her neck, between her breasts, and down to her stomach, where he stopped. "They're inside with baby Trumpet." He glanced up at the kitchen clock. "Holy shmoly. I have *got* to go."

"Another minute," Lizzy said. She knew he needed to leave, but she was tired of being so regimental. So damn Lizzy-like. "Just hold me." She twisted her body so that she faced him, wrapped her arms around his neck, and nuzzled his head between her breasts. His breathing slowed.

She must have dozed off, for the next thing Lizzy knew, Andrew popped up. He called Rachel in a panic and told her he'd be there just in the nick of time for the opening number and that they would have to do the sound checks without him.

"I love you," Lizzy said as he flew out the door, his hand slipping out of hers.

She was alone in her quiet apartment. It looked like it did every other day, and she wondered how that was even possible. Can't walls sing? Floors break apart in celebration? Plates and utensils dance? After all, they do in Disney movies. She picked up the picture, still leaning against the wall, and took it into her bedroom. She placed it on her dresser. *There,* she thought, *baby Trumpet will be in the bedroom with us.* Only then did she realize how much she wanted the baby—girl or boy.

I'm going to have a baby!

Elizabeth Phillips rode that triumphant thought like a saddleless horse.

30

The eastern horizon glowed with the color of the inside of an orange peel. Venus clung to the moon like a lonely child wary of wandering too far from its parent, for the sun's looming rapture and pharaoh entrance to the day had snuffed out the other night lights. I ran as close to the lifeless water as possible—pretending my toe didn't hurt—without giving up the firm sand. But I cut it too close and a mucky goo accumulated on the bottom of my shoes. As I left the lip of the shore, high-stepping over the soft sand and increasing my distance from the resting sea, the air quieted. For even in stillness, the water roars.

I hosed off my shoes, stripped off my shirt, and stood under the pelting stream of water at the outdoor shower. Bickering crows swooped into a palm tree, and the charter fishing boat chugged by on its way to the pier to collect its daily passengers. After changing into shorts and a clean T-shirt, I grabbed two cups of coffee—for John Wayne was again at the end of my dock.

"You're an early bird," I said, taking a seat next to him.

Gulls bobbled in the water and another council of birds gathered on the sandbar.

"I got in late last night. Don't figure you for a night owl. I'm hauling out as soon as we're done."

"Done what?"

"Talking."

"You don't like phones?"

"No."

I waited for elaboration but then remembered who I was talking to. "Coffee?" I extended a cup to him.

He lifted his cardboard cup. "Got one."

"Refresh it?"

He gave his singular nod and peeled back the lid. It was two-thirds empty. I poured it full and he fidgeted the lid back on. "This is a nice spot you have here. A real sense of sovereignty. I prefer land over sea, but I'll grant you this."

The sun's rays snuck around the edge of a solo cloud and bolted beams of yellow across the powder-blue sky. The sky was so smooth I feared a fissure would appear and I would see through to the other side, and the other side would see us. A pod of dolphins less than fifty feet to our left broke the surface one after another. A calf nestled tight between two of them. Sheepshead nibbled at the crusty pilings of the dock, rising and falling in the gentle motion of a boat's wake.

"Have you found out anything about your good friend Andrew Keller?"

My good friend Andrew Keller.

I gave Wayne a recap and told him that Andrew and Elizabeth had a brief affair while she was engaged to Walker. That arched his golden wheat eyebrows.

"Did they see much of each other after they broke it off?" he asked.

"Never again."

"No contact at all?" It wasn't like Wayne to retrace ground.

"Not based on what I know."

The sun broke free of the cloud. He adjusted his hat. "Would Charlie Walker have Mr. Keller killed because an old flame, who is now a new adversary, appears?" He posed the question more to himself than to me. "He strikes us as arrogant but rarely a man to miscalculate."

"Rarely is not never," I said.

He gave me an acknowledging glance. "You've met Mrs. Walker. You've seen them together. What do you think?"

At neither place had I witnessed Elizabeth and her husband interacting, or even talking with each other. I told Wayne that. I also tacked on that I'd met with Walker.

"You did?" he said with a note of surprise. "Just sat down with him?"

"Guilty."

"That's pretty direct," he said, but his tone fell short of condemnation. "Does he have it in him?"

"I don't think I'm capable of reading men like Charlie Walker."

"Your best guess?"

"No. But I wouldn't bet on me."

Wayne took a patient sip of coffee. "You know yourself better than most people. You need to talk to Mrs. Walker."

"I'm working on that."

"She's dying."

My eyes floated over the water. A fishing boat zoomed and scattered the uncountable gulls. I turned back to Wayne. "You didn't come here to give me a pep talk."

"While talking to Mrs. Walker, any information you can

glean off her regarding her husband's business dealings with Limorp would be most appreciated."

"You mean go in under the guise that I'm trying to atone for my good friend Andrew Keller's death but in reality see what dirt she has on Charlie?"

A singular nod. Sometimes I don't like myself, and other times I like myself even less.

"I doubt she knows much," I said.

"Worth a try."

As we spoke, I realized I had a better way to gather information on Limorp than by going through Elizabeth Walker. I didn't tell Wayne my plan, as there was no need to divulge my connection. After Wayne left, I called Garrett and asked him to arrange a meeting.

Then I headed off to visit the prisoner of God.

31

The rear church door was again unlocked, although it wasn't a Thursday. Anna had not contacted me regarding setting up a meeting with Elizabeth. I thought of approaching Elizabeth directly as I'd done with her husband, but that recipe wasn't worth keeping, as that meeting had not been productive. Fearful of positioning myself as an adversary, I redoubled my efforts with Anna. That included arriving with a bouquet of flowers. I made my way through the banner-dripping halls and knocked on the doorframe. Anna had her back to me.

"Come in," she said without turning around.

"Springtime."

She spun at the sound of my voice. "You didn't need to do that," she said, shaking her head with a smile. She took the vase and placed it on a round wood table that was a veteran of many vases over the years without the benefit of a cloth.

"It's the least I can do considering the favor I'm asking of you."

She dabbled with the flowers, pulling some out higher and rearranging the white baby's breath. "She does not want to see you," she said, focusing on her task. "Otherwise, I would have called you."

"Why not? Andrew came—Anna?"

She stopped pampering the flowers and granted me her attention.

"Why wouldn't she want to talk to me? Andrew came to me. He said she spoke to—"

"You don't think I know this?" she said with a gust of unexpected anger, although I didn't think it was targeted at me. "She has given up. There is no hope that she will ever find . . . none of this matters. She is a dying woman, you understand?"

"Did you discuss that Andrew's death might not have been a random act?"

"We did."

"And?"

"She knows nothing and does not want to know."

"Why not?"

She gave me a hurt look. "Why do you ask these things?"

"My friend is dead."

"And mine is dying." She shoved a few white tulips around in the vase. I like white tulips and had selected several for the bouquet. "Sometimes," she said over her shoulder, "there is peace in death. Freedom."

I wandered over to the open window where the sounds of the outside world prattled on, indifferent to our conversation and impasse.

"What do *you* think is best for her?" I said, taking the tack Morgan had employed at our previous meeting.

She gave me a disapproving look. "It is not up to me to decide."

"It is exactly up to you to decide. She needs help. Direction. She wants someone to tell her what to do. We *all* want someone to tell us what to do."

As I spoke my proclamation, I wondered if there was some sort of adoption guru who could sit down with Kathleen and me to cut through all the indecision and illogical wishing. Tell us what to do.

"You do not know her."

"All Andrew Keller spoke about was how Lizzy was the great loss of his life and the vacancy in his heart. You tell me, here and now, eye to eye, that Elizabeth has no desire to speak to me and hear what Andrew said."

Anna bit down on her lower lip. I went in for the kill.

"You know she's battling this decision herself."

"You are a terrible man."

"I know."

"You think flowers can buy me?"

"I hope so."

"I'll call you if she is interested. My case? If I can—"

"Your case has nothing to do with whether I see Elizabeth. Morgan is working diligently on your behalf. You understand that?"

"You are a good man."

"What happened to terrible?"

"I changed my mind. I will try again. I, too, think it would be good for her."

I thanked her and left. The silent walls echoed Wayne's request, and I felt like slime.

THAT EVENING KATHLEEN AND I sat on the

screened porch savoring the turning of the day. For dinner I'd prepared lightly floured grouper, panfried in a thin layer of olive oil in a cast-iron skillet and then placed into a preheated oven. Salt and pepper were the only spices. Fresh bread and cheese grits with diced ham accompanied the grouper. It was a tasty little number but lacked color. That wouldn't do; after all, the first thing you eat with is your eyes. Next time I'd ring the plate with sliced red and yellow cherry tomatoes—such a simple way to decorate a plate that it reeks of cheating.

The eleven streetlights on the road across the bay threaded jiggling lines of white on the water. Hadley III bounded onto Kathleen's lap, patted her paws, and then curled into a ball, making eating a challenge. I'd just finished downloading on Kathleen my visit with Wayne and Anna. She had started strong, but her interest dwindled.

"How's the private adoption quest coming?" I asked. The leading edge of summer had ushered in mounting humidity and, with it, late-afternoon dark clouds. The air smelled like it needed to rain.

"I've got a list," she said in a tone void of promise.

"Any underlined names?" I asked, hoping she'd moved on from her notion that a stork would drop out of the bird-infested Florida sky.

"I've found an attorney who seems to have made a name for herself," she said as she stroked the cat. Kathleen's plate was on the glass table, but she would not disturb the cat by reaching for it.

"Do we make a visit?"

"Not yet." Her breezy voice in no way mirrored the disappointment the previous weeks had brought her. I didn't know if she was slowing down or gearing up.

I asked her.

"Both."

"What's my role here?"

She looked at me, her green eyes catching a flicker from the solitary candle she'd lit on the glass table. She gently picked up Hadley III, who responded with a muffed "mroww," and placed her, still curled in a ball, on the floor. Kathleen stood and motioned for me to slide over. She nestled tight against me. Her hair tickled my neck and it smelled like the moon. A voyeuristic wind came off the bay, and a light rain padded the roof. It was the type of rain that sounded good. A rain that drove you into yourself and kept the world at bay.

"Your role," she said, "is to say yes from the bottom of your heart to whatever I want. But that seems so selfish and self-centered."

"It's not."

"I think I understand that now, but it still feels strange. I'm fearful of breeding resentment."

"At least you're breeding."

She pinched my arm. "Be serious. It could cause bitterness and a sense of entrapment."

"Are you done?"

"I think so. I just don't know. A child conceived in passion is one thing. Starting such a journey with a Google search is another. It's so . . . calculated. So eeny, meeny, miny, moe."

"Moe's a cute kid," I said. "Best-mannered tot in the world and possesses the incredible aptitude to converse with adults. Meeny smiles all day and always has a flower in her hair—even a dandelion. Miny is challenged in math but runs like the wind and leaps like a dolphin."

She twirled my hair. "They are all beautiful. I want to get it right. I want . . ."

"The one," I said.

"That's stupid, isn't it?" She rarely sought reinforcement of her thoughts.

"No."

"Yes, it is." She let her breath out as if to rid herself of indecisiveness. "I don't know why I can't be practical about this. I'm fighting common sense in favor of fantasy. Maybe I need to let that dissolve. Then," she pecked me on the cheek, "I'll contact the attorney."

Hadley III had apparently heard enough. For no reason, as cats are prone to, she stood and slinked away. She turned her head abruptly toward the screen and then, finding nothing of interest there, sulked her insouciance into another room.

"I'm ready when you are," I said because it was true and because I think Kathleen needed to hear me say it.

"I know."

The red channel marker pulsated across the water, and a gecko climbed high on the screen. I wondered if that was what Hadley III had sensed but had not seen, and if so, what a wonderful gift cats have. For as hard as I tried, I cannot see what I cannot see.

When we were in bed, and I thought she was asleep, Kathleen nuzzled up to me. "You forgot Eeny."

"Eeny," I said. "Remember? That exuberant tike totes home every kitten she catches, doesn't see the purpose of shoes, and thinks seashells are fallen stars. That's why she finds more of them in the morning."

Kathleen buried her head in my neck as the rain drummed us to sleep.

VICTOR CAME TO ME THAT NIGHT, BUT I WOULDN'T

let him talk. He was a man I'd killed long ago. I had instructed him—the night I took his life—that he was free to leave, but then I mistook his actions for something else. The hurt and vulnerability in his eyes as his life left him told me that I was wrong. I used to think his haunting eyes would fade, but they surfaced on their own accord with no cultivation. I often wondered if, when I lie dying and am unresponsive to the world, such images will surface. That as others gather around my bed, mute and solemn, squeezing my hand and whispering that it's all right to let go, my mind won't go merrily on its way, rolling highlight reels of all my mistakes, missteps, and failures.

And then this: *When I am dead, who will I visit in the night?*

I woke up, startled. What did Andrew see as he lay dying on a convenience store floor? What were my friend's last images as the corners of his mind hugged the final molecules of oxygen? Were they of Elizabeth? Her touch at the Vinoy after a twenty-year absence? The profit margin on pillows?

The thought stoked my resolve to be the best post-humous friend the world had ever known, as if honoring the dead could redress my actions while he was living.

I swung my legs over the bed. I went back out to the screened porch. The rain had stopped and the world smelled like water. Could I teach Eeny to listen patiently at night for the sound of a dolphin's blow? Could I instruct her how to tie an improved clinch knot and impart upon her to always watch the following sea? To know the direction of the tide by a pair of waves upon a smooth shore? To name the months of the year by the sun's position in the sky? To use her eyes to read timeless words and her ears to hear stirring notes?

I can teach and impart all that without thought or

debate. Without footnotes or hesitancy. Like a migrating sparrow, I can cover those vast terrains with seemingly effortless flight. But that is not all that I do by instinct.

Victor, had I let him talk, would have reminded me of that.

32

"Seven tomorrow night," Garrett said. "He'll be waiting for us."

Garrett flew into Atlanta and drove south while I motored north. We knew Ian McClaskey from our days with the Rangers. He joined Limorp immediately after his discharge. At that time, Limorp had recently been awarded a government contract to protect Iraqi personnel. Guys were rolling right out of the army and into high-paying private jobs. Limorp mushroomed to twelve thousand former combatants at its disposal, and McClaskey rode that wave to the top. He'd recently stepped down, but we were banking on his knowledge and contacts still being fresh. Garrett had briefed him on the purpose of our visit.

Meeting with him was a calculated risk, as I didn't want to undermine Wayne's investigation into Limorp. But if Walker was dealing in arms, McClaskey would know. And if a few of those twelve thousand had hung their shingles out for private jobs—say taking out a furniture salesman in a convenience store—he might be privy to that as well. He could always tattletale on me, but he wasn't cut from that cloth.

Bottom line? I didn't trust my judgment of Charlie Walker. I sought confirmation to either pursue him further or strike him off my list. I hesitated to grant him immunity, as I had no other leads. That was a sorry excuse to keep on his tail. But I do not shun sorry excuses when they are all that I hold.

MY TRUCK'S TIRE CRUNCHED THE GRAVEL parking lot at 6:55 p.m. on a rain-soaked night in southern Georgia. A sign above the building read MISTAKE BAR. FOOD. DRINK. Stiffness had settled in my lower back during the drive. I clambered out of my truck, stretched, and placed my gun in the holster under my jacket. I reconsidered, took it out, and stuck it in the center console. I dodged the rain and opened the front steel door that could pass as a bunker door to a German pillbox. Two metal-detector men stood on either side of the entrance. They patted me down, taking their time around my waist and above my ankles. Satisfied, the brute to my left nodded me through. A few stragglers at the bar kept their heads down.

Garrett and McClaskey sat at a table off to the right. McClaskey kicked out a chair with a dirty boot. I took a seat across from him. Signs cluttered the bar behind him. One of them read DON'T TALK ABOUT YOURSELF, ASSHOLE. WE'LL DO THAT WHEN YOU LEAVE.

"My offer still stands," he said in lieu of a greeting.

"I thought you stepped aside," I said.

"It's a little step. Would it make any difference?"

"No."

McClaskey, while a rising star at Limorp, had offered

me a job. That was after I beat him in a game of chess in which I'd spotted him a pair of eyes—I had played blind-folded. But it was before we were the last two sitting at a poker table in Ramadi, Iraq, at 4:00 a.m. He tried to bluff me with a pair of eights, one of which had gotten marked with a smudge of pecan roll after someone dug up a cache of stale pastries.

"I hear you're hitched," he said.

McClaskey's small, round ears protruded like miniature satellite dishes out of the buzzed sides of his head. It took an effort not to stare at them. His satellite dishes served him well, for he prided himself on his schoolgirl ability to keep tabs on other people's lives.

"I am."

"Leaving the business?"

"Left a long time ago."

"Not what I hear. Word is that you two," his eyes rolled to Garrett and then back to me, "still work for that rogue colonel—Janssen, right?"

"What can you tell me about Charlie Walker?"

A corner of his mouth curled down. "Why are you interested?"

I kept it short. Charlie Walker and an old friend of mine had once both vied for the same woman. Walker won. Old friend reentered the picture, became a donor to the anti–assault rifle movement. Old friend was murdered. Maybe random, maybe not. I left Wayne out. McClaskey might get spooked if he knew a government law agency was behind my interest.

"Why me?" he demanded when I was done.

"I'd like your opinion on whether Walker would contract a hit, and if so, who?"

"You always had a vendetta streak in you."

"I'm—"

"You're not here on your own accord. I looked into Andrew Keller. Two years in the army and then furniture. You met him in the service?"

"That's correct."

He hesitated, a little thrown off by my admission and likely wondering if I'd conceded to his entire statement.

"Janssen running this?"

"No."

"But someone is, otherwise you wouldn't be homing in on Walker."

"Doing it for a dead friend."

"Bullshit."

I remained silent.

"Nothing to offer, yet I am expected to bear gifts," he said.

"If my questions are in any manner a threat to you, then I appreciate your time."

"So damn serious." He broke into a smile that didn't fool me. "I'm just joshing you. But," he raised an eyebrow, "I've got nothing for you."

He sat back. His phone rang. He snatched it off his belt, punched it, and placed it back.

"Walker's clean or you're not saying?" I said.

"As far as I can tell, he's clean."

"I hear he's moving guns."

"Jake-o, Jake-o, Jake-o. Where would you pick that up?"

I spread my hands.

He glanced away, his mind flipping through what hand to play, what might be in it for him. "We heard that someone in Walker's circle might be a snitch. You know anything about that?"

"Just rumors," I said.

"You're bluffing."

"That's your game. I know nothing of substance."

"But you heard Walker might have a leak?"

Someone had to move if there was to be any reason to drive through the Georgia rain. "Might have," I said. He nodded and seemed to process my words. He wouldn't get a morsel more, even if I did have something else to feed him.

He cocked his head in a nonchalant manner, his eyes darting between Garrett and me. "Walker doesn't deal guns —he deals money. If he goes down, it's by himself. He can't touch anyone at Limorp." He shifted his attention to me. "As far as your little issue with Andrew Keller? I can't imagine a guy like Charlie Walker giving two shits about his wife's old flame. If he reached into Limorp for assistance, I couldn't find it. Doesn't mean it's not there. But there's no trail indicating that he contacted us for the express purposes of hiring a hit man."

He leaned back in his chair. I stole a glance at another bar sign. It read TRUST YOUR INSTINCTS. PEOPLE REALLY DON'T LIKE YOU.

"Walker attends our pig roasts," he continued. "Hunts our private grounds, both here and in Montana. He doesn't know an elk's ass from a buck's rack. He just wants to be one of the boys. He's a consummate politician."

He'd given me what I'd come for. We were done. Despite my efforts, I couldn't pin anything on Walker. At least not through Limorp.

"Does he have a hand in moving guns?" Garrett asked.

"You guys have got to let him go," he said, not answering Garrett's question. "He's a fat-cat lobbyist. You know anyone inside his organization who might have turned?"

"I don't."

"Don't or won't?"

"Don't."

He rolled his tongue and gave me a conciliatory nod. I asked him to give me a call if he heard anything. He promised he would and elicited the same promise from me, but we both knew it was a useless exchange. Garrett asked where he was headed and he said he had another meeting scheduled in the bar in fifteen minutes and he'd appreciate if we were long gone.

Garrett offered to follow me to Saint Pete, but I told him there was no need. With Walker off the battlefield, I felt like a warrior with no enemy. I followed a tunnel of white headlights cut into the black Georgia highway. The intermittent windshield wipers could never decide whether it was raining or not.

33

Lizzy

For if loving is the answer then who's the giving for
Do you believe in something that you've never seen before

Thank God it's raining, Lizzy thought. *Too much damn sunshine in Florida.*

Sunny days made Lizzy feel obligated to be outside doing—whatever it is people do. She could never curl up with a blanket and a good book without feeling a tinge of guilt. On a sunny day, such a fine way to idle away the hours was considered lazy, but on a rainy day, the same activity could be conducted without explanation or excuse. (Even now in her head, her mother's chiding voice came back to her. "Why don't you go to the mall with your friends, Lizzy? It's so shameful to waste such a beautiful day inside reading.")

Waste.

She sat on her window seat overlooking the incomprehensibly gray and dullard water of the Gulf of Mexico. Her opened book was laid out flat in front of her. Her waning energy rendered reading a challenge, and that saddened her. She ran her hand over the fabric of the window seat. Less than a year ago, she'd reupholstered it. To think that color selection had consumed her time, been paramount to her days. That shades of blue and gray had ever deserved such scrutiny and debate. It wasn't that it seemed long ago as much as how the intervening time had trivialized her once antagonizing concerns. But Lizzy had learned over the past year that time is a strange and unbalanced chemistry. It obeys no natural laws. It adheres to no formula. It lengthens and shortens itself at will. It can make twenty years pass like a day and a day reverberate for twenty years.

The redecorating bug had revitalized her. Got her thinking about—no, *feeling*—her youth. For unlike the smudge of years that follow, those halcyon border days were never more than a smell, a song, or a glance away. They mauled her shimmering emotions and made her believe that time had been tossed into the path of a hurricane. At first, Lizzy had been puzzled by the sudden urge to jump into her yesterdays. Her mind, sodden with drugs, had forgotten that it was her redecorating urge that had kicked off her backward leap. Memories are like that, drugs or no drugs. Truth is the fluttering flight of a butterfly, and our most ardent beliefs are only a passing and erratic certitude.

And so she had made the decision to do a U-turn. To seek Andrew. To undo what she'd done with Charlie. To right what she always knew was a wrong that could be placed at no one's feet except hers. To honor the young woman who'd sat on a concrete bench on a Florida beach and dug her pastel-pink toenails into the cool sand. A woman surging with confidence. Hope. Enthusiasm. A woman waiting to take a leap of faith and splash herself upon the world.

Whoop-de-doo, she thought. It's amazing what one trip to a doctor's office can do. Just flat-out mind-blowing. There should be a sign above every doctor's door: WARNING! YOU MAY NOT LEAVE HERE AS THE SAME PERSON WHO ENTERS.

She flipped her book shut. She couldn't concentrate. Anna had called. Said Mr. Travis wanted to meet with her. Pitched that it would be good for her to talk with him. Only Anna knew of Lizzy's quest, and Lizzy thought she was scared. Scared that when Lizzy died, it would become her crusade. Her burden. Lizzy had already made the mistake of besetting someone with a far greater weight than anyone should ever be called upon to bear. She didn't want to do that with Anna. Didn't want to make the same boneheaded mistake again.

"*You* care," Anna had said. "And you want peace. Meet with him. Hear what Andrew said to him. Picture how he described him. It will do you good. And maybe he can help you on the other matter as well."

Picture Andrew, Lizzy thought. *My Andrew.* Not that man on the idiot box promising that he will not be undersold. Not the man who escaped to the army. The army! Andrew! Wasn't there some Christmas show about the island of misfit toys? That would be Andrew in the army. And furniture? *Egads! All my fault.* She shook her head at the Gulf of Mexico as if it, too, were scolding her. *Me. Me. Me. My indifference destroyed him. My callousness. When love called upon me—tragic as it was—I didn't answer. Didn't have the goods.*

"That's right, Lizzy," she said out loud. "You didn't have the goods."

But what tragedy she was asked to bear. Who dreamed of such madness? Cruelty and fate twisted together as if bred over a thousand pages of a sprawling Russian novel.

Oh for god's sake, she thought. *Here we go again. Sprinkle a little rain on your mood and it dissolves into syrupy mush. Come on, Elizabeth, remember that it's your last act. Mom did have some good points; head up, shoulders back. Let them see that smile.*

She did it fast. With absence of thought. That is not to say she had not pondered the move ad nauseam. But rather, having fatigued it to the bone, there was nothing more to consider. Lizzy reached for her phone. No more canyons of doubt. No more insurmountable mountains of deliberations. But it was not Anna whom she first called. As she dialed, her toes curled against the hardwood floor as if trying to dig into sand. *Maybe he can help you on the other matter as well.* The thought hit her like a joyous chord. It would not end with her. And perhaps Andrew's good friend was the man for the job.

AROUSED FROM HER BED, LIZZY PADDED INTO THE kitchen at 2:37 a.m. with this sleep-killing thought: Can you love at forty like you did at twenty-three?

She was forty-three but had stopped counting the individual years as they galloped by without invitation. She preferred tracking her age in increments of five years. This was her logic: When you celebrated your eleventh birthday, that was a 10 percent jump in longevity. Age forty would require four years to equal a similar advancement. Age ten to fifteen was a 50 percent jump, and it felt like it. Consider the difference between a gangly ten-year-old girl and a fifteen-year-old who is threatening the crown of womanhood. About the same shock to the system as age forty to sixty, also a 50 percent jump.

But forward math no longer factored into her days. Ever since her doctor's edict, she'd been counting backward, tabulating her remaining days. Her life had become a silent ticking countdown to death, not a celebratory progression from birth. She'd grown to appreciate the closing lines of Alan Seeger's poem "I Have a Rendezvous with Death." *And I to my pledged word am true, I shall not fail that rendezvous.*

No, she thought. Forty was fine.

Now that that was settled, the question, again: Can the body (mind, soul, whatever) love at forty—or fifty or eighty —like it did at twenty-three? Can you burn for the skin of another and give your own without hesitation? Your face might still launch a canoe, but a thousand ships? And no matter how often you pound the gym, your derriere is no longer the Michelangelo marble it was at eighteen. She tried to use Charlie as a point of reference; they had, after all, been making love for two decades. But it was never the same with him as it had been with Andrew. She and Andrew made love as if the rest of the world didn't exist. She and Charlie made love as if they were under a contractual obligation to tumble into bed every so often to ward off doubts about their commitment and feelings and to falsely assure themselves that everything was fine in a life that stretched, bent, challenged, and warped the definition of fine. Who knows, she thought. Sex is bound to fade; at least she wanted to believe that.

But I'm not talking sex. Then what is it, Lizzy? What?

Would the love have lasted, or did we just not have enough time to identify the cracks and succumb to Father Time?

"Oh swell, Elizabeth," she said out loud. "Is that really worth interrupting a good night's sleep?"

Her marriage to Charlie had been a *Revolutionary Road* type of coexistence, albeit without the over-the-top blowups. Little telltale signs along the way that in retrospect clearly foreshadowed, if not a doomed marriage, at least one that struggled to maintain the facade. One that at any moment could implode and in doing so would scorch once-hallowed memories and leave friends shaking their heads. Did you hear? I wonder what happened? Can you imagine?

Is that what lay ahead for Andrew and me? She flogged her mind for telling incidents. Verbal exchanges, long buried, that might have fumed and spread over years, for even the greatest forest fire starts with an unassuming spark. An unanswered question. A wandering eye. A disapproving glance lamely ignored because it takes effort to confront, and who voluntarily walks into a brawl? She reached for a pen and paper. Lizzy relived every negative nuance she could remember with Andrew. Recounted every fore-warning tone. Every innuendo. She wrote them down. *Be honest now.*

Her page looked like this:

He seemed a little miffed that I didn't know toasters needed to be cleaned.

Well, she thought, *I hardly think that would have sunk the ship.* But was that really it? Or was her memory being selective and supportive of her fantasy?

Having nothing else to put on the page, she drew her trademark cat. She'd been drawing the same feline since

Melanie Nash taught her how to draw it in sixth grade. That was the last year Lizzy felt like a little girl, because the following summer her breasts popped out. She thought it was the beginning, but also learned it was the end. Next to being with Andrew, being a little girl was her dearest memory, and no one had told her that her body would slam that door shut without preamble.

She colored a cat of many colors, for Lizzy always felt sorry, a tinge of empathy, for the colors left behind in the box. What if they, too, have feelings? Imagine a blue pencil, standing erect in the box, its tip unused and sharp, lamenting *What's wrong with me? What's wrong?*

She drifted asleep while admiring her colorful cat born in a night of unanswerable questions that followed a day of unbreakable resolve.

34

Florida mornings.

The fanfare. The promise. The joggers and walkers. The seashell collectors. The chorus of birds. The flat Gulf of Mexico waiting for those seeking introspection from her smooth, tan shores and endless water. And the sun. It swells and expands the sky. Its advanced light glows like the forward column of an impending and glorious force. The overture is seldom sustainable, and this day, despite its victories, would die in darkness.

My phone rang as I sopped up egg yolk at Seabreeze with a corner piece of toast preserved for that distinguished purpose. I abandoned my task and hit the screen, smearing it with my fingers. Anna asked if I could drop by and meet with Lizzy at five thirty that afternoon. I told her I looked forward to seeing them both.

Just like that.

I wriggled the phone back into my pocket and stared at the deep-sea diving helmet on the shelf across from me, but my thoughts were as empty as the helmet. It was nine thirty, and I had the ten to two spot at the thrift store. Business was slow, and when I left the floors had never been cleaner. The shelves were polished, the light fixtures were free of a year's layer of dust, and the leaking rear window had a fresh bead of caulking around it. I went downtown and grabbed a late lunch at Mangroves. I browsed the aisles at Daddy Kool's and picked up a few albums, including an original copy of *Judy Garland in Madison Square Garden*, and my empty thoughts swelled with anticipation. There's an indescribable dimension to hearing the first generation of live albums. When the audience explodes with applause on that April night in Manhattan in 1963, I'm there, standing on a bustling New York City street cut with the cool springtime air. JFK is still alive. So is Bobby. So is Martin. They'd all be gone in six years. Judy included.

ELIZABETH WALKER, REPOSED IN the corner of the couch like a sandpiper nestled in a cup of sand on the beach, put down a copy of *Vanity Fair* when I entered Anna's room. She wore jeans and a white sweater with a gold necklace. She appeared to be the embodiment of health and contentment.

All is vanity, nothing is fair.

She struck me as a woman who played down her beauty and who would have been a favorite of central casting. Or perhaps I just had Judy Garland on my mind. Her eyes, still unsure but willing to take a chance, found mine. They did not back down.

She stood and strolled across the floor with graceful fluidity. "Lizzy Walker." She offered her hand. "Without the mask."

"Jake Travis, without the chains." We shook hands and I felt as if I had touched *ma donna*.

"I apologize," she said, "if I came across as rather curt during our previous encounters. Andrew's death had me rattled."

"No apologies necessary. I'm not the gentlest of messengers."

"Nor I the most gracious recipient of tragic news," she said with words meant to ease my guilt and a tone that conveyed an exquisite sense of propriety.

Anna came in and I asked her how her case was progressing. She said she had met with the lawyer Morgan recommended and that lawyer was now working in conjuncture with her own attorney.

"They say her chances are good," Lizzy said. Her eyes shifted from her friend and former maid to me. "But it takes so long as the courts are backlogged."

Anna said, "I'll leave so you two can talk."

"Nonsense," Lizzy said. "It's your home. We can relocate." She turned to me. "Would you like something to drink?"

I told her I was fine.

"I'll fix you a cup, Lizzy," Anna said. She went to a coffee pot perched at an angle on an uneven stone window case. She poured coffee into a cream-colored mug with the icon of the Methodist church on it; a cross with a red flame swirling around it.

"Follow me," Lizzy said with a wink. "I know where we can talk." But her voice did not match her playful gesture. I wondered how heavily she had steeled herself for our meeting.

As we walked down a hall, I said, "You and Anna are close."

"We are. We bonded the first day I hired her. I asked her to change the sheets. She told me she'd rather skip a week's wages and buy me new ones." Lizzy glanced at me. "Charlie always liked stiff sheets. After Anna's comment, the thread count on my sheets rose dramatically."

"And Charlie?"

We stopped in front of a pair of wood doors with arched tops. We had entered a larger hall with tall windows and an ornate outside door, although it wasn't the main entrance of the church.

"I told him he could buy his own sheets. Charlie wouldn't be caught dead buying a household item." She motioned to the door. "We should be fine here. There're all types of activity in the church today—churches like Thursdays as much as they worship Sundays, but this, the original chapel, is rarely used."

I swung open the solid door and followed Lizzy into a hushed, narrow chapel that smelled like an antiquarian bookstore. A stained-glass window in the front canted prisms of sunlight. Dueling choir pews faced each other under the window. She took a seat in a maroon velvet-cushioned pew a third of the way to the altar. I followed her in. She skootched a little farther to allow for a comfortable space between us, our bodies angled at each other. Stained-glass Jesus was our only witness as he battled his decision in the Garden of Gethsemane.

"I didn't used to drink coffee in the afternoon," Lizzy said. "But it slows time down, and, as I believe you know, I have very little of it left. I've become rather stingy with it."

There was a presence about her that I couldn't put a finger on. It was if she was in the moment so effortlessly and so intently that she could break the seconds into pieces and own each piece.

"I'm sorry about your illness," I said.

She flashed me a weak smile. "Trust me, so am I."

"Do you find comfort being here?"

She gave that a second. "Because of the solitude, yes. The other stuff, not so much. My beliefs exist only because I didn't want the burden of starting over if I dismissed them. We have to believe in something, and I'm lazy. So I've stuck to what was ingrained in me like a language when I was young. And you? You appear to be a stranger in a strange land."

"I like your route."

"Come now." She dipped her head. "I won't let you off that easy. If you were to believe, what would trigger it?"

"Being in a foxhole."

"That's taken."

"Music."

"Care to narrow that down?"

"Listening through headphones on a plane—six miles above the earth while the setting sun refracts the curved horizon—is as close as I get. And you?"

She folded her hands in front of her. "Well, when I was a little girl, our family would go out West to ski. It was the only time I would see snow. I had a pair of black mittens. I'd watch the flakes land on them. Before they melted, I would stare at their white and silver-laced purity. They dissolved to nothing of course—but I wasn't into themes. When they first landed, I remember thinking they were God's fingerprints."

"Not many snowflakes in Florida."

"Seashells have taken their place."

We were lost in our thoughts and then she said, "We—Andrew and I—were at an art festival once. He whistled a beautiful tune. I asked him what it was. He said all songs are rivers of memories and then told me the name." She glanced down at her coffee cup, stroking the red flame with her thumb. "I can't remember the tune or the title. It was so pretty and sad and the memory so happy."

"Happiness is a sad song," I said.

She wrinkled her nose. "Please tell me that's not you."

"Charlie Brown—I think."

"You're quoting me *Peanuts*?"

"One could do worse."

She cracked a smile out of the corner of her mouth. "Snoopy and the gang." Her gaze slid off my face and she seemed momentarily lost, as if she'd become unmoored.

"What are the doctors telling you?"

Her eyes came back to me. "I'm sorry?"

"How much time do you have?" I asked, oblivious to tact, although that was not my intent.

"Months. I choose quality of life over extra time. Would you agree?"

"Absolutely. I will pray in every denomination for you."

"But you don't believe."

"I'll pray twice."

She laughed. It was a natural and easy sound, but quick, as if she were conscious of unveiling too much about herself. "Sooo," she drew out. "Andrew came so see you?"

As I talked, Lizzy listened patiently, her lost gaze masking her thoughts, her thumb massaging the red flame. I left out the part about Ella Fitzgerald and Norman Granz, as I didn't think they factored into the story. I omitted one other item as well, mostly to gauge her honesty with me.

"He said that? That I passed out and we never got together again?"

"He did." Then I added, to pretend I knew all along, "It didn't happen that way, did it?"

"Not even close."

"Why would he lie?"

"You tell me. He *was* petrified of complicating his divorce. I think he might have been feeling you out. Did he mention the accident?"

"No. You talked to him about his divorce?"

"Pardon?"

"His divorce. You were aware of it?"

"Yes. We had talked several times on the phone over the past few months. We were—for sake of a better word—plotting to get back together."

It was my turn to allow my thoughts to roam. Not only had Andrew played his cards much closer to his vest than I had imagined but also his true intent in seeking me out still remained a mystery.

"I know that your father and older brother were killed in the same accident. That had to be traumatic for you. For both of you."

She balanced her cup carefully on the worn velvet cushion. "It was . . . very difficult. I reacted terribly to it. I was close to my father and to Benjamin—my older brother. I took their deaths quite hard, and I'm afraid I made it unbearably difficult for Andrew. I felt as if I needed time alone. I went to Europe—Paris initially—for about a year. When I came back, Andrew was gone."

"Was the love gone as well?"

"My, we don't skirt the big issues, do we?" She trailed her left index finger over the top of her left eyebrow. "I don't know. It just—didn't work out."

We were quiet for a moment and then she let her breath out and filled the silence. "The love was—is—always there. That makes me, Anna, and you," she lifted a finger with each name, "who know, not including the unfortunate professionals I paid to enter my mind. Hardly a front-page item."

"But you never saw him again before bumping into him at the Vinoy?"

"It started when I wrote him a letter a few months ago. He called after that. As I said, we talked a few times. He wanted to get together. He said he was getting a divorce, although my letter had nothing to do with it."

"And the meeting at the Vinoy?"

"That was purely by chance. We were both shocked."

"Did he know you have terminal cancer?" Her face pinched in pain. *Terminal.* I'd have to be more delicate with my words.

"I'd like to amend my previous statement," she said. "I was more than just shocked to see him—I was thrilled. Jubilant. No. I wanted to see him so badly. But I couldn't bear to tell him. On the phone, he was so positive. We're still young. We have time." She swayed her head. "What a trash-can dream. It broke my heart, and I kept putting him off. We both still loved each other, had always loved each other. But all I could see was my actions again causing him pain. What's that saying—all the pain that money can buy? Well, nothing buys pain like love."

"That's not *Peanuts.*"

"It most definitely is not."

"And it wasn't a trash-can dream."

"I don't know why I said that."

"Not to belittle the virtues of first impressions and rapid romances, but do you ever doubt your feelings would have withstood time?" My prodding was as much for me as it was intended for her.

"My," she said, tilting her head. "That's a biggie."

"Question withdrawn."

"Too late. No. I've squeezed the doubts out of my life. I'm more confident now than ever before. We don't have complete emotions about the present, only the past."

"Linus?"

"Virginia Woolf. Although I'll grant you it does have a Linus ring to it. I know what you're saying," she said, indicating this was not new territory for her. "That our love fossilized and never suffered natural erosion. Was it sustainable?" She'd been staring straight ahead but now turned to me. "Who knows? But tell me, does that make the ache less real? If it hurts—and it does—how can we imagine physical pain?"

I remembered Andrew's comment: *the physical ache of our mistakes*. I didn't bother to answer, for she'd revealed her position through the phrasing of her question.

She sighed. "Maybe the delusions and illusions are a by-product of the drugs I'm taking." She started to take a sip of coffee but held back. "Or is a broken heart as real as you and I sitting here and not just the stuff of songs and fairy tales?"

"Fairy tales aren't real?"

"You're kind, sitting here and letting me prattle away in my melancholy state."

"I am as agnostic on those affairs as you. But where we return to is never where we left."

She cocked her head back. "The gems you pull off the shelf. Do you live with such conviction?"

"Not even close."

She chuckled. "It's fun to pretend, though, right?" Her eyes roamed over the stained glass of Jesus of Nazareth, his back bent with unbearable weight, his neck craned upward in a position sure to give him a neck ache. "No," she said, although I didn't know what she was referring to. She looked at me. "But that's a cop-out for not believing in yourself. Are you in love?"

She had caught me off guard. "I am."

"When did you fall in love with—the woman in purple, correct?"

I nodded.

"Her name?"

"Kathleen."

"Well?"

I hesitated.

"You think too much," Lizzy said in a flirtatious manner.

"When I laid eyes on her."

"But you have a wandering eye, Mr. Travis. All men do. It is how the species survives. Do you love all women?"

"Desperately."

She laughed and nearly spilled her coffee. "An honest man. Why Kathleen—at that moment?"

I recalled the first time I turned in the barstool at the hotel and saw her standing over me, asking—

"Hey," Lizzy said. "I'm dying to know." I suppressed a smile and she added, "If there's ever a time for dark humor, right? Stop thinking."

I ran my hand through my hair. "I don't know. Maybe—"

"You think I have time for 'I don't knows' and 'maybes'?" she said playfully.

"We looked at each other, and it was as if we'd met long before we really did."

"Next time don't be such a wussy when someone pops a question you know the answer to but don't have the guts to speak."

Well, that stung a little.

"Yes, ma'am."

"Imagine having that look and then blowing it."

"You didn't blow a thing. The accident blew up your world."

She sucked in her cheeks as if trying to contain her composure. The accident, all those years ago, still racking her mind. Its wake rolling her world decades beyond what she could have imagined as a young woman.

"Was Charlie aware of any of this?" I asked.

She drew her head back from me. "Are we finished with the panoply of God and love?"

"That'll be my vote."

"Thank heavens. One can tolerate only so much over-wrought excess. George Bernard Shaw said that on his seventy-fifth birthday he finally knew enough to be a medi-ocre office boy. Let's leave it at that."

"You married Charlie—when?"

She curled up the side of her mouth. "A little over two years after I got back from Europe."

"Did he know you had a fling with Andrew?"

She glanced down and crossed her arms, hugging herself hard. *Fling.* I chastised myself. Again.

"I didn't mean to imply—"

"Don't worry." She waved me off. Lizzy bounced off the canvas as fast as anyone. "He knew. But he wasn't upset, and looking back, that upsets me—that he *wasn't* upset. No to your earlier question. Charlie was unaware of our plans."

I needed to come clean with her in the event that Charlie told her that we had met. I didn't want her to think I was withholding information or sneaking behind her back.

"I had lunch with your husband a few days ago," I said.

Bright eyes. "You did?"

I explained our luncheon, omitting my impression that Charlie Walker was a condescending SOB. She said Charlie never mentioned it to her, but that wasn't surprising as he rarely shared his days.

"Are you aware that Andrew Keller was a major donor to an anti-gun organization?" I asked.

"What are you suggesting? That Charlie had something to do with Andrew's death?"

"*Some*one had something to do with his death."

The door behind us opened, and a boy and a giggling girl wearing a Rays baseball cap burst through. As soon as they were in the chapel, they joined hands. They were no more than ten feet in when they spotted us and came to a halt. The girl covered her mouth with her hand.

"Sorry," the boy stammered, dropping the girl's hand. "We'll . . . we didn't know you were here."

"That's fine," Lizzy said. They scurried out the door that had hardly had the time to close behind them.

Lizzy smiled and shook her head. "Andrew and I met in a church."

"Oh?"

"In a stairwell. That was our moment. He kissed me and said, 'Marry me, my balcony girl.' I'd been sitting in the balcony watching his band perform and our eyes met during a song he was singing." She sighed. "No, I didn't know that Andrew was donating to an anti-gun organization. No, I don't think Charlie would ever be involved in what I think you're suggesting. No, I have no clue who might want to have harmed Andrew. He was kind and gentle. That man on TV?"

She waited, as if to make sure I was on board.

"Yes?" I said.

"The Sofa King of Sarasota? *That* was not Andrew. The girl's perfume smells like a lily. Do you smell it?"

I sniffed the air. "No."

"You can't?"

I felt as if I'd failed some basic test. I gave it another try but shook my head. "Only your perfume," I said. And then not wanting her to think I didn't like it (I did) or that she had on too much (she didn't), I added, "It's faint and pretty."

"It's sweet almond."

I remembered Andrew saying sweet almond was her favorite scent. Our minor diversion over, Elizabeth and I sat in silence on the maroon velvet-cushioned pews of a darkening chapel in downtown Saint Petersburg. Choir practice must have started as voices drifted in from offstage. The angels were back.

"Why do you think he enlisted?" I asked.

"Why do *you* think he did?"

"People join for different reasons. One—and not an insignificant one—is that they are running from something or someone." I looked hard at Elizabeth and was surprised to see her staring quizzically at me.

She swallowed. "You're saying it's my fault."

"There is no fault."

She sniffled and rubbed her hand under her nose. I reached out and touched her arm, giving her a little squeeze, and withdrew my hand. It was the first time I had ever touched her, not counting the throwaway business handshake. Why had I reached out? Was I atoning for the disappointment with myself for not physically comforting her when I broke the news of Andrew's death?

"I told him I needed time. I had to get away for a while. It seemed a sin to rush into marriage after such an unmitigated tragedy." Her chest heaved and her eyes gleamed with moisture. "This isn't my first visit to this musty chapel. It was the original sanctuary before they built the current one in the 1950s. I come here every time I visit Anna."

And then, as if she'd needed that slight diversion in order to get back on track, she said, "He joined when I was away. I think we both knew I'd never recover. That I was damaged goods. But after the years spun by, I wondered if I could have weathered the storm. If I'd reacted too harshly. Too quickly. Do you understand?"

"You doubted your earlier decision."

"Terribly."

"We all do that."

"Well, mine came with heavy consequences."

"Second-guessing does no good."

"You're preaching to the choir."

A silent moment beat by and then I said, "I saw Dylan a few days ago."

Her face fell. "Why?"

"Is that an issue?"

"It's just that I dropped by a few weeks ago. Did he tell you?"

"Nadine did. He refused to tell me what you and he discussed. He said to ask you."

"Not much. I was there partially due to guilt—having not seen him in a long time. I told him I might get together with Andrew, but it didn't mean anything to him. He was so young at the time. I really just wanted to check in on him. A parting goodbye. I wanted to hug him. I *did* hug him.

"He's had a troubled life. But he's doing better. I can't imagine being a ten-year-old boy and losing your father and older brother. We've never been close. I'm not sure whether that's my fault or no one's fault. He was so much younger than Benjamin and I. And after the accident, he spun out of control."

She furrowed her eyebrows as if struck by a sudden and disturbing thought. "How did you find him?" And then without waiting for my answer, she added, "What did *you* talk about?"

That left a pair of dangling questions. "I was retracing Andrew's last week," I said. "His secretary told me that Andrew went out to see Dylan."

"Andrew saw Dylan?" Her face cringed into a montage of fear and confusion.

"He did—after you."

She smoothed her jeans with her hands. "They never really knew each other. What did you and Dylan discuss?" Her voice was distant, as if she were no longer connected to her thoughts.

I recounted my conversation with her younger brother. She listened with her eyes welded to the back of the pew in front of us. Her lips had morphed into a frown, and I couldn't imagine what latent memories had been aroused within her. She asked me if I knew what Dylan and Andrew discussed. I told her that Dylan said Andrew sought him out to inform him that he was planning on getting back together with his sister.

"That's all?" she said. "That we were planning to get together?"

"Dylan said he didn't even know why Andrew made the trip. He admitted, as you alluded, that he and Andrew never really knew each other."

Her shoulders relaxed. "Poor Dylan. He's doing the best he can."

Silence hummed between us like a sustained note. What I was doing in a chapel with a woman I barely knew—

although we were galloping over major issues—and who was dying from cancer? Then it hit me from the other direction. Why is *she* sitting here with me? To relive Andrew's final days, which had been my pitch to her? To help solve his murder? It felt like more than that.

"I appreciate your time, Elizabeth. But why me? Why now?"

"You said he might have been murdered," she said, but her voice was defensive and wary. "I thought perhaps I could help. And I wanted to hear from you what he said."

"I think there's more here than trying to recapture the last days of a fossilized love."

She clenched her jaw. Her eyes moistened.

What the hell is my problem—using her own words against her?

If I can make a dying woman feel a little closer to the love of her life, is that not enough? What if Andrew's death had nothing to do with Elizabeth and Charlie Walker? What if the angry gunman used Andrew to express his girlfriend issues?

Her body shuddered. She wiped her eyes with the back of her hand. "That's it. I'm just . . . goofy and lost." She straightened her posture and faced me with resolve. "Thank you for your time, Mr. Travis. I do so appreciate it." She brought the mug of coffee to her lips and looked away from me.

We'd become derailed. Her armor had slid off her elfin shoulders when we entered the chapel, but now it was strapped back on. She was there for another purpose, and I wasn't worthy. I had failed, and I didn't know why.

And then because I had purposely held it back to see if she would bring it up—and she never had—and omitting the pronoun at the last second because of Kathleen's observation of the capital *T*, and because, let's face it, young

Elizabeth Phillips wasn't the first woman to sail to Europe for a year, or at least nine months, and I was eager to get back in her good graces, I said, "Is Trumpet a girl or a boy?"

The coffee mug hit the floor.

35

I reached over and touched her in the same spot I previously had, but this time I held on, for I was afraid that Elizabeth Walker's shivering body would shatter into tiny pieces of stained glass, and I knew from my experience with Kathleen at the end of the dock that those tiny sparkles could never again be assimilated.

It was the second of three times that I would touch her. Later, when recounting the remarkable effect Elizabeth Walker had on Kathleen's and my life, I marveled that our bodies were strangers to platonic hugs. To light kisses. To pats on the back and comforting fingers. But the moon never touches the oceans, and look what it does. Our words and our silence, our smiles and our frowns, are lunar influences upon each other.

"Take a deep breath."

She exhaled. "It's nothing. It's just the meds. Sometimes they take me. Would you get Anna for me?"

"You OK for a minute?"

She reached out and touched me. Her hand rested on my shoulder, both reassuring and anointing me.

"I'll be fine," she said with a kind smile. "If you could have Anna bring me some water and some paper towels. I'm afraid I made a mess."

I returned a few minutes later with Anna, water, and paper towels, but Lizzy wasn't there. As we dabbed up the coffee spill, Lizzy came in looking fresher. She glanced at me. "Could you give us a minute, please?" It came out like a boardroom order, delivered from someone who was accustomed to being obeyed.

I wandered down a hall, caught a whiff of barbecued beef, and followed my nose to the brightly lit kitchen where several women and a man bustled about. A radio sat on a stainless-steel counter broadcasting the rush-hour traffic report, brought to you by Sarasota Sofa. "What can be better after a hectic commute than your favorite recliner?" the radio asked. Andrew must have secured the rights to the Spanky and Our Gang song "Lazy Day," for what followed matched it note for note. "Laaaay-Zee-Boy." Modulate a key. "Laaaay-Zee-Boy." Back to the original key. "Laaaay-Zee-Boy for you and me. The king promises you a new life. Sale ends Sunday!"

"Would you like a sandwich?" a woman wrapped in a white apron asked. Her penciled eyebrows arched into her forehead. The heat of the kitchen sheened her face.

"You mind?" I said.

"Heavens no," she said. "We get a lot of Oliver Twists on Thursday nights when we put the slow cooker on for the youth and adult choirs."

She snatched a paper plate, plopped a bun on it, forked a glob of meat on the bun, and handed it to me. I barely had time to mutter a thank-you before instinctively taking a bite. It melted in my mouth. Juicy and smoky, it was the culinary offspring of Johnnie Walker and a Kobe beef burger.

"I'm visiting Anna Vargas and her friend," I said, failing to swallow first. "Could I take them a bite?"

"You know Anna?" If her eyebrows could have possibly arched any farther, they would have taken the roof off.

I nodded as I chewed.

"Do you work with her lawyer?" she asked.

"A friend of mine has introduced another lawyer to her. They're collaborating on her behalf."

She checked her wristwatch. "Anna comes in soon. But if you're going up, I'll make you a plate. We pray for her every day. All she wants to do is stay with her family. Twenty years. Can you believe that?"

"Do you mind adding another sandwich? Her friend is visiting."

"Lizzy?"

I nodded, having too much food in my mouth to attempt higher language.

She glanced at a man fiddling with a garbage bag. "Sean, keep that open. We can add more to that." She turned to me. "I ran a restaurant once, so that qualifies me to boss people around. I could write a book on the restaurant business, but it would end at chapter eleven. Poor Lizzy. Beautiful young woman to be stricken with cancer, but we all know someone, right? Don't make it any easier."

"Does she visit Anna often?"

She opened a bag of wheat buns and placed them on a green plastic tray, shuffling them around so that they were neatly stacked. "She does. Sometimes with one of the two attorneys."

"Two?" I wasn't aware that the woman Morgan

contacted had visited Anna yet. Maybe Anna's first attorney came with a partner.

"One of 'em taller than a steeple." She appraised her mountain of buns. Satisfied, she pushed the tray away and started spooning coleslaw into a large plastic bowl. "Anna told me once that one of them was Lizzy's. I'm not sure, though." She glanced up at me. "Let's prepare a tray for you to take to my two favorite women. I don't suppose you would mind another one as well, would you?"

"It's not polite to refuse."

"'Tis not."

She slapped together three sandwiches, a side of coleslaw, and a handful of potato chips. I thanked her and started to leave.

"Hold on. They need something to wash that down with. Lizzy likes iced tea, and Anna's never got over the thrill of diet soda."

She went to the refrigerator and retrieved the drinks. I walked out the door, a hotel waiter being dispatched with room service, except this waiter wondered why Lizzy met her attorney in a church.

36

The two women were huddled in a pew. When I entered, they stared at me, an intruder in their cozy cottage. A stranger in their midst.

"Am I too early?"

"You're fine," Lizzy said. "I see you became acquainted with the Thursday night kitchen staff."

"I did."

"Gianna?"

"Didn't catch her name."

"You caught her food."

The chapel had lost its natural light. Jesus, still frozen in the stained-glass Garden of Gethsemane, was now shrouded in darkness.

"I was just leaving," Anna said in her unique blend of knotted English and Spanish. She took a napkin and arranged her dinner on it. "I'll help Gianna. She has enough cooks in the kitchen when preparing the food, cleaning up as well. But it makes me feel good to be useful and she knows that."

She started out the door.

"Oops," I said. "I almost forgot." I reached into my pocket and handed her a can of diet soda. She accepted it with a shy smile. The door shut behind her. I turned and faced Lizzy.

"Don't make me say it," she said.

Humor was never far beneath her surface. I bustled over to her, took the bottled iced tea out of my pocket, and sat next to her with the same polite distance separating us as before, except now the distance lacked light. The darkness both closed and opened me, and I wondered if it affected her in the same manner.

We munched away in silence and then I said, "What did I miss when I was gone?"

"What I wanted you to miss."

"Gianna said that two attorneys are often here when you visit Anna."

Lizzy let a few beats pass. "I brought in another attorney on occasion, for a second opinion on Anna's case. Do me a favor? Tell me about Andrew—what he was like. I saw him for only the briefest moment at the Vinoy."

She had brushed off my feeble attempt to identify the second attorney. I let it slide and started to explain, again, Andrew's visit.

"Not that," she interrupted me, unable to hide her exasperation. "Tell me his emotions, not just his words."

I told her how Andrew and I had listened to Ella Fitzgerald and how he lit up when discussing the album and Norman Granz. His trademark flowery language in describing his wounded heart. The pain of autumn. How his gaze followed the sails that were billowed taut and smooth with the golden mist of sunset. At first her eyes were intent on mine, but then they drifted away.

In a monotone voice, she said, "I'll read you a chapter and you'll sing me a song."

"Pardon me?"

She looked at me as if mystified by my presence and her surroundings. "Nothing. I'm sorry."

"He knew you married Charlie, right?" She nodded. "He wasn't honest with me. The two of you were talking. Why suddenly come to me?"

She rubbed the palm of her hand over the side of her forehead. "Maybe he was afraid that his wife or Charlie would see our calls. We'll never know."

Her bland response was what I expected. But there had to be more to Andrew's deceit and request than two ex-lovers reuniting and fearing complications from a divorce. I didn't pursue that. Instead, I asked, "Are you going to answer my question?"

"I'm sorry. We launched so many. Which one?"

"Trumpet."

She glanced around the chapel, searching for something to latch onto.

"Boy or girl," I said.

She flicked her eyes to mine. "Girl."

"Does—did Andrew know?"

"That I was pregnant? Yes. That it was a girl? No."

"Charlie?"

"He doesn't know anything."

I let out a low whistle. "Nothing?"

"Zilch." She looked at me. "I'd appreciate it if this stays between us."

"Do you think he found out?"

"I see where you're going. No. Not a chance. It's sealed. Only Anna knows. I've told no one else. The attorney I bring here? He knows."

"He wasn't here for a second opinion on Anna's case."

"No."

She didn't offer an explanation for lying about her attorney's visit, nor could I summon a reason to press her. I wondered if Andrew had told Charlie that he and Lizzy had a child. Would that enrage Charlie Walker enough to silence him? *Damn straight it would.*

"What did Andrew say when you decided to go to Europe and give the child up for adoption?"

"I wasn't the same after the accident. He—we—had no choice."

"There was no need for the accident to ruin both yours and Andrew's life together." It came out as hard and judgmental, which was not my intent. Sometimes my comments are as subtle and accurate as a World War II bombing run.

"I made a mistake," she said, her eyes shiny. "I forgave Andrew, but I never forgave myself." She turned on me, not in anger but as one seeking absolution. "I was young. Confused."

"Don't blame yourself."

"Really?" She drew her head away from me. "You're the one who just said there was no need for the accident to ruin our lives."

"That doesn't mean you crucify yourself."

"What if that is the only way I can feel anything?"

"Regrets are for when you have a choice."

She shook her head. "You and your aphorisms."

"I might overplay it sometimes," I admitted.

"Hardly a grievous sin. There seems to be an immutable law that life begets remorse. Besides, there is always a choice." She sat up erect, as if positioning herself for a charge. "Andrew played a lot of instruments, but not the trumpet. He said he always wanted to learn. He loved the clarion sound. He called it 'the unapologetic king of any ensemble.' When I found out I was pregnant, we named the unborn baby Trumpet."

"And what is it you wanted to tell Andrew about Trumpet? You said at the Vinoy—"

"I'm looking for my child, Mr. Travis. I'm dying and I want to see her and tell her I love her. That both her parents loved her very much, but we just couldn't keep her. But now?" She blew out her breath in one final cleansing motion. "Andrew's dead and I'm out of time."

"You can always—"

"What clowns we are. What festive fools. At least Andrew didn't fake it."

I wanted to say something, felt like I *should* say something, but nothing surfaced.

She repositioned the conversation. "And you? Any children in your future?"

"We'd like to," I demurred, for I didn't want to open that box.

"And what kind of father would you be to a little girl?" she asked in a surprisingly singsong voice. She shifted so that she directly faced me, cocking a knee up on the pew and clasping her hands around it.

I puffed out both my cheeks, thinking of how to avoid the question.

"Don't think about it," Lizzy said. "What would you teach little Jackie?"

Mindful that she had rebuked me for not having the "guts" to answer her earlier question regarding Kathleen, I jumped in. "I'd teach her to fish. To clean the fish and cook the fish. To keep a boat clean and to always watch the following sea. To know the phase of the moon and the direction of the tide."

"Marvelous. But what if all those hold no interest to her?"

"I would encourage her to seek her own passions and to never sit on her dreams."

"Can the tabloid quotes," she batted back at me. "How would you show her to seek passion? How do you teach someone to act on their dreams?"

I was lost, but then I latched onto mythical Eeny whom I had described to Kathleen. "I would clothe her in long dresses with pockets and let her tramp around in bare feet."

"Dresses with pockets?" Lizzy gave me a quizzical glance.

"To collect seashells," I said, winging it. "Toads. Poems. Crabs. Kittens. Sunshine. Every child needs large pockets to put miracles in."

Her hand was on my shoulder, and she seemed as surprised as I by her sudden coronation. She squeezed. In that isolated moment, I felt inexplicably blessed by her presence and my thoughts became unframed. The darkness joined us like a sacred bond, and I had rarely felt so comfortable with anyone in my life.

With immeasurable sincerity I asked, "Is there anything I can do for you?"

"Keep fighting for Anna." She dropped her hand. "And . . ."

"And what?"

I sensed that she was going to ask for something else, but she abruptly pulled up. "Pray three times?" She gave an uncharacteristic nervous laugh.

"What did you forgive Andrew for?"

"Pardon?"

"You said you forgave him long ago, but you never forgave yourself. What did you forgive him for?"

"That's not the point."

"What is?"

"Forgiving others is easy," Lizzy said. "Forgiving yourself is hard."

"Have you?"

"I'm working on it. The advantage of dying is that you finally reach parley with the questions. We're a crooked breed, with anchorless imagination capable of drafting a toyland world that we yearn to be true. That we *have* to believe in. And the sad thing is, we do it so unpardonably well."

"You don't really believe that."

"On a Sunday."

"The other six days."

"I'm fine."

"That's probably the best we can hope for."

I WALKED LIZZY BACK TO ANNA'S ROOM. I OFFERED to escort her to her car, but she wanted to spend time with Anna. As I left the church, the Gregorian chant voices of the youth choir echoed down the halls.

I wandered the streets in the rain, except it wasn't raining; it was a beautiful Florida evening. But sometimes it rains inside and there is nothing we can do about it and no one else feels it. I felt bad for Elizabeth Walker. I felt sad for Kathleen's pipe dream that a child was out there for her. She didn't really believe that, but she didn't want me to feel guilty about tanking our chances of getting an adoption. Lizzy had given her child away and now she couldn't find her. Kathleen was searching for one with her name on it.

When Andrew was alive, he wasn't worth a good bottle of wine, and now that he was dead, I was giving him everything I had. None of it made any sense. I had waited too long in life to ask the right questions. I felt like an Alka-Seltzer tablet dropped into a glass and dissolving into a billion indistinguishable bubbles, all frantically swimming to the surface, gasping for air.

The darkness found me. The Easter morning prelude to the day belonged to a different life. I thought it was the whiskey, but I hadn't had anything to drink and it worried me that it had found me without the guide of alcohol. I stumbled into a bar, texted K, laid a fifty on the counter, and drank the back of Jesus down the River Jordan.

Here's a tip: If you feel that dark curtain coming down, drink a hole in it. At least you can blame it on the booze. There's some fraternal honor in that. Some redemptive hope.

37

Two young women with their fingers interlocked strolled by. The one in tight jeans and an embroidered white shirt said, "Jeepers, are you sure?"

"I'm telling you, sis, it was that fast," her partner replied. Normally Kathleen would have said something like "That's the first time I've heard *jeepers* this year," and we'd be off and running. But the mood wasn't there.

We sat at a high table at Mangroves, perched above the rest of the world. The sun hid behind a wall of condos that loomed over us. I hid behind a tall glass of red wine a little warm for my palate. My cream-colored sweatshirt smothered Kathleen's lap. We faced the bustling sidewalk, choked traffic, and sprinting valets of Beach Drive. Across the street, Straub Park and four hundred square miles of Tampa Bay unfolded before us. The air smelled like an Italian kitchen, but then a gust of wind brought the water in from the bay and it smelled like a damp Italian kitchen.

"How long does she have to live?" Kathleen asked as

she shoved her plate off to the side. A nearly empty bottle of wine rested in front of us.

"Months."

"Did you ask her what medicine she was on?"

"She chose quality over quantity."

"But she's taking something."

"Guess so," I said, cowering from the tone of her question.

"You should have asked," she reprimanded me.

She took a sip of wine and glanced away. I sulked in my high metal chair like a student whose fervent prayer was not to get called out again in class.

"Ask her the next time you see her." She turned her green eyes back to me. "*Are* you seeing her again?"

"I'm not sure." And then, to take the heat off myself, I added, "She doesn't think that Charlie knows anything about Trumpet."

My latest theory, despite what Elizabeth said, was that Charlie Walker had discovered their secret. I'd taken his name off the board, but now that his motivation for murder had afterburners, he was back on. I shared that with K.

"A cauldron of jealousy and love," she said. "Your wife's ex-lover swings around after twenty years, sets course to steal her, and, as a parting shot, declares, 'Oh, and did I mention that we had a child together?' Walker would be nuts *not* be driven mad by it all."

I took a healthy gulp of wine. The waiter walked by and I pointed at the bottle. He nodded. Although we weren't finished with the first one, you always want a man on deck.

"It makes a mockery out of Charlie," I said. "He was nothing but the consolation prize."

"But you said your old friend at Limorp said he saw no evidence of Charlie's involvement."

"He's not a friend, old or new. He might be lying. Or Charlie—knowing that anyone who suspected him of murder would assume he'd go to those in the business—wisely took his request elsewhere."

"Meaning your trip to see—Ian, right?" I tipped my glass to her as it was halfway to my mouth. "Your trip there was only beneficial in that it ruled out the easy answers."

"There's a reason you don't get credit for easy answers," I said.

The waiter uncorked the second bottle. Kathleen ducked her head at it. "You know that soldier is all yours, don't you?"

"Into the valley."

"The hard answers aren't really hard," she said. "Once you find out who killed Andrew and why, it will make perfectly good sense."

The breeze swirled in again. She took the sweatshirt off her legs and twisted it over her head.

"There's no dirt on Andrew," I said. "No call girl or call boy on the side. No heroin habit. No gambling debts. Not a whiff of impropriety."

"Then there is none."

"And his murder?"

"A crime of passion. You need to find the passion. Who hated him and why."

I spread my hands. "I just said—"

"One case, remember. Everything is born in the past."

She went quiet as if struck by her own words and fearful that she had made me a victim of friendly fire. If I'd known Kathleen was waiting for me, I might have—I would have—done things differently.

Kathleen had visited two private adoption lawyers.

They had both indicated that it was "highly unlikely" that they could facilitate an adoption for us. A simple background check would disqualify us (me) from anyone's list. I knew why she'd visited them on her own and feared she harbored an underground stream of resentment, although she gave no indication of incubating any such feeling. I recalled her earlier comment about whether I had asked Lizzy what medicine she was taking—my failure to ask a simple direct question. I thought of asking Kathleen if she forgave me. But I knew she would say yes.

Why ask the question if you don't believe the answer?

WE CORKED THE BOTTLE AND SAUNTERED TO THE bay, Kathleen gnawing her nails into the palm of my hand. A rising moon cast a rippled, pale-yellow road on the water. We stopped under a banyan tree that shrank us, and she kissed me slowly and then with a sense of urgency.

She pulled away. "Never doubt us, Jake."

She rarely called me by my name. When she did, it intensified the moment.

"When did you know?" I asked.

She pursed her face. "Know what?"

"Lizzy told me she and Andrew kissed in a church stairwell and they both knew at that moment."

"They're hardly a stellar example."

"Events beyond their control tore them apart."

"Let's see," she said, and we started walking again. She swung our hands in a large swooping motion. "Have we really not ever talked about this?"

"I'm afraid to say no in the event we have and I've forgotten about it."

"Hmm. Plotting your replies."

"We haven't, have we?"

"I'm not telling. Pass me that bottle, sailor."

We took a seat on a bench and I discreetly extracted the bottle from the bag. You can carry a gun in public—two million people in my state do—but under no circumstances can you uncork a bottle of wine in public. Sometimes I wonder if the country I'd spent five years defending, and was willing to sacrifice my life for, has a brain tumor. No one seems to question mindless and inane laws.

We threw down a couple of quick gulps. I corked the bottle and stuffed it back into the bag.

"Did you and Lizzy exchange this classified information?"

"We did."

"And you told her when you unequivocally came under my spell?"

"Might have."

"And the question is, was it the same moment for us both? A moment that the heart charted the course for two people who had never met but who thereafter would never be apart. But it had to be simultaneous. That is the test, is it not?"

I copped another swig. "That was a little long-winded for me."

She punched me. She hadn't done that for a while, and I wondered if she would be punching me in twenty years.

"You first," she said.

"No, ma'am."

"All right, Chicken Little, I will speak for us both. Let's see," she drummed her finger on my shoulder. "I met you at the hotel bar. The next day I went to your house. You were nervous . . ."

She droned on about her first visit to my house, but I was bummed. It hadn't been when our eyes first met, like Lizzy said it was with her and Andrew.

". . . I picked up that horrendous piece of art you did—hey, are you listening to me?"

"All ears," I said. I was eager to put the topic behind us, as it hadn't gone in the direction I had anticipated.

She swung her head at me. "It was at the hotel bar. I asked if you were who you are. You swung your head around. You nailed me with your eyes and gave me some lame response because you were intimidated and infatuated with my voice. We knew it then."

I'd forgotten. I'd *heard* Kathleen before I saw her. It had been her voice that had turned me around in my stool. I'd fallen for her before I saw her.

Jeepers.

"What was all that other stuff?" I asked.

"Just toying with you. Getting a little nervous there, weren't you? You tuned me out—I made you pay."

"You do that?"

"Straight shootin' I do."

"Why did you know then?"

"Hmm," she cupped her chin in her hand and tapped her fingers on her cheek. "That is not the right question."

"Fine. You pop the question."

"*How* did you know?"

"The difference is subtle."

"The difference is huge," she corrected me. "My heart told me."

"And later?" I said, for I knew there was more.

She stood and stepped in front of me, spread her legs, and then nestled herself on my lap so that our faces were inches apart. She draped her arms around my neck. I kissed her because I'd be a fool not to kiss the girl.

She pulled away. "We rationalize and analyze. We mull our . . ."

She stopped, for it is difficult to speak with someone's tongue down your throat.

WE SPENT THE NIGHT AT KATHLEEN'S DOWNTOWN condo. We'd decided to keep it, as we enjoyed spending weekends in the city. I sat on the balcony, sipped twenty-year port, and promised myself to run an extra mile in the morning and drink less in the afternoon. It was a familiar promise and one that I would willfully break without a hint of remorse.

Flush and reload.

I mulled—Kathleen's word, not mine—Elizabeth and Andrew and Kathleen and Jake. I couldn't imagine Elizabeth losing her father and brother in one sweep of the devil's arm. *But would that tear them apart or bring them closer together?* Who was I to judge?

But that didn't bother me that night high in the Florida sky—this did: Kathleen felt in her heart that a child was waiting for her. What if the only thing waiting for her was a bitter dose of the randomness and rotten luck that had befallen Elizabeth and Andrew?

I went to bed, but Regrets hijacked my pillow. Her nauseous breath and ragged touch caused me to toss and turn. I got up, left Regrets on the pillow, and wandered into Kathleen's Victorian library. I selected a first edition of *To Have and Have Not.* For my money, an underappreciated masterpiece. As I reclined in a chair from Sarasota Sofa, sleep found me. In my untethered dreams, there was no difference between Harry Morgan running rum and Harry the pigeon pecking the floor at Dockside.

THE NEXT MORNING I RAN THE EXTRA MILE IN THE predawn fog of Saint Petersburg. I thought that if I kept running, I might explode out of the other side like a thunderball. That's never happened. All I do is exhaust myself to a footnote on streets that will never know me, that will never acknowledge my searing muscles, my thumping heart, my rasping and labored breath, my debilitated body stripped of its bark. How long do I run before realizing that I will never take wing? That unassailable question caused me to whip myself even harder.

I never knew Andrew. He erased himself before he joined the army, and all that remained were traces of who he used to be. He created the Sofa King of Sarasota. He sculpted himself into a different man from the one who kissed Elizabeth Phillips in a church stairwell, launching both their worlds into an uncontrollable orbit. Unable to shed those impressionable youthful years that accentuate both love and loss, he wrote music deep into the night that no one would hear.

When we met, Andrew needed a friend, so he invented one in me. I begrudgingly played the part. I wanted to think I'd be a better friend now, for he had a younger version of me, a man focused on things that now seemed so foreign. An Arthurian crusader picking a cause without thought while the fertile rain of my youth spiraled down a storm drain. I'm embarrassed to admit to my opening attitude at the commencement of my third decade. My early work for the colonel. A few questionable deaths by your own hand along the way will do that. If not, what monster lies within?

I vowed to be the best friend I could be to the memory of Andrew Keller until the Elizabeth Walker affair was over. One last frantic and impassioned sprint. One final gallant effort to exceed my meager and stretched capabilities.

Then I needed to rest.

38

The rising sun glistened Morgan's chest and glowed his face as it climbed over the rim of the horizon. His thin body, bronzed and curved with muscles shaped from years of sailing, sat straight and cross-legged at the end of his dock. His hair, in a tight ponytail, rested on his upper back. His hands lay casually on his knees. A moon talisman, which never leaves his body, circled his neck. I feared the gods might claim him as one of their own and he would ascend into heaven, leaving me with no north star. Just as Mount Katahdin in Maine is the first American soil to be kissed by the sun every day, Morgan, eager to witness the waking sky, rises earlier than anyone I know. Among his constellation of qualities, he holds the morning dear to him throughout the day, and that is his special gift.

I took a seat on the bench behind him. A crab boat rolled by, and the captain used a grappling hook to snag his trap marked by a green buoy and haul it into his boat. Morgan did not look up. Nor did he raise his head when two dolphins surfaced, blowing their air into the atmosphere and taking in more before returning to their underwater world.

After a few minutes, he lowered his hands to the sacramental platform of the dock. He rose and took a seat next to me, although he did not look at me.

"The sun is warmer every day," he said.

"White man be here soon," I replied.

That earned me a smile. Made me happy. "Coffee?" I handed him a cup. I asked him if there was anything he needed done at Harbor House, although he knew such a topic did not warrant my interruption.

"They want you back," he said.

"They?"

"The class you taught English to."

"You're employing a generous interpretation of teaching."

"They now all carry names of friends in their pockets. They say it gives them confidence. Energy. They said one man did it, and you made the rest do it as well. It's a brilliant idea—to have a reminder of those who are supporting you. Who believe in you."

I tried to pretend that his words didn't affect me, but they did. The dot of time I'd spent with my class at Dockside was swelling—becoming as meaningful, if not more, than anything I had ever done. That seemed illogical. And yet.

"How are things with Elizabeth and Anna?" he said.

I dumped on him. Elizabeth's every word. Every tear she had shed and at what part of the conversation those tears had appeared. He listened with the patience of morning.

"Would such an accident separate two people or draw them together?" I asked. It was a question that had nagged me since my meeting with Elizabeth. It was the reason I'd sojourned to Morgan's dock and sought his tribal wisdom.

He brought the cup to his lips and took a sip while keeping his eyes on the far shore, that mystical place on the earth's surface where the land rises out of the sea. He shrugged. I hate it when Morgan shrugs. It's one thing for us mortals to wallow in the purgatory of uncertainty, but we don't like to see our idols stuck in the same sludge.

"We judge them from now," he said. "There is no way of knowing how they felt then. Do you think this had anything to do with Andrew's murder?"

"I do."

"Why?"

"I don't know."

"It would bring them together," Morgan said, answering my earlier question, but at his own pace.

"And if it did not?"

"Then you have an incomplete understanding of the past."

It sounded a little like gobbledygook to me, but I was the one who climbed the mountain seeking his words, so I couldn't be too critical.

Three hours later, the corner pieces to the puzzle dropped in my lap. Morgan was right—I didn't understand what had happened. It was empty-headed of me not to see it earlier. Sometimes I'm amazed I can even tie a shoe without a diagram. But I was wise enough to seek counsel from my friend, and equally wise to heed his parting comment.

39

"You're late," Rambler said as I took the stool next to him. I'd been at Harbor House installing a handicap ramp when he'd called, asking to meet for lunch. He sat on a backless stool at Victor's Diner in downtown Saint Pete, his spine curved like a quarter moon and his jacket draped over a hook on a beadboard wall. Countertop jukeboxes marked every four spaces. The place buzzed with customers and the frenzied sounds of an open kitchen.

"Iced tea," I said to a waitress who flew past me on the other side of the counter. She managed to give me a quick thumbs-up, which added a few dollars to her tip.

I picked up a sticky plastic menu that lay between us. "What's good here?"

"Hot dogs and milkshakes," Rambler said. "But the milkshake is a killer. It will put you down hard for an afternoon nap, which is fine for you considering you have no visible means of employment."

"Did you invite me here just to gripe about your pension plan?"

"Pointing out the obvious." He gave me a sideways glance I couldn't decipher.

The waitress dropped an iced tea in front of me with a paper straw protruding out of it. "Whatwillitbe?" she asked.

Rambler said, "I'll take the—"

"I know what you want, slinger," she cut him off. "I'm talking to your surfer friend."

"I'll take what he's having," I said. "Maybe it will help explain his mood."

"Cue me in when you crack that one."

She whirled away. He grunted, took a drink, and said, "Tell me what you have on Keller's death."

"Not much."

"I'll be the judge of that."

I give him an abbreviated version. He interrupted a few times, but when the chili dogs came, he zoned out.

A small bowl of chili arrived with the dog. Similar to serving water with whiskey, it was left to the customer to determine the correct ratio. I dumped the bowl into the bun and, anticipating what would come next, tried to snatch a couple of extra napkins from the napkin holder. The holder, stubbornly protective of its children, put up a stiff fight. Rambler reached over and held it with his hand. A group of three came out. I left one between us as a freebie. Halfway through the dog, I flipped through the jukebox dials.

"Ask you something?" I said.

"What's that?"

"You got a quarter?"

He grimaced and squirmed into his pocket, bringing out a green rubber coin purse.

"They still make those?" I said.

"You're the one asking for a quarter."

I shoved his quarter into the slot and selected Bob Marley's "Trenchtown Rock." I wiped my lips with the paper napkin and faced him. "What do you do when you're investigating a crime and the direction you think it's going keeps hitting a wall?"

He worked his tongue between his teeth while pushing the red plastic lattice tray the hot dog had been served in across the counter. "It's one of two things," he said. "Either you're missing something despite being convinced you've turned every stone, or you're on the wrong path."

"How do you find the right one?"

He shifted his weight on the stool. "You tracked his last few weeks—did he see anybody unusual? Break his pattern? Murder is almost always someone the vic knew. If you round up the usual suspects and draw a blank, look for someone who circled back into his life. You may think there's no connection, and that's where you're wrong. Got anybody like that?"

"Not off the top of my head," I lied.

"Look for a one and out. Someone he ran into who was *not* part of his normal routine. They can be hard to find, and the last thing you'll unearth will be the motive. Remember, it's fifty-fifty."

"Fifty-fifty?"

"Forty-six percent of homicides in this city the last three years did not result in an arrest."

"All the lab work. DNA testing. All the—"

"Fifty percent," he interrupted me. "There's luck on both sides of that."

The waitress, a talking blur of activity, reacted to my hand signal and switched out my iced tea. I tented my hands in front of me. "You're not too keen on this lay-low request, are you?"

He grunted in agreement. "It's not my first. They're all the same: Let us handle it for a few days. We got irons in the works and we need to keep a lid on it. When nothing pans out, they tell us we're free to investigate. But by then the trail is cold and it's our fault that it's another unsolved murder. But I don't give a damn about the statistics. The victim? Your buddy Andrew Keller? He's the one who gets the shaft. He's denied a full and," he shot his eyes at me, "professional investigation."

"I didn't seek this," I reminded him. "You called the meeting."

He gave that a second, glanced away, and then dragged his droopy eyes back to me. "Remember I told you we think the perp was driving a silver Honda? That never led anyplace. But then we got a call about people parking cars in front of a house they don't own. No law against it, but one lady in the neighborhood by the convenience store is always complaining. Says it's hard to get out of her driveway. Nothing better to do, right? A rookie gets the honor.

"Last week this tenderfoot is trying to calm our lady friend down. A neighbor comes out to put his two cents in, and our boy finds himself conducting a three-ring circus.

"Turns out the guy owns a silver Honda that he kept in the street. On the day of Mr. Keller's murder, someone stole it, but then brought it back. He saw the cop talking to our lady, so he decided to dump his woes as well."

"I don't follow," I said.

"The perp—assuming it was him—didn't want to drive his car to the scene, so he stole someone else's car. Afterward, he returned the car he hijacked and then drove off in his. Tenderfoot asked the guy why he never reported his car stolen. He said he thought a friend who lives down the street might have used it, although he usually called first.

He suffered through a few minutes of text tag just to discover that his friend didn't have it. And by then, he looks out of his front window and his car is back."

"How did—"

"He'd left his car running while he scooted inside to get his wallet. When he came out, his car was gone."

"The car that was left? The killer's?"

"Maybe. Maybe not. Grumpy lady said there was a blue something parked half a block down, but she doesn't know much about cars except how to bitch about them."

"And the guy whose wheels were missing?"

"Said he did a quick scan of the street, but he was looking for his car. He can't confirm, or deny, a blue car."

He reached for his wallet.

"I got it," I said. He withdrew his hand, fast, like you do when you never had any intention of paying in the first place.

"How do you see it happening?" I asked.

He tilted his head. "Mr. Keller went to the convenience store whenever he visited his showroom that was off the freeway. He went inside and purchased a coffee. Our perp had been trailing Mr. Keller. He had a gun. A mask. All he lacked was opportunity. He follows Keller to the store, or he's waiting for him. But he panics at the last second. He backs out. He spots a car running in the street—or maybe he was going to park and double back on foot. It's like a sign from God. He jumps in and heads back to the store. Parks right next to Keller. That's the car our driver-by witnessed fleeing the scene.

"That tells me this is a crime of passion, not a professional job. No way does a pro rely on luck, and our guy was lucky. And that luck misleads us—makes us think he's better than he was." He swung his head side to side. "Nothing beats luck, especially in murder."

"Did anybody else see him switch cars?"

He shook his head. "We went back, knocked on doors. Nada."

I mopped the water up underneath my sweating glass of iced tea with the extra napkin. I took a sip, letting a cube of ice slide into my mouth. "A blue something car," I said, rolling the ice in my mouth. "That's all we got?"

"Ms. Complaining came around to a late-model two door, but I wouldn't put much faith in that. The killer had a sloppy plan and executed it by the seat of his pants. Your guy tell you anything new?"

"I haven't heard from him in a while."

"Answer the question."

"No."

"The feds don't give a cold crap about Mr. Keller."

"I appreciate what you're doing," I said.

He leveled his eyes on me. "You find something, keep me in the loop. Do not impose your brand of justice."

"There's no need for me to do so."

"I bet you tell yourself that every time."

He slid off the stool and I asked for an iced tea to go. I felt a tinge of guilt for not sharing my new suspicion with Rambler, but it evaporated before I hit the door. I hoped I was wrong. But it had been there all along. One case. Buried in the past.

40

Lizzy

For whenever two or more of you are gathered in His name

F ate.
Lizzy had been stuck on the shitty little word all day. At least *stupid* had finally been dethroned.

What is it, though, she thought? *This snarky, slithery, Machi-avellian creature? It bows to no Geneva Convention. It is incapable of self-recognition. Good or bad, it should be treated with loathing contempt.*

Fate.

It even *sounds* ugly.

Oh for God's sake, Elizabeth. You need to put your words on a diet. Boil them down. She doodled:

Fate = Machiavellian little shit

She considered her scrawl. A little crass. She wondered if she had spelled Machiavellian correctly. Pretty sure she had. She jotted down:

Fate = indifference

That lacked punch and in no manner matched her mood. *And what mood is that?* she chided herself. *What mood derives from a brief and glorious stroll down a love-lacquered path before the earth opens up and you fall a little closer to hell?*

Typical, she thought. Blame it on anything other than yourself. She wrote:

Fate = when you screw up but don't want to blame it on yourself

No—too long. Besides, it reeks of self-examination. Too much time on fate, she thought. It is unworthy of my thoughts. It does not even exist. We make it up. It is . . .

She wrote:

Fate = the bastard child of random events

"There," she said out loud. "I put you in your place, you outcast orphan."

Bored, she tore the page from the notebook, crumpled it, and placed it on the table. She flicked it with her finger, launching it to the floor. But Lizzy didn't like things to be messy. She crossed the room, picked up the paper, and dropped it into an empty waste basket. She went to her study and brought the last of her books, those treasured wordy companions, into her bedroom, including her childhood Bible.

Lizzy couldn't decide where to place the Bible—an

overrated classic that, in her opinion, owed its status only to William Tyndale's translation, or at least what he accomplished before they strangled and burned him at the stake—and ended up shoving it between a Graham Greene book she'd never gotten around to cracking and *A Thousand Splendid Suns*, which she'd read twice, her tears staining the pages both times. *Poor Miriam!* Charlie had stopped insisting that the room was getting cluttered. Charlie had stopped saying a lot of things. He was content to allow Lizzy to live her final days surrounded by whatever she wanted. He'd cut back on his traveling and spent most of his time working out of the house to be with her. They'd grown closer, and even though she attributed that to her impending demise, it still counted, didn't it?

He had even asked if she wanted a hand in her own obituary—a gutsy subject to bring up. She declined, although she did compose the final line. Charlie asked if it was true. Lizzy shrugged him off, saying it was just a favorite quotation of hers from some poet who, at that moment, she couldn't recall.

In the end, she considered Charles Walker a decent choice. And that is what we do. We choose. We move on, foot in front of foot, breath after breath. It had even worked for a while, like everything works when it first starts; a nip here, a tuck there, a compromise, putting in longer hours at work until you realize the sole intent of the extended effort was to produce shorter hours at home. *Think of all the kids who have books because of my mistake!*

Lizzy blitzkrieged the banking industry after her return from Europe. Her work left her with little time to examine her amputated feelings, which made her a prized thoroughbred in the stable of capitalism. Sly Lizzy, thinking she was a step ahead of herself, but knowing she wasn't. Burning a feverish pace year after year. Leaving her male challengers grumbling that their careers coincided with superwoman's and lamenting that they were in the same century as she. The charade ended at two fifteen on a Friday afternoon in March after eleven years and six months with the bank. It was a day she'd punched through seven satellite radio stations on her way to the office before finally settling on silence that curled around her like a warm blanket. It was the day her heart, thought to be mortally wounded, resurrected itself. A day when the rallying truths of her life, crouched in the tall grasses of her mind, pounced.

She'd volunteered to read at 2:00 p.m. to students at the local elementary school as part of a community outreach. Her meticulously constructed defenses down that day—had she known?—she found more enjoyment and fulfillment in fifteen minutes of helping a struggling child read than in 138 months in banking. The student, a young girl, had given her a hug. Horrified at how sensorily austere she'd become, and vowing never to cage her heart again, she quit the following Monday. She did not check her emails over the weekend. Charlie, for all his shortcomings, had been divine in steering her toward establishing a profitable nonprofit. Lizzy always suspected that her volunteer work better suited Charlie's image of a successful lobbyist's wife. A fast-track female banker, after all, might eventually overshadow him. Lizzy had gone on to found A Book for Every Child and eclipsed not only her husband but also the whole damn state. She had only recently been forced to step down due to her—as they say—failing health.

It didn't escape her that the great failure of her life had fueled the great success of her life. A Book for Every Child would outlive her. Out good her. She doubted that if she had married Andrew she would have founded the distinguished and life-changing nonprofit dedicated to childhood literacy that was spreading through the nation faster than cancer cells were multiplying in her body. For her consuming drive was born from a scathing and incontrovertible desire to accomplish something positive with her life, to atone for failing so gloriously at the only thing she ever truly wanted. To counter the seeping sadness that lurked in the evenings, greeted her in the mornings, and plagued her waking hours as the voices of the world receded further each day from the frayed fringes of her sanity.

As for her marriage, it certainly displayed the badge of practicality and respect. In an age when half of eternal loves ended up in a divorce court, she could at least take pride in that, although only the timer's clock saved her in that regard. She was aware that her baggage weighed them down. Charlie deserved better than her. But Charlie, who loved Elizabeth as much as his meager capabilities allowed, never wanted anyone else. It never occurred to Charlie Walker to love someone who loved him.

And as far as not having children?

She couldn't go there. Even now. At the end. Alone in her room. She could say out loud what she just said about her feelings—or lack thereof—for Charlie, but the child door? It was shut. God's mightiest angels, showing pity on her, refused to allow Lizzy in. The demons inside would have ravaged and feasted on her, shameful figure that she was.

She went to her desk with a view of the Gulf of Mexico and extracted a manila folder from underneath a stack of writing tablets. She'd purposely kept everything off her computer. She didn't want Charlie snooping around after she was gone. Anna knew about the folder, but no one else.

Poor Anna. Lizzy felt bad dumping the remnants of her fouled-up life on her good friend, who had her own insurmountable problems.

Anna's two daughters—Kimberly (I say high, she says low. I say eat, she says she's not hungry. I say study, she says why?) and her younger sister, Olivia (the Good Daughter)—were a constant source of worry and pride. Kimberly always dominated their conversations. That's the way it works—the squeaky wheel and all that. Lizzy knew that despite her own problems, Anna's sleepless nights were reserved for her oldest daughter.

She opened the folder and flipped through the pages. There had been nothing new for over a month, and now the hourglass had taken center stage. The odds were increasing that even if she did reach her goal, she'd be gone. But death roused no fear in her. For Lizzy had decided that Shakespeare—or Paul's letter to the Corinthians, or whoever had said it, she couldn't recall—was right; death had lost its sting. Because of Andrew's murder, death was no longer a black door leading to a terror-filled hall. It was the promise of a beginning. A reuniting. Not only with Andrew but also with her father and older brother. We are born with death in us and Lizzy accepted hers.

Her death: It wore no costumes. Bothered with no disguises. It would not be a massive blocked artery while bending over to pick up a seashell, or a brain aneurysm while reading a favorite book, or a plane, scheduled to deliver her to an awards ceremony, hurling itself to the ground. No, her death was a medically calculated event. She had had time to become acquainted with her new partner—and it with her. Elizabeth walked hand in hand with it and when she died, they would exit the world together.

I shall not fail that rendezvous.

She went to the window. For once she wished the goddamned gulf would say something back to her, but it never did. She knew it was too much for Anna, with Kimberly's present state and all. It wasn't fair to ask her to bear the weight of her immoderate obsessions. Not to mention that Anna could be sent packing any day. And Charlie? What a terrible thing to unload on him. *It will have to be Mr. Travis,* she thought. *I should have sprung it on him while we were in the chapel. After all, he knew I was holding back. He didn't ask me the purpose of my attorney when I admitted my lie to him. Oh, Lizzy, be honest,* she rebuked herself. *You were afraid that if you asked him, it would all come out. Maybe that would have been good for me, but Limpy Lizzy didn't take the jump, did she? Too late now. I vowed to take it to my grave, and that is where this train wreck is heading.*

She eased up on herself, for there was always the chance that her phone would ring. That pipe dream, she knew, was a setting sun.

She started to compose a letter in her head. Dear Mr. Travis? Dear Jake? She yearned to call him Jake, for they were approximately the same age, but felt it wise to engage in professional decorum, as she had at the church. But she didn't feel like writing the letter to Mr. Travis, or to Jake, just then. She felt like—she didn't know what she felt like.

She switched to colored pencils. She'd forgotten how much she liked them. On a torn piece of paper, in red, she wrote:

Once, I was kissed under a lamppost.

No. I can do better. Another piece of paper. Now in royal blue:

Once, in the land of Honahlee, a boy kissed me under a
lamppost.

There, she thought. That's as good as any line in any
book in this room. Better. *Funny, I'm not sure I spelled Machi-
avellian right, but I know I nailed Honahlee.* She put the scrap of
paper in the same envelope that she planned to put the
letter in. He'll think it a mistake, she thought.

But Elizabeth Walker wasn't tricked by her casual attitude. She'd fooled a great many people in the world, but
never herself.

41

The day's light was pulling out when I pulled into the graveled parking lot of Nadine's Institute of Southern Cooking. A class must have just finished as a few cars, grinding the gravel, executed sharp turns in tight quarters. At the bottom of the wood steps, two chitter-chattering women, each carrying a dish of food, breezed past me as if I didn't exist.

Nadine sat at the counter conversing with another woman. Her holiday laugh and summer smile filled the room. I retraced my steps and took a seat in a rocking chair. A few minutes later, the woman walked out. I returned to the kitchen and rapped my knuckles on the doorframe.

"Oh, I didn't see you," she said, snapping her head out of the sink where she'd been scrubbing a large pot. She reached for a dishtowel and dried her hands.

"I'm here to see Dylan." And then, not wanting to be rude, I tacked on, "What was this afternoon's class?"

"An old gumbo recipe. A burgundy rémoulade sauce

with boiled shrimp and rice along with French bread for dipping."

"Will you marry me?"

She planted her hands on her hips. "Honey, I think you just want me for my cookin'."

"Any scraps for the neighborhood dog?"

"Have a seat, Rin Tin Tin. And tell me why you have a continuing interest in Dylan Phillips, who, by the way, is planning on moving out next week. Know what that means?"

"The flag is coming down?"

"Oh, that too. No, I've got a contractor ready to roll. A gift shop that will change inventory four times a year to match the seasons. I'll use the upper floor for storage."

"I'm happy for you."

"I'd be happier if you'd tell your women friends to pass the word along that it's worth the drive."

"Guys can't shop here?"

"Don't you start with me. And don't forget to tell them either."

I took a seat that was still warm. "Where's Dylan skirting off to?"

"If he's got an agenda, he didn't nail it on the door. But after dragging his feet for so long, he's mighty anxious to hit the road." She spooned some sauce into a bowl over a bed of rice. "I boiled the shrimp in the sauce. You want the flavors to fuse together. Why are you interested in Mr. Dylan?"

"Why is he in a hurry?"

"He's not much of a talker. 'Bout as good as you are at answering questions." She followed that line with a sassy smile and handed me a piece of baguette.

"Is this a Cajun dish?" I said, picking up a fork.

"Everyone thinks flavor comes from New Orleans. No, that's my grandmother's spice and she never got within a downwind smell of the Big Easy."

I took a bite and four-part harmony exploded in my mouth. I offered my compliments.

She flung a dishtowel over her shoulder "You're not going to make me ask twice, are you? 'Cause I thought you and I got along better than that. A man like you might come around for idle chat once, but not twice."

I put my fork down, glanced around for a napkin, and abandoned the effort. "I need to talk to him about his visit with my friend Andrew Keller."

"I thought you already did that." She handed me a napkin from the counter that was across from me.

"Thank you. I need to do it again."

She rubbed her hand over her apron. Her eyes narrowed in concern. "I told you he was agitated after that man came, remember? But after you showed up, he's been reclusive. I mean, he always keeps to himself, but I can't even coax him out of his hut for food. He sold his car and plans on raising his sail."

"He sold his car?"

She twisted up the corners of her mouth. "Honestly? I'm not even sure he sold it. Some flatbed truck pulled in here one day and hauled it away. Dylan told me it wouldn't start and they were taking it to a garage. But I haven't seen it since and the truck had something about salvage yard on its side."

"Did his use his car much? I noticed it was under a tarp when I was last here."

"He put the tarp on to keep the tree debris off. He never had any problem with it that I know of. Drove it most days."

"Did you ask him where he's going?"

"Said he plans to fly to Mexico. Said he'd never been there and he found some hostel where ten dollars will buy him a day. Livin' cheap is about all that man ever cared about."

I stood. "Is he out back now?"

"Far as I know. Is everything OK?"

"Coming up roses."

Nadine held my eyes with hers, trying to decide what my presence meant.

"OK," she said as if she'd made up her mind. "You go out now, when there's still a little light. I'm not a fan of those woods at night and there's a big swamp beyond that. Remember, that boy's liable to tell you Poseidon's out there."

"You know that's not true."

"You didn't come here to talk to me."

42

Andrew, who had not seen Dylan in twenty years, hunted him down and was murdered two weeks later. Dylan had a blue car. Dylan had a troubled youth, coal-fired by an accident that killed both his father and his brother and ostracized his sister.

But what was his motive?

I think I knew, for a solitary road led to it all being one case. I tried to ignore the vision, for it was something no one should ever see. I wondered why she hadn't told me in the chapel, but I wouldn't have said anything either. I couldn't imagine how Lizzy had persevered. But my beliefs explained why Andrew had visited me and what Lizzy said about forgiving him.

The sharp ping of a hammer striking a metal object echoed from the rear. I looped around to the back of the barn. Headphone wires trailed out of Dylan Phillips's ears. He chiseled away at the same piece of wood that he'd been laboring over during my first visit. But unlike the animals that he sold, this former tree was morphing into an abstract human face. Or a Greek god.

He yanked off his headphones.

"Looks nice," I said. "You getting tired of bears?"

"Thought I'd expand my repertoire."

"Who is it?"

He paused. "Poseidon."

I nodded, calculating how to address that and decided it was best not to. "I talked to your sister last week."

He gave me blank stare. "Who are you, man? Don't give me that shit about being a friend of Andrew's. That cocksucker never had a friend."

A tingle went up my spine. His animosity toward Andrew wasn't warranted by anything I'd been led to believe and certainly not what he'd previously admitted—that he hadn't really known Andrew.

Unless it was one case.

"Why do you hate him so much?"

He shuffled his feet. "I don't hate him. He just broke Lizzy's heart."

"She's the one who split the country after the accident."

"Yeah, really thinking of me, wasn't she?"

"She didn't mean any harm."

"Whatever. He wasn't right for her."

"How would a ten-year-old know that?"

He rubbed his lower lip over his teeth. "You got all the answers, don't you?"

"Just asking a question. Lizzy told me she wanted to get a final hug in. Anything else you two talked about?"

"Nope. Guess no one's interested in you being part of the family. Damn shame you're not buying the message."

"Damn shame I'm not buying your act."

His face contorted and his hand opened and closed on the hammer, white knuckles protruding through the skin. "You gonna bug my sister like you're bugging me? Leave her alone. She doesn't need you in the closing chapter of her life."

"Now you like her?"

"Forget you, man."

"She says you're troubled."

He coughed out a laugh. "Ain't we all? I keep to myself, don't bother nobody, and work on my art. You call that troubled? World would be a far nicer place if we had more troubled people."

"What did you and Andrew talk about?"

"I gotta pack."

He dropped his hammer into a black tool bag and strode past me into the barn. I followed him through the opened sliding door. He started stuffing clothing into a backpack that I presumed he'd brought down from upstairs. Dylan was thin-boned—he could hide in the shadow of a palm tree. I was seized with the urge to leave him. *Walk away, man. Let him run from his past—is that such a crime? Let him swim the seas with Poseidon, each of his feet on the back of harmonized dolphins. Chip dead trees into dead birds and dead bears. All harmless—even admirable. A solitary figure with no quarrels with the world.*

At least not anymore.

The image of Andrew Keller bleeding out on a dirty floor flashed in my aching head. I'd given him cheap wine. Didn't invite him to stay for dinner. Was a little ticked that he smudged my glass table. He came to me for help. Knew he'd made a mistake. Was in danger. I turned him away. He crossed my name out. I felt dizzy. Nauseated. I shook my head trying to clear the cobwebs, but that made it worse. Two gunshots, not one. Then I heard Andrew's answer when I'd asked him what he meant when he said he'd come clean. That he'd set the record straight. The sound of his voice spooked me. Iced my veins.

Nothing. Just running my mouth. Some bullshit about my youth. Hey, I could always lay it on pretty thick, couldn't I?

Dylan spun around. "You just standin' there?"

But Andrew Keller wasn't done with me. *Unloaded the guilt.* I knew then that I should have probed, but I didn't.

"Yo, spaceman, you hear me?"

My mind snapped back. I wiped my sweating face with my hand, but it wasn't sweat, it was Andrew's blood.

"Why did Andrew come to see you?" I felt like a boxer trying to raise himself off the canvas.

He took his hands off his backpack and squared himself in front of me. "Said he was planning on reconnecting with Lizzy. That's it. You happy?" His eyes bulged out. "Sorry to disappoint the amateur sleuth."

"Why would he haul himself out here to tell you that?"

"Ask him. Oops, that won't work, will it? You got me. He shows up and says he was planning on getting back with her. I'm like, why are you here, man? I hardly remembered him. I asked him if he'd talked to Lizzy. He said they'd run into each other and the sparks flew. He just wanted me to know."

"Sort of like clearing it with you first," I said, hoping to lead him on.

"Apparently. God knows why." He pressed a finger to his lips. "But shhh. He's not telling anyone."

"And Elizabeth—when she came out? Do you want to amend that as well?"

"Give it up. There's nothing to amend. Oh, wait. She hugged me. That would have been nice twenty years ago. But no, she flew the coop."

"Where are you flying off to?"

"I've been hitting the hammer for years. Thought I'd take a break and hit the road instead."

"Mexico?"

"Wherever, man."

"Sold your car?"

"Don't need it in Mexico," he said as if it was the most obvious fact in the world.

"Taking off when your sister needs you?"

"Tit for tat."

"It's not too late."

"Don't you need to be someplace?"

"Bet you'd love to never see me again."

"Wouldn't break my heart."

"Mine either," I said. "But I'm stuck. Tell me why the man who dated your sister twenty years ago when you were ten, and who you hardly knew, would drop by to tell you he was considering getting back together with her."

He swung his head back and forth. "Listen, you're just reading far more into this than there is. I feel bad for you. I'm sorry your friend is gone. I *am* sorry my sister got an early call. But I got my life to live, and it has nothing to do with you."

He turned around and shuffled the clothing in his backpack. I took a step deeper into the room and planted myself in front of a picture on the wall. A man, a younger man, and a boy. They held fishing poles and squinted into the sun.

"Is that your father, Benjamin, and you?" I asked.

He carefully placed a folded garment of clothing next to his backpack and walked up behind me. I braced myself for a sarcastic retort.

"That was a month before the accident," he said in a calm voice that pricked the hairs on the back of my neck.

"That must have been hard on you."

"It was a terrible time. Losing your father and older brother in one day is . . . incomprehensible."

He resumed packing but at a more unhurried pace.

"Tell me about that day," I said.

His head dropped as if it had become unhinged. A few silent seconds dripped by. He lifted his head and faced me. "You wanna know? Fine. I'm at a friend's house watching an old Bond film. *Octopussy*. We're in the basement. It's the part of the movie where the bad guys, riding elephants, are hunting Bond. His dad comes down and says he needs to take me home. That there was an accident. I ask if everything's OK, but Mr. Templeton is as white as a ghost and can hardly look at me."

He spoke in the present tense, as if he were there.

"What happens next," I said.

"Mr. Templeton takes me to the hospital, but they don't let me see my brother or my dad."

"Do they explain the accident to you?"

"Accident." He burst out of his catatonic trance. "Like hell. Some guy ran a stop sign. Tire marks showed where my dad swerved to miss him. He never turned himself in. What do you think of that?"

"And if he had turned himself in, would it have brought your father and brother back?"

"Wow—I dig the insight, man. Lemme ask you something—you think you're the first person to preach that verse?" He eyes blazed at me in anger, but I wasn't going to provoke him any further. "My mom, before she drank herself into the grave, paid a lot of money to have people tell me that shit. Who would have known I could have gotten it for free?"

"It didn't do any good, did it?"

"Screw you."

"Where's your car?"

His eyes narrowed. "What?"

"The man who killed Andrew Keller drove away in a silver car, but that wasn't his car. He switched into a blue car."

Dylan opened his mouth and ran his tongue over his lower lip. He gave a single nod, like Wayne's patented move. Frogs croaked in the darkening woods. A clock ticked on the wall. He brought his hand up and rubbed his jaw. "You are one misguided puppy. You think I had something to do with Keller's death? Think I smoked the Sofa King of Sarasota?"

He stepped over to a desk and rummaged through a drawer.

"Where's your car?" I said.

"I sold it," he said over his shoulder. "What'd you think —I was going to drive that rusted bucket to Mexico?"

"Why are you going to Mexico?"

"I need a new venue, so to speak."

"You sold your car to a salvage company. Did you want it destroyed?"

He stuck a hand in his pocket and turned to face me.

"No," he said in a deliberate tone. "The guy who bought it picked it up with a flatbed."

He hadn't shaved for days, but it came across as neglect, not as a fashion statement. He shirt, tucked in on one side, hung out over loose-fitting pants on the other side. His bird eyes, deep in his forehead, darted around the room.

"Why did you kill Andrew Keller?"

He sniffled and swung his head like he had water in his ear. "What the hell, man?" He kept swinging his head, trying to exorcise whatever possessed him.

"Why did you kill Andrew Keller?" I repeated. I took a step toward him.

"You're a crazy fucker."

I took another step. "What did Andrew tell you?"

"I don't—"

"*Was Keller driving the car that caused the accident?*"

"*Fuck yeah, man,*" he raged at me. "He killed my father and brother. Told me he had to get it off his damn conscience before he got back together with her. He destroyed me and my family and told me goddamn Lizzy didn't want to turn him in."

43

Lizzy
Twenty Years Ago

There is love
Oh there's love

S he punched. She kicked. She howled. A horrific gargling sound that would paralyze even the most hardened and ruthless spectral creatures of the night. A vomiting of everything that was ever good and sacred and would never be believed again, so help us God.

So help us God.

So help us, God.

So help us, FUCKING God!

Like gravity from a dark hole, Lizzy and Andrew had collapsed into each other's lives in the church stairwell. Now they were flung apart, an imploding star hell-bent on taking the universe with it.

He tried to console her, but he was weak—destroyed himself, so what strength did he have? Lizzy stared at him but couldn't place his face—this man who was once love incarnate. My future husband? Father of my child? *Lover of mine?* She wailed God's name. And then she withered up into a ball and moaned on the carpet. She rocked back and forth. Andrew paced, for he could not control his spastic and epileptic movement.

He squatted down beside her and touched—

Don't touch me! Don't touch me! Don't touch me!

She whimpered. Groaned. Sobbed. But the language fails, for no matter how gifted or inept with words one may be, there are no nouns or verbs, no fools or kings, that can be rallied and summoned for the cause, for fear of being forever tarnished and soiled with the great tragedy and sadness that occurs when death leaves a young woman standing and fells those whom she loves the most.

Drenched with joy—*I'm going to be a father*—and running late, Andrew's euphoric mind had not been paying attention. He witnessed the carnage in his review mirror. He panicked when he saw what he'd done and hurried back to the scene. He realized, in an out-of-body experience, that it was her father's car, this noodled convulsion of steel. No doors—or what had once been doors—would open. He called 911. Said he'd been behind them—wondered why he lied, but knew why. He fought the metal again, but there was nothing he could do. He raced back to Lizzy's apartment, fleeing the scene, although the sirens were closing in. He told her what had happened. She'd come undone.

But what happened next was not right. It was not of this world. For like a delirious pendulum vaulting the middle, Elizabeth swiftly broke her disfigured emotions. She tamed her tears. Stilled her quivering lips. Her abrupt about-face chilled even her guardian angel.

-You called 911? she said. Her voice was flat. Controlled.

-Yes. They were arriving when I came for you.

-Are they dead?

-It's bad, babe. Real bad. We need to get back to them.

He bolted toward the door but saw that he was alone.

-What? he asked.

-What did you tell them?

-Who?

-911.

-That I was behind them.

-OK. And did you see the car that caused it?

-Babe, it was me.

-No. No. No.

-No, what? Andrew didn't understand.

-You can't implicate yourself. Tell them you didn't see the car that caused it.

-But—

-Listen to me.

-But—

-*Listen to me.*

She plotted ahead. Made her list. What if they died? What if she lost two men in her life? She couldn't bear to lose a third. Double involuntary manslaughter. A child whose daddy would be in prison for years. *Yes, little Trumpet, that's a picture of your grandfather and older uncle. Remember? Daddy caused an accident that killed them both. That's why he wasn't around for a few years.*

She was adamant. Unwavering. They (she) made their decision. They would not implicate Andrew. Nothing good would come from punishment. Practical Lizzy. Sensible Lizzy. Levelheaded Lizzy. Ice Lizzy. Under the most trying and challenging circumstances, her profound intellect carried the day.

(Andrew Keller never forgave himself for not turning himself in. He spoke of this pervasive regret and unutterable sin to no one, but in his mind, it stripped him of any right to pursue happiness. Born that night, not in a manger, but in a car wreck, was the Sofa King of Sarasota.)

-We need to go to them, he said.

-I know, she said, suddenly horrified at her delay. -I know. Let's go.

When they arrived, the ambulance was gone. The only thing that remained was her father's car, a crushed accordion against a noble and proud oak. They sped to the hospital. Lizzy swearing her life to God if she, he, or it would allow them to live.

Her father.

He'd taught her to ski on both crystallized and liquid water. He'd impressed upon her that if she swooshed down a white mountain of snow and broke the placid surface of a lake before the early-morning fog lifted, if she read great books in the morning and listened to stirring music in the evening, if she was accepting of and kind to all people— well, he said one day when sharing a pumpkin doughnut with her—there was more to the world but that was all he took from it. She was fourteen. She pretended to understand.

When she was twelve, her mother layered her with perfume one Saturday. Her father hosed her off in the driveway while she bitterly complained about the cold water. He told her that nothing at the cosmetic counter could ever compete with flowers. They went for a walk, sniffing everything in sight. Lizzy could close her eyes and pick out a rose, tulip, gardenia, honeysuckle, wisteria, lily . . . sweet almond.

At age eight, during a soccer match, Lizzy got kicked above a shin guard. She played on as blood ran down her leg and leaked into her squishy shoe. It wasn't until afterward that her father saw how nasty the gash was. Lizzy hadn't cried. Not even a whimper.

-You have a high tolerance for pain, her father said. She had taken his comment with pride. When older and recalling his words, she wondered if she'd detected a note of worry in his voice. Wondered if he knew, even then.

At age seven he had discovered her reading under the covers one night with a flashlight.

-Elizabeth, he'd said as he entered her bedroom. -Are you in there?

-Yes.

-And what are you doing?

Pause.

-Elizabeth?

-I'm in my Reading Tent, she replied, hoping she wouldn't get in trouble.

-Reading Tent, he said. -Can I come in? After that, he crawled in at least once a week and, by flashlight only, he would read to her in the Reading Tent.

Benjamin.

The confidence he bestowed upon her just by being in the same building when she walked through the doors her freshman year of high school. He was three years ahead of her, a champion fueling her self-esteem. A protective wing over those crazily bizarre years when her body mushroomed ten years ahead of itself, and it felt as if the whole world was staring at her as if it had never seen a shapely woman before.

Benjy! An ace up the sleeve if there ever was one.

It is one thing to lose the light of one's life gradually to the friction of age, the natural cloudiness of the eyes' lenses. It is another to have it zapped away at the apogee of youth.

She stayed with her father and brother, sprinting between hospital rooms, until the family was officially reduced by two-fifths. The remaining three-fifths, while still a majority, could not assimilate into a whole. The center of the circle was gone. Her father and older brother were dead.

SO WERE LARRY AND EARL, THE FISH SHE AND Andrew had brought back from the art festival. They flopped to their demise on the tile floor. Lizzy didn't remember knocking them over the night before. And while she never mentioned it to anyone (not even the shrinks pried this gem out of her) when confronted with the realities of her decision the next morning, and destroyed with remorse for not rushing to her father and brother's side when Andrew had first told her, she nearly took her own life. Their (her) posturing had consumed critical seconds. Weren't there tales of people having superwoman strength at such times? Maybe she could have pried a door open. Lifted the car with one arm. They said her father was in a coma, but maybe he could have heard her. Felt her hand. Smelled her.

Could he have smelled me?

Oh God! Oh great God! Could he have?

Her father told her during a summer beach vacation that she smelled like the morning waves. She'd believed him. What if he could have smelled morning waves when he was in the car? He loved nothing more than starting his day by the sea. A cup of coffee. A breathless air incapable of rousing even a single page of his beloved *New York Times*. Would it have made a difference? The thought strangled her. She'd been by his side at the hospital, but not at the accident. No. She had dawdled. She'd left them to die like Larry and Earl. She thought of the closing line of a Christopher Logue poem her father read to her once in the Reading Tent: "Where is the snow we watched last fall."

Gone for good. Oh, the world! It's gone and it's my fault!

Elizabeth Phillips stood in front of a mirror, a razor blade in her fingers, her being—and the nascent start of another deep within her—dangling on a thread. Only the pressure of her deceased father's hand upon her left shoulder allowed her to escape the moment. She took a breath. And another. And then another. Like Andrew's regret for fleeing the scene, she shared this darkest hour, this nadir of her being, with no one. Not a word would be spoken to another breathing soul about the touch from beyond. Her forgiving father's hand upon her shoulder steadied her breathing, quelled her anguish, and became the nucleus of her life.

AFTER THE FUNERAL THEY POUNDED THE contorted issues until there was nothing left to say. A part of Lizzy had died with them, and she hadn't been prepared for that. For her own flatline heart. She needed to be alone. She *had* to be alone. Someplace where no one knew her name. That wouldn't be hard, for she no longer knew herself.

-I'll go with you, he pleaded.

-No. I need my time.

-But what's the purpose?

-I need to be alone.

-We need to handle this together. We—

-I need to be alone.

It would be years before Elizabeth realized what a terrible thing she had forced upon Andrew. That it was easy, as she had done, to run. But it was suffocating to stay behind, especially without her. Andrew Keller had no choice but to create another life. Elizabeth saw the aftermath of her selfish action too late—along with a long list of other unpredictable and inarguable consequences, including this biggie: she had deserted her younger brother during his time of great need.

They did an airport goodbye. A hurried hug. An empty "I love you." A quick kiss and then a vacant seat. Nothing beside you when only recently there had been heaven. She'd flown to Paris by herself. Andrew slammed the door on his past, threw away the key, checked into prison (army), and resurrected himself as a new person. And Elizabeth Phillips, her emotions in permanent retreat and her intellect on a goose-step march, never sang again.

44

Dylan Phillips swayed his head, overcome by a life that struck him down when he was ten. Cut him in half during an elephant chase scene in a Bond film. That laughed at his wasted folly as he struggled and tripped and failed to ever fully right himself. I felt a great pity for the man. For what had happened to his family. For what it had turned him into.

His sobs quieted. He rubbed his hand over his forehead and then raked it through his hair.

"Does she know?" I said. I could not bear the thought of Elizabeth Walker learning that her younger brother had murdered her life's true love—and Trumpet's father.

"She's got no idea. That was between me and him."

"Jake? Dylan?" Nadine stood behind us, her hands gripping her thighs. She spoke as a child. "I heard yelling. Is everything all right?"

"It's fine. Dylan and I are just having a discussion."

"I heard you asking him . . ."

I went to her, took her elbow, and guided her toward

the back porch. "It's something we need to work out. I won't be here much longer. Are you getting ready to close up?"

"I want to go home," she said, as if home was something she once took for granted but never would again. She stopped at the base of the steps leading to the porch, resisting my efforts to go any farther. "Did he kill someone? Should I call the police?"

My mind blazed out of control. I realized that I needed to inform Wayne that whoever he was protecting in Walker's camp was fine and to hand the investigation back to Detective Rambler. I was perturbed that the thought commandeered my mind—it was the least of my worries.

"Not yet," I said. "Let me talk to him."

"OK."

I turned and walked back to Dylan. He stood silhouetted under the doorframe. Hand in his pocket. Calm. Poised. Relaxed. Nothing like himself. I stopped halfway. I should have kept walking.

"You gonna call the police?" he asked.

"No plans to. When did you learn that Andrew caused the accident?"

"The day he told me. I hadn't seen the man in decades. Didn't even know him when he drove up. He introduced himself and said he wanted to have a few words. I said sure. What the hell, right? We took a couple of chairs and he started talking about those days when he was dating Lizzy. Said he was thinking of getting back in touch with her, some crap about mending old fences."

"What did you think of that?"

"I couldn't figure out why he was coming to me. Hell, I didn't know him then or now. He got real nervous, started pacing, and then—poof—he tells me. Says, 'Remember the accident.' Like I'm going to forget it, right? Then he says he was the one who ran the stop sign. Caused my dad to swerve. Hit that oak tree and kill himself and my brother."

He paused and I stole a glance over my shoulder. Nadine stood directly behind me on the porch.

"He said he wanted me to know before he and Lizzy got together. Bawled how sorry he was. Said he wanted to turn himself in, but my sister couldn't bear the thought of him going to jail and losing the 'three men in her life.'"

Before I could say anything, he added, "What do you think of that—the three men? Like I wasn't even born."

"I'm sure she didn't mean it like that. You said you were just ten. That—"

"That I was the afterthought of the family. That man took them from me, and my sister allowed him."

"It was an accident, Dylan. Andrew had no intent. You know that."

"Tell that to their tombstones. Try living with a dead brother and father your whole life. What would that be—an accident living with an accident? Their voices are fading now. Know what I mean? I can't hear them like I used to. I got a few videotapes, and I use them like boosters, but it doesn't come from inside anymore."

"Lizzy?" I said.

His face grimaced. "Like I said, she came by for a hug and to say she was getting back with Andrew. Meant nothing to me. Damn good thing, though, that she came before he did." He swung his head as if trying to empty it. "You've seen him on TV, right? Well, I got the Sofa King of goddamn Sarasota crying his eyes out in my yard. Telling me he was late for a gig and ran a stop sign. That he recognized the car, knew it was Lizzy's father, and that he stopped and went to them, but they were twisted pasta. He called 911 and hightailed it out of there to my sister's."

"What did—"

"And then he begs my forgiveness. Problem is—I'm not too keen on that shit. And you know what? He knew it, man. He wanted retribution. Damn straight he did. He knew he was signing his death warrant by coming here. All I did was comply with his wishes. I followed him. Evened the score. Made my father and brother proud of me. What do you think of that?"

"I think he caused an accident that weighed heavily on him, and—"

"He didn't seem too worried prancing around in that stupid king outfit on TV."

"—you committed premeditated murder."

What a brainless thing to say. But I felt compelled to protect Andrew. He had no intent to cause harm, unlike the man who faced me. I wrestled with how to get Dylan to stay so that Rambler could arrest him. I stole another glace over my shoulder to check on Nadine. When I turned back, Dylan Phillips had a gun to his head.

"Don't," I said.

Nadine squeaked. I dropped my right hand across the corner of my back where my gun was. I couldn't move left or right without exposing Nadine to the line of fire should Dylan decide to take someone else's life instead of his.

"Why? So you can haul me in? Stick me in the chair?"

"You had a traumatic childhood. A good attorney can get you a reduced sentence."

"Wrong, wrong, wrong, wrong, wrong. Plead insanity, right? No way I'm gonna let some quack back inside my head. I've checked out of that roach hotel for good."

"Dylan," Nadine said. "Put the gun down. You're a good man. I know that."

"This is none of your business, Nadine."

"They can help you."

"While I sit in jail? Don't think so."

The moon broke free of a cloud and our scene brightened. A ghostly white bathed the air and cast tepid shadows upon the ground.

"Think of Elizabeth," I said.

Dylan's face contorted into pain. "She knew, man. She knew."

"What she knew was the punishment had to stop. It has to stop now. Put the gun down. Don't take another life."

"You're going to take mine," he said, swaying his head. "I ain't going to let that happen."

Nadine started walking toward me. "There are good people who can help you, Dylan. Remember, that's how we met. How you got into your art."

I waved my hand behind me, keeping my eyes on Dylan. "Stay where you are, Nadine." I slipped my hand on my gun.

"That's right, Nadine," Dylan said. "Don't get close to the bad man."

"You're not bad, Dylan," Nadine said. "Bad things happened to you. Bad things that we can't even imagine, but that doesn't make you bad."

"Whoop-de-doo. Man, I have *never* heard that one before." He leered at me, his face pallid. "What do *you* think?"

"You want to do this to Elizabeth? She doesn't have long."

"Always about Lizzy, isn't it? She helped cover up the cause of my father and brother's deaths, left me with a mom who loved booze more than me—and what? I'm supposed to be concerned about her? And you think I'm the one who needs help?"

"She didn't cover anything up," I said. "She tried to stop further damage resulting from a terrible accident. That's what you need to do now. Put the gun down, Dylan. Don't punish yourself."

"Let me see your hand," Dylan said.

I kept my hand low, like the gunslinger I was.

"You got a gun," he said. "I seen it on you before."

"Put your gun down, Dylan."

"No." He shoved his gun up hard under his chin.

Nadine's hoarse breathing, the croaking frogs and the chirping crickets, had been on the pixelated edges of my consciousness. Then something inside me latched into place and the world popped. Everything was clear. Accentuated. The frogs. The crickets. Nadine's every breath and the space between those breaths. My broken toe throbbed in syncopation with my heartbeat. My eyes focused. My hand steadied. I wished like hell Nadine wasn't directly behind me, but she was. I saw us as from above, the three of us lined up. Any sharp move either left or right would expose her to Dylan. I thought of the promise I made on the beach as the bright moon set over the water and waves of corn rolled upon the shore. Maybe I should've moved my hand a little higher. But I wanted to be able to draw if I needed to. That's the only option I understood.

I took a step toward Dylan.

"Don't," he said.

"Put the gun down, Dylan."

"I'm not letting you take me."

"I'm not taking you anywhere."

"You gonna call the police?"

"Just put the gun down."

"You are, aren't you?"

"Don't do this to yourself. You and Elizabeth are the only family left. You think this is what your father wants? What Benjamin would want you to do?"

"You gonna let me go? Settle this after she's gone?"

"That can be arranged."

"Then you should have been the one who thought of it. Problem is, I don't see you being that type."

"We can—"

His eyes popped wide. "Hey! I know what type of guy you are."

"Who's that, Dylan?"

He swung his gun at me.

45

Robert Frost said, "In three words I can sum up everything I learned about life: it goes on."

It was a weekday afternoon at the hotel, and while I waited for Elizabeth, it was going on: A bearded guitar player strumming about unrequited love, sunbaked bodies on toweled lounge chairs, muted TVs beaming down from the white-canvas bar ceiling, two women babbling and double-thumbing their phones, flashing each other their screens, laughing and sipping dizzy-colored drinks rimmed with slices of tropical fruit clinging to the cups, a distant siren, loud men pounding beers, strutting women wearing not much more than thin smiles on knowing lips, squeaky-voiced children splashing in the pool who reminded me that life not only goes on but also regenerates with glee. I sat there in my triumphs and crushed dreams, and it didn't give a damn; it went on cocky and full of itself, surging, pushing, stumbling, and slamming itself into the next second, year, decade and insignificating everything that came before.

The hotel is a pink Moorish structure built in the 1920s by an Irishman from Virginia, named after a character in a play by a French dramatist that was turned into an English opera, and is located in a city named for its Russian counterpart. You can find me there most days, a stand-in from a cut scene in a forgotten film.

An irritable man to my left unloaded on the woman next to him. His life going on in frivolous contention, ignorant to the thinness of it all.

"You gotta use your head, OK? The money doesn't work that way. Can't you think? You understand what I'm talking about?"

"I see," she replied in a meek voice, not wanting to draw attention to their quarrel. Her head hung down and black hair curtained her face. An ice-sludged rainbow drink sat in front of her but it was an ocean away. Life going on, but under no obligation to go in the direction you envision.

"Use your head." His voice cracked with contempt. "Think you can do that? You see what I'm talking about, right?"

"Yes."

"*Do* you?"

"Yes. I do." She stared at the frozen illusion on the bar.

I wanted to bash his head in and ride into her life. I took another sip of beer.

The police had held me for hours regarding the death of Dylan Phillips. But with Nadine backing up my story, and with Rambler's help, I was exonerated. Wayne and I met again at the end of my dock, and I informed him that Andrew Keller's death had nothing to do with Charlie Walker. I'd asked him if he was still investigating Walker. He said they were "winding down" their case.

Two days later, Charlie Walker was charged with violating state laws by failing to disclose payments from his organization while lobbying on behalf of the NRA. He had neglected to file any compensation reports for the previous eight years. Garrett called and said the inside scoop was that Walker also aided in laundering money through Limorp, but nothing ever came of that.

Roger DeRomo, his trusted lieutenant, took a position in private industry. I suspected DeRomo was the inside man Wayne was protecting when he asked me to look into Andrew's death. I wondered if that was why DeRomo had warned me at Walker's house. Was he afraid I'd find dirt on Walker and foul up his efforts? I didn't know and didn't care. I felt deflated thinking I'd chased Walker and all they had on him was failure to file.

I had not talked with Elizabeth. No one had told her of Dylan's confession—that he had killed Andrew. She only knew, through Rambler, that her disturbed younger brother had used me for assisted suicide and that Andrew had paid him a visit before his death. She had to have her suspicions. Rambler, over another hot dog, had asked me to tell her. "Better she hear from you than from me," he'd said. This time, he picked up the tab. Rested his hand on my shoulder when he slid off his stool.

That was the second assisted suicide for me. A cardinal of the Catholic Church, while I was in London, had used me to arrange and stage his death. Like my empty promise to drink less, I seemed incapable of escaping my life's flight path. Self-pity tried to move in, but I met it at the gate. I was finished with the switchback trail of doubts and regrets. I keep telling myself that.

Andrew had dropped by my house because he

suspected his confession to Dylan might have had fatal repercussions. He knew he'd made a mistake. I should have probed, but I didn't. I failed my friend. I felt greater remorse for letting Andrew down than for the consequences of defending myself against Dylan.

Elizabeth scraped back a barstool, its metal legs grating the bricks. I hopped off my stool and helped scoot her closer to the bar. Her eyes, once eager to take a chance, could no longer leaven a face that was embroidered in sadness.

She ordered water "with a twist of lemon." We discussed her husband's predicament, a topic that was not on the forefront of either of our minds. She indicated that Charlie felt confident that at most, he would end up with a pile of attorney bills and pay a fine, but nothing more.

I asked her how she felt.

"Top of the world."

"What world might that be?"

"The make-believe one in my head," she quipped with a smile. "I'm comfortable and—incredibly, considering what's going on internally—without pain. But I'm not good for anything over an hour. The medicine makes me loopy, and it gets harder to concentrate. Sometimes I feel as if I could just sleep and . . ." She waited until a ripping blender completed its annoying job. "It's nice to be in a vibrant place."

"I wish there was something I could do."

"You prayed twice, right?"

"I did."

"You've done your duty."

I reached into my pocket and brought out a flash drive. "Marcy—Andrew's wife—sent me this. It's songs that he composed. I thought you might like it."

She stared at it as if she were afraid to touch it. "You keep it." She cut her eyes to mine. "You'll know what to do with it."

"Meaning?"

She dismissed my question with a weak smile. I stuck the flash drive back in my pocket. "I'm sorry about Dylan."

Her eyes roved my face. "I knew he had issues, but he never displayed suicidal tendencies. It's tragic that he used you in the manner in which he did."

"Did Andrew tell you he was going to see Dylan?"

"No. But he did ask me how Dylan was doing. I told him that I'd lost touch with him—that I'd lost him to drugs long ago. That was such a terrible thing to say to Andrew. I suspect all I did was to dump even more guilt on him— something I turned out to be inexcusably good at."

I expected a question about what Dylan and I discussed. But instead she surprised me. "I lied to you in the chapel."

"The girl's perfume didn't smell like a lily?"

She laughed. "No. I wouldn't have misled you on that."

I searched my memory for what she might be referring to. She hadn't told me that Andrew had caused the accident, but that possibility had not been discussed.

"You told me that Andrew didn't know your child was a girl. But you admitted that you two had talked. You told him."

"I did."

"Why that one?"

She humped her shoulder. "I'm not sure. I was still evaluating you. It was something I'd never told anyone before. Throw in a dozen more senseless reasons if you'd like."

"It's not necessary."

"So little is."

"He went all those years without knowing."

"You didn't need to say that," Elizabeth said. She wasn't afraid to put me in my place. "I did refrain from telling him that I was searching for her. I was afraid that I would sound like the pathetic figure I am. A dying woman trying to atone for past sins. To see my daughter before my last breath escaped me. Reunite with a lost lover; perhaps the three of us having lunch together overlooking a sun-drenched lake. All the ingredients for the final scene of a corny movie."

"Are you close to locating her?"

"Inching along. The laws are different there. It took a while for the man I hired to locate someone competent in French adoptions. Everyone should go to Paris when they are young. Unfortunately, I was there for the wrong reasons."

The singer took a break, and the sound of children laughing and splashing in the pool ascended without the competition. The woman with the curtained face had yet to touch her drink. Her companion paced by the hot tub, his phone flattened to his ear, the frustrations his life showering someone else.

"Tell me about the night of the accident," I said, hoping to get it in before we shifted back to Dylan.

"You know, don't you?"

"Dylan told me." I wondered if she realized the implications that lay behind my answer. That the only way Dylan would know would be if Andrew had told him.

Elizabeth stared ahead for a few beats. She took a fingernail over the top of her left eyebrow. *She knew.* "It was an accident. Fate." She paused and leveled her weary eyes on mine. "I couldn't tell you this at the church. You understand?"

I nodded.

"But I should have," she said, her voice faltering. "I wanted to. So badly. But the words just wouldn't come out. I . . ."

Her eyes fell. I thought she might melt and slide off the stool. I rested my hand on her shoulder, touching her for the third and final time in our lives. She rallied and pinned her shoulders back, as if annoyed that she conveyed the image that she needed someone else's strength to proceed.

"I'd just told him I was pregnant. But we had no time to celebrate. He had a gig that night and was running late. He dashed out the door. He bolted back in fifteen minutes later." Her eyes tried to unpeel my face, as if there were more of me than there really was. "Do you know that, outside of Anna, I've told this to no one?"

"You don't have to."

"Oh no. You are so wrong. I do have to. I made a plan that night. I *insisted* on it. I didn't want Andrew to go to jail if they died, and if they lived, I'd worry about our story later. So I made him say that the accident was there when he approached the stop sign. He kept to that story, although I'm not certain the police entirely bought into it. But when they saw that he was with me, and it was my family in the car, they didn't push.

"Andrew wanted to confess, take the high road, but I held firm. My life was unspooling before me. All I could see was if they died, I'd be a single mother with a husband in jail for double involuntary manslaughter."

"You can't—"

"I deserted my father and brother."

"You made a decision."

"With cold-blooded, audacious calculation."

She delivered her last line with thrust. I fidgeted with

my beer. She glanced away as if both stunned and shamed by her own admission. Her eyes fell to the tiled counter. "He used to make us promise to laugh at his funeral, to celebrate his life. But he thought that would be when we were older and he was ancient, not when he was being buried with his son. There was no laughing."

She raised her head in a defiant move. "The sheer enormity of what happened crashed down on Andrew and me. We had a terrible scene. Our rationale, driven by me, was that there was nothing to gain by Andrew turning himself in. We didn't realize that by doing nothing, we lost everything. We lost who we were."

I thought about tossing out what she and I had discussed in the chapel. That regrets are for when you have a choice. But we were beyond that.

"The morning after the accident, after my father and brother died in the hospital, I went back to my apartment. We . . . had bought two fish at an art show." Her voice faltered. She touched her left shoulder. "I'm sorry. I can't do this."

"I shouldn't have asked."

"No, you had to." Her breath escaped her and she took her hand off her shoulder. "End of story. I told him I needed to be alone. That it was all too much to bear. I went to Paris, had our baby, and gave her up. Andrew hung up his guitar and joined the army—what a joke that must have been. That was his way of punishing himself."

I felt I should say something, but my thoughts were scattered and would not assimilate.

"Why did you go to see Dylan for a second time?" she asked.

"I received a tip that a blue car was at the scene of

Andrew's death. I'd noticed on my first trip that he had a blue car. He had it removed by the time I returned. I knew Andrew had gone to see Dylan. Beyond that, it was a hunch."

She kept her gaze steady on the shelves of liquor bottles in front of her. Her fingers massaged her plastic cup of water, but there was no red cross today. No flame left in her life. We sat in silence, the thrumming world swirling around us.

I said, "The only person new in Andrew's life prior to his death was Dylan."

Elizabeth took a sip of her water. She tented her hands in front of her. "They say stress can kill you. What do you think of that?"

"It certainly does no favors."

"Charlie didn't want children. He was too absorbed in himself and his lust for power. And I'd already seen what type of mother I was. But deep inside, in those smoldering embers of truth, I knew I'd made a mistake. Both in how I treated Andrew and in my decision to marry Charlie. All those years—I knew the stress was winning. But I didn't have the spine to break free. Not until I started A Book for Every Child did my life start to right itself—did I catch the wind—but it was too late."

She'd purposely veered off topic. I thought I should offer a placating comment, especially about her mother-hood putdown. Instead, I sat there and contemplated whether the stress I carried would one day manifest itself in mutant and renegade cells.

"When they told me I had terminal cancer, all I could think was that I'd been terminal for years. My life was over before I created another."

"And if you had?" I said. "Turned him in? What would that road have looked like? We know only the road taken."

She gave me quick smile. "You're back at it. Oh, trust me. I've played that game ad nauseam. Double involuntary manslaughter. I imagined our life with a reduced sentence and who knows?—possibly even with no time served. What the friends and cousins would say at holiday parties. How Andrew and I might glance at each other—how others would look upon us. At what age we would tell Trumpet.

"I spoke a minor mistruth earlier. Others know of what happened. A phonebook of psychiatrists. Their soft voices and murmured sympathies helped, but ultimately," she glanced at me, "only you can forgive yourself."

"You've done wonders with your life. A Book for Every Child is a tremendous accomplishment. An incalculable benefit to society."

"It is kind of you to say so. But I know my motive. It's amazing how fast one can run, what one can accomplish, when running *from* something. You said in the chapel that Andrew joined the army because he was running away, remember?"

"I do."

"I, too, sprinted into another life, trying to forget the old. My drive, my prolific oeuvre, if I had any, stemmed from inner dissatisfaction. My desire to create something out of the devastation. The obituary triumphs of my life were born from grief and tragedy."

"That doesn't disparage your accomplishments."

Elizabeth took a sip of her water and positioned herself higher on the stool. "I'm ready now."

I said it fast to get it over with. I told her they were testing Dylan's gun but that he had confessed to killing Andrew. That Andrew had sought Dylan out to tell him that he was getting back together with his sister and that he had caused the accident. I explained the scene to her: Dylan in front of me. Nadine directly behind me. That when Dylan pointed his gun at me, I drew like it was high noon. That I hadn't wanted to kill him, but I feared it came down to him or me. Or Nadine.

Allison's jeering words dropped out of the Florida sky: *Bullshit. Guns kill and that's what you'll do with it.*

I didn't dive between the lines. That Elizabeth's one-sentence letter was the catalyst for events that had ultimately resulted in Andrew's death and the death of the only remaining member of her family.

As for me? My successful quest to find Andrew's killer had resulted in my failure to distance myself from my past. A hollow victory—but I don't give a damn what it's called.

She kept her eyes focused on the liquor bottles. Her right hand had found its way to the top of her left shoulder, where it rested as if she were crossing her heart with her arm.

"I was afraid of that," she said. "But I needed to hear it. I hope you don't blame yourself."

"His gun wasn't loaded."

"What?" Her hand dropped off her shoulder.

"No bullets."

"Oh my." Her face twisted in pain. "Oh dear God. But you had no way of knowing, right?" It was kind of her to rally to my defense on such short notice.

"I did not. Nadine occasionally cleaned his room for him. She told the police that she found his gun a few days earlier and took the bullets out for his—and her—protection. Said her brothers had guns and she knew her way around them."

"Do you think he knew? That it wasn't loaded?"

"You can tell by the weight when you pick it up, but I doubt your brother was that familiar with it."

"Nadine didn't say anything, even though she was behind you?"

"She was afraid he'd put the bullets back in. She had no choice but to remain silent."

"We'll never know."

"No."

"Did he . . . I'm sorry. I don't know how to ask this."

"Did he pull the trigger?"

"Can you tell?"

"A pair of yeses."

"You did the right thing," she said, her eyes drilling my face. "You had no choice as well."

I did have a choice. I could have tried to talk Dylan out of it. That's what Morgan would have done. He would never have taken another person's life.

There was no need to tell her that my breathing was easy, my stance relaxed. That it played out in my mind before it happened, and I followed my role without debate or hesitation. That Dylan had murdered Andrew Keller in cold blood as Andrew lay on the floor. That I never bought into Nadine's claim that he was harmless. Could I have successfully negotiated the situation to a peaceful conclusion? Possibly. Could Dylan, with Poseidon drowning the last morsel of rationality in his damaged mind, have killed himself? Me? Nadine?

Well, not without bullets.

Nadine made my decision easy; I told myself I did it to protect her. But I knew, in that ironclad box where you keep guarded thoughts, that her presence didn't alter my decision. I had one thought and one thought only when Dylan

Phillips swung his gun at me: no policeman would knock on Kathleen's door.

"Neither did you," I said before my thoughts pulled me under. "You had no good choice."

She let out a heavy sigh. "You want to know what the shrinks never heard, what I never even told Anna? What I misled you about earlier?"

"If it's something you—"

"It was my fault Andrew was running late that night. I told him I was pregnant and he was ecstatic. We both were." She shook her head as if disgusted with herself. "I was always the practical one. But that evening, I begged him to stay. To lie with me just a moment longer. We made love. Lingered in our happiness. It wasn't providence that took his speeding car to the intersection where my father and brother were waiting, it was me. I orchestrated the event. I sent Andrew out the door at the prerequisite moment."

"You can't think—"

"Every day of my life. Every morning I wake, I have a minute—maybe five, never ten—that is free and then it snaps back."

"You told me in the chapel that you forgave Andrew long ago."

"I forgave him that night. It was an accident, and I couldn't bear to see him in pain. I don't think I ever loved him more than when I saw him hurt."

"Why treat yourself differently?"

"Because that is what we do. I did eventually forgive myself—when I realized that my father forgave me. That he wouldn't want me to feel guilty. That his love was not altered or weakened by the circumstances of his death, or my reaction to it. Want a freebie from a pro?"

"I'm all ears."

"Don't let the wisdom of the grave be your only path to redemption."

She died five weeks later, the quest to breach the unscalable wall of her past laid to rest with her bones.

46

Morgan, Kathleen, and I marched into Anna's room in the church, knowing we were bearers of grand news. She had a court date. With a little luck, by the end of the year, she would no longer be trapped with God. She would need a new job, as Elizabeth had died two weeks before. Morgan insisted that Kathleen be there—although he stammered for a reason, settling on Anna wanting to meet my wife. Not that it mattered, for Kathleen, after hearing us talk about Anna, wanted to meet her as well.

Anna welcomed us in, and as she and Kathleen talked, Morgan shifted his weight like a kid who couldn't contain his excitement. Anna still had a long battle in front of her, but the tide had turned. Morgan gave her the good news. Anna was appreciative but seemed nervous and not as relieved as I would have expected. She'd likely heard promising reports in the past only to be disappointed. I asked her about Elizabeth's death.

"I was with her when she passed," she said. "I was fearful of being picked up by the ICE, but Charlie said not to worry. It was good of him to allow me to be there. He did what was right for her."

"That must have been difficult for you," Kathleen said.

"Yes." Anna reached over and touched Kathleen's hand. She gazed hard into her eyes. "I am so glad you are here. We—I am just so pleased to meet you."

Morgan checked his watch and glanced around the room.

Anna said to Kathleen, "My daughters, Kimberly and Olivia, are coming for dinner. Can you stay?"

"We don't want to impose."

Anna's hand still held Kathleen's. "Please," she implored her. "We'd love to have your company."

"We'd be happy to," Morgan said, making the decision for us all.

Kathleen asked Anna about her daughters, and Anna barely came up for air. Ten minutes later, Gianna appeared pushing a stainless-steel cart piled with food. Morgan and I arranged the food on the table. It was certainly more than Anna and her daughters would need. Anna had planned to have us stay before she extended the invitation. Morgan had likely vouched for our acceptance.

While Kathleen and Anna discussed the perils of raising a daughter—unfamiliar territory for Kathleen—two young women tentatively entered the room. Anna sprang up and greeted each with a hug. She turned to Kathleen and me.

"These are my daughters." She touched the serious-looking younger girl on the shoulder. "This is Olivia. She is in eighth grade."

Olivia took a step forward. She extended her hand with confidence admirable for a girl of her age. Anna made no introduction to Morgan, and I sensed that he'd previously met them both.

"And this," Anna said, as if presenting a prize at a state fair, "is Kimberly. She is a senior."

Kimberly stood like a stubborn mule. Her eyes, under dark bangs that needed trimming, darted about the room searching for nonexistent options.

"I'm so pleased to meet you. When are you due?" Kathleen asked, for Kimberly was about seven to eight months pregnant. Morgan leaned forward, his hands clasped in front of him. I cut him a look, but he kept his attention on Kimberly and Kathleen. My mind jumped the fence. I hoped Kathleen was more disciplined with her thoughts.

"Six weeks," Kimberly said, her eyes darting to her mother.

"You must be very excited," Kathleen said.

"I am."

"It is hard," Anna said. She went and stood by her daughter. She took Kimberly's hand in her own. "She's been admitted to USF. I am so proud of her. She has already completed more education than anyone in our family."

A silent yet deafening moment ticked by. In a measured and controlled voice, Kathleen said to Kimberly, "I'm sure you'll manage with your mother's help."

I tried to swallow, but my mouth was dry. Like a detached observer in a dream, I'd become uncoupled from the scene. The main narrative flow of my life was taking a sharp turn and I was paralyzed. I wanted to mumble a prayer for Kathleen—for us—but my thoughts were in tongues and all I could come up with was *please, please, please.*

"My daughter is seventeen," Anna said, her voice shaking. "She is not married and does not intend to marry the child's—it is a girl—father. She is an excellent student and wants to go to college. We've had very serious discussions."

No one spoke. We stood like actors who had forgotten their lines, each waiting for someone else to come in.

Anna looked at her daughter. "Go ahead."

"No, Mama, you tell her."

Anna took a step toward Kathleen. The two women's pairs of hands joined together at their waists as their hands spoke what their voices could not say. My eyes were fixated on their hands, for I could not look at Kathleen. They massaged and squeezed each other.

Anna said, "Lizzy told us Mr. Jake believes little girls should wear dresses with large pockets to put miracles in. Mr. Morgan said you and Mr. Jake are wanting—"

Kathleen unraveled. It was Morgan who went to her side as I stood there stoned.

47

She had been delivered to our house between ten and twelve on a Saturday—*Will someone be home?* That tells you what I know about life. We struggled with names until Kathleen, who wanted to pay homage to Elizabeth and Anna's relationship, inquired of Anna if Elizabeth and she had ever discussed a name for Kimberly's child. If Elizabeth had ever moved past 'Trumpet.'

Nothing had prepared me for the way she flopped around when I cleaned her tushy, her little hands clutching at air and her stubby legs lolling on the changing table that in another life had been my desk. Or the way, at six months old, Joy smiled at me with glee and unfathomable innocence, as if no flower in the world could match my face. How she cooed and babbled and created all sorts of sounds, this tiny woman who owned no words but who had captured my heart. Kathleen and I had created a family, and the concept was as unknown and intimidating to me as any creature to spew forth from the deep sea. Yet I was eager to embrace it, consequences unknown and without delay.

I finished changing her diaper and laid her in her crib staring at a rotating zoo. My phone rang. It wasn't a number I recognized, and it went to voice mail. It was the second time the number had rung. The first time had not been followed by a voice mail.

Elizabeth had been on my mind during my morning run. She had carried her burden well, but she'd had a hell of a burden to carry. She bottled her passions for twenty years, but when she'd opened the lid, the sultan of fate had come swirling out of the hellbroth. Both Andrew and Dylan were nothing more than belated victims of its original dark plan. Who was I to fence with such a demon? To dance with such an unbalanced partner?

I'd called the colonel and told him to strike my name from his list. He pestered Garrett. Garrett told Janssen that I spoke for both of us, although it had not been Garrett's decision. While I had never doubted Garrett's support on the battlefield, it was reassuring beyond articulation to know it extended to unchartered theaters.

The insurance company buzzed me. Said a seventy-foot cruiser was missing. The owner, a Miami attorney known for defending drug lords, was demanding full restitution. I thanked them for the opportunity and requested that they never call again.

I taught ESL classes five days a week.

I wound up the crib mobile. It rotated dolphins and birds and friendly lions above Joy's head. Her eyes widened. Hadley III stalked in the room and took up her position by the door. She, too, kept her watchful eyes on the rotating dolphins and birds and friendly lions.

I hit my voice mail.

"Mr. Travis. My name is Yankee Conrad the Fourth. I was retained by the late Elizabeth Walker to look into her affairs. I have concluded my work for her. However, part of that effort entails that I present you a letter. If you would be so kind, please give my office a call so that we can arrange a time that I may present you with the document."

He left his number.

I dialed him back. A snarly secretary asked the purpose of my call, as if my intrusion on her time was a most unwelcome part of her day. I politely told her that I was returning Mr. Conrad's call, although her attitude grated on me.

"Mr. Conrad can see you at ten tomorrow morning."

"How is eleven?"

"He can see you at ten."

"What is this regarding?"

"I do not know."

"You must have some idea."

"Is ten manageable?"

"It is."

I hit my phone and looked at my heavy-eyed daughter. "Think that's manageable for you, kiddo?"

YANKEE CONRAD THE FOURTH WORKED OUT OF an old house with a deep front porch in downtown Saint Pete that fronted Tampa Bay. The snarly secretary offered me a drink, and when I declined, I ceased to exist. After a quarter of an hour, and without apparent prompt, she stood.

"He will see you now." She led me to a closed door, opened it, but did not enter.

I stepped into a shipping magnate's library from the

turn of the previous century. The walls were solid built-in bookcases. The shelves were of a dark and gnarly uneven wood, as if cut with a hand plane. They held thick books and models of sailing ships and steamers. A round glass table, supported by a massive ship's anchor, dominated the center of the office. The only technology was a thin, closed laptop that rested behind him on a credenza crowded with nautical pictures. Not a single photograph of a person. No fishing trips. No golfing buddies. No smiling women or children. Only a heavily framed and aged oil painting of a woman in a red dress, her sheening breasts nearly tumbling into the room.

Yankee Conrad roosted high above a small, weathered desk. Behind him, a floor-to-ceiling paned window overlooked a Monet garden and pond.

"Nice digs," I said.

"One must surround oneself with those items that grant one comfort."

"One must."

He stood and we introduced ourselves.

He was a tall man—*taller than a steeple*—and stood like an unbent tree. He wore a vest and a pink bow tie. His suit jacket hung on a valet stand. He peered from behind wire-rimmed glasses, his New England face surveying me like a stoic and timeworn lighthouse casting for danger. He reclaimed his chair. Without invitation, I took a seat across from him in a leather chair.

"How did you happen to come to know the late Mrs. Walker?" he asked.

"I'm not sure."

"I beg your pardon?"

I flipped open my hand. "I was asked to investigate the death of . . . a man she was once in love with."

"Mr. Keller?"

"That is correct."

"By a U.S. marshal; Mr. Wayne, I believe."

My body stiffened. *Who was this guy?*

He showed no delight in his omniscience, but instead delicately opened a folder on his desk, as if in some manner the deliberation of his move contributed to its sacred contents. He adjusted his glasses as he spoke. "You spent five years in the army and received the Purple Heart as well as the Distinguished Service Medal, both sealed. You spent time with the Defense Intelligence Agency. In the course of retrieving a stolen boat numerous years ago, you killed two men. You were rumored to be involved in the death of four professional hit men from Chicago executed in Fort De Soto Park—the city did an admirable job of keeping all that extremely low key—and you were present at an Old West shoot-out at the home of Raydel Escobar, who is now serving time in prison. More than one body was carted out of his house that night. Yet," his eyes ascended over his glasses, "I believe you and your wife remain close with his wife. And, of course, our matter at hand. You killed Mr. Dylan Phillips, my client's harmless and psychologically impaired younger brother. Assisted suicide, whatever form of murder that may be. Have I missed anything?"

If it was his intent to show his muscle, he'd succeeded. Yet his nonjudgmental tone carried not a hint of accusation or implied impropriety on my part.

"Quite a bit," I said.

"Yes. I wouldn't doubt that. Wouldn't doubt that at all."

"Did you summon me here just to kick me out of school?"

He closed the folder and clasped his hands together.

"Those who know you speak highly of you. And a judgment of peers is the only report card worth noting."

"It's a ship's desk, isn't it?" I asked.

"Pardon?"

"That ridiculously small desk that makes you look like a great blue heron. It's a captain's desk from a ship."

"The *Scarlett*." He tipped his forehead. "She is to your immediate right." I stole a glance at a Baroque-framed oil painting of a ship in perilous seas. "She was the last of a breed. A magnificent sailing vessel that ran out of Tampa harbor. My great-grandfather was her captain. This was his desk in his quarters."

"That would have been the first Yankee Conrad."

"Correct. Although he went by Conrad Yankee. My grandmother reversed the names."

"I'm sure there's a story."

"Yes, but not for today."

"And the anchor under the table?"

"The *Scarlett*'s anchor as well. The bookcases that surround you were cut from her hull."

"Not by you?"

"My grandfather."

"You're from a line of merchant marines?"

"Yes, and I still maintain interest in that area."

"Interest as in curiosity or in capital?"

"Both. I am blessed that my curiosity generates capital."

"You mentioned you had a letter for me."

"She—Mrs. Walker—had great faith in you." He paused as if that was a cue for me. When I remained silent, he continued. "I believe she mentioned to you that she was searching for her daughter."

"She did."

"That well-endowed search did not end with her death.

That was not her wish. My instructions were to find the young woman, and if successful, to present you with a letter. It contains a request that we shall get to later should our conversation proceed smoothly and without contention."

He opened another folder on the desk, extracted a large sealed envelope, and handed it to me. I tried to pry it open. He handed me a knife. "This may be of assistance."

It had a pearl handle and a thin blade nearly ten inches long. I slid it inside the envelope and handed it back to him. "That's quite a letter opener. It's underutilized in such a capacity."

He placed it back into the middle drawer of the desk. "It has served dual purposes. My grandmother used it to kill my great-grandfather, an act for which the family is eternally grateful."

"Great-grandfather or grandfather?"

"I spoke correctly."

"Anything to do with the name change?"

"Perhaps you should read the letter. That is the original, Mr. Travis. I, of course, will retain a copy. If you do not choose to honor her wishes, I will need to explore other methods of meeting her request. Do not let my concerns taint your decision."

A scrap piece of paper was at the bottom of the envelope. I ignored it and pulled out a heavy stock paper that had never been folded.

DEAR MR. TRAVIS,

As you are reading this, I assume you have met Mr. Conrad. A fascinating man out of a Dickens novel. He has no listing and is invisible to any search. A tall man who, indeed, retains a low profile.

Despite the outcome, Andrew was wise to go to you, and I hope that I, too, have made a sagacious decision. You are under no obligation to comply with my wishes, of course, but I have the utmost faith that you will. You have a great capacity for caring and empathy, although I suspect you are unaware of these fine attributes. I found that charming in you.

Mr. Conrad has located Trumpet. While in a perfect world, he would share that news with me, it is you who he has summoned. What I would give to be in the chair you are sitting in.

Before my request, I'd like to express the simple enjoyment I experienced by talking with you in the chapel. I found it difficult to know people. Whether this was a curable disease or something that would have plagued me until I reached ninety-two, I'll never know. But in many ways, I don't think we left much out that day. My father once told me that he took only a few things to enjoy from the world. I didn't live long. I can count my friends on one hand, my blessings on the other. But I don't believe extra decades would have added anything to what I took from the world. Or gave.

I sense you share this sentiment.

Trumpet.

I would be most appreciative if you delivered a painting to her. Tell her that her father and I are in that cottage with her as a child. That I am brushing her hair. That no two people could possibly love a child more, although that may seem so incongruous with my actions. Tell her that she has music in her, and wild and leaping stories. Tell her that when she gazes at the stars at night, I am there, just past the second star to the right. It's all so silly—corny—isn't it? You'll know what to say.

Thank you.

Affectionately yours,

ELIZABETH PHILLIPS WALKER

PS. The picture. See the shoreline in the distance? That is Honahlee. I know that now. I know that more than anything.

I placed it back in the envelope, but not before I stole a glance at the piece of paper on the bottom.

Once, in the land of Honahlee, a boy kissed me under a lamppost.

Had she'd known it was with the letter? I glanced up at Conrad and was surprised to see his quiet face studying mine.

"She left a stipend for your travel costs," he said.

"What painting?"

He rose from his desk, a giant and gangly king, and crossed the room. Conrad was easily midway between six and seven feet tall. His trousers were without crease, his pace without haste. He went to a closet and took out a painting bundled in cloth. He carefully unwrapped it. He turned it around.

It was a yellow cottage by the sea with opened blue shutters and a covered front porch. A bird, perched on a beached rowboat, stared with anticipation at the cottage. A pair of oars angled out of the rowboat. Across the water, in the distance, stood a deserted shore—Honahlee, apparently. It was good street art, brightly colored and unfaded.

"I am to deliver this to Trumpet?" I asked.

He gave me a quizzical glance "Who?"

"Elizabeth's daughter."

"That is her wish. You, naturally, are under no obligation. If you choose to, she has left more than ample funds to cover your expenses."

"I believe her obituary mentioned in lieu of flowers to make contributions to A Book for Every Child. Is that correct?"

"It is."

"I'll deliver the picture on my own dime. Take her stipend and donate it to them."

"I will be happy to put your name as the donor, as they are your funds to direct as you please."

"It will be anonymous."

"Very well."

"You said you had other methods, should I refuse. What might those have been?"

"You misunderstood me. I said I would explore other methods. Mrs. Walker had no doubt as to your willingness. Are you sure you won't accept the stipend?"

"Would you like me to report back to you in any manner?"

He paused, as if considering my question, or how I framed it. "There is certainly no legal consideration here. But I have been searching for Mrs. Walker's daughter for some time, and at considerable expense to her. I would appreciate the courteous gesture of knowing that it ended well."

"It never ends well."

"No. It does not."

He wrapped the picture and gave it to me.

"I'll be in touch." I headed for the door.

"Mr. Travis?"

"Yes?"

He took a step toward me. He hesitated, although he was not a man to hesitate. "Often, in the course of my business, I need . . . a man. One who is comfortable with himself in extenuating circumstances and does not condemn nor defend his moral judgment. Certain ones of us are called upon for the more trying situations. And while we all have our doubts, this man should be an individual who, while questioning his untiring conscience, does not shy away from the hard and difficult task."

"Good luck with that."

"Luck has never held my interest. I was privileged to get to know Mrs. Walker quite well during her quest. She was a pragmatic person in the best sense of the word. A woman stamped with tragedy and left to bleed by the world, but whose high tolerance for pain allowed her to persevere where mortals were expected to fail. A woman who embraced her sorrow and forged it into meaningful and lasting achievement. A remarkable woman, and I am most respectful of that word. I found her judgment and reasoning to be impeccable. She spoke highly of you, and I have heard nothing this morning, or from my sources, to render her judgment false. May I call upon you from time to time? The pay is good, but, in fairness, the situations are often dangerous and fraught with ambiguity."

I thought of the warm secret of Joy's face. The pledge I made to myself on the bench as the moon set over the Gulf of Mexico. The giggles my class suppressed when I struggled to teach them a new language in which to express old

357

thoughts. Those images and promises vied and jostled for recognition and confirmation in my mind. They circled like dolphins and birds and friendly lions above wide, uncomprehending, and heavy eyes. There was something inherently attractive about Yankee Conrad, and he was too interesting a character to leave behind, and, perhaps—remembering what Kathleen had whispered to me in the boat—I needed him. For as eager as I was to let the world go, what would take its place? Where would the magic come from?

As though I were a voyeur to my own life, and with startling indifference to my exhausting morning run when I pledged to rest, my voice floated into the room.

"I don't pack a gun anymore."

"That is entirely your decision."

"Sure. Give me a ring anytime."

48

We met at Louis Bar inside the Montana Hotel, in Lucerne, Switzerland. The hotel overlooked a mirror lake, and the jagged snowcapped Alps circled the lake and jutted into the blue sky. We took corner seats under a large window. Her eyes were unsure but willing to take a chance. Our only audience was our reflections in the window. I tried to keep my attention on her, but it was hard to ignore the high and cold mountains. They stood gallant and bored, and I had to look through myself to see them.

The painting rested beside me, the flash drive containing Andrew's music in my pocket.

Her name was Michelle, but in my mind, she would always be Trumpet. She was poised and well spoken, although that would be a product of her upbringing and not her siring. A great sadness enfolded me as I realized the doomed lovers never saw the miracle in front of me, who, except for her eyes and effeminate lips, shared her father's features. Her dangly arms. Her thick hair the color of a football, with a cowlick where it parted on her forehead. I juggled with what to leave out and what to leave in and then decided to tell it to her straight and as best as I could remember. But memory is a complicated and porous patchwork of thoughts and emotions designed to create permanence where there is none. It took a conscious effort just to recall the shade of Elizabeth's eyes. It was all fading, and questions sprouted like weeds on a deserted playing field— the participants gone, the stands empty, the lights dark. Had Elizabeth contacted Andrew prior to her diagnosis? Was her overpowering drive to resuscitate the past the offspring of a failed marriage, or does the heart truly harness more power than the sun? Not that it mattered, for no audience would ever see our shooting star. Trumpet would take my words, my earnest yet feeble attempt to reconstitute events, and forge her own tale. She would cultivate her own conclusion, because that is what we do.

And as for me?

Billowed sails filled with the golden mist of sunset swept Elizabeth and Andrew into a horizon that we are not permitted see. It was all decided for them. They had no choice. Nor did I.

I believe this.

Walker, Elizabeth Phillips

Elizabeth Phillips Walker, 43, passed away peacefully into the gentle arms of her Lord on June 12, 2019, in her home by the sea that she loved. She enjoyed a rich life with her husband, Charles Edward Walker, who will miss her fondly.

"Lizzy" was born on January 12, 1976, in Gainesville, Florida, to parents George and Carolyn (Brecher) Phillips. She graduated summa cum laude from the University of Florida with a BA degree in English literature. She went on to receive her MBA from the University of Florida, where she graduated in the top 10 percent of her class.

After graduation, Lizzy and Charlie married and settled in Tallahassee and later enjoyed a second home in Tierra Verde, Florida. She worked in banking for eleven years, where she rose to senior vice president of marketing of BB&T. While at BB&T, Lizzy was credited with raising the bank's profile from a strong local name to a regional brand that materially expanded its presence in the southeast United States. She was the firm's Banker of the Year in 2005 and a past member of the American Bankers Association. She was the youngest person, and first woman, to be appointed president of the Florida Bankers Association. She left the banking industry to engage in nonprofit work.

Combining her business acumen and lifelong love of reading, Lizzy was the founder and past president of A Book for Every Child (ABC). A nonprofit, ABC is dedicated to establishing literacy in preschool and pressing its importance during the first three years of elementary school. ABC became a standard for similar programs throughout the nation. Under Lizzy's guidance and vision, ABC now has chapters in all of Florida's sixty-seven counties and an endowment approaching $50 million. Over two hundred thousand books a year are provided free to those Florida children who otherwise might not have access to them. Lizzy was especially proud of her Reading Tents that have become a staple in county fairs. ABC's army of enthusiastic volunteers staffs the white tents, marked with colorful Renaissance banners. They sell secondhand books, conduct readings, and encourage children to write stories, presenting a ribbon to every composition. Lizzy could often be heard asking a child how a story made her or him feel. She believed that reading was knowledge and that knowledge would prove to be the world's unifying force for peace, ultimately triumphing over ignorance and prejudice.

Failing health forced Lizzy to step down from the post she created, but she continued to work tirelessly until her death, generously donating her time to sister causes. Her last effort was to host an event in her home for Pinellas Early Reading. Her warm spirit, driving commitment, and unwavering support of education will be missed but never forgotten. The many close friends she made at ABC, the bank, and through her husband's work as a lobbyist will greatly miss her easy smile, her sly wit, and her challenging humor. She and Charlie had wonderful years together. They traveled extensively. Lizzy was especially attracted to the Cotswolds in June, Napa Valley in the fall, and a Florida beach at the bookends of any day, where she always wore a shirt with pockets in which to place seashells. She lived a full and happy life and left the world a better place.

Elizabeth Walker was preceded in death by her father, George, a former attorney in Gainesville, her mother, Carolyn (Miss Florida, 1971), her older brother, Benjamin, and her younger brother, Dylan.

Calling hours will be at the First United Methodist Church of Saint Petersburg on Thursday, June 20, at 10:00

a.m. with a memorial service to follow at 11:00. A private funeral will be held in Tallahassee. In lieu of flowers, donations may be made to a local chapter of A Book for Every Child.

Rest, sweet angel, like summer upon a meadow, for your heart is joyful, your travels complete, and now with your lover, forever sleep.

ABOUT THE AUTHOR

 Robert Lane is the author of the Jake Travis stand-alone novels. *Florida Weekly* calls Jake Travis a "richly textured creation; one of the best leading men to take the thriller fiction stage in years." Lane's debut novel, *The Second Letter* won the Gold Medal in the Independent Book Publishers Associations (IBPA) 2015 Benjamin Franklin Awards for Best New Voice: Fiction. Lane resides on the west coast of Florida, and escapes in the summers to the deciduous hardwoods of Ohio. Learn more at Robertlanebooks.com

To receive your free copy of the Jake Travis Series prequel, *Midnight on the Water,* **sign up** for Robert Lane's newsletter. Equal parts mystery and love story, *Midnight on the Water* is the saga of how Jake and Kathleen meet, tumble into love, and the drastic measures Jake, Morgan, and Garrett take to save Kathleen's life—and grant her a new identity. *Midnight on the Water* is available only to those on Robert's mailing list. The newsletter contains book reviews across a wide range of genres, both fiction and non-fiction. It also includes updates and excerpts on the next Jake Travis novel.

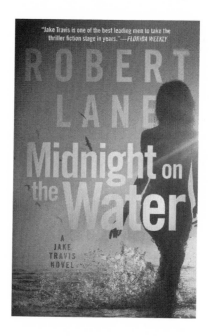

If you enjoyed reading *The Elizabeth Walker Affair*, please take a moment to leave an Amazon review. Your time and effort are most appreciated.

Thank you,

Robert

Be sure to read these previous stand-alone Jake Travis novels:

The Second Letter
Cooler Than Blood
The Cardinal's Sin
The Gail Force
Naked We Came
A Beautiful Voice

In chapter 22, Rachael Stone sings a verse of "Do You Think of Me?" to Jake. She mentions that it was "One of my favorite songs," that Andrew composed. Listen and download "Do You Think of Me?" at: https://robertlanebooks.com/music/

Visit Robert Lane's author page on Amazon.com: https://www.amazon.com/Robert-Lane/e/B00HZ2254A/

Follow Robert Lane on:

Facebook: https://www.facebook.com/RobertLaneBooks

Goodreads: https://www.goodreads.com/author/show/7790754.Robert_Lane

BookBub: https://www.bookbub.com/profile/robert-lane?list=about

Learn more and receive your free copy of *Midnight on The Water* at http://robertlanebooks.com

Made in the USA
Columbia, SC
29 May 2020